T0304527

I AM
STONE

The Gothic Weird Tales of

R. MURRAY GILCHRIST

I AM STONE

The Gothic Weird Tales of

R. MURRAY GILCHRIST

Edited by

DANIEL PIETERSEN

This edition published 2021 by
The British Library
96 Euston Road
London NW1 2DB

Selection, introduction and notes © 2021 Daniel Pietersen

Dates attributed to each story relate to first publication.

Every effort has been made to trace copyright holders and to obtain their
permission for the use of copyright material. The publisher apologises
for any errors or omissions and would be pleased to be notified of any
corrections to be incorporated in reprints or future editions.

Cataloguing in Publication Data
A catalogue record for this publication is available from the British Library

ISBN 978 0 7123 5400 4
e-ISBN 978 0 7123 6773 8

Frontispiece illustration by Sandra Gómez, with design by Mauricio Villamayor.
Photographs by Fay Godwin © The British Library Board.

Cover design by Mauricio Villamayor with illustration by Sandra Gómez
Text design and typesetting by Tetragon, London
Printed in England by CPI Group (UK) Ltd, Croydon, CRO 4YY

This book is dedicated to my wife, Cat,
without whom it would not exist.

I would also like to thank Dr Sam Hirst and Dr Jen Baker
for their support and encouragement of my early research into
the life and work of R. Murray Gilchrist.

CONTENTS

INTRODUCTION

'He liked candles and Elizabethan thickness of atmosphere and, if possible,
the rain beating on the leaded panes.'

HUGH WALPOLE,

The Apple Trees: Four Reminiscences

We know frustratingly little about the life of Robert Murray Gilchrist (1867–1917) but this quotation from the memoirs of Hugh Walpole, Gilchrist's friend and a descendant of *The Castle of Otranto*'s Horace Walpole, offers one of the most evocative insights into his personality. Walpole remembers a man who wasn't especially shy—he tells us that Gilchrist 'had a passion for coloured pocket handkerchiefs; he generally carried three, all of different colours'—but who does seem to have preferred cosy routine to unfamiliar surroundings. Walpole continues his anecdote by recounting trips to Gilchrist's family home of Cartledge Hall in Holmesfield, near Sheffield, where 'in the evening after dinner we paid a ceremonial visit to the other part of the house, carrying our candles through dark and winding passages'. Here they would sit with Gilchrist's mother 'talking there to the old lady as though we had but just arrived from China and had exciting tales to tell'. There is a strong impression that Gilchrist enjoyed these imaginary journeys, undertaken on his own terms and for whimsical reasons, far more than the infrequent trips to promote his writing in the bustle of cities like London or Paris. This duality, a love of both the fabulous and the familiar, is also reflected in another important aspect of Gilchrist's life. In addition to his mother and two sisters,

Gilchrist shared his home with George Garfitt, often euphemistically referred to in contemporary accounts as a 'male companion'. Garfitt was Gilchrist's life-long partner and the two lived together for almost thirty years, a relationship ended only by Gilchrist's early death from pneumonia in 1917. Cruelly, the pair lived in a time when their relationship could not be spoken of publicly and it may simply have been easier for Gilchrist to keep to himself, enjoying the life he preferred in secluded surroundings even if it was to the detriment of his literary career.

Gilchrist's tendency to introspection did not go unnoticed by sympathetic friends. William Sharp wrote to him in March, 1894, advising that 'I think you should see more of actual life: and not dwell so continually in an atmosphere charged with your own imaginings'. It speaks to his affection for Gilchrist that Sharp took pains not to offend his friend; 'It is because I believe in you that I urge you to beware of your own conventions,' he continues. Despite Sharp's advice, however, Gilchrist's reticent nature persisted. Indeed, it persists even beyond his death as Gilchrist's grave, which he shares with his sister Isabelle in the graveyard of St Swithin's Church in Holmesfield, makes no note of his accomplishments as a writer.

Yet accomplished he was. In his short life of fifty years, Gilchrist wrote twenty-two novels, four regional guide books and six short story collections. He was published in periodicals like *The Idler*, *The Windsor Magazine* and even the notorious pages of *The Yellow Book*, alongside illustrious names such as William Hope Hodgson, Robert W. Chambers and Henry James. However, none of this writing, apart from the few stories collected in this volume, now remains in print.

So, why revisit Gilchrist's work after all this time? Critics of the period, especially those only aware of his novels, may well have asked the same question. *The Literary World* called *Passion the Plaything* (1890), Gilchrist's debut novel, 'crude and unnatural' while *The Spectator* simply derided it as 'an unpleasant book, containing far too much in the way of sensuous descriptions'. As he honed his skill over subsequent novels his technical ability as an author became accepted by the establishment, but always begrudgingly. *The Spectator* described *The Labyrinth* (1902) as 'a book with an atmosphere of nightmare' where 'characters, mostly bizarre and some repellent, live in a mist and move in a maze' before finally admitting that 'the morbid extravagance of the plot is in a measure redeemed by the skill of the literary treatment'. Another review in *The Spectator* is slightly more positive but still manages to damn Gilchrist with faint praise by asserting that his eighth novel, *Beggar's Manor* (1903), took 'a disagreeable subject, and treated it with adequate taste and skill'. The overriding opinion is very much that Gilchrist has competence as a writer but his choice of subjects, despite his reticent nature (or, perhaps, because of it), are too 'unreal and morbid' to be sustained over a novel. *The Literary World*'s critic, for example, ends their thoughts on *Passion the Plaything* with a stinging comment: 'The author began and was not able to finish'. Even Walpole, an ardent supporter, laments that Gilchrist's novels 'never sold very greatly'.

We do see critical praise, however, for Gilchrist's short stories. The majority of these are often described as 'tales of the Peak'—picturesque works that describe vignettes from the lives of Peak District countryfolk, often written in near-impenetrable dialect—but a small handful are of a different, darker lineage. In 1894 Methuen and Company published *The Stone Dragon and Other Tragical Romances*, which they described in promotional matter as 'a volume of stories of power so weird and original as to ensure them a ready welcome'. A reviewer in *The Academy* concurred, saying that 'the book is sinister, enveloped in gloom—yes, and decadent; but it is strong, it has authenticity; the effect sought is the effect won'. The anonymous critic continues with further praise which provides an insight into the importance of Gilchrist's short fiction: 'There is nothing quite like *The Stone Dragon* in modern English fiction: but in it you may distinctly trace the influence of Poe, and perhaps also of Villiers de l'Isle-Adam and Charles Baudelaire'.

Gilchrist's work is worth revisiting and celebrating because the short stories included in *The Stone Dragon* are not just a unique blend of the decadent and the gothic but because they are early glimpses of what we would eventually come to know as weird fiction. Gilchrist is a nexus of these three strands of fiction, never existing fully in any of them but drawing from all of them. Stories like *The Crimson Weaver* predate the strangely oneiric weird fiction of Clark Ashton Smith as much as *The Basilisk* looks back to the fated inevitability of Poe. *My Friend* takes what could easily have been a rather formulaic work of decadent transgression and transforms it into a hauntingly melancholy piece of queer introspection while *The Return* usurps and softens the predatory nature of that most gothic of creatures: the vampire.

Modern readers should be warned, however, that as much as Gilchrist uses elements of decadent, gothic and weird fiction he does also occasionally fall foul of their more unhelpful stereotypes. Despite his own otherness, for example, he is sometimes guilty of relying on the trope of the Sinister Other, where foreignness or madness are equated with either personal failings or intentional malice. This is most evident in *The Noble Courtesan*, where 'blackamoors' with 'staring eyes' are reported to have 'gibbered sleepily', but both *Roxana Runs Lunatick* and *The Madness of Betty Hooton* show insanity as an almost immediate, inevitable result of trauma. Whether this is due to Gilchrist's insularity, his own intolerances or simply the ignorance of the times makes it no more acceptable but I feel these stories are still valuable and offer context for more sympathetic elements like Mary's selflessness in *The Stone Dragon* or the bereaved parents' charity of *A Strolling Player*. Additionally, a more subtle problem for the modern eye is Gilchrist's persistent use of terms and references which were archaic even in his own day; few stories pass without the appearance of culvers, pleasaunces or passing nods to the artworks and people of many centuries ago. I have included a Notes on the Texts section at the end of this collection to explain some of these references and, hopefully, add depth to Gilchrist's elaborate world.

In his study *A Century of Weird Fiction*, Jonathan Newell outlines how weird fiction did not simply appear fully formed but instead erupted out of its gothic ancestor, 'composed of the same tissues but unfamiliar, alien and yet not-entirely-so, at once part of its progenitor and curiously foreign to it'. Gilchrist's writing, and the shadowy figure we can sometimes glimpse behind the writing, embody that sense of 'alien and yet not-entirely-so'. I believe the stories contained in this volume—the entire contents of *The Stone Dragon* and a handful of works from other publications, including three never-before reprinted tales: the weirdly distanced narrative of *The Holocaust*, the gothic horror of *Sir Toby's Wife* and the mournful Peak tale of *A Strolling Player*—are a crucial part of weird fiction's history and allow us to more deeply understand where weird fiction came from—and, where it might go.

I opened this introduction with a quotation from Hugh Walpole and it seems fitting to end it with the words which he himself uses to end his reminiscence of his friend, an overdue wish that I like to think this collection goes some way to grant.

'I hope that someone soon will rediscover him, as others far less worthy than he have been rediscovered. I salute with reverence, admiration and deep affection one of the kindest, gentlest, most affectionate artists I have ever known'.

DANIEL PIETERSEN

FURTHER READING

Machin, James, *Weird Fiction in Britain 1880–1939* (London: Palgrave Macmillan UK, 2018)

Newell, Jonathan, *A Century of Weird Fiction, 1832–1937: Disgust, Metaphysics and the Aesthetics of Cosmic Horror* (Cardiff: University of Wales Press, 2020)

Walpole, Hugh, *The Apple Trees: Four Reminiscences*, (Leominster: Golden Cockerel Press, 1932)

A NOTE FROM THE PUBLISHER

The original short stories reprinted in the British Library Tales of the Weird series were written and published in a period ranging across the nineteenth and twentieth centuries. There are many elements of these stories which continue to entertain modern readers; however, in some cases there are also uses of language, instances of stereotyping and some attitudes expressed by narrators or characters which may not be endorsed by the publishing standards of today. We acknowledge therefore that some elements in the stories selected for reprinting may continue to make uncomfortable reading for some of our audience. With this series British Library Publishing aims to offer a new readership a chance to read some of the rare material of the British Library's collections in an affordable paperback format, to enjoy their merits and to look back into the worlds of the past two centuries as portrayed by their writers. It is not possible to separate these stories from the history of their writing and as such the following stories are presented as they were originally published with minor edits only, made for consistency of style and sense. We welcome feedback from our readers, which can be sent to the following address:

British Library Publishing
The British Library
96 Euston Road
London, NW1 2DB
United Kingdom

PART I
Dead Yet Living

I've started this collection with my own first encounter with Gilchrist's gothic weird fiction. 'The Crimson Weaver' is perhaps one of his most florid and fantastical works—in only a handful of pages we encounter birds with the blank faces of mannequins and human-animal hybrids cavorting in 'steaming, sanguine pools'—but it also is dense with his repeated motifs of plant and flower symbology, obscure classical references and a cloying, baroque atmosphere. More fundamentally, 'The Crimson Weaver' demonstrates his penchant for taking a Gothic trope—in this case a predatory vampire—and adding a weird twist; the Weaver is well-named, her tastes more cultured than a simple lust for blood. Other tales of Gilchrist's also deal with vampires of a more subtle kind. In the decayed and gaunt characters of 'The Return' we see the withering effects of loss and despair whereas the 'curious radiance—greenish, cold' encountered by the protagonist of 'The Lover's Ordeal' invokes the envy that the dead have for the living. Gilchrist also summons ghosts and apparitions into his tales. 'A Night on the Moor' outlines Warmsworth's experiences as he unwittingly slips through a gap in time to witness, potentially to cause, a calamity from many years ago while 'Midsummer Madness' implies that the main characters are ghosts to each other, not quite aligned in space and time; Phyllida, when questioned by her betrothed about the strangely erratic passing of time, whispers 'I cannot explain, unless that we have dreamed'. At the end of this section 'The Pageant of Ghosts' and 'The Priest's Pavan' conjure up visions of the long-dead, benevolent and malevolent respectively, while in the sinister and haunting 'Dame Inowslad' Gilchrist turns his attention to a disquieting version of the third of Gothic fiction's 'dead yet living': the revenant.

THE CRIMSON WEAVER

y Master and I had wandered from our track and lost ourselves on the side of a great 'edge'. It was a two-days' journey from the Valley of the Willow Brakes, and we had roamed aimlessly; eating at hollow-echoing inns where grey-haired hostesses ministered, and sleeping side by side through the dewless midsummer nights on beds of fresh-gathered heather.

Beyond a single-arched wall-less bridge that crossed a brown stream whose waters leaped straight from the upland, we reached the Domain of the Crimson Weaver. No sooner had we reached the keystone when a beldam, wrinkled as a walnut and bald as an egg, crept from a cabin of turf and osier and held out her hands in warning.

'Enter not the Domain of the Crimson Weaver!' she shrieked. 'One I loved entered—I am here to warn men. Behold, I was beautiful once!'

She tore her ragged smock apart and discovered the foulness of her bosom, where the heart pulsed behind a curtain of livid skin. My Master drew money from his wallet and scattered it on the ground.

'She is mad,' he said. 'The evil she hints cannot exist. There is no fiend.'

So we passed on, but the bridge-keeper took no heed of the coins. For awhile we heard her bellowed sighs issuing from the openings of her den.

Strangely enough, the tenor of our talk changed from the moment that we left the bridge. He had been telling me of the Platonists, but when our feet pressed the sun-dried grass I was impelled to question him of love. It was the first time I had thought of the matter.

'How does passion first touch a man's life?' I asked, laying my hand on his arm.

His ruddy colour faded, he smiled wryly.

'You divine what passes in my brain,' he replied. 'I also had begun to meditate... But I may not tell you... In my boyhood—I was scarce older than you at the time—I loved the true paragon. 'Twere sacrilege to speak of the birth of passion. Let it suffice that ere I tasted of wedlock the woman died, and her death sealed for ever the door of that chamber of my heart... Yet, if one might see therein, there is an altar crowned with ever-burning tapers and with wreaths of unwithering asphodels.'

By this time we had reached the skirt of a yew-forest, traversed in every direction by narrow paths. The air was moist and heavy, but ever and anon a light wind touched the tree-tops and bowed them, so that the pollen sank in golden veils to the ground.

Everywhere we saw half-ruined fountains, satyrs vomiting senilely, nymphs emptying wine upon the lambent flames of dying phoenixes, creatures that were neither satyrs nor nymphs, nor gryphins, but grotesque adminglings of all, slain by one another, with water gushing from wounds in belly and thigh.

At length the path we had chosen terminated beside an oval mere that was surrounded by a colonnade of moss-grown arches. Huge pike quivered on the muddy bed, crayfish moved sluggishly amongst the weeds.

There was an island in the middle, where a leaden Diana, more compassionate than a crocodile, caressed Actaeon's horns ere delivering him to his hounds. The huntress's head and shoulders were white with the excrement of a crowd of culvers that moved as if entangled in a snare.

Northwards an avenue rose for the space of a mile, to fall abruptly before an azure sky. For many years the yew-mast on the pathway had been undisturbed by human foot; it was covered with a crust of greenish lichen.

My Master pressed my fingers. 'There is some evil in the air of this place,' he said. 'I am strong, but you—you may not endure. We will return.'

''Tis an enchanted country,' I made answer, feverishly. 'At the end of yonder avenue stands the palace of the sleeping maiden who awaits the kiss. Nay, since we have pierced the country thus far, let us not draw back. You are strong, Master—no evil can touch us.'

So we fared to the place where the avenue sank, and then our eyes fell on the wondrous sight of a palace, lying in a concave pleasaunce, all treeless, but so bestarred with fainting flowers, that neither blade of grass nor grain of earth was visible.

Then came a rustling of wings above our heads, and looking skywards I saw flying towards the house a flock of culvers like unto those that had drawn themselves over Diana's head. The hindmost bird dropped its neck, and behold it gazed upon us with the face of a mannikin!

'They are charmed birds, made thus by the whim of the Princess,' I said.

As the birds passed through the portals of a columbary that crowned a western tower, their white wings beat against a silver bell that glistened there, and the whole valley was filled with music.

My Master trembled and crossed himself. 'In the name of our Mother,' he exclaimed, 'let us return. I dare not trust your life here.'

But a great door in front of the palace swung open, and a woman with a swaying walk came out to the terrace. She wore a robe of crimson worn into tatters at skirt-hem and shoulders. She had been forewarned of our presence, for her face turned instantly in our direction. She smiled subtly, and her smile died away into a most tempting sadness.

She caught up such remnants of her skirt as trailed behind, and strutted about with the gait of a peacock. As the sun touched the glossy fabric I saw eyes inwrought in deeper hue.

My Master still trembled, but he did not move, for the gaze of the woman was fixed upon him. His brows twisted and his white hair rose and stood erect, as if he viewed some unspeakable horror.

Stooping, with sidelong motions of the head, she approached, bringing with her the smell of such an incense as when amidst Eastern herbs burns the corse… She was perfect of feature as the Diana, but her skin was deathly white and her lips fretted with pain.

She took no heed of me, but knelt at my Master's feet—a Magdalene before an impregnable priest.

'Prince and Lord, Tower of Chastity, hear!' she murmured. 'For lack of love I perish. See my robe in tatters!'

He strove to avert his face, but his eyes still dwelt upon her. She half rose and shook nut-brown tresses over his knees.

Youth came back in a flood to my Master. His shrivelled skin filled out; the dying sunlight turned to gold the whiteness of his hair. He would have raised her had I not caught his hands. The anguish of foreboding made me cry: 'One forces roughly the door of your heart's chamber. The wreaths wither, the tapers bend and fall.'

He grew old again. The Crimson Weaver turned to me.

'O marplot!' she said laughingly, 'think not to vanquish me with folly. I am too powerful. Once that a man enter my domain he is mine.'

But I drew my Master away. ''Tis I who am strong,' I whispered. 'We will go hence at once. Surely we may find our way back to the bridge. The journey is easy.'

The woman, seeing that the remembrance of an old love was strong within him, sighed heavily, and returned to the palace. As she reached the doorway, the valves opened, and I saw in a distant chamber beyond the hall an ivory loom with a golden stool.

My Master and I walked again on the track we had made in the yew-mast. But twilight was falling, and ere we could reach the pool of Diana all was in utter darkness; so at the foot of a tree, where no anthill rose, we lay down and slept.

Dreams came to me—gorgeous visions from the romances of eld. Everywhere I sought vainly for a beloved. There was the Castle of the Ebony Dwarf, where a young queen reposed in the innermost casket of the seventh crystal cabinet; there was the Chamber of Gloom, where Lenore danced, and where I groped for ages around columns of living flesh; there was the White Minaret, where twenty-one princesses poised themselves on balls of burnished bronze; there was Melisandra's arbour, where the sacred toads crawled over the enchanted cloak.

Unrest fretted me: I woke in spiritual pain. Dawn was breaking—a bright yellow dawn, and the glades were full of vapours.

I turned to the place where my Master had lain. He was not there. I felt with my hands over his bed: it was key-cold. Terror of my loneliness overcame me, and I sat with covered face.

On the ground near my feet lay a broken riband, whereon was strung a heart of chrysolite. It enclosed a knot of ash-coloured hair—hair of the girl my Master had loved.

The mists gathered together and passed sunwards in one long many-cornered veil. When the last shred had been drawn into the great light, I gazed along the avenue, and saw the topmost bartizan of the Crimson Weaver's palace.

It was midday ere I dared start on my search. The culvers beat about my head. I walked in pain, as though giant spiders had woven about my body.

On the terrace strange beasts—dogs and pigs with human limbs—tore ravenously at something that lay beside the balustrade. At sight of me they paused and lifted their snouts and bayed. A while afterwards the culvers rang the silver bell, and the monsters dispersed hurriedly amongst the drooping blossoms of the pleasaunce, and where they had swarmed I saw naught but a steaming sanguine pool.

I approached the house and the door fell open, admitting me to a chamber adorned with embellishments beyond the witchery of art. There I lifted my voice and cried eagerly: 'My Master, my Master, where is my Master?' The alcoves sent out a babble of echoes, blended together like a harp-chord on a dulcimer: 'My Master, my Master, where is my Master? For the love of Christ, where is my Master?' The echo replied only, 'Where is my Master?'

Above, swung a globe of topaz, where a hundred suns gambolled. From its centre a convoluted horn, held by a crimson cord, sank lower and lower. It stayed before my lips and I blew therein, and heard the sweet voices of youths chant with one accord.

'Fall open, oh doors: fall open and show the way to the princess!'

Ere the last of the echoes had died a vista opened, and at the end of an alabaster gallery I saw the Crimson Weaver at her loom. She had doffed her tattered robe for one new and lustrous as freshly drawn blood. And marvellous as her beauty had seemed before, its wonder was now increased a hundredfold.

She came towards me with the same stately walk, but there was now a lightness in her demeanour that suggested the growth of wings.

Within arm's-length she curtseyed, and curtseying showed me the firmness of her shoulders, the fullness of her breast. The sight brought no pleasure: my cracking tongue appealed in agony: 'My Master, where is my Master?'

She smiled happily. 'Nay, do not trouble. He is not here. His soul talks with the culvers in the cote. He has forgotten you. In the night we supped, and I gave him of nepenthe.'

'Where is my Master? Yesterday he told me of the shrine in his heart—of ever-fresh flowers—of a love dead yet living.'

Her eyebrows curved mirthfully. ''Tis foolish boys' talk,' she said. 'If you sought till the end of time you would never find him—unless I chose. Yet—if you buy of me—myself to name the price.'

I looked around hopelessly at the unimaginable riches of her home. All that I have is this Manor of the Willow Brakes—a Moorish park, an ancient house where the thatch gapes and the casements swing loose.

'My possessions are pitiable,' I said, 'but they are all yours. I give all to save him.'

'Fool, fool!' she cried. 'I have no need of gear. If I but raise my hand, all the riches of the world fall to me. 'Tis not what I wish for.'

Into her eyes came such a glitter as the moon makes on the moist skin of a sleeping snake. The firmness of her lips relaxed;

they grew child-like in their softness. The atmosphere became almost tangible: I could scarce breathe.

'What is it? All that I can do, if it be no sin.'

'Come with me to my loom,' she said, 'and if you do the thing I desire you shall see him. There is no evil in't—in past times kings have sighed for the same.'

So I followed slowly to the loom, before which she had seated herself, and watched her deftly passing crimson thread over crimson thread.

She was silent for a space, and in that space her beauty fascinated me, so that I was no longer master of myself.

'What you wish for I will give, even if it be life.'

The loom ceased. 'A kiss of the mouth, and you shall see him who passed in the night.'

She clasped her arms about my neck and pressed my lips. For one moment heaven and earth ceased to be; but there was one paradise, where we were sole governours...

Then she moved back and drew aside the web and showed me the head of my Master, and the bleeding heart whence a crimson cord unravelled into many threads.

'I wear men's lives,' the woman said. 'Life is necessary to me, or even I—who have existed from the beginning—must die. But yesterday I feared the end, and he came. His soul is not dead—'tis truth that it plays with my culvers.'

I fell back.

'Another kiss,' she said. 'Unless I wish, there is no escape for you. Yet you may return to your home, though my power over you shall never wane. Once more—lip to lip.'

I crouched against the wall like a terrified dog. She grew angry; her eyes darted fire. 'A kiss,' she cried, 'for the penalty!'

My poor Master's head, ugly and cadaverous, glared from the loom. I could not move.

The Crimson Weaver lifted her skirt, uncovering feet shapen as those of a vulture. I fell prostrate. With her claws she fumbled about the flesh of my breast. Moving away she bade me pass from her sight...

So, half-dead, I lie here at the Manor of the Willow Brakes, watching hour by hour the bloody clew ever unwinding from my heart and passing over the western hills to the Palace of the Siren.

THE RETURN

ive minutes ago I drew the window curtain aside and let the mellow sunset light contend with the glare from the girandoles. Below lay the orchard of Vernon Garth, rich in heavily flowered fruit-trees—yonder a medlar, here a pear, next a quince. As my eyes, unaccustomed to the day, blinked rapidly, the recollection came of a scene forty-five years past, and once more beneath the oldest tree stood the girl I loved, mischievously plucking yarrow, and, despite its evil omen, twining the snowy clusters in her black hair. Again her coquettish words rang in my ears: 'Make me thy lady! Make me the richest woman in England, and I promise thee, Brian, we shall be the happiest of God's creatures.' And I remembered how the mad thirst for gold filled me: how I trusted in her fidelity, and without reasoning or even telling her that I would conquer fortune for her sake, I kissed her sadly and passed into the world. Then followed a complete silence until the *Star of Europe*, the greatest diamond discovered in modern times, lay in my hand,—a rough unpolished stone not unlike the lumps of spar I had often seen lying on the sandy lanes of my native county. This should be Rose's own, and all the others that clanked so melodiously in their leather bulse should go towards fulfilling her ambition. Rich and happy I should be soon, and should I not marry an untitled gentlewoman, sweet in her prime? The twenty years' interval of work and sleep was like a fading dream, for I was going home. The knowledge thrilled me so that my nerves were strung tight as iron ropes and I laughed like a young boy. And it was all because my home was to be in Rose Pascal's arms.

I crossed the sea and posted straight for Halkton village. The old hostelry was crowded. Jane Hopgarth, whom I remembered a ruddy-faced child, stood on the box-edged terrace, courtesying in matronly fashion to the departing mail-coach. A change in the sign-board drew my eye: the white lilies had been painted over with a mitre, and the name changed from the Pascal Arms to the Lord Bishop. Angrily aghast at this disloyalty, I cross-questioned the ostlers, who hurried to and fro, but failing to obtain any coherent reply I was fain to content myself with a mental denunciation of the times.

At last I saw Bow-Legged Jeffries, now bent double with age, sunning himself at his favourite place, the side of the horse-trough. As of old he was chewing a straw. No sign of recognition came over his face as he gazed at me, and I was shocked, because I wished to impart some of my gladness to a fellow-creature. I went to him, and after trying in vain to make him speak, held forth a gold coin. He rose instantly, grasped it with palsied fingers, and, muttering that the hounds were starting, hurried from my presence. Feeling half sad I crossed to the churchyard and gazed through the grated window of the Pascal burial chapel at the recumbent and undisturbed effigies of Geoffrey Pascal, gentleman, of Bretton Hall; and Margot Maltrevor his wife, with their quaint epitaph about a perfect marriage enduring for ever. Then, after noting the rankness of the docks and nettles, I crossed the worn stile and with footsteps surprising fleet passed towards the stretch of moorland at whose further end stands Bretton Hall.

Twilight had fallen ere I reached the cottage at the entrance of the park. This was in a ruinous condition: here and there sheaves in the thatched roof had parted and formed crevices through which smoke filtered. Some of the tiny windows had been walled up, and even where the glass remained snake-like ivy hindered any light from falling into their thick recesses.

The door stood open, although the evening was chill. As I approached, the heavy autumnal dew shook down from the firs and fell upon my shoulders. A bat, swooping in an undulation, struck between my eyes and fell to the grass, moaning querulously. I entered. A withered woman sat beside the peat fire. She held a pair of steel knitting-needles which she moved without cessation. There was no thread upon them, and when they clicked her lips twitched as if she had counted. Some time passed before I recognised Rose's foster-mother, Elizabeth Carless. The russet colour of her cheeks had faded and left a sickly grey: those sunken, dimmed eyes were utterly unlike the bright black orbs that had danced so mirthfully. Her stature, too, had shrunk. I was struck with wonder. Elizabeth could not be more than fifty-six years old. I had been away twenty years; Rose was fifteen when I left her, and I had heard Elizabeth say that she was only twenty-one at the time of her darling's weaning. But what a change! She had such an air of weary grief that my heart grew sick.

Advancing to her side I touched her arm. She turned, but neither spoke nor seemed aware of my presence. Soon, however, she rose, and helping herself along by grasping the scanty furniture, tottered to a window and peered out. Her right hand crept to her throat; she untied the string of her gown and took from her bosom a pomander set in a battered silver case. I cried out; Rose had loved that toy in her childhood; thousands of times had we played ball with it... Elizabeth held it to her mouth and mumbled into it, as if it were a baby's hand. Maddened with impatience, I caught her shoulder and roughly bade her say where I should find Rose. But something awoke in her eyes, and she shrank away to the other side of the house-place: I followed; she cowered on the floor, looking at me with a strange horror. Her lips began to move, but they made no sound. Only when I crossed to the threshold did she rise; and then her head moved wildly from side to side, and her hands pressed close to her breast, as if the pain there were too great to endure.

I ran from the place, not daring to look back. In a few minutes I readied the balustraded wall of the Hall garden. The vegetation there was wonderfully luxuriant. As of old, the great blue and white Canterbury bells grew thickly, and those curious flowers to which tradition has given the name of 'Marie's Heart' still spread their creamy tendrils and blood-coloured bloom on every hand. But 'Pascal's Dribble,' the tiny spring whose water pulsed so fiercely as it emerged from the earth, had long since burst its bounds, and converted the winter garden into a swamp, where a miniature forest of queen-of-the-meadow filled the air with melancholy sweetness. The house looked as if no careful hand had touched it for years. The elements had played havoc with its oriels, and many of the latticed frames hung on single hinges. The curtain of the blue parlour hung outside, draggled and faded, and half hidden by a thick growth of bindweed.

With an almost savage force I raised my arm high above my head and brought my fist down upon the central panel of the door. There was no need for such violence, for the decayed fastenings made no resistance, and some of the rotten boards fell to the ground. As I entered the hall and saw the ancient furniture, once so fondly kept, now mildewed and crumbling to dust, quick sobs burst from my throat. Rose's spinet stood beside the door of the withdrawing-room. How many carols had we sung to its music! As I passed my foot struck one of the legs and the rickety structure groaned as if it were coming to pieces. I thrust out my hand to steady it, but at my touch the velvet covering of the lid came off and the tiny gilt ornaments rattled downwards. The moon was just rising and only half her disc was visible over the distant edge of the Hell Garden. The light in the room was very uncertain, yet I could see that the keys of the instrument were stained brown, and bound together with thick cobwebs.

Whilst I stood beside it I felt an overpowering desire to play a country ballad with an over-word of 'Willow Browbound.' The words in strict accordance with the melody are merry and sad by turns: at one time filled with light happiness, at another bitter as the voice of one bereaved for ever of joy. So I cleared off the spiders and began to strike the keys with my forefinger. Many were dumb, and when I struck them gave forth no sound save a peculiar sigh; but still the melody rhythmed as distinctly as if a low voice crooned it out of the darkness. Wearied with the bitterness, I turned away.

By now the full moonlight pierced the window and quivered on the floor. As I gazed on the tremulous pattern it changed into quaint devices of hearts, daggers, rings, and a thousand tokens more. All suddenly another object glided amongst them so quickly that I wondered whether my eyes had been at fault,—a tiny satin shoe, stained crimson across the lappets. A revulsion of feeling came to my soul and drove away all my fear. I had seen that self-same shoe white and unsoiled twenty years before, when vain, vain Rose danced amongst her reapers at the harvest-home. And my voice cried out in ecstasy, 'Rose, heart of mine! Delight of all the world's delights!'

She stood before me, wondering, amazed. Alas, so changed! The red-and-yellow silk shawl still covered her shoulders; her hair still hung in those eldritch curls. But the beautiful face had grown wan and tired, and across the forehead lines were drawn like silver threads. She threw her arms round my neck and, pressing her bosom heavily on mine, sobbed so piteously that I grew afraid for her, and drew back the long masses of hair which had fallen forward, and kissed again and again those lips that were too lovely for simile. Never came a word of chiding from them. 'Love,' she said, when she had regained her breath, 'the past struggle was sharp and torturing—the future struggle will be crueller still. What a great love yours was, to wait and trust for so long! Would that mine had been as powerful! Poor, weak heart that could not endure!'

The tones of a wild fear throbbed through all her speech, strongly, yet with insufficient power to prevent her feeling the tenderness of those moments. Often, timorously raising her head from my shoulder, she looked about and then turned with a soft, inarticulate, and glad murmur to hide her face on my bosom. I spoke fervently; told of the years spent away from her; how, when working in the diamond-fields she had ever been present in my fancy; how at night her name had fallen from my lips in my only prayer; how I had dreamed of her amongst the greatest in the land,—the richest, and, I dare swear, the loveliest woman in the world. I grew warmer still: all the gladness which had been constrained for so long now burst wildly from my lips: a myriad of rich ideas resolved into words, which, being spoken, wove one long and delicious fit of passion. As we stood together, the moon brightened and filled the chamber with a light like the day's. The ridges of the surrounding moorland stood out in sharp relief.

Rose drank in my declarations thirstily, but soon interrupted me with a heavy sigh. 'Come away,' she said softly. 'I no longer live in this house. You must stay with me tonight. This place is so wretched now; for time, that in you and me has only strengthened love, has wrought much ruin here.'

Half leaning on me, she led me from the precincts of Bretton Hall. We walked in silence over the waste that crowns the valley of the Whitelands and, being near the verge of the rocks, saw the great pinewood sloping downwards, lighted near us by the moon, but soon lost in density. Along the mysterious line where the light changed into gloom, intricate shadows of withered summer bracken struck and receded in a mimic battle. Before us lay the Priests' Cliff. The moon was veiled by a grove of elms, whose ever-swaying branches alternately increased and lessened her brightness. This was a place of notoriety—a veritable Golgotha—a haunt fit only for demons. Murder and theft had been punished here; and to this day fireside stories are told of evil women dancing round that Druids' circle, carrying hearts plucked from gibbeted bodies.

'Rose,' I whispered, 'why have you brought me here?'

She made no reply, but pressed her head more closely to my shoulder. Scarce had my lips closed ere a sound like the hiss of a half-strangled snake vibrated amongst the trees. It grew louder and louder. A monstrous shadow hovered above.

Rose from my bosom murmured. 'Love is strong as Death! Love is strong as Death!'

I locked her in my arms, so tightly that she grew breathless. 'Hold me,' she panted. 'You are strong.'

A cold hand touched our foreheads so that, benumbed, we sank together to the ground, to fall instantly into a dreamless slumber.

When I awoke the clear grey light of the early morning had spread over the country. Beyond the Hell Garden the sun was just bursting through the clouds, and had already spread a long golden haze along the horizon. The babbling of the streamlet that runs down to Halkton was so distinct that it seemed almost at my side. How sweetly the wild thyme smelt! Filled with the tender recollections of the night, without turning, I called Rose Pascal from her sleep.

'Sweetheart, sweetheart, waken! waken! waken! See how glad the world looks—see the omens of a happy future.'

No answer came. I sat up, and looking round me saw that I was alone. A square stone lay near. When the sun was high I crept to read the inscription carved thereon:—'*Here, at four cross-paths, lieth, with a stake through the bosom, the body of Rose Pascal, who in her sixteenth year wilfully cast away the life God gave.*'

THE LOVER'S ORDEAL

ary Padley stood near the leaden statue of Diana on the terrace at Calton Dovecote, gazing towards the stone-arched gate that barred the avenue of limes—sweet-scented, with their newly opened bloom—from the dusty high-road.

She wore white—a mantua of thin silk, a stiff petticoat spread over a great hoop, and a quaint stomacher, lilac in colour, and embroidered with silver beads.

Her hair was cushioned and powdered, Madam Padley, her grandmother and guardian, insisting that, since she would probably soon change her estate, she must cease playing the hoyden, and devote herself to a careful study of such fashions as leaked from town to the Peak Country.

It may be stated, however, that the dame, in calling her a hoyden, spoke tenderly enough, since she knew that her sole living descendant had sterling and admirable qualities, combined with a physical loveliness that promised to make her a reigning toast after her union with Mr Endymion Eyre, heir-presumptive to my Lord Newburgh.

Madam, herself being high-spirited, doted upon—though she outwardly condemned—the maid's too fervent love of the romantic and uncommon.

But, at the present moment, Madam Padley had very kindly fallen asleep beside her embroidery-frame, and Mary had stolen from the house to watch for Mr Eyre's coming.

She held in her right hand a folded sheet. A ray of the westering sun touched the words: '*The Spectator*, No. 557. Wednesday, June 23, 1714.'

The minutes dragged. She opened the first page, and began to peruse, for the twentieth time, a letter which her lover, who was gifted with some literary power, had addressed to Addison, partly for the sake of eliciting one of that master's wise disquisitions.

'Mr Spectator,' she read softly—'Since the decline of chivalry, a man has no opportunity of proving his devotion to the lady of his choice. Why not permit her to name some ordeal through which he must pass, and by whose performance he might win from her the fullest trust and faith, without which a true marriage is impossible—'

She read no more, for she heard the sound of his mare's hoofs in the distance. A bright smile lighted her face; her colour rose faintly. 'Here comes my author,' she said, 'speeding to hear my yea or nay. Heigh-o! I wish my heart would not beat so wildly! For all the world 'tis as if I'd stolen a fledgling and prisoned it in my bosom!'

He dismounted at the foot of a mossy staircase. A groom came forward to take the bridle. Mary curtsied her prettiest, then gave him her hand to lift to his lips.

'This evening,' he said laughingly, 'this evening you promised to tell me whether you'd marry me or no. Of course, the asking's but a formality, for I'm fully resolved to make you.'

'Alack,' she cried, 'you've a pretty fashion of showing me that I've met my master! Well, good Mr Eyre, you have courted me for a full year, and I've known you all my life, and, as you are aware, I've no aversion for your person. Yes—yes, I'll marry you—on one condition.'

'And that—' he began.

'You've set my heart upon making you pass through an ordeal. Don't suspect for a moment that I'm ignorant as to who wrote this.' She held her *Spectator* aloft. 'You've asked to be tested—'

'The deuce upon my scribblings!' he exclaimed. 'Well, mistress, whatever you wish I'll do with the utmost expedition, on one condition—that being that it does not take me long from you. Tell me the ordeal, sweet. I'm eager to pass through it—to have you swear that I'm a worthy man.'

Their eyes met fondly.

'I ne'er doubted that,' she said; 'but all girls have their whimsies. Come down into the park. 'Tis a night made for lovers.'

Then she gave him her hand again; and they went together through the narrow walk of the rosery, where the beautiful flowers were all wet with dew, to a knoll about half a mile from the Dovecote, whence one could see almost forty miles of rough moorland and wood passing upwards towards the North Country.

A crescent moon hung overhead. There was no sound save the sighing of the wind and the churring of the moth-hawks.

Mary paused when they reached the summit, and pointed to another hill about three miles away—a strange conical place covered with great trees, from whose tops rose several stacks of twisted chimneys.

'You wish, then, to pass through the ordeal?' she said. 'You are no coward, and that which I set you to do needs a brave spirit. 'Tis—'tis to spend a night at Calton Hall, where no living creature has been after dark since my folk left it eighty years ago. The place is haunted—or so 'tis said—and 'twill require all your courage to pass the midnight hours in those deserted suites.'

He interrupted her by taking her into his arms, quite in an informal fashion, and silencing her lips by the pressure of his own.

'May it be done tonight?' he asked. 'Let me perform this valorous deed at once, and so become a hero in your eyes.'

'Ay,' responded Mary. 'I have the key of the door—I took it unseen from my grandmother's basket. If I had asked for it, be sure she'd not have consented. There's none has a keener belief than she in the mystery that haunts the place o' nights. So, since you sup with us, I'd have you say naught concerning the ordeal, or she'd at once forbid it.'

They returned to the house now. Madam Padley, who had awakened some minutes before, met them in the hall.

She was a stately old woman, still comely despite her seventy years. In youth she had been a lady-in-waiting to the Duchess of York; and her manner still suggested the atmosphere of a Court. As she possessed both fine wit and intuition, she read aright the radiance of the lovers' faces.

'I offer my profound congratulations,' she said. 'Mr Eyre, I'm vastly proud that you're to enter our family. In short, there's no gentleman I've e'er met whom I'd liefer receive as grandson. But, putting the blind god aside, supper is already served; and I am amazingly hungry. Your arm, Endymion. Young miss shall walk behind.'

Throughout the elaborate meal she talked incessantly, preaching a dainty homily on the duties of married folk.

Afterwards Mary and Endymion confessed to each other that they remembered nothing of what she had said, their own thoughts being engaged in rosy pictures of the future.

When the meal was over, they passed to the withdrawing-room, where Mary sat to the new harpsichord and played sweet songs from Purcell's operas.

At ten o'clock Madam Padley rose from her chair and signified courteously that 'twas time for the gentleman to retire, but cordially invited him to spend the following evening in the same fashion.

Mary accompanied him to the courtyard, where a groom waited with his mare. Now that he was starting for the ordeal, the girl's heart failed of a sudden; and she begged him to forget her words. He laughed merrily, and shook his head.

'Too late,' he said. 'I go now to Calton. Not for the world would I renounce the adventure. When I see you again, I shall have wonderful stories of ghosts for your ear alone. If they be harmless things, why, you and I'll go together afterwards to pay 'em a visit of ceremony! Now, adieu, mistress. Sleep well, and dream pretty dreams.'

He turned thrice in his saddle, and waved his hand. She stood watching until he was out of sight. Then she went back very sadly to the house, and, finding that her grandmother had already retired, sought her own chamber, where, instead of undressing, she sat in a deep window-recess, peering through an open casement at the moonlit chimneys of the distant house.

Meanwhile, Eyre rode on leisurely over moor and through copse until he reached the neglected pleasaunce, where the undergrowth had matted together until there was scarce space to reach the stairs leading to the colonnade.

He left the mare in a small courtyard, where dock and nettles had covered the stones with a thick carpet; then, making his way to the front, opened the door and entered the musty hall.

There he took out his tinder-box, and struck a light, finding, much to his relief, a tall wax candle standing in a sconce near the mantel. This he lighted, and, holding it high above his head, made his way up the oaken stairs, and through a long gallery, at whose further end stood an open doorway that led to the suite of staterooms. These were hung with moth-eaten tapestry. In places the decayed canvases of ancient portraits trailed from their frames to the floor. The movement of the light brought around him clouds of evil-smelling bats; two owls on the sill of a broken oriel hooted loudly, and then fluttered out into the night.

On and on, through countless chambers whose antique magnificence was veiled with dust and cobwebs, until he came to another and greater door, which stood slightly ajar. And as he pressed the panel with his palm he saw that the place beyond was lighted with a curious radiance—greenish, cold—not unlike the moonlight on a frosty evening.

The door fell back easily. He found himself in a great chamber, the walls adorned with coloured bas-reliefs; the ceiling, still bright and vivid, covered with a gorgeous fresco wherein one saw the gods at play. On the two hearths fires burned—inaudible fires with greedy, lambent flames whose tongues licked the mantel-stone.

'By the Lord!' he exclaimed, 'there are folk living here! This is no place for ghosts! As handsome a—'

His voice died, for something had moved at the further end— something hidden in the shadow of a canopy of velvet embroidered with gold thread.

The muscles of his heart tightened. He moved forward, almost unsteadily, holding the candle at arm's length, until he came to the lowest step of a low platform, whereon, in a lacquered chair, rested a form shrouded in a veil of black gauze. And, as he paused there, this veil stirred again, disclosing the figure of a young woman, whose long, white hands moved slowly from her face.

Her eyes opened. They were large and luminous, gleaming as if a steady fire burned behind the pupils. She was wondrously beautiful; her loveliness was greater than that of any woman he had ever dreamed of—greater even than that of the maiden to whom he had given his heart. She was strangely pale, the only colour—a vivid scarlet—being in the plump, curved lips.

'I bid you welcome, signor,' she said. 'The long, long sleep has not been wasted since you are the awakener. Your hand! Weariness is still in my body. I'd fain rise and walk.'

Her voice was exquisitely soft, exquisitely glad. 'Twas not the voice of an Englishwoman. There was a quaint accent, as if she had come from a Southern country. And the hand Endymion took was cold and damp at first—as cold and damp as the hand of one prepared for burial; but, as it lay lightly in his own, it became warm, and the fingers closed tenderly upon his own.

'Your name, signor of whom I have dreamed?' she said.

The blood began to run quickly through his veins. 'Endymion, madam, at your service,' he replied.

'And mine shall be Diana,' she said. 'Diana, who kissed Endymion in the night. Prythee, now, your arm. I'll lean upon you, being but a weak creature. Ah me, but your country's sad! I'd give all for the warm skies of Tuscany—for the vineyards under the hot sun! I like not the moonlight.'

Something impelled him to talk foolishly. ''Tis not the warmth of skies or the sight of vineyards that makes for perfect happiness,' he said. 'There's a rarer warmth—the warmth of love.'

She laid her right palm upon his lips. 'Hush!' she said. 'At this our first meeting why should you talk of love? Doubtless there's some cold, pretty girl living for you alone in the world—some green creature who dotes upon you—who looks to the day when she may call you spouse, unless 'tis so already.'

Then, with a swift movement of the left arm, she drew aside the tapestry from a great window that stretched from floor to pargeting.

Beyond, through glass clear as crystal, he could see the moor, white in the moonlight, as if covered with hoar-frost.

'Behold the winter!' said the lady. 'Behold the cruelty of your country! Alas, I am outdone with the cold! Let's to yonder fire for warmth.'

The curtain fell back again. Together they went across the chamber.

Not once in all that time did he bestow one thought upon the girl he loved—the girl whose promise he had won that very night. Past and future were blotted from his mind. He lived solely in the present.

The beauty chose a great chair, covered with crimson silk—a chair with carved arms and legs and padded face-screens.

'I sit here, my cavalier,' she said; 'and you rest at my feet. Yonder's a stool. Your head shall lie upon my knee.'

She drew from a tissue bag that hung from her girdle a handful of dried petals, and flung them between the andirons. The fire engulfed them silently. A blood-coloured flame rose high up the chimney.

A strange commingling of luxury and dread came over Endymion. He sank to her feet.

She drew his face, with both hands, to her lap. Then she bowed her head until her soft lips touched his neck.

Mary found herself unable to sleep—unable even to prepare for bed.

In less than an hour after Endymion's departure her disquietude became so painful that she left her chamber and hastened to Madam Padley's bedside.

The old lady was sleeping placidly. Her white horsehair head-dress had been replaced by a decent cap of plaited linen.

The girl laid a trembling hand upon her shoulder. 'Waken, grandmother,' she said. 'Waken, I am miserable. I have done something that I had no right to do. I am bewildered. Some evil thing is happening!'

The dame started, and sat up. 'What is't child?' she said. 'Art troubled with a nightmare?'

Mary spoke disconnectedly. Madam listened, piecing the broken sentences together; then she flung aside the bedclothes.

'My God,' she cried, 'you have done wrongly! I had never wished to tell you, but the reason—the reason why yonder house is deserted is that your great-grandfather wooed and wed for second wife a foreign woman, who fed upon human blood! And the place grew foul with strange crimes!'

She rang for her abigail; but before the worthy woman could appear Mary had fled from the chamber and from the house. In another minute the great fire-bell of the Dovecote was clanging wildly, and the servants leaping from their beds. Madam Padley could not speak for excitement. Her gestures alone bade them follow with all speed in the girl's tracks.

Mary reached the hall long before the others, and, entering through the open doorway, ran up the gallery and passed from room to room, calling passionately upon her lover's name. The moonlight shone now through the latticed windows. Everywhere she saw bats flying into the corners. At last she reached the great chamber, not lighted now with mysterious fires, but dark and dusty, and fetid of odour.

Endymion lay prone upon the floor; beside him crouched a woman's figure, the head pressed close to his own. And Mary took the thing madly by the shoulders and thrust it aside, and linked her arms around the young man's waist.

His eyes opened; she heard the sound of his breathing.

'There's naught for it save that I drag you from the place,' she whispered. 'Who knows that she may not bring others stronger than I?'

'I have dreamed terribly,' he muttered; 'dreamed of things that I dare not tell.'

In the gallery he rose awkwardly to his feet, and, leaning heavily against her, stumbled to the staircase. 'Had you not come, dearest one,' he said, 'all the blood had left my body.'

There the servants met them, and prepared a rough litter, in which he was carried back to the Dovecote. Mary followed, but not until after she had done something that ere another night had blotted Calton Hall out of existence. As she left the place she set fire to the tapestries, and the woodwork took flame almost instantly. Since 'twas her own heritage none could complain. When Madam Padley and Endymion heard they said nothing; but it was easy to see that they approved.

And when, two days afterwards, he was permitted to leave his room and sit with Mary in the sunlit garden, and she took his hand and held it to her bosom, and begged him to forgive her for submitting to such a weird ordeal, he put his disengaged arm around her neck and begged her to be silent.

'For, sweet,' he said, 'there's shame in my happiness. That night hath shown me how nobler is your love than mine.'

A NIGHT ON THE MOOR

he sun had set in a dull red glow, and twilight fell with odd swiftness. Although the sparse thorns of the moor, all inclining from west to east, in obedience to the prevalent winds, were scarce tinged with the bright hues of autumn, a few thin flakes of snow were falling gently.

Lindsay Warmsworth, who had rented the shooting from Squire Greenleaf, buttoned his coat, and finally discharging his gun, prepared to return to the Lodge. That afternoon, since his friends had passed on to other places and a new party was not to arrive until the following day, he had been obliged to tramp alone. Barton, the old keeper, had complained mysteriously of rheumatism in his shaky knees, and after begging him on no account to be benighted, had tottered homeward when they reached the confines of the park. The bag which was slung over Warmsworth's shoulder was heavy with slaughtered grouse; a brace of woodcock, too rare a prize to be carried in such plebeian company, bulged in his right-hand pocket.

This great stretch of tableland in the very heart of the Peak country, was covered chiefly with ling and sphagnum. Here and there, round beds of rushes, wet and blood-coloured, disclosed the existence of treacherous marsh. Warmsworth, after passing a Druid's Circle, found an ancient bridle-path of hollowed slabs, which he had never seen before, and surmising that it passed in the direction of his resting-place, he began to hurry, thankful to be relieved from the necessity of carefully picking his way over the sodden ground. As far as he could understand, he had more than three miles to cover before reaching comfortable shelter; but being young and hot-blooded, he felt no tremors, and lifting a powerful voice in a popular hunting song, he shaped the rhythm to the muffled sound of his footsteps. After a while, however, so intense grew the blackness and so heavy the snowfall that he stopped short in his elegy of 'John Peel,' and with a sudden uneasiness drew out his compass, struck a match, and strove to discover if he were on the right track. A gust blew out the light immediately, but not before he had seen that the needle had fallen from its pivot; without further delay he continued to proceed, trusting to a keen sense of locality which he had never known to fail.

After he had proceeded for at least an hour, and now not yet reached the sloping clough at whose lower end stood the Lodge, he found that he had left the path and was straying knee-deep in heather, whose branches were so tough that no firing could have been done for years. The snow was still falling, and the wind rose in low soughs. He began, unwillingly, to realise that he was lost, and, in spite of Barton's deprecations, in all probability must remain on the moor until daybreak. Fortunately, just as he had resigned hope of finding any shelter, his outstretched left hand touched a stout wooden door, and after a brief struggle with the latch he entered a shepherd's hut, mud-walled and thatched with turves. On striking another match, he discovered, to his great relief that the place was waterproof, and that, in readiness for the winter, a huge faggot of fir-boughs lay in a corner, beside a great stone, above which rose a narrow chimney. To set light to a few twigs was the work of a moment; soon a brave fire was crackling lustily. A bed of dried bracken was spread on trestled boards; he sat down, drew out his pipe, and thanked the gods for a harbour of refuge. The resinous sap of the fir-wood diffused a fragrant odour that overpowered the fumes of the tobacco, and the flames cast dancing shadows on the dark brown walls.

Ere long the heat of the place made him drowsy; he lay full length on the bracken, and with his face turned towards the glow, fell fast asleep. He was awakened very soon, however, by the distant barking of a dog, and in the belief that someone was searching for him, he sprang to his feet and threw open the door. Outside the blackness was denser than ever; the firelight struck against a barrier of mist. The downfall had ceased, there was no longer any moaning of the wind. Half-convinced that the noise had existed only in his own fancy, he placed his fingers again on the latch, when it was repeated, and peering in the direction whence it came he saw, near by, the greenish light of a lantern. In another moment a young woman glided forward and stood, like a gorgeous shadow, on the threshold. The lantern swung from one hand, the other held a gauzy handkerchief, slipped through the collar of a timid white fawn; in the background crouched a huge old mastiff, whose eyes gleamed sullenly.

The lady's beauty, coupled with the quaintness of her attire, numbed Warmsworth's faculty of speech; he did naught but gaze stupidly on the strange picture. Her skin was very fair, touched with a faint pink in the cheeks; her eyes were deep blue and lustrous, her mouth archly curved. On either temple hung a cluster of black curls, connected across the smooth forehead with a jewelled trellis-work; above rose a turban of gold gauze (one fringed end of which fell to her neck), surmounted with the plumage of a bird of Paradise. Her gown, of carmine velvet, was not of the present fashion; the bodice tight to the waist and heart-shaped at the bosom, the skirt swelled over a great hoop. This was nearly covered with a long white satin-lined mantle of beet-red with vast sleeves; a collar and cape of sable lay lightly on her polished shoulders, unclasped so that a brilliant necklace was visible. There were no signs of travel in her costume; her bronze sandals were not even damped with the snow.

'La!' she cried, in dismay. 'I had hoped to find shepherd Nawe here, to beg him to shelter my poor fawn. Marlowe turned her out on the moor, hoping, perchance, she'ld die before daybreak. He hates all gifts that others offer me. I took Lightfoot and went a-seeking her. Not a long task, the wretch lay under my chamber window!'

Warmsworth was still tongue-tied; the stranger shrugged and pouted. 'Lord, what an outlandish costume!' she cried. 'Prythee, good gentleman, art come from the shores of Greenland?'

He flushed, and found his speech. 'No, madam, but from Calton Lodge,' he said. 'I am belated here, after a day's shooting; I have kindled a fire to rest by till morning.'

'A *monsieur*!' she exclaimed, with a merry laugh. 'No Englishman spoke with such an accent. But you are wrong, sir, in meditating a night spent here. My own house of Offerton lies not half a mile away, and Marlowe, my husband, shall play host at my bidding. So—no demur, I entreat—come with me now; we'll leave Crystalla, the fawn, in your stead, and you shall bring life to a deadly dull place.'

There was something so fascinating in the beauty's aspect that Warmsworth had no thought of declining. The mode of her garments perplexed him somewhat; never before had he seen a woman gowned so strangely. Yet there was no doubt that what she wore became her vastly. In some odd way she reminded him of an eighteenth century painting of a belle of the Georgian

Court. A brief glance at her hands showed him that they were daintily kept and extremely small; she displayed a fine ring upon each finger.

'I shall be very grateful,' he replied. 'I had no knowledge of a house so near the Lodge—'

'Why,' she said, 'if 'tis Calton Lodge you speak of—you are full seven miles from 't! I am taking you to Offerton Hall, in Barley Clough—surely you've heard of the place. My husband, Stephen Marlowe—the last of the Marlowes—compels me to live in this barren Peakland.'

'Forgive me,' said Warmsworth, 'but I am almost a stranger here, I know naught of this country. This season I rented Squire Greenleaf's shooting for a whim—'

'Heavens!' interrupted the lady. 'Will Greenleaf's shooting! And I saw him but yesterday, and he said not a word of't. But he was ever a sly, cunning lad! His eyes tell me that—when he seems to be looking at the wall, Lord! he's noting everything that passes! Now, sir, I beg of you, let us go on to Offerton; I'm warm by nature, but this night's enow to strike one dead.'

The white fawn (it was evidently accustomed to the shelter of a roof), lay before the hearth; Warmsworth closed the door, and the lady, who refused to relinquish the lantern, walked a few paces in front, with the dog at her side.

'I must tell you that Steve is a man of odd fancies,' she observed. 'As jealous a rogue as was e'er begotten—he cannot bear those whom he loves to give word or look to another! But you, an outlandish stranger, benighted, he won't fail to offer you a hearty welcome.'

There was a shade of doubt in her voice; she paused, as if reflection told her that she had been better advised to leave Warmsworth in the shepherd's hut. She sighed lightly because of her fleeting cowardice, then hurried on again.

'Tonight he had a whimsie for turning my Crystalla loose. I doted on her too much, said he, and 'twas because my lord the Earl of Newburgh bred her. If I had not unchained Lightfoot and donned my cloak and ran out, the poor angel would have frozen stark. I'll send her back to my lord tomorrow, if I can find in my heart to part with her. Yet Steve's a good soul, though there's black blood in his veins. Sometimes, I protest, he makes me tremble like to an aspen leaf. He was in one of his wildest humours an hour ago, but I ne'er show that I'm daunted, and I gave him word for word—told him naught should hinder me from having my own way. Yet, though I prattle on with other men, in my heart his roots twine everywhere.'

Her fantastic excitement and tantalising confidences wrought Warmsworth to great curiosity; but he dared ask no questions. At a gateway in a lofty arch of limestone, she fitted her master-key in the lock.

''Tis the nearest way,' she said, 'though there is no boundary betwixt the garden and the moor on the eastern side. Were it not night-time, and over-cold, we would loiter here and you should tell me of life in town. Ay, me, Steve has not let me leave this prison for two dreary twelvemonths! None but country joskins to talk folly with—the overflow of my love to fall on such silly creatures as Crystalla and old Lightfoot.'

Ere they had passed half-way up the broad path the valves of a great door swung inward, and a man appeared on the topmost stone of a staircase that descended to a terrace. To Warmsworth's bewilderment, he was attired as quaintly as the lady, in black satin coat and knee-breeches, and vest of embroidered green. A white-periwig covered his head, in peculiar contrast with the jetty curved eyebrows. His sparkling eyes were of a hue to match; the corners of his mouth were drawn upward, uncovering small white teeth. Despite the malevolence of his expression, it was impossible to deny that his beauty was equal to the lady's.

She caught Warmsworth's sleeve and drew him forward. 'Steve,' she said, in a voice that quavered perceptibly, 'in my journey for the fawn's safety, I came across a wayfarer, poor gentleman, who had taken shelter in Nawe's hut, and knowing that you delight in showing hospitality to all, I brought him here.'

Her husband lifted his forefinger to his brow, as if to smooth out a gathering frown, then giving Warmsworth a cordial welcome, led the way to the hearth of a dining parlour.

'I am vastly wearied of the folk I know,' he said, 'and 'tis indeed a pleasure to see a stranger in this house. For my wife's sake' (the lady gave a little cry of surprise) 'I live here and make the best of't. This is her inheritance, remote from the world of gaiety; I warrant Sophia loves the seclusion.'

'Bah!' she exclaimed. 'I do not love it—I shall never love a gaol-house, although I may love my keeper.'

She flung off her mantle and glided across the room to an opened spinet; still standing, she used her right hand to draw out a few chords, then sang the first words of 'Phyllida flouts me':

> 'Oh, what a plague is love! I cannot bear it;
> She will inconstant prove, I greatly fear it.'

Warmsworth, glancing at his host, saw in his countenance a look of agonising pain, that changed instantly into an agreeable smile. The wife left her spinet and went to an oaken buffet that bore, amongst bright pewter-ware, a stone flask and a silver loving cup. She drew out the stopper of the former, filled the vessel to the brim, then drank lightly.

'Here's to a happy meeting!' she said. 'Here's to a joyful break in our dulness!'

She passed it to Warmsworth, touching meaningly that part of the edge which her lips had pressed. Stephen Marlowe's back was turned for the nonce, and the young man, unaware that he faced a mirror, nodded and drank, ending with an audible kiss, at sound of which the husband swung round suddenly upon his heel. Sophia thereupon made a demure curtsey, her hands clasped over her bosom, where the velvet met the frilled muslin of her chemisette.

'Alack and well-a-day,' she sang. 'She loves me to gainsay—'

Stephen strode forward and caught her by the wrist. 'Damn you!' he muttered huskily, 'you *have* met this man before!'

'And if I have, what then?' she responded. 'Surely I met men before I met you. At the Court, indeed, I knew *gentlemen*, ere I was fool enough to listen to your prayers. I command you to release my hand! I have no liking for purple bracelets made by your iron fingers!'

'My God!' he groaned, as he thrust her roughly aside, 'you go too far, Sophy—to speak thus in a stranger's presence!'

Then, without waiting for her reply, he averted his face and abruptly left the chamber. She sighed wearily, motioned Warmsworth to rest by the fire, and putting down her rebellious hoop she sank into the recesses of a heavy gilt-framed brocade-covered armchair.

'Alas!' she said, almost whimpering, ''tis very hard to live with such a housemate. Had I known that Marlowe'ld use me thus, I'ld have stopped my ears with wax—as Ulysses did when the Siren chanted. A belle—the most famous toast of three years agone, to be kept barred in a cage—to be slighted afront a foreigner! See, his violence hath already marked my poor skin—there's five scarlet spots growing darker every instant.'

She held out her hand; Warmsworth knelt and drew it nearer the firelight. Curiously enough the quaintness of their manners reflected itself upon him, he began unconsciously to mimic demeanour and speech.

'Prythee, Mistress Sophia,' he said, 'do not blame me, though I be the cause—'

Her merry laugh rang out again! Perhaps that was why the tapestry curtain of another doorway, opposite to that by which they had entered, fluttered convulsively.

'Not Mistress!' she cried, 'Lady Sophia—Sophy to my friends and to my jealous husband. A marquis's daughter, wedded to a commoner!... Ah, I do not blame you, sir; I ask but a penance—each stain to be kissed. A kiss is the best salve in the world.'

A low moan came from behind the tremulous curtain as the young man's lips touched the warm satiny skin. Doubtless Lady Sophia heard it, for the light in her eyes danced very fantastically, and she stooped until her face was very near his own.

'Hist,' she whispered, 'let you and me play a comedy, such as Mr Wycherley wrote ages ago. I'll do the talking—your part is but to smile and languish and say "Ay" every time I pause. Now for't—the curtain rises!' Her voice rose, she began to speak in tones brimful of feigned tenderness and delight.

'La! Sir Michael, to think that tonight we should meet so unexpectedly, when tomorrow, by assignation at the Druid's Circle, which I described in my summons, you were to wait my coming, whilst Steve was a-hunting the fox. He never knew of your existence, by Gemini! he never shall know what passed between us. There's an infinitely keener joy in stolen kisses—such as you wot of in Nawe's hut.'

'Ay,' said Warmsworth, 'Ay.'

'Dost remember at my aunt's ball, the Bath Assembly Rooms the place—after young Mr Beckford had led me through the minuet, you fumed and fretted (foolish boy!) and swore that you would spit him on your rapier. There was budding down on your upper lip then, and your skin was fair as mine. And to appease you, dearest, I promised to wed you some day, but sure I was not in earnest. Why, heart o' me, I was scarce sixteen at the time, and you were but three months older! When your folk sent you on the Grand Tour, we both wept like bantlings!'

She linked her arm around his neck, hollowed her palm to support his chin, and turned his face upwards. A rebellious fever heated his veins; he would have given much for her words to have been sober truth.

'Why play comedy any longer?' he murmured, hoarsely.

'Nay, you'll spoil my pretty mischievous plot,' she whispered in return. 'Be your old self, Sir Michael,' she cried. 'Steve hath no inkling of whom you are, or how we loved—and still love!'

'Ay,' he said.

'I vow,' she continued, 'that you're as goodly to look upon as you were eight years ago. Many and many a night have I awoke in my bed, thinking that no comelier man was ever created since the days of Adam. We were made for each other—there's conceit for you... Can you say in earnest that I am still as beautiful as in those days when you called me your little wife, and we broke asunder a silver ring?'

'Lovelier,' said Warmsworth, with an enthusiasm that was not pretended, 'infinitely lovelier.'

Her cheek was pressed against his, her breath stirred the tiny curls on his temples.

'Had I known that time would work no change in your affections,' she said, 'I'ld ne'er have harkened to Steve's protestations. But he swore to kill himself if I said him nay—he followed me like a spaniel—battered at my door till in very hopelessness I let him enter. And you were flaunting abroad with your tutor, loving the maids of Italy and France and Allemagne, whilst I had naught of you save a broken bit of silver.'

She drew hereby to her full height and stood apart, casting a mischievous look at the further doorway. Warmsworth rose from his knees and confronted her; his eyes bright as hers and as vivid a colour in his cheeks.

'Steve is far away,' she said, 'working off his fury in a flight over the moor. He has never learned—shall never learn—what is hidden in the trinket I keep warm against my heart' (her fingers began to toy with the laces of her bosom), 'for I kept it sacred to you and swore no other man should e'er open it.'

Warmsworth no longer remembered his injunction to say naught but 'ay.' He moved nearer; she retreated a step. 'Let me see it?' he cried.

The coquette laughed for the last time, and thrust out her arms, as if to fend his touch. 'Nay,' she said. 'Of my own will, I'll ne'er show it.' She plucked from her bodice a loop of sky-blue ribbon. 'You shall not make me do what I would not!'

He came nearer still and clutching the ribbon strove to draw the locket from its nest. Of a sudden she grew white and faint, reeling back against her chair.

'The comedy is played,' she faltered.

Marlowe strode forward, tearing the tapestry from its hooks. So fearful was he to behold that Warmsworth shrank aside, as if in grim earnest the man was possessed with a demon. Sophia strove to regain her composure, and grasping one of his clenched fists essayed to relax its tension.

'My dearest,' she stammered, piteously, ''twas but a piece of acting; I ne'er saw the man before tonight, and I knew that you were present all the time. I saw the curtain shake; I heard you gasp and groan.'

Then she quailed in silence before the madness she had evoked. Warmsworth laid his hand on the lappet of Marlowe's coat.

'The lady speaks the truth, man!' he cried.

But Marlowe, paying no heed to his words, pointed to the door by which they had entered, and his wife crept from the chamber, with him following stealthily in her wake. The door slammed, and Warmsworth heard the turning of a key. He beat upon the panels, but nobody came; he hastened to the other door, to find it barred with an invisible spring. Beyond the heavily-mullioned oriel window a faint ray of moonlight showed him two mist-cloaked figures—one in pursuit of the other—scurrying over the snow-covered garden...

He began to pace restlessly to and fro, ever and anon striking the door and the floor, in the vain hope of summoning some servant.

At last, wearied with over-excitement, he flung himself in a chair by the sinking fire, and fell into an uneasy slumber, from which, after curious dreams of mingled joy and horror, he was awakened by the creaking of rusty hinges.

His eyes were dull and heavy; some moments passed before he recognised old Barton, the keeper, who stood at his side. Instead of the panelled walls of Marlowe's dining-parlour, he saw piled clods, with chinks that admitted a dim daylight.

'How did I come here?' he inquired in a voice that sounded peculiarly rasping.

'Lord hev' mercy, sir,' said the relieved gaffer, 'yo've been lost on th' moor, on a neeght when no folk o' these parts'ld dare to venture aat. Et's ten o'clock—at dawn I tuk th' cob an' started a-seekin' yo'. Yo' be grey as death!'

'Have you a flask?' said Warmsworth. 'I feel cramped and sick.'

He drank and rose from the bracken. At the door stood a grey pony, which Barton helped him to mount. Neither spoke as they moved slowly through the rain, until they came to some rough piles of stone, where Barton, who was a good Catholic crossed himself devoutly.

'Theere's Offerton Owd Hall,' he remarked in a low voice. 'At least theer et stood. Et's been i' ruins for more nor a hunnerd year—sin' Mr Marlowe draaned hes lady i' th' marsh, through jealousy.'

MIDSUMMER MADNESS

I

The Marriage Eve

he had never looked fairer, for the full moonlight fell on her bosom and arms, and threw into her sweet face a statuesque quietness. For a while the curious question of whether the garden were or not a fitting background for her beauty puzzled me; but soon, with a self-pitying smile, I gave my attention again to her whose inspirations governed mine. She was leaning against a great vase, from whose margin toad's flax and creeping violets—flowers she loved—hung in clusters, with odours floating about in almost tangible clouds.

We were to be married on the morrow, and I was excited and was scarce myself. I dared not think of my courtship; for the knowledge that her affection was too great a gift—that I was indeed unworthy to approach that white, delicious creature whose subtle potency forced me against my will to love her—this knowledge, I say, confounded me beyond belief.

Fate had thrown us together, ironically matching a woman whose story was irredeemably sad with a man wounded in a thousand struggles, who bore no other trophy to lay at her feet than a dead youth. She had stooped with more than human tenderness, and had raised me to her breast, and pressed my head there until the heated brow had cooled, and the temple-throbbings ceased.

As time passed I essayed a question. Had it not been desecration I would have leaned forward and pressed that bare shoulder with my lips. As it was, the purity hindered me: I could as soon have kissed the heavens.

'Once more, Phyllida, for the last time in our unwedded life,' I said, 'tell me, with all your heart, if you love me?'

I looked for her simple assurance, accompanied by the fond chiding that maddened me; and waited tremulously for answering. None such came, and looking into her face I saw a strange air of abstraction. Wounded by her indifference, I repeated my question.

She turned wearily. 'Why do you ask?' she said. 'I have often said that I love you. Let me be silent for awhile—not alone,' (seeing that I was hurt, and that I moved away)—'your presence is enough for me: to know that you are here, and that I may touch you when I will.'

Vainly enough, jealous perhaps of her thoughts, I now strove to compare Phyllida with the splendour of her surroundings; and pained by her apathetic humour, I fancied as my eyes glanced over the landscape that her beauty suffered in comparison. Behind us lay the half-ruined gables of Colmer Hall. Hebe's urn in the terrace fountain was brimful of clear water, and the mantle of scarlet moss that time had spread over the statue seemed trebly luxuriant in the clare-obscure of the moonlight. The windows of the morning parlour were thrown open, and the lamplight showed those quaint thread-embroideries of fabulous beast and fowl and fish; one outcome of the over-exuberant fancy of Phyllida's ancestress, Margot Colmer.

In front lay the choked fish-ponds, with their pretentious water-stairs and sleeping reeds. To the right the beech-planting with its vistaed alleys sloped down to a brawling river. To the left, through great elms, stretched the long barren view of fields and hills, chequered by mortarless limestone walls.

Then I looked again at Phyllida. I cannot attempt to describe her countenance in full. It did not approach any conventional type. White and still and languid, with lips arched in the fashion old poets loved; clear-cut brows and perfect in fancifulness; in the chin power and voluptuous ease combined.

Hers was more than a woman's height. Her gown was of snowy silk; one of those ancient costumes of which there was such store in the presses; the style was of the time of Anne. Gorgeous arabesques were woven in metal thread on bodice and petticoat; pictures of woodbine-covered lattices, idylls of cornfields, of spring flowers budding. Twisted about one arm was a long string of glittering sapphires: clasped on the other a Javan bracelet of rich filigrain inwrought with rubies.

I stood feasting greedily on the sight, whilst I scorned myself for attempting to compare her to anything earthly. Her bosom had moved more freely since she had discarded the bloodstone heart. I was glad of its disappearance, for she would never disclose, although I had often begged to hear it, the story of how it had become hers; and of late its presence had angered me unreasonably.

At last she looked up, and stretched her right hand to fondle mine.

'Mad genius,' she said gravely, 'can you burst into no wild ode about me? You are in the humour for tragedy. Remote as my thoughts have been, yet I have felt that you have wavered angrily and striven to drive me into nothingness. But after all I am paramount.'

What could I do but lift her hand to my lips and press it until I was lost in the ecstasy of touching her flesh so for the first time. She withdrew it, seeing that I quivered from head to foot.

'Come,' she cried, with a mirth that I had never known her affect before. 'Come, let us return to the house. Tonight, Rupert, of all nights, I have something to tell: something concerning the past I must make known.'

And she lifted her eyes to the moon, and held her hands fantastically forward, as if she expected the orb to fall from its setting. When she was wearied, she took my arm within hers and, leaning, walked to the entrance of the hall.

There the moonlight fell on the armed figures. The damascene breast-plates worn four centuries ago in French battles gleamed like Phyllida's gown. The bloody mort-cloth with the stained opals, that hung dusty and tattered by the door, twisted as if a strong current of air stirred behind. The lamp in the morning-room had burned so low that the air was tainted.

Phyllida left me, whilst I gazed at Anne Killigrew's portrait of James the Second and his queen. Was ever picture more ludicrous? Each crease of the royal draperies concealed a demon of dulness; in each feature of the royal countenances was an excessive, wooden minuteness that deprived the dark, ugly faces of the faintest suggestion of life. The lacquer-framed tapestry to the left of the window offered as ever only a conflicting relief, for the enigma of the aureoled woman, who bore in her hand a bag of gold with the inscription *Holy Barbara bringeth Help*, could never be un-riddled.

Suddenly a cry of wonder burst from my lips. A bust modelled in red clay had taken the place of the devotional book on the reading-table. It was the head of a man in the early prime of life, suave, handsome, and priestly: the brow was high and narrow, the mouth painfully compressed, the tonsure of such curls as would have graced a bacchanal. The crudeness of detail, and the luxuriance of fancy, showed me that Phyllida was the modeller.

A fierce murmur, like a wounded animal's, checked me as I laid my hand on the forehead to gauge its lack of breadth.

'Touch anything but that! Do not let your hands corrupt it! Profane! profane!'

I turned aghast, to see Phyllida at my side. Her face was wan, her eyes red and swollen with tears. She seemed a pious witness of some random sacrilege.

'What is wrong?' I said. 'What have I done? Am I so unworthy?'

Without heeding me she unfastened the bundle of papers she had brought, and having extracted several, she laid them on the table. Then, touching my arm, she motioned me to a chair, and in lamplight that dimmed and dimmed as the moon prevailed she began to read:—

> 'Sensuous hopes trampled upon; visionary joys despised. There is no future gladness. Destiny works. What are we more than a handful of faded leaves, tossed by the early winter wind? Some speed—others are checked and lie until corruption. I have reached a splendid goal; you, poor flower—poor slug-a-bed!... Alas! why should I chide, I of all men?'

'I do not understand,' I interrupted. 'Explain, Phyllida!' She gave no sign of hearing, but continued:—

> 'For our love had seemed impossibly great before. O heart of mine! is it that passion is dying—leaping high before burning out? I cannot breathe as I think of you—cannot sit, nor walk, nor lie, but must everlastingly fall with my spirit ebbing from my lips.'

At this I bowed my head and covered my eyes with my hand. What talisman gave Phyllida power to evoke such mental agony. The very fragmentariness of the selections maddened me. Each word seemed as if it might have been forced from me, or from one of my impossible heroes.

> *'You are mine for ever. Strive as you will against the gossamer network that I have flung over you; call on your God for assistance; curse me until you hate, and yet there is no remedy.'*

The voice that had grown so soft as to be almost a whisper ceased now, and looking up I found that I was alone.

II

The Marriage Morning

The roofless building where Phyllida had desired our marriage to be solemnised lies in the outermost corner of the Colmer estate. I had only seen it once before; on a spring twilight when, reckless with undeclared passion, neither knowing nor caring whither I went, I had stumbled into the enclosure, where the scent of withering snowdrops filled the air.

Dreams that were beautified by traditions half understood before swept through my brain in the short disturbed sleep of the marriage morning. I saw Patrick Drassington killing the last wolf in England on the Wyke Quicksand, saw him staggering homeward to the manor-house with the monstrous head in his arms, and the wound in his side vomiting life-blood. Legends I had gleaned from the Colmer records came on in rapid succession:—I traced the histories of the Princess Ursula from Ravenna, who married

Elizabeth's favourite, and slew herself so that on her deathbed she might hear her husband declare his love revived; of Margot Colmer, who laid down her life for Charles the Second; of faithful Driden, the steward, who, like Catherine Douglas, strove to save his master at the cost of his right arm. A thousand other pictures followed. Indeed, I was just in the act of mounting a pillion to ride before a woman in sea-green paduasoy when I woke to find the sun risen, and the clock in the house-place striking four.

My wedding clothes lay beside the bed; I gazed at them for some time ere I rose, scarcely believing my own happiness; then, when I sprang to the floor, I drew aside the window curtain and looked down into the orchard. The cherries had ripened in the night; they were large and lush, with wasps a-grovel in the bursting sweetness of their sides.

Never before had I been so slow or so proud about my toilet. The waistcoat my father had worn at his own nuptials was held up to the light at least twelve times so that I might catch the scintillations of the diamond buttons, and admire the white roses my mother had embroidered. There was a shade of vanity in my eyes as I stood before the mirror. After all, I was not ugly; for something in my face relieved its grotesque outline, and the change that had come of late—the flush that breathed in my cheeks, and the glad dilation of the eyes—charmed me almost into egotism.

I had no friends to attend me to the chapel, for years ago I had broken with all the country gentry, and had lived like a recluse in Drassington Manor. Sometimes, but always vainly, I asked myself the true cause of this isolation; for the charge of infidelity was not of itself sufficient, and my writings, if they corrupted, corrupted out of the reader's wickedness. God knows that I wrote with a pure mind.

The world was glad, but drowsy withal; the songs of the birds were deadened, the chirpings of the grasshoppers less shrill, and even the shallow canal in the Pleasaunce (the canal I had planted with willows, in imitation of the Dean's work at Laracor) exhaled a sleepy odour. The path lay across ripening cornfields. Poppies were full-blown. I gathered a great bunch, for Phyllida loved them, and I fastened them in my waistcoat, intending to weave them in her hair.

She met me at the east entrance of Colmer Park. I ran open-armed to embrace her, but she drew back coldly.

'What do you mean?' she asked, looking into my face.

'How?' I cried. 'I am not late. I am here at the very moment!'

'You know what I speak of,' she replied coldly. 'What do you mean by *being* at all? I was contented, happy even, before you came. The past had died and you have revived it. I am going to break the most sacred vows.'

'Phyllida!' I exclaimed in amazement. 'What vows? I know that you have a past. Let us forget all our unhappiness—'

At this she raised her arm swiftly, as though she would strike me, then with a dull, heartless laugh she came nearer and caught my hand.

'Sometimes,' she said, 'I am as mad as you. It is well to be mad: we can suffer and enjoy a thousand times more keenly. Yes, Rupert, dear Rupert, lover, husband, mournful already, I can tell of what you are thinking. You are white now—there are red circles round your eyes.'

'Hush!' I faltered. 'If you read me well you will be silent. This morning: I cannot endure at once to see your beauty and to hear your words!'

If I were nearly mad before, the sight of Phyllida, as she stood filled with conflicting emotions, was sufficient to blast for ever the few shreds of reason left me. She no longer wore a virginal colour, but a long rippling gown of flame-coloured silk, whose lowest hem was wrought round with yellow tongues. Her face was more tender, her chin trembled, and those eyes, into whose depths I had gazed for hours, and seen no change in their coldness, were filled with warmth and light.

When I had feasted on the sight I leaned forward, and clasping her neck and waist drew her to my bosom. There I held her until she cried out; but even then my arms would not relax, and she was compelled to extricate herself with a charming force. Being my first full embrace it made me delirious. She began to laugh again, childishly, silverily, and taking my hand she paced slowly at my side along the way that led to Stony Mountgrace.

We reached the ruined doorway, and stood beneath its wealth of carved foliage. The sound of boys' singing came from within. Phyllida herself had arranged everything with the old vicar of Drassington. How she had conquered his scruples against reading the ritual in a roofless building I never knew; but the place was still consecrated, and the altar tomb of Elizabeth Colmer, which in past days had been used as the holy table, still stood in the chancel under the east window, where the stained glass of Saint Anthony, with the human-faced swine crawling up his pastoral staff, cast subtle hues on the broken floor.

The words of the marriage hymn were indistinctly sung: the choristers' voices sounded cold and sharp, and the vicar looked almost frenzied with impatience.

'How is this, madam?' he said, with his bearded face drawn into the severest lines. 'Yon beg me to come here as a favour, and when, after the considerations laid before me I agree, you keep me waiting until an hour after the appointed time!'

'An hour?' I gasped, looking not at the vicar, but at Phyllida. 'An hour late! Why we met at the moment—'

Phyllida was triumphant. 'Silence,' she whispered. 'I cannot explain, unless that we have dreamed.' She turned to the ascetic. 'I am ready to atone in any way for my fault,' she said contritely. 'Forgive me, sir, it was unavoidable.' And she made her eyes so pleading that he had been no man had he not calmed instantly and forgiven her for her guiltless offence.

'Enter,' he said. 'It is almost too late. Had you been absent five more minutes you would not have found me here.'

As we reached the apse the voices of the choristers swelled loudly, before dying in a long sustained murmur, and the vicar, with his tattered black-letter book held near his eyes, began to read the marriage service. Not a word did I understand: I repeated automatically when I was bidden to repeat, I forced the ring on Phyllida's finger at the ordained time. But all the while I thought of naught, or spiritual or sensual, save her incarnate loveliness.

Phyllida was mine now! Phyllida was mine now! Daintily I lifted her hand to my arm, and with the echo of the vicar's shrewish congratulations ringing in our ears we moved into the midday sunlight, and began to walk towards Colmer.

'You are my wife,' I said. 'Mistress Drassington, we are out of everybody's sight—these trees will hide us—you need have no shame in kissing me here.'

She made no reply: I turned towards her, imagining that she was wrought beyond speech. We had reached the Syne Marie Wood, where the great conifers screened off the sun. But one dusky shaft crowned Phyllida, and sliding from her head struck her fingers and danced there. Her face was set, her eyelids had fallen.

'Tell me, love,' I murmured. 'Let me help you: you know you are mine now. One kiss, just one, my meed if I have ever given you an instant's happiness.'

Neither word nor movement responded. She was impenetrably silent: her flame-coloured gown became a barrier of defence: I dared not touch her.

'Phyllida,' I entreated. 'My wife!'

Those woebegone eyes were raised slowly. 'Wife,' she said, like one in a dream, 'I am no wife. I am true, true as Heaven itself. Do not write again, I will be true.'

Suddenly her face changed terribly, and she drew herself to her full height. 'For God's sake, Rupert Drassington!' she cried, 'for God's sake tell me that it is not so!'

'What, dearest?' I said.

'My terror—that we are man and wife.'

'I am yours and you are mine—my wife—my wife.' And my tongue dwelt on the words with delight.

But Phyllida left my side, and, sitting on the trunk of a newly-felled tree, wept as her poor heart would break.

III

The Marriage Night

A dull fear troubled me from the moment when Phyllida, with many piteous words, begged me to leave her to herself until evening. Her face was averted all the time, although I strove to make her look at mine, in the belief that my agony at this phase might excite her pity and compel the confidence she withheld.

Assured that she loved me with all her soul, I had no distrust of her. Phyllida was the perfection of purity; in what I knew of her past she had shone with a splendid chasteness, and not a breath had sullied her repute. The curious letters she had read the night before told of nothing but the holiest love, and the insinuation concerning an influence that would prevail was nothing more than a poet's fancy. I had conceived many such: in my story of *Hope Deferred* Michael strives to bind Mary so, and despite her fears of being his bond-maid for ever, at the dawn of a stronger passion, a stretching of the limbs, a higher inspiration breaks lightly asunder the shrivelled withes, and Michael becomes a memory and no more.

Thus, to a great extent, must it be with Phyllida. At the birth of her love for me she had broken most of the bonds—broken them unwittingly: for today she was unaware of her freedom, fancying that the past still held her and that she had sinned against fidelity. I knew otherwise; the few films of gossamer that remained would soon disappear and leave her entirely mine.

Yet was I depressed; and when, after her entreaties had wrung the promise from me, and she had begun to return to Colmer alone, I took her seat and followed with my eyes, as with a step uncertain and often lingering, she threaded the intricacies of the wood. When she had disappeared I prepared for a disinterment of memories.

The aromatic scent of the resin, as it oozed from the heated bark, overburdened the air. In a distant glade the light played so daintily that I amused myself by picturing seraphim sliding down the beams. I moved there and rested amongst sun-stricken trees, whose perfect silhouettes fretted the ground. A ripe-berried mountain-ash grew near—how it came in a fir-wood I cannot imagine—and a culver, undisturbed by my silent presence flew to the key-twig and perched there crooning, until the leaves shook, and then all the boughs, and finally the trunk itself.

Had I been prophetic in my early writings? Had I suffered in the anguish I felt when writing the last chapter of *Hope Deferred* (in which Mary Blakesmoor loses her wifely love and becomes self-concentrated) a foretaste of my own doom?... Moreover in *Alnaschar's Bride* the fairest hopes were blasted...

But Phyllida was different—was stronger and purer than any of these visioned heroines; and surely I had a firmer purpose than their lovers? Nay, as much as she excelled the women in beauty, I excelled the men in strength of will. I would not be thwarted. Who grapples with fortune conquers, and I would conquer!

What folly ramping in my brain made me imagine that such puppets could resemble my living wife! I began to accuse myself of faithlessness, and grew desirous beyond endurance to touch her hands.

How slowly the afternoon faded! The day had been too fine for a gorgeous sky, so the sun, contented with his work, descended quietly into the tops of the distant trees, shook himself there for awhile, and then sank out of sight, leaving the clouds stained bright yellow. Soon after his departure a grey curtain crept up to the zenith, and blotted out the few stars that had already appeared.

I rose, determined to return to Colmer at a snail's pace. If I walked speedily I should reach the house before the time Phyllida had appointed: I might disturb her in the act of conquering her last few remembrances, and cause the past to rise drossily. My sadness left me, and I grew happy once more. As I loitered I drew one by one from my vest the withered poppies, and detaching the petals, let one fall at every step, giving to each flower a verse from some ancient ballad.

When all my poppies were destroyed I bethought myself of an image from Spenser's 'Ruines of Time,' and laughed again and again. It was of the ivory harp with golden strings that the poet saw borne up to heaven. Ah, my joy—*mine!*—was assured! No malicious intervention could hold me from it now. In one short hour, in one short hour!

Twilight deepened into evening as I walked; soon large drops of rain began to fall, and the parched vegetation cried aloud with joy, as its fibres relaxed and its thirsty flowers drank their fill. There was a numbness in the air that foretold a thunderstorm before morning.

Thrice a light blanched the heavens, showing me the distant avenue that led to the garden. The lime-trees were in full bloom, and the heavy shower beat the flowers to the ground. Scarce had my foot touched the velvety grass ere from the distance came the sound of voices in impetuous discussion. My wonder was great at any human creature's daring to walk in these weird precincts after nightfall.

The voices were those of a man and a woman; the one commanding, the other pleading earnestly. They were coming rapidly towards me. Indeed I could already distinguish something black moving beneath the limes.

A flood of bombast rushed to my lips. The desire for something discordant almost overpowered me, forcing me to rack my brain for some bizarre sarcasm wherewith to distract the love-making of these country sweethearts. Soon their speech resolved into distinct words; it seemed as if they lingered.

'Nay, leave me! Take me no further! Was ever woman so tortured?' one cried loudly.

'Was ever woman so false? was ever woman so unworthy?' the other replied.

'But I swear, Cuthbert, I will not come. Oh, let me return! I love him—this very moment he is waiting for me. My darling Rupert, my husband. I *will* return.'

At these words I felt my stature lengthen: then sight, speech, everything left me save the quickened sense of hearing.

'Do you remember the old promises? Fool! to think of contending against my influence—to dream of setting that dullard's power against mine! You are mine, planned so by God, joined to my soul in implacable union. Come, Phyllida.'

Silence followed.

Phyllida was false and I was wifeless. I leaned against the trunk of a lime, waiting for the last sight of the woman who had betrayed me so pitifully.

The footsteps approached nearer, and erelong a man passed. He was more fragile than I, and his long form was shrouded in a black cloak. His arms waved from side to side in magnetic rhythm, and his white face and hands shone like those of a corpse. I watched him, spellbound; and when he had gone a little way I heard the voices begin anew. It was illusion—magic—anything but the terrible thing I had feared. The relief made me fall, face downwards, to the sodden grass.

In less than half an hour I entered Colmer Hall. Hester, Phyllida's old nurse, came to me at the foot of the staircase, and laid her hand upon my shoulder.

'Madam—nay, pardon me—my lady, bade me say that she would be in the morning-parlour. She has waited long.'

I turned the handle of the door, and was confronted by darkness. Yet was I not appalled, for I could understand Phyllida's delicacy in wishing that our first meeting should be where her blushes might go unseen. I stole to the window, and sat on the

73

praying-stool, with my eyes travelling through the gloom to her place. For the fourth time the sky blanched, and I saw her beside the table, resting her head on her hands, with her hair spread over shoulders and bosom in rippling swathes.

At last, wounded by her indifference, I spoke, and destroyed a delightful hope that she would bid me welcome.

'Phyllida!'

The old silence. I knew that she must be in one of those wonderful depths of feeling that she sometimes sounded, and felt proud of a woman of such strange charms. But what had swayed in the mistress troubled in the wife.

'Are we not in perfect sympathy?' I cried.

Afraid of I know not what (the air in the room seemed turbulently struggling to pass through the closed windows), I opened the door and took one of the candles from a sconce in the hall.

'Phyllida! Phyllida! Phyllida!' I whispered, holding the light above my head. 'I am here, sweet one, look at me!'

Still silence. Fiercely, perhaps, but still lovingly, I placed my hands beneath her forehead, to make her look upwards. At my touch a bundle of papers fell from her breast, and lay scattered on the floor. The clay bust I had seen on my marriage eve stood near: I thrust out my right hand angrily and broke it into fragments. The past was done with now! I had conquered! My victory made me exultant. Phyllida's gossamer bonds were torn away for ever.

As I drew back the hair and let the candlelight fall softly on my wife's face she sighed heavily.

'Dead love has slain my passion,' she said.

THE PAGEANT OF GHOSTS

late twilight in June. A woodlark rippling in mid-air. Drowsy-scented ladies' bed-straw in a marsh that was once a garden. On the terrace wall, beside the cedar, a stone urn with a lambent flame.

The casement hung open, and the excess of beauty and perfume drugged me: so that, with a sigh, I sank back into a moth-eaten sedan that had borne four generations to Court. Dried dust of lavender and rue filtered through the brocade lining, and grew into a mist, wherethrough the bird's song waxed fainter and fainter. Indeed, I was just closing my eyes when the tuning of fifes and viols roused me with a start.

A shrill titter from the further end of the ballroom drew me from my seat. At the outer extremity of the oriel hung a curtain of Philimot velvet, lined inwardly with pale green silk: behind this I stole, and, parting the draperies from the wall, gazed towards the musician's gallery. Five men, dressed in styles that ranged from the trunk-hose and collared mantle of Elizabeth's day to the pantaloons and muslin cravats of the third George, were arranging yellow music-sheets on the table. The youngest forced a harsh note from his viol, then struck another's bald pate, and set all a-laughing. A grave silence followed. Then began just such a curious melody as the wind makes in a wood of half-blighted firs.

All the sconces were lighted of a sudden, and the martlets and serpents in the alt-relief above the panelling sprang into a weird life.

Resting between the firedogs on the open hearth were three logs, one of pine, another of oak, and a third of sycamore. The grey flame licked them hungrily, and the sap hissed and bubbled. The carved work of the walls was distinct: Potiphar's wife wrapped her bedgown about Joseph, Judith triumphed with the bloody head aloft, and in the centre Lot's daughters paddled with his withered jowls.

I felt but little wonder at the change from stillness to life. As the last of my race, treasurer of a vast hoard of traditions, why should I be disturbed by this return of the creatures of old? I dragged forth the creaking sedan, and sat waiting.

A rusty, half-unstrung zither that hung near quivered and gave one faint note to the melody. Ere its vibration had ceased, Mistress Lenore entered through the arched doorway. Hour after hour had she plucked those wires that cried out in welcome.

Her fox-coloured tresses were wrought into a fantastic web, each separate hair twisted and coiled. A pink flush painted her cheeks, and her lustrous blue eyes were mirthful. She wore opals (unfortunate stones for such as love), and hanging from a black riband below her throat was the golden cross Prince Charles had sent her from Rome.

The legends of her character came in floods. Wantonly capricious at one moment, earnest and devout as a nun's at another, her expression changed a thousand times as I beheld. Now she was racking her soul with jealousy; now pleading—as she alone could plead—for pardon; now, when pardon was won, laughingly swearing that her repentance was only feigned. As she neared my heart beat furiously, and I cried, '*Lenore! Lenore!*' My voice was low and broken (the music gave a loud burst then), but she passed without a word, her ivory-like hands almost hidden beneath jewels and lace. The further door stood open, and she disappeared.

Nowell the Platonist followed; a haggard middle-aged man in a long cloak of sable-edged black velvet. Forgetful of all save desire, he bore a scroll of parchment, whereon was written in great letters *To Parthenia*. This was the only outcome of his one passion. At the second window he paused, with a wry mouth, to gaze on that statue of Europa from whose arm he had hanged himself. Then his hands were uplifted to his head to force away the agony of despair; for hurrying towards him came the Mad Maid, who could not love him, being devoted to the memory of one wrecked at sea.

'Why art thou in anguish?' she said. 'See my joy; laugh with me, dance with me. He returns tomorrow—the boat's coming in. Ah, darling! Ah, heart's delight!' And she held up her arms to a girandole whose candles fluttered; but her face grew long, and thin, and pale, and she rested on a settee and drew from her pocket a dusky lace veil, which being unfolded, discovered a ring with a burning topaz and a heart of silver. She leaned forward, resting her brow in her hands, and talked to the toys in her lap as if they understood.

To the veil she said, 'No bride's joy-blushes shalt thou conceal!'

To the ring, 'Thou last gift of him who died and left me!'

To the heart, 'O heart, thou hast endured! Thou art not broken!'

After a few tears she refolded all, and unbuttoning her bodice took from the bosom a miniature framed with pearls; but, as if afraid lest it should grow cold, she replaced it hurriedly, and seeing that Nowell beckoned towards her, glided on, sighing and with downcast looks.

Then passed a cavalier in azure silk and snowy ruffled cravat and long-plumed cap of estate. He was whistling a song that threw all bachelors into humorous ecstasy. Who he was I know not: unless the courtier who had fought a duel with my Lord Brandreth, and had died in the wood near St Giles's Well, pressing convulsively in his right hand a dainty glove of Spanish kid. A merry fellow, quoth the legend, who loved the world and all in it, but who was over fond of his own jest.

Fidessa, the singer, entered next. She had brought her little gilt harp, and her lips were parted to join harmonies of voice and instrument. Bright yellow hair plaited in bands that formed a filigrain-bound coronet; eyes half-veiled, with sleepy lashes, hands fragile as sea-shells. It was the 'Verdi Prati', Mr Handel's celebrated song, that she adored most, and on the morrow she would sing it at Lincoln's-Inn-Fields Theatre. At least she purposed to sing it then and there. Fate, however, had otherwise ordained: the tomorrow would never come, and the sweetheart at the upland grange might well write on her letters, 'Darkness hath overcome me.'

Thin and pale Margot, her wanness heightened by dishevelled black curls, came forward in her scarlet cloak. Silent reproach was in her every feature; her eyes were stern and long-suffering. The prophecy that bound up her life with that of her dying twin was rapidly approaching consummation. Another moment and the direst pain filled her; for a loud cry from an outer chamber told her he was dead.

As she disappeared in the gloom, Nabob Darrington, himself in life the lover of a ghost, paced slowly along. A beau of the last century, wearing a satin flowered waistcoat and a coat and breeches of a plum-coloured kerseymere, between his finger and thumb he held the diamond which he had brought from the East as a spousal gift for the woman who, unknown to him, had died of waiting. He was anticipating the meeting with her, and his brown cheeks flushed blood-red at the sound of a light footstep. He turned, saw one with violet eyes and tragic forehead; and with one joyous murmur they enfolded each other and passed.

Althea approached; a massive creature gowned in white and gold. In one hand she held a tangle of sops-in-wine, in the other, as symbolical kings hold globes, a bejewelled missal. The contention between the two lovers—the old, who had tyrannised until her life was of the saddest, and the new, who filled her with such wild happiness—was troubling her, and she was pondering as to which should gain the victory. She was just beginning to understand that to wait in passive indecision is to be torn with dragon's teeth.

Barbara, with eyes like moon-pierced amethysts, followed, singing Ben Jonson's 'Robin Goodfellow' in a sweet quaver that was only just heard above the music. How strangely her looks changed—from maiden innocence to the awakening of love! From the height of passion to the abyss of despair!

But as she went the horizon was ripped from end to end, and a golden arrow leaped into the ballroom. Dawn had broken. The scent of ladies' bed-straw was trebly strong; the tired woodlark sank lower and lower.

The room was empty—the pageant had passed and done.

THE PRIEST'S PAVAN

esternight I took my viol, and made my way over the limestone cliffs to the concave where stand the ruins of Woodsetts, the house Vignola—he who designed Saint Angelo's Castle in Rome—had built beside the fallen abbey, for his boon-fellow, Bateman de Caus. And as I sat, drawing the strings together, nigh the pedestal of the Goddess of Plenty in the white summer-house, behold, the overgrown yew and privet bushes that had once been clipped in forms of dragon and hippogriff, shrank again to their old preciseness, and the terminal statues rose from the grass, and the wreathed columns bore again their garment of midsummer roses.

I played 'The Priest's Pavan' that I had learned from the 'Book of Airs,' and at the first note the fire-stains on the frontispiece vanished, and one by one the gaping windows donned their lattices, and the leaden roof shone above the parapet, and the light of a thousand sconces fell about me in broken rillocks of gold.

... It was no longer the burr of my viol that rang in my ears, but the chirping of a virginals in music that was conceived by a divinity.

One noontide, more than ten years ago, my lord came to the town and found me by the table in my chamber, copying in fair hand the suite of dances that I had made for Daphne's wedding. His tumid red face shone unctuously; his attire was disordered with the heat.

He flung a parchment book upon the table, and laughed, as he ever laughed, like one drunk with wine.

'T'other morning, when they took up a stone that had cracked in the monk's chapel,' said he, 'my steward found this in a brazen casket. A set of dances such as are not used nowadays—of music far superior to aught such crickets as you create!'

I could not demur, for my lord was a *cognoscento*, and although he oft-times affected liking for my work, and professed to find genius therein, I knew that 'twas but humble in his regard. His life had been spent in the great world; players and singers had been damned by his frown. So I took up the book, and opening its pages saw quaintly-shapen notes ranged up and down like little coffins draped in scarlet and black.

''Tis in lute tabulation,' I said. 'A book of the airs ecclesiastics loved ere the Reformation brought them low!'

'Ay,' commented my lord. 'Mayhap the work of the white monk who haunts the precincts o'nights—him, the humble folk call Ambrose. The very sight of that page evokes pictures of woodmen's wives, oddly gowned, hey-trix-come-go-trixing in the cloisters! But farewell to this light talk! Madam, when I put it in her hand (she hath a rage for antiquities), sat her down to the harpsichord, and played things that drove away the scene before our eyes and set us a-wandering in strange places. She fell a-longing, and by her whim all the plans for music at our little mistress's nuptials are changed. That which you have done shall be brought to light when the lass gives her master a fine boy. Her mother hath sworn to revive all the dances—see, here at the end is the description—and our guests are being taught galliards, lavoltas, pavans... What I have come to tell is that nought will content her save that the musicians (receiving their due pay) be disbanded, and that you alone will sit in the gallery and tinkle an ancient virginals from sunset to midnight, whilst we, poor fools! hop and scurry like grigs.'

My heart was burdened with disappointment, but I held my peace. Daphne had been my pupil; I had taught her rosy fingers to dash like fire-drakes over the keys, to draw softer notes than the wood-dove's, I had not seen the bridegroom (the match was made at Court), or perchance the excellence of my music might have been marred. As it was, I had thrown into each chord a speech of my devotion to the maid. She had ever known that I regarded her with great tenderness; and being endowed, despite her green youth, with a keener insight than her fellows, had twined wreaths of laurel for my grey head, and made my chamber ever bright with flowers. The knowledge that he whom her parents had chosen was a man of advanced years and more than evil fame, had distressed me for the while; but the child, from her very innocence, had hitherto displayed no distaste when she spoke of the future.

My lord gave me a folded paper. 'Madam hath writ here the order of the dances,' he said. 'There is but short time for you to study, since, the wedding-day being Thursday, the book must be returned to her on the morrow. "The Priest's Pavan" is the last— 'tis the wildest thing in the world—all strutting and curtseying and twisting the arms and pointing downwards with the thumbs! Anan, master fiddler, I must leave you, for my son-in-law waits below, too gouty to climb your stairs. Be sure no harm comes to the book; for, if I may believe madam, it has worth above rubies.'

He descended, panting, to his chariot; peering from my case-ment, I saw, beside the opened panel, the face of the bridegroom, wrinkled, yellow and unholy, with the dull eyes that only sparkle at the sight of the table or of a woman's loveliness. His lace cravat hung beneath his chin like the beard of an African ape. He poked his fingers betwixt my lord's ribs, and cackled foolishly.

''Tis a wench you keep there!' he cried. 'To the deuce with your talk of music-men! A sweet morsel, red and creamy as Temple's nectarines, and with hair soft and light as tow! Send for her down, so that I may look on your choice. A minx, I vow! Madam shall know—'

I heard no more, for the stone-horses leaped forward and the chariot lurched away towards the market-place, where the fresh huckster wenches from the uplands stood beside their stores. When the by-street was quiet again, I passed to my harpsichord, and played the music of the 'Book of Airs' from end to end, finding at the very first that a masterpiece of either good or evil genius lay before me on the stand.

... Never before had I dreamed of melody so exquisitely pleasurable, so bitterly painful. In each were two things—the flitting of white angels over the lawns of Heaven and the dancing of fiends around the tormenting fires of Hell. The fragrance of ever-blooming flowers, and the stench of brimstone hovered about in ghostly clouds. I heard the laughter of pure children, and the cachinnations of imps. Ere long half my chamber was filled with a radiance infinitely brighter than the dying sun's; the other half was lost in impenetrable blackness. My body was sick and trembling; but my spirit was full of eager delight.

At 'The Priest's Pavan,' I was overcome with frenzy and with ecstasy. This told of the war between Heaven and Hell, of the clashing of archangel's lances—of devils rushing forward and falling back—of breaches made in golden ramparts—of Apollyon leading his myrmidons almost to the battlements. But the voice of God was lifted in thunder; and Hell with its warriors sank seething together through Chaos.

My fingers curled like the talons of a bird; my head sank till my chin lay upon my breast. This was no budget of dances, no toy to please madam the countess withal, but an epic of Divinity. Perchance it had passed from generation to generation of churchmen, as our Bible in later years hath passed to us. 'Twas music such as is heard at the triumphal feasts of Cherubim.

'I will not play it,' I said. 'Although I lose my lord's favour, I'll be no party to profanity. 'Tis not meet that such as group about the Court should caper to its passion!'

In the night-time, as I lay sleepless, the parchment shone like touchwood. I rose—hid it in a coffer, yet still I knew of its glittering, and the obsession remained. At dawn I enclosed it in my leathern wallet, and prepared to start for Woodsetts. But on the threshold I was met by Daphne, hooded so that until she had unknotted the throat-strings none might have known her for the bride.

'The women rose betimes, to gather midsummer dew,' she said, 'and I stole apart and ran, so that I might bid my master farewell, and tell him how that I shall ever pray for his fame.'

The maid was pale as death; her eyes were red with restlessness and weeping. I drew her into the chamber, and there, as she had still the ways of a child, she sat upon my knee, and passed her fingers through my hair and kissed my forehead.

''Tis a long farewell,' she whispered. 'Who knows that I may ever return? I have fear at times that my life must shortly reach its term. I would fain have you think of me sometimes.'

'I am old and withered, Mistress Daphne,' I made answer, 'and there is no hope of fame for old men; but as long as I have breath you shall lie in the innermost cabinet.'

Big tears rolled down her cheeks. 'Ah, master,' she sighed, ''tis hard to go away from the folk here to a strange country with one I understand nothing of, and to know that he will be with me always! My mother tells me to have no fear, for my husband will hold me as the apple of his eye. Alack! to be without young playmates!'

She dried her face with her kerchief, and rose; her glance fell on the book in the wallet.

'Will not you play to me of that music?' she said. 'Tomorrow night all dance to it. We are being instructed in the oddest steps.'

I shook my head. 'Nay, little one, you must never hear it. This morning I take it back to your lady mother with word that I cannot follow her behest.'

Daphne sank to her knees and clasped my neck. 'Then play it to me but once,' she pleaded. 'I was ever an apt learner, and it may be that I shall understand. When I heard before, out of the harshness came a curious joy; but you will turn each note into a strung jewel.'

I gave her no naysay, but moved to the harpsichord and played. And behind me at first I heard a sound of moaning, then of breath leaping after breath; but when I came to 'The Priest's Pavan,' Daphne was silent as the grave. I turned, to find her standing erect, with rapt countenance, her hands clasped over burgeoning breasts.

A while passed ere she spoke; her voice came low and trembling. ''Tis my desire, master, that you play thus at my nuptials.' And she left the chamber with no other word.

So it was that on the appointed night I sat alone in the musicians' gallery of the ballroom at Woodsetts. This place had in long-past times been the refectory of the monks, and the master-builder, Vignola, had chosen that save for the new floor of oak that swung on iron chains, all should remain unaltered. Behind the tapestries of the Gobelins, which my lord's father had purchased, still might be found dim wall-pictures of Christ at Gethsemane, of the Virgin, and of the Apostles; the light of the candles showed the company from the Court, all bedizened with trinkets and plumes and brocades, moving to and fro in clusters.

Madam came secretly up the narrow staircase, and beckoned me into the shadow, not deeming it fit that the wedding guests should see her converse with one so inferior. The lines of her forehead were eloquent of caprice and satisfaction.

'No chance had I to speak with you before,' she said. 'The whirl of this merry day hath held me every moment. What think you of the bride—almost a woman now, tomorrow on the way to matronhood?'

Looking down, I saw Daphne, quivering affrightedly, like a white culver amongst ravens. At hand sauntered the groom, simpering, whispering to the men-folk behind screening fingers.

'I know not what to think,' I said.

Madam gave no heed. 'Impatient for the signal of withdrawal, I protest! See how restlessly she stirs! But, master, what of the music? What of my plan of giving life again to these ancient dances? 'Tis vastly taking. Duchess Mary (she who wears the sombre gown with yellow leaves) declares that her recollection tells that not according to the teachings of the book were galliards and lavoltas danced! They say her age exceeds the century! The beldam dotes; but, even if she be right, why, 'tis a fine thing to dance in styles past human memory. And even if, as she fears, they be enchanted dances, 'tis so much the better. It may be that ghosts will rise!'

Whereat she made her mocking curtsey and withdrew, and anon I began the first air, and the floor swayed under mad caprioles. And in the pause I looked downward again, and saw that each face save Daphne's had grown wan and pregnant with unutterable wickedness. But the maid was blushing, as if the breeze of April clipped her cheeks. She had stolen apart from the rest, and, bride though she was, all were so intent upon their performance that she passed unobserved.

Methought, as dance followed dance, a thin sulphury vapour rose and wrapped about these revellers, so that their bodies grew vague, and little was to be seen but their lustful blinking eyes... Still Daphne stood alone and neglected, toying with the rose at her girdle.

The voice of the virginals swelled so that all other sound was hidden; the mist grew ever thicker and thicker. Ere the playing of 'The Priest's Pavan,' it seemed as if horny wings had risen from the shoulders of each dancer, and the skin of each had swarthened under the powder.

Then, to the first notes were made the magic twists and down-turnings of the thumbs; and of a sudden, with one accord, the dancers ceased all movement and my hands fell numbed; for the tapestry of the eastern wall was drawn aside, and one clothed as a priest in shining vestments entered through an arched doorway, and moved to the place where Daphne waited. A hallowed light emanated from his face and hands, so that none might see; as he approached the maid, this radiance wound about her in tender embrace. She showed no sign of blenching; but sank before him as the Magdalene sank before Christ. He raised her with infinite gentleness, and put his arm about her waist, and led her to the place whence he had come.

There followed no murmur of anger or surprise; but, as I gazed, smoke and tongues of fire leaped from every crevice of the floor; and, in another minute, there came the noise of iron chains snapping, then, as flames leaped to lick the roof, one hoarse wail of agony.

DAME INOWSLAD

ycamores and beeches surrounded the inn; elders, still green-flowered, leaned over the grass-grown roads. The belt of sward was white with lady-smocks, but in the damp hollows marsh-marigolds radiated essential sunlight. The blackbirds sang, and loudly, yet without the true strain of mirth: sang like blackbirds that must sing, but of rifled nests. Even the grasshoppers had some trouble: never had they chirped so pathetically before.

On the green the gilded figure of a bull hung from two uprights; it swung from side to side in the light breeze. The copper bell on a twisted pole hard by was green with mould: a-swing from it was a rusty chain; it had been used in the old posting days, and many a yeoman had haled himself into his saddle from the worn mounting-block beside it.

For the inn itself, it was vast and rambling, dwarfed by the towering trees. For miles in every direction lay the old forest of Gardomwood, a relic of primeval woodland, rich in glades and brakes, in streamlets and mizzies: hazy in the clearings, where sheer-legs, like the trivets of witches' caldrons, and tents and blue-smoking heaps told of charcoal-burners and their ever-shifting trade.

The Golden Bull with its beautiful precincts took me back to that fading Arcady whose shepherdesses and swains felt the end of the joy-time coming. It was utterly sad; but I was caught in the meshes of its melancholy, and for the while could not escape.

Twilight fell, and I ceased from exploring, and went indoors. In the parlour was a great square piano. Its music, while acidly discordant, was yet plaintive with the curious speech such old things often own. I played a few Robin Hood ballads—of the Outlaw and Little John, of the Bishop of Hereford and Robin's pleasing escape. Then the hostess entered with a great Nottingham jar full of white lilac. She set this down between the firedogs, and stood leaning one hand on a chair-back and listening to the music. When I stopped she sighed heavily: I left the piano, and offered her a chair. She was middle-aged and deformed; her shoulders were humped, her face was shrivelled, but she had large grey eyes and a wistful smile.

'I thank you, sir,' she said. ''Twas the music drew me in. Nobody's played since last summer, when Sir Jake Inowslad stayed here. His taste was sonatas and fugues—things pretty enow, but only pleasing at the time. Give me a melody that I can catch—almost grasp in my hand so to speak.'

'Do you play?' I asked, half-hoping to hear some air she had loved in her youth.

'No, I cannot play. I was still-room maid at Melbrook Abbey, so I never had opportunity.'

As she spoke, a girl came in with the snuffer-tray and candles. She was pale and tall and of a tempting shape. Beautiful she was not, yet the sad strangeness of her face impressed me more than great beauty would have done. Her eyes were like the other woman's, but clearer and more expressive; her lips were quaintly arched; long yellow hair hung down her back. She seemed, although she walked erect, to be recovering from some violent illness. When she had gone the hostess spoke again. 'My niece is not strong,' she said, laying an unnecessary emphasis on the word *niece*. 'The air does not suit her.'

'Was not she bred in the country?' I inquired.

'Ah, no! She is not without money—her father endowed her well. Until two years back she was at the convent of the Sisters of Saint Vincent de Paul for her education. 'Tis in the hill-country, and I think that coming to the flatness of Gardomwood has done her harm.'

The girl came in again: this time I noted her grace of movement; it had something of the wearied goddess. 'Aunt,' she said quietly, 'I wish to go into the woods—you can spare me? All I had to do is done; the women are sewing in the kitchen.' She went to the further end of the room, where a cloak of rose-coloured silk hung, ermine-lined, from a nail in the panelling. She donned it at her leisure; her long and narrow hands were of a perfect colour. She tied the broad ribands of the collar; she lighted two candles that hung before a tarnished mirror, and gazed at her shadow; then, her lips moving silently, she left the room.

'Ever the same,' the elder woman said. 'Night after night does she leave the house and travel about like an aimless thing. Come back, Dinah,' she called, 'come back.' But the thin voice went wavering through the empty passages unanswered. So the hostess rose and with a half-apologetic 'Good-night,' left me alone. I sat down in the deep recess of the window behind a heavy curtain. A copy of Denis Diderot's *Religieuse* lay on the little table. I took it up, and was soon engrossed in it: for of all books this is the most fascinating, the most disappointing, the most grim. A light came glimmering at the end of the vista before me: it grew and grew, and the moon uplifted herself waist-high above the trees. And when I had watched her thus far, I returned to my nun and reached page twenty-two of the second volume, where I read the following sentence: 'After a few flourishes she played some things, foolish,

wild, and incoherent as her own ideas, but through all the defects
of her execution I saw she had a touch infinitely superior to mine.'
Then in the shaded window-seat I fell asleep...

The striking of a tall clock near the hearth awakened me: I had
slept till midnight. The candles had been removed from the table
to the piano; those in the girandole had guttered out or been
extinguished. A young man sat at the piano on the embroidered
stool. His back was towards me; I saw nothing but high, narrow
shoulders and a dome-shaped head of dishevelled black hair plenti-
fully besprinkled with grey. From the road outside came a noise
of horses whinnying and plunging. I looked out, and there was a
lumbering coach drawn by four stallions which, black in daylight,
shone now like burnished steel.

The would-be musician turned and showed me a long painful face with glistening eyes and a brow ridged upward like a
ruined stair. It was a face of intense eagerness: the eagerness of
a man experimenting and praying for a result whereon his life
depends. Without any prelude he played a dance of ghosts in an
old ballroom: ghosts of men and women that moved in lavoltas and
sarabands; ghosts that laughed at Susanna in the tapestry; ghosts that
loved and hated. When the last chord had sent them crowding to
their graves he turned and listened for a footstep. None came. He
lifted a leather case from the side of the stool and, unfastening its
clasps, took out a necklace which glistened in the candlelight like a
fairy shower of rain and snow. 'Twas of table diamonds and marga-
rites, the gems as big as filberts. He spread it across the wires, and
after an instant's reflection began to play. The carcanet rattled and
jangled as he went: it was as an advancing host of cymbal-women.
When he listened again, great tears oozed from his eyes. He took
up the jewel and played a melody vapid at first, but so subtle in

its repetitions that none might doubt its meaning: thus and not otherwise would sound a lyke-wake sung in a worn voice after a night of singing. And whilst he played, the door opened silently, and I saw Dinah, there in her nightgown, holding the posts with her hands. She took one swift glance, then disappeared again in the darkness, and came back carrying in her arms a bundle swathed in pure linen and strongly redolent of aromatic herbs. Holding this to her breast, she approached the man. Her shadow fell across the keys, and he lifted his head. From both came a long murmur: his of love and joy and protection, hers of agony. He rose and would have clasped her, but she drew back and placed her burden in his outstretched hands.

'It is the child,' she said. 'Three months ago I gave birth to her, none knew save myself... She was all that remained of you: all that I had, and I dared not part with her... But now—now that I have seen you again—take her away—leave me—leave me in peace.'

'Dinah,' he said proudly, 'listen to me.'

'Nay,' she whispered, 'not again. If I listen I may forget your wickedness; I might be weak again. Leave me, Jake.'

'Dinah, you must hear me. Why, out of all the love you held and hold for me, can you condemn? When I left you I fell mad; for the year I have been mad, and only yesterday did they set me loose. See, I have brought you all the diamonds; tomorrow you will be Dame Inowslad.' And he laid the dead thing on a table, and caught the mother to his bosom. Her figure was shaken with sobs.

'Oh,' she cried, 'it has been hard; but my trial has brought the true guerdon of happiness. Only once have I missed seeing the place where you promised to meet me—the place where you said you loved me; and that was on the night of my lonely travailing.'

Outside the horses plunged and snorted: a shrunken postillion swaying at the neck of the off-leader. In the hollows of the road lay sheets of mist, and the moonlight turned them into floods. A long train of startled owls left the hollow sycamores and passed hooting... hooting... down the glade.

'Let us go,' Sir Jake said; 'by morning light we shall be in sight of Cammere, where Heaven grant us a happy time;—a year of joy for each week of pain. Do not wait to dress; rich robes and linen are inside the coach; I have brought many of my mother's gowns.'

Dinah extricated herself from his embrace, and went to find her cloak. During her absence a strange and terrible look came into Inowslad's face and he smote his forehead. He smiled at her re-appearing. 'Dinah,' he said, looking downwards, so that she might not see his eyes, 'Dinah, I am so happy that I can scarce see. Lead me from the house.'

He took up the dead little one in his right arm, and carried it as believers carry relics. The outer door closed softly; they descended the moss-grown steps, and entered the coach. The horses leaped forward, half drowning the sound of a chuckle. A glint of the moon pierced the coach windows, and I saw a brown hand, convulsed and violent, gripping a long white throat.

PART II
Useless Heroes

Another pervasive element of Gilchrist's short fiction, and another he shares with the Gothic, is the concept of fatal flaws leading to an inevitable, inescapable tragedy. Many of the tales in this collection manifest a sense of creeping doom that, chillingly, the characters often appear all too aware of and Gilchrist gives this an interesting twist by making the flawed parties his male narrators and protagonists. Not only this but where many of his major female characters are active, both emotionally and physically, the men in Gilchrist's stories are flawed through their indecision, apathy and passivity in the face of the world. In 'The Manuscript of Francis Shackerley' Gilchrist even has Lady Millicent chide these 'useless heroes' in a way that foreshadows the tale's brutal finale. This is compounded in 'The Basilisk', where it is doubtful whether the narrator's innocence is salvation for Marina or an unwitting sacrifice to her 'wearied demon-god', and in the short-sighted incompetency of the would-be witch-finder in 'Witch In-Grain'. Even the well-meaning Peregrine allows his wife to dwindle away in 'The Grotto at Ravensdale' through his own inaction; 'forbiddances shall never come from me,' he announces rather grandly as her spirit is consumed by her obsession with the grotto's 'cruelly familiar' denizens. Pliny Witherton, as we learn in 'Excerpts from Witherton's Journal', is simply a self-aggrandising, manipulative wastrel who is happy to benefit from Anne's inheritance and yet abandon her when he subsequently discovers her in poverty, blissfully unaware that it is his co-option of her fortune which has lead to her downfall. 'Bubble Magic' is an interesting tale as it features Gilchrist's repeated use of a male narrator caught between two potential lovers but includes the additional, disruptive inclusion of Norreys, the protagonist's 'bosom friend' and childhood bedfellow whom he loves 'more than a brother'. The slight 'Dryas and Lady Greenleaf' is reminiscent in many ways of Clark Ashton Smith's more quasi-medieval writings but also shows the interconnected world of Gilchrist's fiction; Squire Greenleaf is mentioned briefly in 'A Night on the Moor' as is Crystalla, the name of Lady Sophia's pet fawn and also a pseudonym used by Lucy in 'Excerpts from Witherton's Journal'. I've concluded this section with 'The Stone Dragon', perhaps Gilchrist's masterpiece of Gothic Weird storytelling. Here the male narrator is almost inconsequential when compared to the battle of wills between Rachel, who 'feels everything too acutely' yet delights in her gloves made from the flayed skin of a murderess, and her reserved, selfless sister Mary. The cloying scent of honeysuckle pervades this gloomy, Poe-like tale of betrayal, anguish and murder.

THE MANUSCRIPT OF
FRANCIS SHACKERLEY

(Being a True Account of the Most
Noble Lady, the Lady Millicent Campion.)

ince that news has come this day of Sir Humphreville
Campion—a death strangely caused by the bursting of
an alembic—there is naught to hinder me from taking
up my drowsy pen and writing a true history of certain matters that
caused no small wonder in their day. True it is that I would liefer
work in my garden amongst the simples and flowers, for since the
last affairs to be narrated in my history, all thought has been painful to me, and the world a place rather to endure than to dwell in.
There is a quiet joy in the breeding of small cattle and the growth
of crops; but to one who has tasted of life's sweetness such pleasure
is wondrously pitiable.

We met first in 1611. My father's coach, as we were travelling
to Sherenesse Manor, where dwelt my aunt Bargrave, broke down
outside the village of Stratton—the left sling being overchafed.
How it came about I know not, but in the scuffle, when my folks
were hastening back to the inn, I stole unnoticed across the road to
a mossy wall, and, filled with arrant mischief, leaped over and ran
panting along the sward. Monstrous elms, with contorted boles,
stood about: it was springtide and the leaves were freshly green;
in the branches overhead squirrels played and squeaked.

Soon I heard two sounds, cuckoo and a child mocking cuckoo; turning abruptly past a high jetto, as thin in the lower part as a needle, but towards the top breaking into mist which the sun made orange and purple and blue, I reached a tennis-court, where a girl danced, an odd pretty creature, with a pale face and ringlets so deeply hued that they might have been washed in blood. She was all alone, tripping round and round in a ring, first on one foot, then on the other, and singing to herself in baby language. The cuckoo marked time: at every note little mistress drew herself upright, clasped her hands, and cried *cookoo*, then continued her dance. I stood by in silence, till, as she passed for the third time, she lifted her eyes, showing how they were hazel and big.

'Ah,' she said in a proud fashion, ''tis not Humphreville! Day after day have I thought to see him. They said last summer he had flown away with the cuckoo, and I know that with the cuckoo he must return. It is lonely here with no playmates. Who are you?'

'Frank Shackerley. My father's coach broke down, and I ran away.'

She held out a tapering brown hand, on whose marriage finger gleamed a golden ring. 'And I am the most noble lady, the Lady Millicent Campion, wife to Sir Humphreville Campion.'

'You tease me,' I said vexedly. 'You are not nearly as old as I, so you cannot be a wife.'

The Lady Millicent came nearer, tears gathering in her eyes; she put her arm around my neck. 'Dear heart,' she murmured, ''tis true. I know not how it came, but in the summer Humphreville stayed here with his parents, and I was wedded to him. At night when I was put to bed they brought him to kiss me, and when I awoke in the morning he had gone with the cuckoo. Why does not he stay with me and keep house like other husbands?'

At this moment an elderly woman came through the yew arch-way: she leaped almost off her feet with surprise. 'Bless us!' she cried, 'an elvling!' And she caught little Millicent in her arms; but the child laughed and patted her cheeks.

'Nurse Granmodè,' she said, 'Master Shackerley hath stole away from his friends to visit me. Put me down at once, for I must speak with him. At once, I say! Dear nurse, do!'

The woman obeyed, and Millicent came again to my side. 'Now let us kiss, for you must go back to your people,' she whispered. ''Tis very good to meet you. I shall often think of you when you are gone.'

She brought her smooth lips to mine, and kissed with evident delight. The nurse separated us. 'Madam, your mother will be uneasy if we do not return now,' she said. 'The bell has rung: we must go at once.'

Her charge took up the seams of her green skirt, and made a courtesy, then with a strange grace walked quietly away. In some manner she made me feel that I was utterly unpolished in com-parison: her gait—her way of speaking—might have been copied in courts.

When she had passed out of sight I hurried back to the coach, where I found the men taking out the valuables. My parents and sisters had gone back to Stratton, imagining that I had preceded them; so I hastened along the road and soon reached the 'Bull and Butcher,' which we had left only an hour before.

In the inn-yard a set of mountebanks was playing 'The Merriments of the Men of Gotham'; but though I loved these shows. I did not pause till I entered the presence of my mother, who was in high unrest at my absence. My father stood conversing with the innkeeper, a comely, well-proportioned dame, who put me in mind of the portrait of Anne Bullen at Amnest. ''Twas more than strange—'twas wicked,' I heard him say, 'the lass to have no choice!'

Mistress Nappy-ale replied, 'A sweet child if ever there was any!' My mother's curiosity conquered. I was sitting on her knee—all fears were allayed. 'Pray, husband, what is the purport of your long conversation?' He took her hand lightly. 'A pitiful story, indeed!' he said. 'Mistress here is telling me of Lord Dorel's mad freak about his daughter's marriage. Will you not repeat it to my wife? Dorel's Park was where the sling broke.'

Our hostess then began an account of how the Earl of Dorel, who had lost much of his fortune at the court of Elizabeth, had slightly retrieved his position by selling his child as wife to Humphreville Campion, a lad of thirteen: his father, Sir Withers Campion, being desirous for him to interwed with one of the purest stock in England. The Earl was old and profligate: he desired to shine amongst the gallants of Scottish James. Lady Millicent was seven years old at the time: her mother, a simple creature, so browbeaten that she dared not oppose any wish of her lord. After the ceremony, which was performed by the Bishop of Exeter, Sir Withers took Humphreville away to dwell at Campion Court until both parties attained ripe years. The act had made Lord Dorel very unpopular in the country, and since that day, now eight months ago, he had not once appeared at Dorel's Park.

This story made a deep impression on me. I remember that I was silent about my meeting with the baby-wife, not even telling the truth to my mother. When the coach was repaired and we went on to Aunt Bargrave's, my quietness was construed by my sisters into a sense of shame because of my escapade. For some weeks I was dull and heavy: I desired a companionship that was not attainable, and was regarded for a time as wasting. Nature, however, took mistress-ship, and before midsummer the subtle influence of Millicent seemed to have worn away.

Then intervened seventeen years, which, since they have little or naught to do with the Lady Millicent, I may pass over without excess of detail. I was educated at Salisbury Grammar School, and in 1617 became gentleman commoner at Christchurch, where, in 1622, I took the degree of Master of Arts. My father dying about this time, left me the estate of Amnest. My three sisters were married, one to a French noble, the others to men of position in our own county. Unaccustomed to the use of money, I set to squandering my fortune, and, being drawn into the vices of the court, kept wenches and horses both for myself and my less endowed friends. Time came when I discovered that half my money was dissipated: all my land mortgaged. I had some talent for writing: at Oxford I had composed many satires; so, with some wild view of retrieval, I wrote a play, which was often acted with great applause by the High and Mighty Prince Charles's servants, at the private house in Salisbury Court. Three other comedies followed; then a tragedy, then an epic of *Mars and Venus*, then *The Mother*, a tragi-comedy, on the presentation of which, before the king and queen, at the 'Red Bull' in Drury Lane, I first met Humphreville, now Sir Humphreville Campion.

His repute had often reached me, for he was accounted one of the maddest men in England. In his youth he had spent some years on the continent, and had there imbibed a love of occult things. 'Twas even said that he discovered the philosopher's stone. Darcy, my schoolfellow, who was murdered in Italy on his first tour, wrote once from Paris, where he had visited Sir Humphreville, who showed him a richly-coloured water, which he declared would turn any metal into gold. Then, doubtless by some sleight of hand, he performed an experiment whereby two ounces of the great metal were found in a crucible where lead had been before. Darcy had begged for a piece, but had been denied on the plea that all was not perfected.

Seeing that I had often wondered about him, it will amaze none to find that I examined him from top to toe. He was very tall—of at least six feet; his frame was thin; his hands and feet were small, the former exquisitely kept; his face was speckled like a toad's belly; his eyes deep brown—the left one with a slight cast; his hair black and crisp; his lips ripe red, very full and voluptuous, and his teeth of dazzling purity.

He seemed to favour notorieties. Hearing that I was the playwright he came to me, and, on the next seat's being left unoccupied, sat there and watched. He dispersed a rich smell of violets—it was said that his skin by some artificial means had been impregnated lastingly with their odour. When the play was done I bade him to a supper I had made for the actors; and there, though his language savoured of the empiric, he discoursed most interestingly, particularly on antipathies: in France he said he had kept a mistress who fainted at the sight of velvet; and even if it were drawn over her face in sleep she would instantly fall into convulsions. This, and such like information, kept us together till late in the morning. On parting he entreated me to visit him at his house at Hampstead, where, he told me, the Lady Millicent was lying. I kept my own counsel about our former meeting, thinking it might give him some displeasure.

On the morrow I went, to find Sir Humphreville away from home, but expected shortly. I was shown into his library, a spacious chamber, lighted by a louvre of many-coloured glass, and lined with a collection of books such as I had never seen before in the house of a private gentleman. It consisted chiefly of modern poets and dramatists, memoirs in divers foreign languages, works on witchcraft, chemistry, and astrology: on the whole being of more pretence than worth.

As I took up a new copy of Michael Scott's *Quaestio Curiosa de Natura Solis et Lunae*, I heard the rustling of a woman's gown, and turning, saw Lady Millicent gazing at me with a mirthful face. She was much changed. As a child she had seemed sad and fantastic, now at twenty-four she had developed into a woman of heavenly beauty. Her face was white as snow, an admirable oval; her grey eyes clearer than crystal; her hair, which had not, as hair is wont, changed with the passage of years, fell in heavy curls down her back and over her bosom, held from her brow by an ornament of pearls.

'So we meet again,' she said. 'You were my fairy prince. I almost doubted that you had ever really existed. It is very sweet to find you here. When they brought your name to me, years seemed to roll away. Ay me, for those long past days at Dorel's Park!' she sighed.

Somehow her words brought back the hollowness of my manhood. Would that we two were children again! That once more I might run through the Park, where the jetto played and the squirrels squeaked, and the stately little maid kissed me. Lady Millicent noted my depression.

'Childhood is sweeter than barren knowledge,' she said in a low tone. 'For one year of unalloyed happiness I would sell all the rest of my life.'

As she spoke a curtain swung back, and one entered in the guise of a Saracen; turbaned and bedecked with many precious stones. He passed round the room by the wall; not until he reached the further door did I observe his face. It was the most terrible I had ever seen. Heavy brows leaned over green and yellow eyes: the skin was puckered in huge wrinkles: a few silver hairs swayed from his chin. His mouth was loathsome; by some preternatural means the lips had been drawn almost to the ears, and in the gulfed space lay a hedge of black teeth, which being opened—the jaw hanging loosely on his breast—showed me in that short space that the tongue was missing, and its place taken by some white snake-like roots. At the door he made his obeisance, accompanying it with a hoarse, frightful sound.

'It is Sir Humphreville's mute eunuch,' she said frowning. 'He has the leave of the house. My lord bought him from the Soldan. He is reputed to have stores of forbidden knowledge—Sir Humphreville sets a high value on him: they work for hours in the laboratory together.'

When the creature had gone she laid her hand on my arm. 'I have a fond belief that yonder gelding pollutes the air. Let us sit in my own chamber: there at least he is forbidden to enter.'

She accompanied me to a cabinet furnished in the richest, most extravagant fashion. The walls, where not hung with white satin, were of alabaster, fretted with moresks of finely-beaten gold; the ceiling, also of white, but pierced with a crescent moon and stars that by some arrangement of changing mirrors and lights glittered more brightly than the real firmament. Tripods of silver with smouldering spills sent out dainty clouds that massed beneath this mock sky and filtered through its orifices.

There we sat and discoursed of our lives. She had heard of my fame; had even seen one of my comedies at White Hall. She made no attempt to glose, but begged for information as simply as a begging child. When I had told her all, she began to relate her own history since her marriage. Sir Humphreville (whom, as I had already noted, she spoke of in a constrained fashion) had returned from the Continent in her sixteenth year to take possession. The Earl of Dorel had died meanwhile; and her husband, after a year of quiet life, had been appointed ambassador to Naples. There she had passed three unhappy years, the women of Italy not being companionable, and Sir Humphreville overmuch engrossed in his philosophical researches. After that they had resided in England; at divers seats of the Campions; and now, Sir Humphreville being called to the Court, where he was in high favour because of his proposal to turn all the copper of the kingdom into gold, he had bought the house at Hampstead. Day by day, she said, he worked with the king in the royal laboratory.

When she had done, the noise of a coach in the yard made her rise. 'He has arrived. We will go back to the library,' she said timidly. So we returned thither, and almost before I could kiss her hand she retired. As I turned towards the window I caught sight of the mute, half hidden behind a heavy crimson curtain, with his foul face drawn into one most filthy grin. A curious fascination—as is felt of him that looks upon a cockatrice—took possession of me; and I stared until Campion's appearing, who came forward with a wry smile of welcome. I heard afterwards that some most precious liquid had been spilled that morning by the king's carelessness.

When we had conversed for a while on the matters of playwriting—he himself was one of those discontented characters who aspire to everything, and he would ask much of me concerning the general make and conduct of a drama—the mute came forward, after sundry signs of impatience, and speaking as it were with his fingers, imparted some news to his master. From a motion of his head I understood that he was telling of my encounter with Lady Millicent; and my fears proved too well-founded; for Campion turned to me with a suspicious face, and, immediately, though with courteous words, he brought our interview to a conclusion, pleading that an important experiment would be destroyed if it were not viewed at once. He expressed no desire to see me again, whereat I was sorry; for my meeting with the woman whose memory I had cherished so long had filled me with a hope of many exquisite hours. But I went back to my house, and that same day gave Arbel Strype, my mistress, a small farm in Dorsetshire, and liberty to marry: then dismissed her, glad that it had lain in my power to make her becoming provision.

In the evening I went again to the play, and, as before, I saw Sir Humphreville Campion in attendance on the royal party. I saluted him; but to my surprise had no acknowledgment. It seemed either that he had forgotten me altogether, or that some jealous fear had so blinded him that he could not force himself to be courteous. Next day the illness of my mother, who was living on her dower at Amnest, called me to her bedside, where I remained until the end, which took place a se'nnight afterwards. The arrangements for her obsequies and the winding up of her affairs so engaged me that I had little time to think of other matters: indeed, I had half resolved to withdraw altogether from town life when news came that Sir Humphreville Campion had been despatched on a secret mission to the Court of Spain, and in the hope of meeting his lady I repaired to my house in Gracious Street. Here, to my amaze, I found an epistle, with the Campion crest of a dragon on the seal. It was from Lady Millicent herself.

'Sir,' it read, 'if it be true there are reasons why you should not visit me, I pray you explain them. I am alone here: Campion at this moment is in Madrid. I have little to tell except that every available word of your writing I have perused, and won great pleasure therefrom; that I would willingly play student to your better intelligence: there are many things I would choose to learn from you. Write to me on your return from the country, and tell me that we may meet, and that shortly. All my old friends are alienated: you alone are left to remind me of an innocent past. But of this no more.—MILLICENT CAMPION.'

I went: she received me in state. The old Dowager-Countess of Dorel, blind and deaf by reason of her years, sat with us through the interview, and we talked to our hearts' content. A pretty fable Lady Millicent told me; called by herself *The New Andromeda*, which she had writ for a fancy of her own. 'Twas of a young child tied to a rock for a warlock to devour—another Dragon of Wantley, forsooth. The babe, innocent of her fate, plays and frolics; Perseus—or More of More Hall, or what you will—comes by,—is too innocent to understand the danger—and little mistress is left for the warlock. I could see that she meant her own history: I was the useless hero—she, the victim. Old madam nodded in her chair the while. When the time came to depart Millicent said she was leaving London on the morrow by Sir Humphreville's command, to retire to a country seat in the Yorkshire fells until her master's return. Byland Grange was the place: if I would honour it with a visit, she would herself show me the riches of the hills and valleys. That there was little of the really happy in the world she made no doubt: let each choose his own joy. When I took her hand she said, ''Tis the same ring I wore at Dorel's: as years passed it chafed and was enlarged: now it chafes again.'

Three days afterwards I started to follow her, half in hopes to come up with her equipage, but it seemed she had the advantage and ever kept a day in front. I rode the two hundred and forty miles in four days, and it was on a Sunday afternoon when I led my horse into the yard of the Campion Arms, and bespoke a chamber. My man followed by post with mails; but I did not wait for ceremony, and having eaten in haste, I passed through the stately gates of the park. A spacious wilderness lay before me, netted with undergrowth green in the spring's triumph. Rivulets leaped across the clean stoned path, and crags frowned, their feet laved in clear pools, where strange waterfowl swam, their sides almost hidden beneath mosses and tangles of dove's-foot. Here and there belvederes watched down vistas, terminated by fish-ponds or stairlike ranges of peaks.

So great was the loveliness that I paused: in my most lively dreams I had never imagined aught like so perfect. As I stood I heard the cry of *cuckoo*, then from the distance the laughing mockery of a voice. Years rolled away like a mist, I was a boy again, she a girl; vice and dishonesty and sadness had all disappeared, and life was fresh and sweet as in those days of old. I ran clapping my hands to a coppice of firs, which, as firs are used, had caught about its trunks a golden mist, and there I found Millicent, knee-deep in bracken.

There is a certain tremulous joy whose remembrance pains me almost too much to describe. When I said before that we were boy and girl again I spoke rashly, though children we were in a sense. But we were weaker because of our age: children love for very joy of heart and innocence, men and women love for love's sake. There was no reticence in either, we gave ourselves to each other with freedom and without shame. Neither had lived so long as to be unconscious that true love—true passion—is the completion of existence. She loitered at my side through the open park, where stands a ruined abbey, and along glades to the terrace of the house. Byland Grange is one of the strangest mansions in our country, standing against an abruptly rising cliff which mountain ashes and silver birches cover with greenery. The building is of red brick, with two wings and a court garden, and so covered with ivy that from the distance it seems like a cluster of rare trees with ruddy trunks and branches. The sun had taken the windows, and the whole front was chequered with glittering lights.

The great door stood open: we went into a hall where stood wooden knights in complete panoply. At the end were two flights of stairs, which joined to a corridor that pierced the house: in niches fountains fell with pleasing music from satyrs' heads and dolphins' mouths. In a chamber of faded colours we sat together on the same settee, silently, heedless of the hours. Through the window we saw the moon disentangle herself from the tree-tops, the stars twinkle out one by one. Not until candles were brought did I take my leave, and then I entreated my mistress to meet me early on the morrow.

At parting she looked at me long and earnestly. 'We are carried away by some hidden current,' she said. 'Passion has entrapped us; we must be happy and we must suffer! Thus!' And she stood tiptoe and kissed me; her warm sweet tresses falling on my shoulder. At my inn I tossed all night awake—a battlefield of hopes and fears; so that when I arose in the morning I was haggard and languid. Of that I took no heed; but hastily donning my clothes, I ate, and hurried to the meeting-place. I had not waited a minute before she swept down, tired-looking and big-eyed. She wore a royal gown, somewhat like one I had read of in a description of the Princess Elizabeth's wardrobe. It was of a pure satin, in colour betwixt apple green and rose; once it shone the one, again the other; and the skirt was embroidered with eyes of amethyst and seed pearls.

In our talk we made no mention of Campion: 'twas as if each were in a little world some genius forbade him to enter. But as time passed we grew less and less masters of ourselves. This day our tongues were loosened, but neither rhyme nor reason came, and we babbled like hoyden and hobble-de-hoy. In a little arbour near the abbey she had ordered a collation of fruit and wine to be placed, and at noon we ate and drank together; then strolled on amongst the giant beeches. The heat of the sun overpowered us, and we sat to rest; she unlaced her bodice to breathe the freer, and, like me, weary for lack of sleep, let her head sink back to the green grass. With the movement the kerchief fell loosely from her throat, and showed me, lying upon her breast, a curious miniature of myself, wrought by some unknown hand and framed in rubies. My hand caught hers; I grew drowsier and drowsier until we slept. We lay thus for three hours, when both were awakened rudely by the sound of a thunder-clap. We sat up and beheld the skies of a uniform blackness. Heavy drops of rain began to fall; almost ere we had reached the open we felt water on our skin. But the sight of the storm was so terrible and tragical that we took no care for ourselves. My mistress was not frightened: the gods were holding a chariot race, she said, and indeed the rumbling sounded as if it were so.

The forks leaped across the fells: when they passed over water, it seemed to hiss; avenues of flame opened from one end of the park to another. The strong wind caught the trees and made them kiss the ground; the evening was pregnant with inquietude. We sheltered in an archway of the abbey: in mortal peril there, for stones that steamed with the uncooled heat were cast about our heads. It was well-nigh dark before there came a lull; and Millicent was so outworn with the strife of the elements that she could scarce move. So I took her in my arms and stumbled across the wilderness to the Grange. There the servants, who were old and careless, had not so much as taken note of their lady's absence.

She hastened to her chamber, and sent dry clothes to me; some grandsire's garments taken from an ancient press and heavy with the odour of musk. I donned them, and saw myself a courtier of Henry's time in doublet and hose of slashed velvet. The storm did not abate; and when I descended from the place where I had shifted to a parlour on the ground floor, I had given to me a hasty note. 'I am tired,' it ran, 'tonight I cannot see you; a bedchamber is prepared; honour me by spending the night here.'

My heart sank now at the thought of times apart from her; but I strove to wile the hours with a lute I found; and I made verses on my lady's beauty, which I wrote on some tablets that lay in the window-seat. At midnight I retired to bed, where, being still exhausted, I fell asleep immediately—to dream that terrible and most sweet day all over again. I woke in an hour. Outside the wind shrieked and howled: it shook the mullions; strange things rattled across the panes. My candle, which I had forgotten to blow out, was guttering in the socket.

Suddenly I heard a woman's cry—it was repeated—it rang above the noise of tempest: '*Francis, O Francis, help me! they are killing me!—they are killing me!*'

I sprang from bed and ran into the corridor, my feet clapping loudly on the plaster floor. At the further end was an open door, with a brilliant gleam. All indoors was quiet: on the threshold I paused, seeing a golden bedstead, hung with curtains of tissue, and the shape of a woman beneath the covering.

Again came that frightful cry—fainter and fainter, '*Francis, my Francis, help me!—help me!*'

Then I went to the bedside and tore aside the fabric; to behold my mistress's face all contorted as with fear and pain. Forgetful of all save my desire to drive away her torturing fancies (for I saw that she rode the wild mare), I leaped upon the pillow and caught her head to my lap, where the grey eyes opened in wonderment, and a flush spread over the cheeks. She gave one laughing sigh—a woman's whinny; then thrust out her arms and clasped my waist...

At that moment came the sounds of bolts undrawn and doors banging; then followed a loud tumult in the hall below—then a quavering of voices hushed by one sharp and loud. I would have drawn away for her sake; but her hands were locked.

'It is he,' she whispered. 'How he comes I know not. Stay with me to the end.'

The clamping of shoes, the clinking of spurs moved along the gallery; then Sir Humphreville and the mute came through the open door. Jealous hatred flashed on us from the knight's eyes; he held his sword before him; I could see him tremble.

'ADULTERESS!' He spoke no more than the one word.

Lady Millicent smiled—still from my lap. 'Think you so?' she said.

At a motion from him the Saracen came forward, holding a knife. The garments of both dropped water on the floor. The mute pricked those white fingers till they unclasped, then dragged me away. I flung myself upon him, naked as I was, but his long arms held me like serpents, so that hardly might I breathe. Then Campion tore down one of the curtains and bound me to a chair. He seemed to meditate. Millicent his wife gave no sign of fear, but lay watching from her disordered pillow. At last he locked the door and stood between us.

'In all things I chose refinement,' he said. 'If I were a boor, both of you should die—both be sent into lasting damnation together. But as I hold that those who love meet in the next world, one of you shall go, the other be left, so that such joy you may not have.

For my own easement, and the better that I may attend to my particular work, I think best that you, Madam Whore, should be the one to bleed.'

She stepped from the bed. 'Wonderful man, wonderful genius,' she said scornfully, 'I am ready.'

Campion tore off her lawn smock, so that she stood before us in naked beauty. 'Fie upon you!' she said, 'to treat a woman thus.'

He drew her towards a large silver bath that lay in an alcove, there he forced her to lie in the water. I began to struggle, but the gelding tied a kerchief round my neck, and offered the point of his knife at my heart. I tried to press forward on it, but he broke the skin, and then withdrew it. Again and again I strove, ever without success.

Then Sir Humphreville took from his breast an emerald pencil, which, being opened, revealed a tiny lancet. He knelt where Millicent lay, and breathed a vein in her lovely arm. A fountain of blood pulsed out, discolouring first the water around her shoulders, then circling in clouds to her feet.

She turned and brought her eyes to mine, they were laughing still.

'When we come together again, Frank,' she said faintly, ''twill be in God's sight.'

Dimness overcame my eyes, and for a while I could scarce see, but on my brain was printing the form of a naked woman lying on a mattress of blood and silver...

'How we met boy and girl! how I loved you in my heart of hearts! Speak to me, Frank. Shall we... shall we be young again some day?'

I sought to answer, but my tongue forsook its office; at my side the mute made his horrid attempt at speech. Sir Humphreville drew himself upright and folded his arms waiting for the end. From the bath a steam began to rise, the smell of blood filled the room.

She made effort to turn on her side, but she could not. From her lips came the word *cuckoo*—just as she had mocked the bird at Dorel's... Campion knelt again and clapped his hand over her mouth, thinking haply she was jeering him in death. Moan came after moan: such a sound as a weeping angel might make. There was a faint splashing, then silence.

... It is all told.

What spells and charms were worked on me, I cannot tell. When six months after I found myself at Amnest, brought by means I knew nothing of, all desire of vengeance as of life had gone. It seemed to me, while Sir Humphreville lived, I could not publish this history to the world: for—perhaps by some enchantment learned in his pursuit of hidden knowledge—he had gained a great power over me. No will was left: I was doomed to feebleness both of mind and body.

Yet this scripture must be done, for traduction hath been at work with a most noble lady, and before I go to her I would fain have the world to understand.

THE BASILISK

arina gave no sign that she heard my protestation. The embroidery of Venus's hands in her silk picture of The Judgment of Paris was seemingly of greater import to her than the love which almost tore my soul and body asunder. In absolute despair I sat until she had replenished her needle seven times. Then impassioned nature cried aloud:—

'You do not love me!'

She looked up somewhat wearily, as one debarred from rest. 'Listen,' she said. 'There is a creature called a Basilisk, which turns men and women into stone. In my girlhood I saw the Basilisk—I am stone!'

And, rising from her chair, she departed the room, leaving me in amazed doubt as to whether I had heard aright. I had always known of some curious secret in her life: a secret which permitted her to speak of and to understand things to which no other woman had dared to lift her thoughts. But alas! it was a secret whose influence ever thrust her back from the attaining of happiness. She would warm, then freeze instantly; discuss the purest wisdom, then cease with contemptuous lips and eyes. Doubtless this strangeness had been the first thing to awaken my passion. Her beauty was not of the kind that smites men with sudden craving: it was pale and reposeful, the loveliness of a marble image. Yet, as time went on, so wondrous became her fascination that even the murmur of her swaying garments sickened me with longing. Not more than a year had passed since our first meeting, when I had found her laden with flaming tendrils in the thinned woods of my heritage. A very Dryad, robed in grass colour, she was chanting to the sylvan deities. The invisible web took me, and I became her slave.

Her house lay two leagues from mine. It was a low-built mansion lying in a concave park. The thatch was gaudy with stonecrop and lichen. Amongst the central chimneys a foreign bird sat on a nest of twigs. The long windows blazed with heraldic devices; and paintings of kings and queens and nobles hung in the dim chambers. Here she dwelt with a retinue of aged servants, fantastic women and men half imbecile, who salaamed before her with eastern humility and yet addressed her in such terms as gossips use. Had she given them life they could not have obeyed with more reverence. Quaint things the women wrought for her—pomanders and cushions of thistle-down; and the men were never happier than when they could tell her of the first thrush's egg in the thornbush or the sege of bitterns that haunted the marsh. She was their goddess and their daughter. Each day had its own routine. In the morning she rode and sang and played; at noon she read in the dusty library, drinking to the full of the dramatists and the platonists. Her own life was such a tragedy as an Elizabethan would have adored. None save her people knew her history, but there were wonderful stories of how she had bowed to tradition, and concentrated in herself the characteristics of a thousand wizard fathers. In the blossom of her youth she had sought strange knowledge, and had tasted thereof, and rued.

The morning after my declaration she rode across her park to the meditating walk I always paced till noon. She was alone, dressed in a habit of white lutestring with a loose girdle of blue. As her mare reached the yew hedge, she dismounted, and came to me with more lightness than I had ever beheld in her. At her waist

116

hung a black glass mirror, and her half-bare arms were adorned with cabalistic jewels.

When I knelt to kiss her hand, she sighed heavily. 'Ask me nothing,' she said. 'Life itself is too joyless to be more embittered by explanations. Let all rest between us as now. I will love coldly, you warmly, with no nearer approaching.' Her voice rang full of a wistful expectancy: as if she knew that I should combat her half-explained decision. She read me well, for almost ere she had done I cried out loudly against it:—'It can never be so—I cannot breathe—I shall die?'

She sank to the low moss-covered wall. 'Must the sacrifice be made?' she asked, half to herself. 'Must I tell him all?' Silence prevailed a while, then turning away her face she said: 'From the first I loved you, but last night in the darkness, when I could not sleep for thinking of your words, love sprang into desire.'

I was forbidden to speak.

'And desire seemed to burst the cords that bound me. In that moment's strength I felt that I could give all for the joy of being once utterly yours.'

I longed to clasp her to my heart. But her eyes were stern, and a frown crossed her brow.

'At morning light,' she said, 'desire died, but in my ecstasy I had sworn to give what must be given for that short bliss, and to lie in your arms and pant against you before another midnight. So I have come to bid you fare with me to the place where the spell may be loosed, and happiness bought.'

She called the mare: it came whinnying, and pawed the ground until she had stroked its neck. She mounted, setting in my hand a tiny, satin-shod foot that seemed rather child's than woman's. 'Let us go together to my house,' she said. 'I have orders to give and duties to fulfil. I will not keep you there long, for we must start soon on our errand.' I walked exultantly at her side, but, the grange in view, I entreated her to speak explicitly of our mysterious journey. She stooped and patted my head. ''Tis but a matter of buying and selling,' she answered.

When she had arranged her household affairs, she came to the library and bade me follow her. Then, with the mirror still swinging against her knees, she led me through the garden and the wilderness down to a misty wood. It being autumn, the trees were tinted gloriously in dusky bars of colouring. The rowan, with his amber leaves and scarlet berries, stood before the brown black-spotted sycamore; the silver beech flaunted his golden coins against my poverty; firs, green and fawn-hued, slumbered in hazy gossamer. No bird carolled, although the sun was hot. Marina noted the absence of sound, and without prelude of any kind began to sing from the ballad of the Witch Mother: about the nine enchanted knots, and the trouble-comb in the lady's knotted hair, and the master-kid that ran beneath her couch. Every drop of my blood froze in dread, for whilst she sang her face took on the majesty of one who traffics with infernal powers. As the shade of the trees fell over her, and we passed intermittently out of the light, I saw that her eyes glittered like rings of sapphires. Believing now that the ordeal she must undergo would be too frightful, I begged her to return. Supplicating on my knees—'Let me face the evil alone!' I said, 'I will entreat the loosening of the bonds. I will compel and accept any penalty.' She grew calm. 'Nay,' she said, very gently, 'if aught can conquer, it is my love alone. In the fervour of my last wish I can dare everything.'

By now, at the end of a sloping alley, we had reached the shores of a vast marsh. Some unknown quality in the sparkling water had stained its whole bed a bright yellow. Green leaves, of such a sour brightness as almost poisoned to behold, floated on the surface of the rush-girdled pools. Weeds like tempting veils of mossy velvet grew beneath in vivid contrast with the soil. Alders and willows hung over the margin. From where we stood a half-submerged path of rough stones, threaded by deep swift channels, crossed to the very centre. Marina put her foot upon the first step. 'I must go first,' she said. 'Only once before have I gone this way, yet I know its pitfalls better than any living creature.'

Before I could hinder her she was leaping from stone to stone like a hunted animal. I followed hastily, seeking, but vainly, to lessen the space between us. She was gasping for breath, and her heart-beats sounded like the ticking of a clock. When we reached a great pool, itself almost a lake, that was covered with lavender scum, the path turned abruptly to the right, where stood an isolated grove of wasted elms. As Marina beheld this, her pace slackened, and she paused in momentary indecision; but, at my first word of pleading that she should go no further, she went on, dragging her silken mud-bespattered skirts. We climbed the slippery shores of the island (for island it was, being raised much above the level of the marsh), and Marina led the way over lush grass to an open glade. A great marble tank lay there, supported on two thick pillars. Decayed boughs rested on the crust of stagnancy within, and divers frogs, bloated and almost blue, rolled off at our approach. To the left stood the columns of a temple, a round, domed building, with a closed door of bronze. Wild vines had grown athwart the portal; rank, clinging herbs had sprung from the overteeming soil; astrological figures were enchiselled on the broad stairs.

Here Marina stopped. 'I shall blindfold you,' she said, taking off her loose sash, 'and you must vow obedience to all I tell you.

The least error will betray us.' I promised, and submitted to the bandage. With a pressure of the hand, and bidding me neither move nor speak, she left me and went to the door of the temple. Thrice her hand struck the dull metal. At the last stroke a hissing shriek came from within, and the massive hinges creaked loudly. A breath like an icy tongue leaped out and touched me, and in the terror my hand sprang to the kerchief. Marina's voice, filled with agony, gave me instant pause. '*Oh, why am I thus torn between the man and the fiend? The mesh that holds life in will be ripped from end to end! Is there no mercy?*'

My hand fell impotent. Every muscle shrank. I felt myself turn to stone. After a while came a sweet scent of smouldering wood: such an Oriental fragrance as is offered to Indian gods. Then the door swung to, and I heard Marina's voice, dim and wordless, but raised in wild deprecation. Hour after hour passed so, and still I waited. Not until the sash grew crimson with the rays of the sinking sun did the door open.

'Come to me!' Marina whispered. 'Do not unblindfold. Quick—we must not stay here long. He is glutted with my sacrifice.'

New-born joy rang in her tones. I stumbled across and was caught in her arms. Shafts of delight pierced my heart at the first contact with her warm breasts. She turned me round, and bidding me look straight in front, with one swift touch untied the knot. The first thing my dazed eyes fell upon was the mirror of black glass which had hung from her waist. She held it so that I might gaze into its depths. And there, with a cry of amazement and fear, *I saw the shadow of the Basilisk.*

The Thing was lying prone on the floor, the presentment of a sleeping horror. Vivid scarlet and sable feathers covered its gold-crowned cock's-head, and its leathern dragon-wings were folded.

Its sinuous tail, capped with a snake's eyes and mouth, was curved in luxurious and delighted satiety. A prodigious evil leaped in its atmosphere. But even as I looked a mist crowded over the surface of the mirror: the shadow faded, leaving only an indistinct and wavering shape. Marina breathed upon it, and, as I peered and pored, the gloom went off the plate and left, where the Chimera had lain, the prostrate figure of a man. He was young and stalwart, a dark outline with a white face, and short black curls that fell in tangles over a shapely forehead, and eyelids languorous and red. His aspect was that of a wearied demon-god.

When Marina looked sideways and saw my wonderment, she laughed delightedly in one rippling running tune that should have quickened the dead entrails of the marsh. 'I have conquered!' she cried. 'I have purchased the fulness of joy!' And with one outstretched arm she closed the door before I could turn to look; with the other she encircled my neck, and, bringing down my head, pressed my mouth to hers. The mirror fell from her hand, and with her foot she crushed its shards into the dank mould.

The sun had sunk behind the trees now, and glittered through the intricate leafage like a charcoal-burner's fire. All the nymphs of the pools arose and danced, grey and cold, exulting at the absence of the divine light. So thickly gathered the vapours that the path grew perilous. 'Stay, love,' I said. 'Let me take you in my arms and carry you. It is no longer safe for you to walk alone.' She made no reply, but, a flush arising to her pale cheeks, she stood and let me lift her to my bosom. She rested a hand on either shoulder, and gave no sign of fear as I bounded from stone to stone. The way lengthened deliciously, and by the time we reached the plantation the moon was rising over the further hills. Hope and fear fought in my heart: soon both were set at rest. When I set her on the dry ground she stood a-tiptoe, and murmured with exquisite shame: 'Tonight, then, dearest. My home is yours now.'

So, in a rapture too subtle for words, we walked together, arm-enfolded, to her house. Preparations for a banquet were going on within: the windows were ablaze, and figures passed behind them bowed with heavy dishes. At the threshold of the hall we were met by a triumphant crash of melody. In the musician's gallery bald-pated veterans stood to it with flute and harp and viol-de-gamba. In two long rows the antic retainers stood, and bowed, and cried merrily: 'Joy and health to the bride and groom!' And they kissed Marina's hands and mine, and, with the players sending forth that half-forgotten tenderness which threads through ancient song-books, we passed to the feast, seating ourselves on the dais, whilst the servants filled the tables below. But we made little feint of appetite. As the last dish of confections was removing, a weird pageant swept across the further end of the banqueting-room: Oberon and Titania with Robin Goodfellow and the rest, attired in silks and satins gorgeous of hue, and bedizened with such late flowers as were still with us. I leaned forward to commend, and saw that each face was brown and wizened and thin-haired: so that their motions and their epi-thalamy felt goblin and discomforting; nor could I smile till they departed by the further door. Then the tables were cleared away, and Marina, taking my finger-tips in hers, opened a stately dance. The servants followed, and in the second maze a shrill and joyful laughter proclaimed that the bride had sought her chamber...

Ere the dawn I wakened from a troubled sleep. My dream had been of despair: I had been persecuted by a host of devils, thieves of a priceless jewel. So I leaned over the pillow for Marina's con-solation; my lips sought hers, my hand crept beneath her head. My heart gave one mad bound—then stopped.

WITCH IN-GRAIN

f late Michal had been much engrossed in the reading of the black-letter books that Philosopher Bale brought from France. As you know I am no Latinist—though one while she was earnest in her desire to instruct me; but the open air had ever greater charms for me than had the dry precincts of a library. So I grudged the time she spent apart, and throughout the spring I would have been all day at her side, talking such foolery as lovers use. But ever she must steal away and hide herself amongst dead volumes.

Yestereven I crossed the Roods, and entered the garden, to find the girl sitting under a yew-tree. Her face was haggard and her eyes sunken: for the time it seemed as if many years had passed over her head, but somehow the change had only added to her beauty. And I marvelled greatly, but ere I could speak a huge bird, whose plumage was as the brightest gold, fluttered out of her lap from under the silken apron; and looking on her uncovered bosom I saw that his beak had pierced her tender flesh. I cried aloud, and would have caught the thing, but it rose slowly, laughing like a man, and, beating upwards, passed out of sight in the quincunx. Then Michal drew long breaths, and her youth came back in some measure. But she frowned, and said, 'What is it, sweetheart? Why hast awakened me? I dreamed that I fed the Dragon of the Hesperidean Garden.' Meanwhile, her gaze set on the place whither the bird had flown.

'Thou hast chosen a filthy mammet,' I said. 'Tell me how came it hither?'

She rose without reply, and kissed her hands to the gaudy wings, which were nearing through the trees. Then, lifting up a great tome that had lain at her feet, she turned towards the house. But ere she had reached the end of the maze she stopped, and smiled with strange subtlety.

'How camest *thou* hither, O satyr?' she cried. 'Even when the Dragon slept, and the fruit hung naked to my touch... The gates fell to.'

Perplexed and sore adread, I followed to the hall; and found in the herb garden the men struggling with an ancient woman—a foul crone, brown and puckered as a rotten costard. At sight of Michal she thrust out her hands, crying, 'Save me, mistress!' The girl cowered, and ran up the perron and indoors. But for me, I questioned Simon, who stood well out of reach of the wretch's nails, as to the wherefore of this hurly-burly.

His underlings bound the runnion with cords, and haled her to the closet in the banqueting gallery. Then, her beldering being stilled, Simon entreated me to compel Michal to prick her arm. So I went down to the library, and found my sweetheart sitting by the window, tranced with seeing that goblin fowl go tumbling on the lawn.

My heart was full of terror and anguish. 'Dearest Michal,' I prayed, 'for the sake of our passion let me command. Here is a knife.' I took a poniard from Sir Roger's stand of arms. 'Come with me now; I will tell you all.'

Her gaze still shed her heart upon the popinjay; and when I took her hand and drew her from the room, she strove hard to escape. In the gallery I pressed her fingers round the haft, and knowing that the witch was bound, flung open the door so that they faced each other. But Mother Benmusk's eyes glared like fire, so that Michal was withered up, and sank swooning into my arms. And a chuckle of disdain leaped from the hag's ragged lips. Simon and the others came hurrying, and when Michal had found her life, we begged her to cut into one of those knotted arms. Yet she would none of it, but turned her face and signed no—no—she would not. And as we strove to prevail with her, word came that one of the Bishop's horses had cast a shoe in the village, and that his lordship craved the hospitality of Ford, until the smith had mended the mishap. Nigh at the heels of his message came the divine, and having heard and pondered our tale, he would fain speak with her.

I took her to the withdrawing-room, where at the sight of him she burst into such a loud fit of laughter that the old man rose in fear and went away.

'Surely it is an obsession,' he cried; 'nought can be done until the witch takes back her spells!'

So I bade the servants carry Benmusk to the mere, and cast her in the muddy part thereof where her head would lie above water. That was fifteen hours ago, but methinks I still hear her screams clanging through the stagnant air. Never was hag so fierce and full of strength! All along the garden I saw a track of uprooted flowers. Amongst the sedges the turmoil grew and grew till every heron fled. They threw her in, and the whole mere seethed as if the floor of it were hell. For full an hour she cursed us fearsomely: then, finding that every time she neared the land the men thrust her back again, her spirit waxed abject, and she fell to whimpering. Two hours before twelve she cried that she would tell all she knew. So we landed her, and she was loosened of her bonds and she mumbled in my ear: 'I swear by Satan that I am innocent of this harm! I ha' none but pawtry secrets. Go at midnight to the lows and watch Baldus's tomb. There thou shalt find all.'

The beldam tottered away, her bemired petticoats clapping her legs; and I bade them let her rest in peace until I had certainly proved her guilt. With this I returned to the house; but, finding that Michal had retired for the night, I sat by the fire, waiting for the time to pass. A clock struck the half before eleven, and I set out for King Baldus's grave, whither, had not such a great matter been at stake, I dared not have ventured after dark. I stole from the garden and through the first copse. The moon lay against a brazen curtain; little snail-like clouds were crawling underneath, and the horns of them pricked her face.

As I neared the lane to the waste, a most unholy dawn broke behind the fringe of pines, looping the boles with strings of grey-golden light. Surely a figure moved there? I ran. A curious motley and a noisy swarmed forth at me. Another moment, and I was in the midst of a host of weasels and hares and such-like creatures, all flying from the precincts of the tomb. I quaked with dread, and the hair of my flesh stood upright. But I thrust on, and parted the thorn boughs, and looked up at the mound.

On the summit thereof sat Michal, triumphing, invested with flames. And the Shape approached, and wrapped her in his blackness.

THE GROTTO
AT RAVENSDALE

hree weeks after the wedding of Peregrine Fury and Lady Mary Tufton, daughter of the Earl of Thanet, the young couple left Newbottle (my lord's Northamptonshire seat), and journeyed in a new coach and six to Ravensdale, the bridegroom's estate in one of the most remote Peakland valleys. Of the journey they knew but little, each being vastly in love, and deeming no prospect in the world comparable with the reflection to be found in the other's eyes.

Mrs Tryphena Wilbraham, a kinswoman of the young lady— one of those useful spinsters upon whom devolve the smoothing of other folk's paths—had been sent, the day after the nuptials, to see that the house was set in readiness for one who had been accustomed to luxury from her birth. Peregrine Fury had not visited the place since his infancy, the late owner, his uncle, Sir Agabus Webbe, having alienated the affections of all his relatives by a middle age marred by eccentricity of no very pleasant nature.

For a life of Sir Agabus, one must consult the third volume of *The British Magazine, or Monthly Repository for Gentlemen and Ladies*, wherein is a brief biography, entitled: 'The Character of a Miser, founded on fact, though veiled under a fictitious name'. There it will be seen that a conjugal catastrophe changed a harmless gentleman into a parsimonious hermit, whose whole energy was devoted to almost incredible cheeseparing. For well-nigh twenty years no fire burned on the hearths of Ravensdale Lodge; the doors and gates of house and garden were ever kept locked and barred; only one servant (an elderly female) was permitted to sleep beneath the roof. Eggs with cresses from the stream made the baronet's usual diet, though it was occasionally varied by a partridge or rabbit trapped in the garden. Throughout those years 'Fuscus' (so the Grub Street writer called him) never stirred beyond the confines of his park, or looked upon a stranger's face. He died of some slight complaint, which any country chirurgeon might have remedied. And after his demise, it was discovered that he had tripled his securities, and, dying intestate, left enough to make his heir one of the wealthiest men in the kingdom.

At the time of his uncle's death, Peregrine was page-in-waiting to Frederick, Prince of Wales, and at Leicester House had frequently met Lady Mary Tufton. His position, however, was not such as found favour in the eyes of my Lord Thanet; since his patrimony consisted of naught save a few hundred acres of Lincolnshire marsh, and a green-lichened, moated house overrun with rats. But the great windfall caused the father to veer round suddenly (in sober truth the earl often played weathercock), and welcome young Master Fury with a stately blessing.

Lady Mary had inherited considerable beauty from her mother, the Marquis of Halifax's daughter. She was tall and slender— indeed, her height came to within an inch of Peregrine's—with a dainty silken skin and languishing, melting blue eyes. She had loved him for a full twelvemonth, and had been much troubled by her father's strenuous endeavours to wed her to one of her own rank. She had little of the virgin's foolish meekness—more than once she had threatened to enter a convent unless she could have the man of her own choice. When the death of Sir Agabus set all matters right, I dare swear that no happier girl could be found anywhere.

Peregrine was, in man's fashion, as pleasant to look upon as she—a strongly-built lad, with the frankest, handsomest face, quite unspoiled by the time he had spent in the artificial atmosphere of the Court. He bade fair to become a greatly respected country gentleman, who would sit in Parliament, and maybe towards his latter end be rewarded with a barony.

At Newhaven Inn, a great posting-house on the Manchester road, within two stages of home, Mrs Tryphena herself, who had been to the county-town to arrange about the repairing of some hangings, joined them, and shared their carriage for the remainder of the journey. They did not resent her presence as they would have done that of a less kindly woman; for she was mistress of consummate tact, and had ever been noted for her pleasing blindness to the foibles of young lovers. During the greater part of their drive together, she sat very primly gazing from the nearest window, and not until they came in sight of the river Darrand for the first time did she make any remark beyond comments upon her delight in seeing them again. Then, in a pause of the young couple's 'little language', she leaned forward and took the wife's hand.

''Tis the strangest house I ever dreamed of,' she said. 'Sir Agabus, whatever may have been his faults (and I hold miserliness one of the worst that any man is capable of), possessed a virtue which atones for much, according to an old woman's way of thinking. When I reached Ravensdale, I found not as much as a footstool unswathed in brown holland! 'Tis true that dust lay thick upon everything; but the fabrics wherewith the furniture's covered are fresh as when he bought anew for his wife's homecoming. The dame who played housekeeper—lacquey—God knows what to the late master—assures me that the dust-sheets had not been removed for a score years, and that her chief duty in autumn was the making of little bags of lavender (there's thousands of 'em all piled now in an empty chamber), to keep away the moths. The garden's in as perfect order as the house; on all the temples and belvederes—I vow there's as many here as at Stow Park—the roofs are as perfect as if built but yesterday.'

Lady Mary turned happy eyes upon her husband. 'And yet you never told me—' she began.

'I remember naught of Ravensdale,' he replied; 'since I was not more than a year old on my former visit. All will be as new to me as to you; we shall spend many merry hours in peering into every hole and corner.'

'A new Adam and Eve in a formal Eden!' cried the spinster, who was something of a wit. 'With not even a blindworm to play tempter! But, to speak plainly, the domain is vastly pleasant—all that I hold against it is its entire seclusion amongst the limestone hills. You'll be as far removed from the world as if you'd crossed the seas to Virginia... And now we're about to climb Black Harry—in my belief the highest hill of these parts. Another four miles and we're at the Lodge.'

They crossed the Darrand, low with summer drought, at an ancient ford, and began to ascend the steep deep-rutted road, which soon became little more than a track across the open heath. A magnificent prospect opened—north, east, and west rolled the billowing expanses of primeval moorland, the south being occupied by the bright Darrand valley and the serrated Edge of Stanage. The red sun was setting behind a conical mound; a soft breeze swayed the white cotton-grass in the hollows.

To the right of the hilltop a narrow clough descended to Ravensdale, whose concave was now filled with a mist faintly rose-coloured, pierced with the tops of heavy-foliaged trees and the grotesquely twisted chimneys of the Lodge. Peregrine and his wife (his arm around her waist) leaned from the open window and looked downwards. They had passed out of the warm sunlight now; Lady Mary shivered; he drew her closer to his side.

''Tis like an enchanted world!' she said. 'Aunt Tryphena was right in calling it an Eden. There's no sign of life here.'

'We're to bring life,' whispered the lover. 'We're to people this world. And there'll be no angels with flaming swords...'

The coach passed suddenly through the rising curtain of mist, and at last the strange beauty of the valley became visible. The house, built in the latter part of Elizabeth's reign, was stately and large—its frontispiece containing more of window than of wall; around lay gardens and a park where the sward was green as moss in winter, and where a shallow stream meandered level with its banks until it threaded a ravine that clove the rocky bank of the Darrand. A lake nearby the terrace was full of yellow and white lilies; in the centre a tall Neptune spurted thin jets from the end of his trident.

The young husband and wife talked in low voices now (somehow it seemed as if the time for idle prattle were past), until the coach drew up afront the colonnade, where an old, old woman, gowned in sober black with white apron and cap, stood curtseying.

'This is Law, the housekeeper,' said Mrs Tryphena. 'She holds it her duty to lift her mistress across the threshold, according to the custom of the family. The good soul—as faithful a creature as ever lived, for she starved in Sir Agabus' day, rather than leave him in utter solitude—hath rehearsed the scene more than once.'

The dame, smiling as genially as a face whose nose and chin almost met would permit, took Lady Mary in her arms and tottered with her from the coach to the hall.

''Twas so I bore Sir Agabus's lady,' she said breathlessly; 'a beauty, too, though not to be spoken of with you. I bid you welcome, sir and madam, and may God grant this be a happier house!'

Mrs Tryphena now led the way, past the smirking newly-hired servants, to the dining-parlour, where, lighted with wax candles in silver sticks, the table was laid for supper. There, only doffing their travelling cloaks, they sat and spent the next hour in refreshment and talk. Afterwards Peregrine drew his wife to the window, and they stood with linked arms looking out upon the formal garden, white beneath the crescent moon.

'Eden in night-time!' said Lady Mary. 'In truth I believe there's no finer home in all the world than ours! What think you of a walk amongst yonder flowers? A good housewife'd not be content till she'd passed through every chamber of the place, but I'm no good housewife. And I'm cramped with our long journey—'twould refresh us both.'

He tied the strings of her cloak, and, with her arm still in his, conducted her from the house and down a great stone staircase to the French garden, where they walked to and fro for more than an hour, till both yawned sleepily, and were minded to go bedward.

As they reached the terrace, Peregrine saw a young gentleman, dressed in garments of antiquated cut, standing beside the mounting-block, holding in his right hand a rose that glowed like a living ruby. He was watching them intently, his eyes lighted with a yellow gleam. The young husband, curious because of a stranger's presence, moved towards him; but he glided in perfect silence to the shadow of a gigantic cedar.

Lady Mary gave a little cry. 'Tell me why you started!' she said. 'You have seen someone...'

'Ay,' he replied, 'the oddest creature—see, there he walks down yonder yew-path, quivering like to a leaf! Some friend, perchance, of Sir Agabus—come to pay compliments, and taken with shyness.'

'Let's follow,' she cried. 'No visitor must go unwelcomed on our first night.'

Then hand in hand they ran along the path, catching ever and anon glimpses of the stranger, who, despite Peregrine's halloos, went on and on without turning.

'As deaf as an adder!' exclaimed Peregrine. 'By the Lord! The fellow is as eccentric as old Sir Agabus himself!'

They stopped short, each with a gasp of surprise; for the yew-alley terminated abruptly there, at the entrance of a cave whose roof and sides were covered with great shells. The man was no longer visible; nothing stirred in that mysterious archway save a tiny stream that wound, clear as crystal, over the floor of variegated pebbles.

'He's gone!' cried Peregrine. 'How, I cannot tell—unless there's some opening in the hedge!'

Lady Mary's face had grown of a sudden very strained and haggard. 'Let us go back,' she said. 'I am afraid. I saw him pass into the grotto. Oh, come, Peregrine,' (her voice broke foolishly) 'I do not like this place in the moonlight... I am weary—cold—'

He lifted her in his arms and carried her to the house and up to her bedchamber. Whilst the abigail undressed her, he wandered aimlessly through the suites, until by some odd chance he came across the housekeeper's parlour, where good Mrs Law sat sipping her nightcap of sloe-cordial. She rose as he entered; but being of a genial nature, he bade her resume her pleasant occupation, and chose for himself a chair at the further end of the hearth.

'We came upon a stranger in the garden,' he said. 'A young man attired in the quaintest clothes, who disappeared in a way I cannot account for, nearby a grotto with a stream.'

'Dear God!' muttered the woman, lifting her hand to her heart. 'Dear God! There's no way by which anyone could have entered after your honour's coming; for at edge-o'-dark all the gates were locked. It must have been the trees—the clipped yews cast marvellous shadows.'

'Not shadows with eyes that burn like coals,' said Peregrine. 'Nay, 'twas a living man, who carried a rose in his hand. Moreover he was not a little handsome both of face and figure.'

Mrs Law crossed herself. 'Sir Agabus' lady once spoke of such an one,' she said; 'but none of the housefolk e'er came upon him. And 'tis more than twenty years since she died.'

'So it could not be Sir Agabus' lady's friend,' said her master laughingly. 'Tomorrow, maybe, the gentleman will come again in full daylight, and we shall jest over our first meeting. Prythee, what cave is that we came to? There's shells there, and the inmost wall's made of stones roughly piled.'

The woman's forehead puckered like the shell of a walnut. ''Tis the grotto made by Sir Agabus for a whim of his lady's,' she replied, 'and 'twas there that she died... Lord, sir, I entreat you not to speak of't to my mistress—sure 'twould set her against the place. My late master built the screen himself, afterwards—carrying each stone from the Holy Circle on the hilltop.'

She promised loquacity; but Peregrine, mindful of his wife, bade her good-night, and returned to the chamber, where he slept soundly until the valley was warm with morning sunlight.

The greater part of that day the young folk spent in Mrs Tryphena's company, rambling through the house, and wondering at the many curious portraits of long-since dead men and women. Sir Agabus' wife proved most to Lady Mary's liking; for the painter had depicted to perfection her exquisite pride of countenance and bearing. There was a marked resemblance between the two women—both had the dainty colour and long tapering fingers of patrician inheritance; but the living wife was lacking in a peculiar aloofness of the eyes, which in the other suggested that the mind dwelt overmuch upon something vague and distant. A picture of earlier date hung beside—that of a comely youth with a Roman nose and a pouting red mouth, whose right hand held a rose, whilst the other toyed carelessly with the diamond buttons of a white waistcoat embellished with fantastical needlework.

'How strange 'tis,' observed Lady Mary pensively; 'here are two full of life, and yet gone for ever, with scarce a trace left of aught they did!'

Just then one came with word that the bailiff desired an interview; so Peregrine left his wife and went to the gun-room, where he was soon deep in discussion concerning a suitable breed of cattle wherewith to stock the park. Lady Mary and Mrs Tryphena left the house and loitered through the garden, pausing at last before the grotto at the end of the yew-alley, where the girl told the odd experience of the preceding evening.

Mrs Tryphena declared herself a believer in ghosts. 'Surely 'twas some restless spirit—a bachelor, perhaps, whom love of you hath driven to the shades!'

Lady Mary shook her head. 'The only suitor I ever had opportunity of denying was corpulent and elderly,' she said. 'My Lord Wollaston still lives in the flesh—he gave me the wedding gift of Indian diamonds... This is the place where the gentleman disappeared—see the shells over yonder are wrought in the motto: "Love once, love ever!"'

After a while she began to examine the barrier of stone that formed the inner wall, and touching one of the topmost, caused it to fall, leaving a hole as big as a child's head. Thereupon Mrs Tryphena, being of a curious nature, peeped through, then fell back with affected dismay.

'La!' she cried. 'I could have sworn that a man stood there! One with a face as white as death itself!'

Lady Mary, all eagerness, pressed her own face to the opening; but saw nothing but a dim avenue of grey stalactites, lighted by reflections of sunlight from the stream, that came through the chinks of the loose masonry.

''Tis like to a cathedral aisle!' she said. 'I'll bid Peregrine order the removal of these boulders, and this shall be my own retiring place. What if the passage goes into the very entrails of the earth!'

But Mrs Tryphena laid a hand upon her sleeve. 'I could have sworn that someone laughed as you were speaking,' she whispered. 'Come back into the garden, my pretty—'

Lady Mary drew aside almost petulantly. 'Dear aunt,' she said, 'I dote upon the place. There's the posy, which'll always remind me of Peregrine, and the air's cool and fresh and sweet—'

At that moment her husband appeared; and telling him of the vista that lay beyond the stones, she won from him a promise to have the cave reopened ere another day had gone by, and to explore it in her company—with clues and torches, if need be.

So, on the morrow, the barrier being removed, they went there together, and for more than two hours were lost to the upper world, thridding the countless galleries of a marvellous *lusus naturae*, where the floors were of fine dry sand, and the walls of limestone smooth as ivory. The place was so full of windings that at last both wearily declared that a month might be passed ere its wonders were exhausted.

In the following week the weather grew extraordinarily hot and sultry; and since Peregrine was much occupied with necessary business, Lady Mary found herself at liberty to spend many hours in her grotto, which in truth was the only cool place in the valley. Her embroidery frame was carried there, and at first she worked laboriously upon a cravat for her spouse's wearing. Mrs Tryphena, whom both had entreated to stay permanently at Ravensdale, was assiduously occupied in examining and repairing the contents of the great linen-presses, or supervising the conservation of fruits; whilst Law, in consideration of her faithful services in Sir Agabus' day, still retained nominally the post of housekeeper.

One morning, in the still-room, the old woman found herself constrained to speak of her former mistress's strange ending.

'I like not her ladyship's going so oft to yon cave,' she remarked; 'since 'twas there Sir Agabus' lady used to go, whilst she peaked and pined away almost to an anatomy!'

Until now she had been reticent concerning the lady's tragedy; but today, as if stirred with dread lest a like misfortune should overtake the young wife, she waxed very confidential, and told Mrs Tryphena the oddest story... It had the effect of sending the spinster hotfoot to the grotto, where she found her niece fast asleep by the embroidery frame, her upturned face smiling mysteriously, as if she dreamed of matters pleasant beyond human ken. She touched her somewhat roughly on the shoulder.

'You are unwise to sleep here,' she said—'the air's cold enough to strike a chill to your bones. Come out into the sun, my dear— why, you have lost all your colour!'

Lady Mary rose, passing her hand drowsily over her eyes. 'You cannot let me be!' she said, with a new querulousness. 'Is there something wrong in my dreams, that you must spy upon me day after day?'

Mrs Tryphena stared in wonderment. ''Tis I, Mary,' she said—'I, your aunt—you know that I have never spied—'

The girl began to laugh confusedly. 'My head's all bewildered,' she said. 'I thought—I thought 'twas Peregrine himself! And I was far away from here—in a world of my own—a wonderful world, all full of romance.'

After they had returned to the Lodge, Mrs Tryphena contrived a private conversation with the husband.

'I beg of you,' she said, 'to forbid your wife to frequent the grotto. The place is ill-omened—'twas there that the lady of Sir Agabus lost her strength—her life; indeed, there's something—I know not what—of the unfortunate—'

He dismissed her objections lightly. 'How could I cross one whom I love so well?' he said. 'Forbiddances shall never come from me, whose sole desire is to make her happy. Nay, good aunt, listen to no more old-wives' tales—'

'Ay,' interrupted Mrs Tryphena; 'but sure you have not forgotten how on the night you came here, you saw an unknown gentleman?'

''Twas some hapless fellow with a greeting he was too shy to make, or perhaps some Scotch rebel, making his way across country to the Border. Our sympathies are with such.'

So Mrs Tryphena went away very discontented, resolved to neglect the household duties that she had taken upon herself, and to accompany her niece whenever she went to the grotto. This, however, met with Lady Mary's disapproval, and ere long the officious spinster found the place entirely deserted save for herself; and with a satisfied mind returned to the thousand avocations of the great house.

But Lady Mary went there privately, and day by day her beautiful colour faded, and she grew more and more listless. The wise elderly folk wrongly attributed this to a natural cause; more than once speech was made to Mrs Tryphena of the day when Ravensdale Park would echo with *feux-de-joie*, and the distant bells of Hassage Church would chime in blithe announcement to the countryside of the birth of Peregrine's heir.

It was not until autumn was far advanced that the great tragedy occurred. One night, when the air was very still, and the skies covered with a black cloud, Peregrine woke to find himself alone, and after hastily donning his clothes made a fruitless search through the wing devoted to their use, then hurried to Mrs Tryphena's bedchamber.

'Mary is gone!' he stammered. 'I can find her nowhere!'

The aunt rose from her canopied bed, and huddled on a wrapper.

'She cannot have left the house,' she said, incredulously; 'she must be restless... I will come with you—prythee, do not rouse the servants.'

They passed through many other chambers, calling faintly; but found no clue until they came to the hall, where, to the amazement of both, the door hung ajar.

'If she be not indoors,' faltered Mrs Tryphena, 'there's but one place where she would go on such a night—'

A lantern stood here upon a table; she lighted its candle and led the way through the garden to the grotto. And in the yew-alley their hearts grew very cold and heavy; for they heard the sound of voices speaking softly.

Peregrine stumbled against Mrs Tryphena. 'She is here, and not alone!' he muttered. 'My God! what does it mean?'

The spinster trembled so that she could scarce stand. ''Tis no living man who's with her,' she said bravely; 'I'll not believe such wickedness—'

But still the voices murmured; one sweet and low and bewitching; the other a faint and incoherent echo of the wife's. The words of both were indistinguishable; but the tones were laden with burning passion. Peregrine caught the lantern from Mrs Tryphena's hand, and staggered forward into the blackness; then fell back at sight of Lady Mary sitting on the ground beside the stream, her head bowed to her bosom.

A sharp, bitter cry came from the inner recesses of the place— 'twas a woman's voice raised in agony—then a dimness came into Peregrine's eyes, so that he saw his wife no longer.

He leaped forward; two figures hurried ever before him—one cruelly familiar, t'other that of a tall dark man, who laughed and laughed and laughed.

They sped along passages where hitherto no human foot had ever trod; they climbed the steep sides of monstrous caverns; they slipped through narrow apertures, bending almost double where the roof hung low—until at last they reached a vast vault filled with the noise of falling water. There they stopped short where the sandy floor broke, on the verge of a pit, into which a cataract fell from the lip of a jagged rock overhead.

Peregrine put out his hand to grasp the loose sleeve of the woman's gown; ere his fingers closed she turned, discovering a countenance fretted with an unendurable grief. The man stood with face averted, an arm firmly encircling her waist.

'Ah, do not leave me!' cried the husband. 'Come back—come back—'

The ashen lips moved in silence; one hand strove feebly to remove the imprisoning arm. But her companion drew her closer still, and sprang into the utter blackness of the pit, and Peregrine was left alone.

Hours passed ere Peregrine left the place; hours in which he heard naught save the roaring of the water. The candle guttered—the last spark died as he reached the grotto at the cave's mouth. The sun had risen; all the east was rich with purple and amber clouds. A heavy mist hung over the park; cattle were lowing for milking-time.

Mrs Tryphena sat on the pebbles beside her niece, whose cheek rested against her shoulder. The old lady did not observe him until his foot touched her skirt.

'Thank God!' he cried hoarsely. ''twas but a nightmare—the cruellest nightmare man ever knew! I believed that she had gone for ever!'

He knelt at their side; Mrs Tryphena held him back with a trembling hand. 'Oh, I am worn with waiting!' she moaned. 'How could you leave me?'

'I have been tricked—some devilry forced me to see... Ah, speak to me, wife!'

'Hush!' faltered Mrs Tryphena. 'She has never stirred—she will never stir!'

EXCERPTS FROM
WITHERTON'S JOURNAL:
ALSO A LETTER OF
CRYSTALLA'S

he principal events of Pliny Witherton's life are written at length in Goodwin's *Records of English Painters*, a
volume published by Dodsley in 1752. He is described
therein as one whose genius went beyond his achievement; who
suffered ecstatic pain in conception, yet brought forth little worthy
of remembrance.

Personally he was small and ill-formed: of that sallow countenance
and red skein-like hair wherewith tradition has gifted Judas Iscariot.
His gait was felinely nimble, his voice harsh. Notwithstanding his
great defects, he was a favourite with women.

He died at his zenith. His celebrity was ephemeral; for, possessed of a curious medium, the secret of whose preparation he
refused to share with any contemporary, he used it with such fatal
effect that his works, which were strangely rich at first, became
almost colourless after the lapse of a few decades. The only picture
still existent is at Hambleton; where is also preserved the journal
whence the following extracts are taken. It is a 'Boadicea,' faded
to a sober brown.

*

Jan. 12, 1700.—This morning my uncle chose the story of Jacob wrestling with the Angel. I know not how I bore his tedious droning. He pictured the dullest scene, put into their mouths the dullest words. And there came something that thrust a hand through my breast and caught about my heart, and forced tears down my cheeks. Oh to have shown them what I beheld!

Little Anne saw me through the broken panel of the Earl's pew, and put her fingers to my knee to feel the thrilling. But I thrust them away, for the child is a bastard and as ugly as a toad—yet not so ugly neither, but foreign (her mother came of the Rouvigny's) and pale and quiet. She is downtrodden by madam the Countess. May be I was hard upon her.

The lass blenched, for had she not but yesternight slyly given me her father's present—a golden guinea—to buy colours for my work? What if she give me no more! Alack! So after the *Amen* was mumbled I stole with her to the pools amongst the groove-hillocks, and showed her rush-tips covered with hoar above the ice. As we stood she put her arm about my neck and said: 'We are both lonely, none loves us.' And I fell angry again and struck her face. 'I am not lonely, I shall be famous,' I cried; 'but you, Mistress Craven-spirit, are fit for naught but nursing madam's brats.'

May 1, 1703.—Too terrible Fortune, prisoning me in an iron cage; from between whose bars I see thy wheel turning, turning, turning! Today is my twentieth birthday, and I have done no work for all these years. Creations enow have stirred my brain. I see heroes in jewelled harness; ruddy-hued and beautiful dames. They play their parts, yet when I take the crayon, 'tis to depict a crowd of malkins. God, never was being so ill-fated!

Anne brought me a purse woven of her own coarse hair; it held eight crowns and a posy-ring. Yesterday I had threatened to leave this accursed house and never send word. She hath now sold all her trinkets. The office of secretary to such a dotard as the Earl I loathe; and the continual buzzing of my hummer-bee-uncle frets my very soul.

I walked with Anne on Danman's Moor, and the strong wind blew a colour into her hollow cheeks. Moreover, her eyes looked very big and lustrous. But she wore such a faded gown as any village alewife would have scorned; and the looseness made her shoulders seem huckled. Withal on her lips was such a smile as I shall give Christ's Mother in my masterpiece. As I gazed the rosiness deepened, and she murmured in a voice half-moan, 'Is there aught worthy there?' So, being malicious of humour, I praised that smile, and saw her bosom rise and fall like a wild beast's panting apart from the hunters.

Jan. 9, 1704.—At last I have left Hambleton. There was no money there, and my lord strove to repress my ambition with his eternal 'Thy uncle on his deathbed wished it so. For, leaving thee not a penny, he commended thee to my care. The chaplainship shall be thine, an' I need no secretary-work save what thou canst do at odd times. Alas! nine daughters have I to dower!' And Anne had given me all, so I rolled my pictures in a bundle and am come to seek the patronage of our great men, who, as I have learnt, are ever ready to help on struggling Wits.

July 27, 1704.—O Heaven, that this world should be so cruel! Flouted in rich fools' antechambers; turned roughly from door after door! Shame devours me today; for though poverty no longer pricks me I have sold my honour. Twenty golden pieces earned with bloody sweat lie on the table. The signs were delivered scarce two hours since. The first I wrought had some solace, for the Angel was a careful presentment of Lucy, as sweet a maid as

England holds. But twelve years old, and yet with the wit and loveliness of Sheba's queen, how she shrivels her base-born half-sister! A hundred times since I came to this town has her proud excellence disquieted my slumbers. The beauty that daunts a man's the beauty for me.

Accursed be this vile place where art and genius crouch together in the alleys!

Septr. 30, 1704.—The last page I may write in this poor journal shall contain naught of anger. Once I read that he conquers who strives with circumstance. No greater fallacy was ever writ. The last coin is spent; utter ruin in store. The certainty of my gift hinders me from pandering again to the vulgar. Life and I nearly parted at the great humiliation. Those terrible pictures, to whose doing desperation forced me, haunt me like ghosts. I dared not pace the streets lest I should see my handiwork swinging over the causey. It is better for me to die.

To Anne I bequeath all good and tender wishes, for she alone would aid me in my early strugglings. In this my last hour I fully acknowledge her kindness...

Oct. 1, 1704.—Dolt that I was to lose courage! At last the goddess hath smoothed her frown. When I rose at the sound of knocking 'twas to find a cloaked and hooded woman at my door. The domino fell open and discovered Anne's face, haggard and stained with tears. In her hands she carried a heavy bag. 'My Aunt Rouvigny is dead,' she cried, 'and since she might leave me naught by will this she gave me in private. None knows of it save myself. It is yours—all lies before you now. Take the road to Fame.' And though we had not met for so long, she waited for no word.

Dear heart, to resign that fortune for my sake! When I have seen all that Europe boasts, and studied the works of the dark masters,

I will return and make her my wife. Here is a copy of what I writ to her at Hambleton:—

'Mistress, I entreat you would be pleased to receive my very great thanks for the largeness of your generosity. I have warmer dreams of my work than ever, and with travel and the instruction of Italian artists I hope to do wondrous pictures. You have been my staff, and when the day comes that I already foresee, I shall cast myself a willing slave at your feet.—I am your humble Servant,   PLINY WITHERTON.'

*

[The journal contains an accurate narrative of adventures on the Continent. Anne's gift was a thousand guineas. The relation of Witherton's amours in France and Italy is worthy of Smollett. Anne's constancy is noted at intervals. Her father and the tyrannical Countess had died, and left her guardian of their nine children, and she spent the years at Hambleton fostering the estate.

Witherton suffered anguish before the Titians at Venice, and swooned in the Sistine Chapel. English art being what it was, his work won him some notice in Rome. Success strengthened his imagination, and his creations became more virile.

At the Russian Court, whither he travelled from Italy, he was made painter-in-chief, and found his emoluments so large, and his position so vastly improved, that at the end of the fifth year he returned to England, with the intention of fulfilling his promise to Anne.]

*

Jan. 1, 1710.—'Tis no longer the Hambleton of my boyhood; 'tis a centre of wretchedness and parsimony! Then all was lavishness—open house—the whole world welcome. Even whilst the leather hung rotting from the walls, came tuns of wine and rare fruits for each season. Now a new order ruleth;—to the deuce with such cheeseparing! 'Mistress orders the fish from our own ponds; mistress orders the gorcocks to be killed on Danman's Moor.' The meanness of habit that sickened me in earlier times has now reached head.

And yesternight I made her understand. In the days before the *cognoscenti* acknowledged my genius, we had been wont to watch the New Year in from the windows of the Grecian temple that lies a quoit's-cast from the hill-walk.

When we had supped together she rose from the table, and courtesied with an old maid's awkwardness.

'You play hoodman-blind when I am by,' she said. 'Do you not see my gown? From Firenze you wrote that purple becomes pale faces best.'

But one at table had worn damassin of pale green, woven with gold and silver arabesks—Lady Lucy, a debonair maid, rosy-lipped and eyed like Venus—and I had sight for no other.

Mistress drew me to the bay, and pointed to the clearing beyond the pines where seven squares of light fell on the frosty grass.

'In your honour, O painter mine, a fire has burned there all week, and now five hundred candles are lighted! When we went before 'twas as downtrodden children. Tonight let us sit and watch and listen to the bells.'

She laid her hand on my arm, and drawing over her shoulders the rich furs I had brought as a spousal gift, passed with me from the house. When we reached the temple steps, she ran forward and flung the valves open, so that, even ere we entered, we were bathed in the glow. Inside much reparation had been done: the walls shone in white and gold, and the ceiling-fresco of 'Aurora pursuing Night' was newly cleaned and restored. The chamber was warm and sweet with burning logs. We closed the door and sat on the pigskin stools by the fire, the length of the hearth lying betwixt.

Drifting against the glass came the noise of Edale Bells. The lads were drunk as ever, lashing out the old tempestuous jangle.

'We are crowned,' she said. 'We have ever fought side by side, and now we are victors.'

I looked at her, and saw that the frost had pinched her face and reddened her eyes. Then I gazed at Aurora, juicy and fresh. On the hearth lay a withered leaf that had tapped in after us: on the table a great yellow rose. And I was moved by these things to speak the truth.

'Anne, let it be all over between us. We have grown apart; life together would be miserable... I have my art, and you would bind me to earth. From this night we will be cordial friends; lovers we have never been... I cannot love you.'

After a while she turned her eyes from mine and bowed her head. 'Better so,' she murmured. 'I am not worthy.'

For an hour she sat in silence, flushing and twining her hands...

CRYSTALLA'S LETTER TO THE *SPECTATOR*

JAN. 19, 1712.

Mr Spectator,

As I have dwelt in these wilds since my birth, and, though an Earl's daughter, have never been permitted to show myself in

London, a description of my face and figure must needs give you pleasure. 'Tis not my own, but that of Pictor, read to me from this Journal.

'Of a full, ripe beauty, such as none but Virgins of high birth possess. A face neither round nor oval, but something between, touched with the softness of an apricock's sunside. Eyes lupin-coloured; in sober moments half-hid behind velvet lashes, but when roused sparkling azure fire. Lips such as a god might pasture on. Shoulders pure and white and smoothly dimpled; and a waist of most admirable shape. A foot so arched that Philip, her pet sparrow, cowers 'neath the instep.'

Methinks, sir, if you but saw me, spite of your melancholy, you also would fall in love. Though I be modest, I protest that the picture is nowise over-coloured. The simple country folk are so enamoured of my person that the louts line the way to church, and swear when 'tis fine, "Tis Crystalla's weather.'

That your humble servant may receive advice concerning the disposal of her person, she begs to lay her case before you. For two years she has been courted by an aged nobleman, who offers her a position of highest rank, and such wealth as only pertains to princes. There are many stains on his character, but he is old and not like to live long.

And now Pictor himself comes forward and sighs at my feet. He is a man of great fame, and, moreover, one attached by old kindness to my family. He is strangely ugly, being livid-skinned and orange-tawny-haired; but, notwithstanding, it has never fallen to me to meet a man of so many attractions. Maybe his stealthiness charms me, for he is like a cat treading softly and creeping from all manner of places; and I vow I would rather wed him than the handsomest man made since Adam.

He hath had love passages with a poor relation of mine, whom my parents, in return for fancied services, made guardian of my sisters and myself. She is a vixen and a shrew, who fancies to keep us within bounds; but I'll have none of her! Pictor, coming from a foreign land, brought her many gifts, utterly forgetting your handmaid, but their meeting was the quaintest and coldest thing (on his side) that I have yet beheld.

When he saw me his humour changed, and he put himself forward to delight, and his witless creature wept for very joy. With time, however, I saw his distaste grow and grow, till I could scarce forbear twitting both.

Now I see her going quietly about her work, but sighing in odd corners as if her heart would break.

So, dear Mr Spectator, I desire you to inform me whether, being an Earl's daughter, it would be great folly in me to choose the painter and flout the duke. The one holds me in chains of fascination; the other, though I don't hate him, wakens no tender feeling.

I am, Sir, your dutiful and obedient servant and admirer,

CRYSTALLA.

P.S.—I entreat you let me know soon.

BUBBLE MAGIC

he last hind had left the booth. The Ambassador, the Page, and Clarinda were spreading supper on the trestled table behind the tattered stage-curtain. Yesternight had been a benefit, and we were now to eat the remnants of the feast. We had played Phillip Massinger's *Maid of Honour*, and though our acting was stirring enow, few of the country folk had ventured.

We sat at table in our players' clothes. I, the master, was Bertoldo; Mary Perceval, Camiola; Mrs Brookwith, the Duchess of Siena. Robert, Ferdinand, and the rest were made up of recruits from Town. Stupid prattle came from the further end; but where we three sat there was nought but whispering. Camiola's nut-brown hair lay adown her back; my fingers stole amongst it, and made a nest; there was no expression in her colourless—almost haggard—face, save that of passion. She would not taste the viands; but once, when I had drunk, and turned to speak with the Duchess, her hand stole to my beaker, and her lips pressed where mine had pressed.

Mrs Brookwith's gorgeous colouring put me in mind of an old-fashioned garden. She was not without beauty; but 'twas the beauty of peonies and Turk's-caps. Moreover, her eyes were bright and sparkling as the toad's that lurks beneath such flowers; they hinted of vast knowledge acquired by a placid contemplation of the strange.

Our talk turned on love. Camiola said with a shudder that, though she had never suffered, such a thing must be horrible, must burn out the heart, must leave a woman nought but an empty shell. The Duchess laughed drily, and passing one plump, beringed hand behind my shoulder, stroked the girl's neck.

'Dear child,' she said, 'when you are old as I, and have passed so oft through the flame, you will know that 'tis not love, but falsity, that burns and destroys.'

I interrupted her with: 'I hold love to be nowise great as friendship; a friend who preserves a perfect faith is the best gift Providence bestows.'

For I was thinking of Norreys, who even that day had written, for the hundredth time proffering help if my affairs were disordered. As children, we were bed-fellows, and, though he had heired a great estate, he had ever held me as his bosom friend. Twice already had he rescued me from poverty, calling me *Quixote*, and taking away all shame. I loved him more than a brother.

'Ah, you have never loved—by some rare chance you have escaped the fire,' retorted the Duchess, drawing her hand from Camiola's neck and laying it on my breast. 'This heart awaits its torture!' she added.

Camiola, sighing querulously, threw in: 'Men cannot understand women.'

Just then one drew aside the curtain that oped to the field, and showed us the bright hues of the setting sun. The chain of talk grew brighter and brighter as the ale and wine went round. Unobserved we stole from the table, and went through the court of the *Green Man*. No sooner had we reached the herb-garden, that lies east of the archway, when the Duchess turned to me, somewhat abruptly.

'You have perchance not forgotten that Earl Russetwell carried me to Italy, and detained me there five years?' she said... 'In that time I gathered forbidden fruits... I know much of love. Would you that I showed to yourself, Bertoldo, and to our sweet Maid of Honour here, some little trick of the near future?'

Camiola in haste assented for both, and Mrs Brookwith hurried up the stone stairs to the gallery where lay the women's chambers, to return with a white silken case, which presently disclosed a tiny pipe of gold and a crystal phial half filled with rosy liquid.

'Let us remove to a more secret place,' she said.

She led the way down the ill-kept alley of box to a lawn, where the yew fowls had lost all shape. In an arbour adorned with portraits of long-mouldered gamesters we sat, the waning afterglow hanging overhead.

''Tis nought but the blowing of bubbles in magic water,' she explained. 'You, Camiola, shall have the first sight. Observe me, and when the bubble attains its largest, peep into the picture.'

Wherewith she poured into the hollowed palm of her left hand a shallow pool, and bedabbling the bowl, blew and blew until the bubble swelled to the size and form of a citron. She motioned with her head for Camiola to look, and the girl bent forward.

A cry of rapture leaped from her lips; a rich colour filled her cheeks. The bubble burst, but her inspired loveliness remained. She clasped her hands; she gazed upon me; I read new-born joy in her eyes. She would have spoken, but her heart beat far too quickly. She took up a flower I had culled in the garden, unfastened her laces, and let it fall to her bosom.

'What did she see?' I asked in jealous eagerness.

'Nay, that is not in my lore. I saw only floating colours. 'Tis your turn now.'

Again she stirred the water with the bowl, and this time blew a bubble big as a child's head. At her nod I stooped, and peered into the thing, and saw the garden, amethyst, scarlet, sapphire, yellow, crystal-green, blood-colour. And, as it were, the yew-birds fought.

But, within the moment, the garden disappeared, and in its place came a moor where curlews flew and a mountain river threshed into spume, and afterwards a squat thatched house with many dormers. The door of this opened, and Penthea herself—the one woman for whom my feeling resembled passion—stood on the threshold, and held out her arms towards me.

'Sure, 'tis Penthea!' I cried unconsciously.

The bubble burst.

Mrs Brookwith smiled. 'Whatever you have seen—and I have small desire to know,' she said—'depend upon't 'tis true. If Madam Penthea were in the picture—'

'She stood as waiting to clip me!' I faltered. 'Prythee show me another bubble that I may know more.'

'Not so, my friend—there'd be no virtue in't. And I must return; you have forgotten that I'm to design a new gown for mine honourable daughter, Margaret Overreach. Fare-thee-well.'

She poured back the drops that lay in her palm, and dried the golden pipe; then rose, and with the curtsey that she used so admirably in the plays, moved from the arbour. I followed, with many entreaties; but she was implacable; and at last I went to my chamber, and began to write a long letter to my mistress, telling her of the sweetest vision. Ere long, however, my eyes lifted and fell on a yellowed map that hung between mantel and window, and looking carefully upon it, to my amaze I found that Bleaklow was but fifteen miles distant. So I tore up the sheet, and having studied the way, without a word to any of my folk set out to visit her, though 'twas but a fortnight since we had parted, and our next meeting was to have been soon.

Mine hostess lent me a tinder-box and a horn lantern, declaring that I should need them in the woodland; and then, having ascertained the road to the next village, I set off in haste. Darkness had already fallen; one by one the stars blinked into being. My repeater told me 'twas ten by the clock. The white line of the road kept me from straying, till I reached Hunter's Manor, where the hamlet lies at the entrance of Gardom Wood.

Most of the villagers were abed; but a decrepit gaffer, already half-stripped, had bethought himself that his toll-gate was not yet locked for the night. Of him I inquired the way to Bleaklow; but 'twas long ere his dimmed brain could take in my question, and at the first wave of his hand toward a bridle-path that struck directly to the heart of the forest, I hurried onward, and in the hollowed bole of the first great tree, struck a light and fired my lantern.

Gardom Wood was in its rarest beauty. Autumn had tinged the leaves all imaginable shades of red and brown and green; the cold air (methought it froze) was pregnant with the rich smell of withering leaves. Here and there as I went, reremice, that haply had never beheld a lantern before, beat down and rattled the horn; owls wailed out their melancholy; up in the branches were squirrels with glistening teeth, and in the damp vistas will-with-the-wisp was jerking. The place was full of life; ripples of mirth came from the streams that prattled across the path; in one grove of half-withered cedars that was threatened by a falling gable, moans and sighs crept from the tips of the boughs.

Of a sudden one in pure white tripped from behind an undergrowth of young poplars, and a sweet breath touched my cheek.

'Twas Camiola, dressed as I had seen her last, and still adorned with courtly gew-gaws.

'I have waited for long,' she said, with a shiver; 'but now that you are come, it seems scarce a moment since we parted. I go with you—as your page—as your lantern-bearer.'

I dissented. 'The walk is far too long, child,' I said. 'Go back— take the lantern. You have no covering for your head... I insist...'

Feigning contrition, she stooped, but caught the iron ring of the lantern, and no sooner had she possession when she flew for some paces in front, nor would she permit me to lessen the space between us until I had vowed to use no more persuasion, but to permit her to have her will.

In truth she made a very dainty picture...

We linked arms, she still swaying the lantern by her skirt, and so in silence passed through the forest of Gardom Wood, and reached an 'edge' traversed by many a pack-horse track. There, as I pondered on the right way, Camiola spoke:

''Tis this,' she said, pointing to the least worn. 'Already I hear the water.'

Listening, I, too, heard the sound of a hissing river, thrown into flood by storms in the upland. Yet was I bewildered by Camiola's knowledge.

'How comes it, mistress, that you know the way?' I asked.

'The bubble magic showed me, and I have the keener ears,' she made answer. 'Now, since I have replied frankly, tell me who is this madam we go to see?'

Her tone was somewhat contemptuous; I was affronted. 'The woman I love—she, who is to be my wife.'

Camiola's limber fingers twined about mine. 'Poor soul, poor soul!' she sighed, whether for pity of Penthea or of me I knew not.

A flock of curlews flapped overhead, whistling and hissing, and Camiola shrank closer to my side. I had not divined that her nearness would enchant me so subtly. We reached a narrow clough that sloped to the river. There, as we crossed the flints, I heard her quench a moan, and, seeing that she walked lamely, asked if she were in pain.

'My feet,' she said—above the noise of the river—'my feet were not shod for such a journey.'

In the lantern-light she raised her left foot and showed me the once white satin stained with the green juices of the grass—and the sole flapping apart from the rest.

'You go no further,' I said. 'See, I will leave my coat to cover you, and the lantern also shall be yours... I will send from the house... Surely it cannot be very far.'

Camiola laughed merrily, as if she prisoned some secret. 'You will never send from her house to me,' she replied. 'I can walk—'twas but a pebble got underneath my heel. I will bind it with my bodice-lace—thus!' She drew out one of her silken cords, and strapped it cross-wise about her instep. 'I am ready,' she said.

At the stepping-stones, I caught her to my heart, and with one arm of hers encircling my neck, and the other outstretched in front with the lantern, we crossed the perilous place.

On the further bank I struck my repeater again, and found that midnight was past by two hours. There was no path visible now, so perforce we made our way through the stunted beech-spinney. On the summit of a limestone hill, where grey ghostly things peeped from the thin sward, I saw the gables of Bleaklow, with a light burning in Penthea's window.

Camiola grasped my arm convulsively, and then held the lantern so that I might see her face.

'Tell me,' she whispered fondly, 'is mistress beautiful as I?'

My tongue was on the point of declaring rashly that Penthea was peerless, when it was borne upon me, with some uneasiness, that the loveliness of her with whom I travelled could not be excelled. For there was a wonderment of gay beauty in her face; it seemed as a virgin's soul played there. Erstwhile I had deemed her coldly charming; now I wondered how she had come to preserve through so many trials that exquisite passion.

'Not more beautiful,' I hesitated.

She lowered the lantern, and again we progressed until we came to the bed of rushes beside the long pool. There the herons were beginning to stir.

Camiola gazed, as in some fashion afraid, along the old road that runs from Silence village to Bleaklow. Near us lay a rock basin, where the water gushed down on pebbles and yellow sand.

'My feet are hot and tired—let me bathe them here,' she said. 'But for a minute... I would fain see the lady... A constant woman's heart—'

Sitting on the ground she undid her shoes and drew off her stockings. She dabbled her feet in the rillock, crying out in delight; and though I craved so keenly for sight of Penthea, in truth I felt no impatience now.

'Why not rest beside me, Bertoldo?' she said. 'Sure there's no harm in staying a while. I am very weary.'

I sank to a tussock, setting the lantern betwixt us. She curved her neck so that the breeze might bring with it the lightest sound; ever and anon she looked toward the road. Once she paled, and smote her breast; but the moment afterward her colour returned, and she took off her kerchief, and dried her feet, and donned her stockings and shoes.

'I hold love to be nowise great as friendship,' she said, repeating in a mocking voice my words of yestereven. 'A friend who preserves a perfect faith is the best gift Providence bestows.'

My hand moved to take the lantern; on my fingers fell a hasty shower of tears. Camiola wept, wherefore I could not understand.

'Dear child!'

She recovered herself soon. 'Oh, that I had never come!' she murmured.

Before us in the gloom whinnied a mare that galloped eastward as to welcome the dayspring. Then the curtain lifted, and the sky flushed with all the hues I had seen in the bubble, and soon the sun, gigantic and ruddy, lifted himself from the fork of a hill.

Morning came in strides; from the thorn-bushes rose birds, piping autumnally. We stole along the depressions of the ground; for I was anxious that Penthea might not behold me till I had reached the garden. The light in her window was extinguished—or was it that the blaze of the sun dazzled my eyes?

At the gate of the wood-close I turned to Camiola.

'Sweetheart,' I said, 'My mistress—'twould be best for me to see her first and explain your company. Stay here a while—I will return very soon.'

All rosy was she in the first light; so rare, indeed, that I was loth to part.

'Ay, leave me, dearest!' she cried, with tender cajolery. 'Leave me if thou canst!'

Even as she spoke, Penthea threw open her door and gazed eastward along the grass-grown road, and held out her arms, as to draw one bosomward.

I moved forward. Camiola caught my cloak with one hand, and with the other pointed to where Norreys approached, spurring his great white stallion.

DRYAS AND
LADY GREENLEAF

ady Greenleaf crooked her arm through the handle of a shallow wicker basket, and fluttered from the still-room to the garden. Noel was sitting there on the grass beside the statue of Ceres—a Renaissance monstrosity begirt with impossible fruits and flowers. When his wife appeared, the clerkly old man rose, closed his volume of 'Hakluyt,' and pushed back his gold-rimmed spectacles. Although they had been wedded two years, he still found something irresistibly tempting in her childishness; and as the morning air was brisk and full of sunshine, his sluggish blood moved less slowly than usual.

'Let us race together?' he said, drawing out his shagreen-covered repeater. 'To the bowling-green—I will give you two minutes in advance.'

She shrugged her shoulders, pursed a mouth quaintly beautiful. 'I'll not race today, little one,' she said laughingly; 'but, if you wish you may help me to gather roses. I need this basket brimful.'

He sauntered beside her, past the knots of herbs to the court where the water-roses grew. These flowers were very big and heavy, although each had only five petals. No thorns rose from the plump stems—velvety to the touch as her own smooth fingers. The fragrance spread about like the breath of a perfumed brazier; of late Lady Greenleaf had perused the 'Eastern Tales,' and this sweetness reminded her of the joyous life of that sultana (the mother of White

Hassan) who held sole dominion over a stalwart spouse's love. And so intent was she upon the moving pictures, that when Noel's hand toyed with the laces at her throat she forgot even to pout.

When the basket was filled, she lifted it to a balustrade, and drawing back her loose sleeves, buried white arms in that fragrant bed, and moved them fantastically, so that it seemed as though two Cupids struggled there. Noel watched her intently, his pale grey eyes alight with pleasure. Ere the marriage, which he had made after a life spent in intrigue and mild devilry, he had known many fair women, and heretofore had thought with gentle lightness of her beauty; but as she stood there smiling, ivory-skinned, flushed, small-breasted—a semblance of ripening fruit, for the first time he acknowledged her perfection. Her prune silk gown hung in loose folds, the skirt uplifted so that her little feet in their green shoes and stockings with silver clocks were discovered; her lawn chemisette scarce veiled the warmness of her neck and bosom.

Of a sudden it seemed to him that the plump arms curling amongst the roses were young babes that she had borne.

'Ah, if 'twere God's truth!' he murmured.

She understood, and withdrew her arms sharply, as if a snake had lain amongst the flowers.

'I do not wish for children!' she cried. 'You are my little one. Sure you are happy?'

'Ay, child, a thousand times more happy than I deserve. You are the paragon of wives!'

Again his hand plucked her laces; this time she drew away.

'Carry the roses for me, little one,' she said.

On the way back to the house, they passed a niche in the box hedge, where stood a leaden statue which of late had been newly gilded. It was of Dryas, the son of Pan and Venus; Girardin, the

Frenchman, had made it for a gift to Noel's great grandsire, that time he was Ambassador at Paris. The sunlight fell hotly upon it; the brilliancy threw out a metallic vapour. And through the trembling of this vapour, Lady Greenleaf noted for the first time the virile comeliness of the faun—the god-like head with its wreath of green vine-leaves that almost hid the sire's gift of goatish ears—the massive neck with jutting Adam's apple.

As she paused, one came with a letter for Noel. He unfolded it very tediously, and found word that his sister, of Stoney Marlbro', had been stricken with palsy, and that it was imperative for him to visit her at once. He read this aloud to his wife; but she could scarce withdraw her attention from the bewitching faun.

'I must ride at once,' he said wryly; ''twill be the first time you and I have been apart since our nuptials. Wilt be afraid, child?'

She shook her head and turned to watch him out of sight. The basket of roses lay on the ground; when she was alone, she chose the finest flowers and, tip-toeing on the pedestal, stuck them between the leaves of the wreath. Then, with a murmur of shame, she hastened after her husband so that she might speed him on his journey.

Late that afternoon, as she sat reading her book of romances, a coach drew up in the forecourt, and, looking from a window, she saw a gallant youth alight and mount the balustraded staircase. She returned to her book, and waited with some curiosity until the arrival was announced by the house-steward.

'If it pleases your ladyship, a foreign gentleman begs your hospitality. He declares himself godson to my lord. He is bound for the Court—in two days he is to be received by the King. He reached the Quay only this afternoon, and if 'twill not incommode your ladyship overmuch, desires to rest here till the morrow.'

Ere he ceased, the stranger entered. She rose and curtsied, watching him from demurely lowered eyes. He was tall and fair-skinned; there was a soft, almost invisible, down on his upper lip. Moreover, he was dressed admirably, in a fashion such as she had never seen, for Noel resolutely kept her away from the temptations of the world.

'This house is at your service, sir,' she said courteously. 'My husband has been called away to his sister's bedside; but what poor hospitality we can afford is yours. Pray, Mr Mompesson' (this to the house-steward) 'see that the gentleman is shown to a guest-chamber.'

When they were gone, she began to make preparations for his entertainment. Such responsibility had never before fallen to her share; but she ordered a dainty supper, and when all was ready lighted the table-candles with her own hand. In the with-drawing-room, she found him indolently strumming on Noel's guitar. She had chosen to wear a new gown of ivory and silver brocade, and had twisted the Greenleaf ropes of pearl around her neck. The stranger started with amazement; he had imagined nought so exquisite away from his own country.

'But—truly—you are my lord's daughter?' he said.

She laughed gently, lifting her fan to hide a pretty blush. At table she strove to make him talk; but he was curiously embarrassed, and could only respond foolishly to her gay sallies. Nevertheless, his eyes sought hers continually. Afterwards they built pagodas of cards—or rather, she attempted to instruct him in the art; but his fingers trembled so that the great chamber rang with her mirth-ful protests. Finally, she bade him tune the guitar and play a duet with her, and then sat to the new harpsichord Noel had bought her for her last—her eighteenth—birthday. So full of tenderness was that music, that her gaiety disappeared, and she grew silent as her guest.

When she retired, the moon was shining brightly through the windows. At the door he kissed her hand, and would not release it for a few moments. She hastened to her chamber and disrobed, to lie tossing from side to side of the bed. The time crept on very slowly; she heard the clocks strike eleven, then twelve. A subtle fever burned in her veins, a fever that troubled her so acutely that ere long she found unendurable the close air of the house. Passionate thoughts flocked to her brain; she painted warm-hued vignettes in which she saw herself tasting a happiness hitherto unknown.

At last, overwrought with excitement, she rose suddenly, and donned her pantoufles and threw about her shoulders an Indian shawl; then she went down to the garden. Another was there— one who, like herself, was unable to rest; on her approach he hid behind the screen of clipped box.

She paced to and fro, murmuring. The night air was cool and sweet with the dewy roses. The glittering of the gilded statue startled her once more; she went to the niche, pressed the smooth forehead with her open palm.

''Twas thou who wakened this folly in me!' she said. 'Thou, who art nothing but a leaden image!'

She thrust away the withered roses, replacing them with fresh buds wet and heavy. When this was done, she went to the tall jet d'eau, and leaning over the rim of the basin strove to catch reflection of her face. The moonlit ripples shook beauty into grotesqueness; she returned again to the hedge and threw herself on the sward at Dryas's feet.

'Surely there is some truth in ancient tales,' she said. 'Why should it not be that the thing which hath wrought this strangeness in me, may at times be warm with human life... 'Tis the likeness of a perfect man—a god!'

She rose, raised her arms and caught the faun about the neck, kissing the brow where her hand had pressed. The metal was key-cold to her lips; with many sighs she went away again.

A boy's laughing face moved in the shadow; his eyes followed her past the fountain to the sunken court where the cedars grew; then, seeing her rest there on the lowermost stair, he moved to the niche and swung the gilded Dryas aside and stood himself upon the pedestal...

Lady Greenleaf was tortured with fantastic madness. Her breast rose and fell quickly; her hands were out-thrust as if to embrace. About her shoulders, from which the shawl had slipped, her hair hung in long tresses, swayed to-and-fro by the light breeze.

Ere long she began to weep and to beat her bosom. 'True happiness is denied me!' she whimpered. 'Only today hath the sleeping love awakened!'

Once more she hastened to the niche. The wind had scattered the roses, the faun's head was unadorned. She knelt, her hands pressed to her face. 'Waken! waken!' she prayed.

The strenuous note in her voice startled her; her head drooped; the tears trickled faster between her fingers and fell to the grass.

'Have compassion on me! Thou alone hast brought forth my love!'

There came a sound as if one near by sighed in deep delight... surely 'twas the soul, coming down from that pastoral heaven, where the demigods sing and play in everlasting noontide. She redoubled her clamours.

'Waken, 'tis a woman who cries!'

She rose fearfully; she threw her arms around his neck—found it no longer cold, but pulsing with living veins. For the first moment she was awed; then her voice rose with sharper pleading.

The glittering arms were outstretched slowly; she felt the motion, but saw nought, for her eyes were dimmed. She heard the beating of a heart; she felt a warm breath touching her cheek.

'One kiss, such as thou givest the nymphs of heaven,' she murmured.

The faun's lips met hers; one hand buried itself in her hair. At the contact an odd fear overcame her; she remembered the story of Jove and Semele, and with a sudden motion freed herself and flew, trembling, back to the house. Another time, perchance, when the glory had grown more familiar... who knows? She closed her chamber door, threw herself upon the bed, and fell into a heavy sleep, from which she did not waken until noontide.

She looked around strangely. Her pantoufles lay at the bedside, as when she had first retired; nothing in the place was changed. She went to the window and gazed along the vista of the rose-garden, and saw the gilded Dryas still resting in his niche.

She began to laugh so loudly that her waiting-woman was alarmed, and ran in from the ante-room.

'I have had the oddest dream!' cried Lady Greenleaf. 'A miracle of a dream!'

The abigail pressed her to reveal it, bidding her hurry meanwhile, for the guest was leaving; but she laughed again.

'Nay, 'tis all mine own; none shall ever know it.'

She dressed hastily, lest her husband's godson should suspect some discourtesy. As soon as she was made ready, she went to the library where he waited, and made due apologies to him.

'An incubus hath troubled me,' she said. 'I slept ill and woke late.'

Her eyes met his; he was smiling and blushing.

'The most wonderful dream woman ever had!' she continued, drawing him to the window. 'You see yon gilded statue? Methought 'twas tenanted by a soul—a god's soul.'

'Such things are possible,' he replied. 'Have not we the precedent of the sculptor and the maid of stone?'

'Ay, but that was in the days when the gods really visited the earth. My dream was stranger.'

He grasped her fingers roughly; she withdrew them with some sharpness.

'We countrywomen are simple,' she said. 'The little courtesies of your world are unknown to us. Ah, they have brought your coach!—is it not in your power to stay longer? I am afraid that your visit has been unconscionably dull. Will not you dine—perhaps my husband may return soon?'

'I should be most happy if I could; but tomorrow I must be at Court. I bade your servants not waken you, though I hated the thought of leaving *sans adieu*. As for your entertainment, I was never so well content; I shall bear to my death the recollection of your kindness.'

'My lord will be sorely disappointed,' she said. 'He hath often spoken of you.'

For reply he stooped and gave her a warm kiss. She drew back, white with annoyance.

'You are officious!' she cried.

'Do not you remember?' he whispered.

She had regained her composure. 'It was indeed an honour to entertain you,' she said, in a voice filled with wonder. 'And now, when I reflect on my endeavours to instruct you in the art of building pagodas, I can only praise your patience.'

The house-steward came to the doorway.

'Your lordship's coach waits.'

The lad offered his arm; Lady Greenleaf touched it lightly and accompanied him to the forecourt. Ere taking his place, he murmured in her ear: 'Do not you remember?'

She frowned, racking her brains. 'I cannot understand, unless it be that the music was excellent.'

So he smiled gravely, and kissed her hand in a very formal way. Inside the coach he leaned back on the cushions, gazing with perplexed eyes into nothing...

Noel returned mourning before nightfall; but she drove away all his grief for the loss of his sister, with a thousand quaint descriptions of the gambols of fauns and nymphs, of the shower of coins that fell upon Jove's mistress, and of Venus's shame in the golden net. Such scenes Verrio had depicted on the ceilings, and the walls of the staircases; but Lady Greenleaf talked as if her own eyes had beheld.

'You might have dwelt in classic times!' said Noel.

He held her at arm's length, wondering at the beauty that had ripened even since yesterday.

'Who knows that I was not a goddess or a nymph?' said she.

THE STONE DRAGON

I

y father's account of his last visit to Furnivaux Castle, which I found in his journal some years after his death, enlightened me concerning the cause of his disagreement with my great-aunt Barbara. In response to an imperious summons he had travelled hurriedly from the south of France to the remote corner of Westmoreland where her estate lay; no sooner had he reached the portico than the old woman confronted him, and began to discuss a new plan for restoring his shrunken fortunes, by a marriage compact between myself and one of her great nieces, either Rachel or Mary, both of whom were children in the house. I was fifteen years old then, Rachel thirteen, and Mary ten. The ceremony was to take place at once; and I was to travel for some years before claiming my child-wife.

My father refused indignantly: scarce had, his decisive words been spoken ere Lady Barbara turned away angrily.

'Fool, is there no changing you?' she cried.

He understood her peculiarities, and despite his acknowledgment that she was a gross and materialistic woman, who held no views beyond this world, and whose chief enjoyment was to interfere mischievously with the affairs of other folk, his kinship made him treat her with respect.

'None,' he replied. 'My boy shall not be forced into bondage before he knows what love means. I would rather he begged for his bread than wronged body and soul.'

She swung round and showed a menacing face. 'You have refused what I had set my heart on!' Her voice softened: ''Tis for the love I bear you, Alston. I want to help you; remember that I am your mother's sister. Don't refuse me.'

'Aunt,' he said painfully, 'it may not be. I cannot sin against my son.'

She came still nearer. 'Well, so be it,' she muttered in his ear. 'Others will suffer for your obstinacy. I know what my project meant; but you, with your blind gropings after light, will never see. Nay; you come no further into my house; this is no place for you!'

The door was closed violently, and my father passed along the dark avenues to the village. He was with me in two days; but, although I pressed him often (being curious to hear all about Furnivaux, which I had never seen), he refused to disclose either the cause or the result of his visit.

Before two years had passed, however, I found myself, by a curious trick of fortune, in the vicinity of Furnivaux Castle. I had suffered from an acute attack of brain fever, and when convalescent had been ordered by the doctor to taste the air of Marlbrok-over-Sands, a quaint watering-place at the mouth of the Lamber estuary. My father was engaged at the time in preparing for the press his volume of *Philosophical Discussions*, and, although he would willingly have accompanied me, I chose rather to take Jeffreys, a man who had been his valet in former times, but who held now the posts of confidant, secretary and checker of the domestic accounts—a faithful old servant of a type unknown to the present generation.

At first my father was averse to my visiting Marlbrok. He had suggested Nice or Mentone, fancying that the bustle of foreign life would act as a tonic; but as he heard of the marvellous strengthening virtues which, according to Doctor Pulteney, belonged to the Lamber water, he consented, and after strictly enjoining me not to go within at least a mile of Furnivaux, travelled with me, and left me with Jeffreys at an ancient inn.

On the fourth evening of my stay I strolled with Jeffreys to a large hill whose seaward side is perfectly precipitous, but which is easily climbed landward by a winding sheep-path. When I had reached the summit I threw myself on the grass and rested for a while, gazing at the misty outline of Man; then when my dimmed eyes had cleared I turned and saw high on the side of a far-distant inland hill an enormous building, which at first sight appeared on fire, for the westering sun struck full on the great square windows. A grove of majestic trees gloomed to the left, and a park besprinkled with herds of deer sloped downward to the furthermost recess of the estuary.

A shepherd was training a dog near the place where I sat: regardless of Jeffrey's deprecations, I called to him, and inquired the name of the house.

'Furnivaux Castle, young sir. Lady Barbara Verelst's place,' he replied.

'What?' I cried. 'Tell me all about it. Have you ever been there? What is it like?'

Before he could answer Jeffreys interposed. 'Come, Master Ralph, it is growing chill; we shall have Doctor Pulteney here if you take cold.'

But I took no heed of him, and despite his attempted hindrance obtained all the necessary information concerning the way. An evil desire to disobey my father filled me: it seemed as if the glamour of the house had cast a spell over me, and as I was hurried away by Jeffreys, I resolved to take advantage of him in the early morning, and to visit Lady Barbara.

I slept little that night, but lay watching the dawn creep over the sea, and listening to the plaintive chirping of birds. As the cracked bell of Marlbrok-St-Mary's struck six I sprang from my bed, dressed hurriedly, and after a quiet laugh at the thought of what Jeffreys' consternation would be when he discovered my absence, I slipped from the house, and followed the path the shepherd had described.

It led through a long wood of small trees, matted with bracken and sedge, and crossed by many rivulets that ran down to the sea. There was much honeysuckle—so sweet that life grew absolutely perfect: I gathered a large bunch, wherein lay many bees; and chanting extempore rhymes I hurried onward.

When I reached the terrace of Furnivaux it was nearly breakfast-time. The hall door, half open, revealed a vista of ancient pictures. As I knocked there timidly, an ancient serving-man in fawn livery appeared. Something, perhaps my resemblance to my father, amazed him, and he bade me enter at once.

'I wish to see Lady Barbara Verelst,' I said.

He ushered me into a small, white-panelled room. 'Her ladyship will be with you very soon,' he replied.

Meanwhile I arranged the honeysuckle in a large china dish. As I was doing this a slight noise disturbed me, and looking up I saw a white-frocked little girl eyeing me very intently. A black Persian cat lay in her arms, rubbing its head on her shoulder.

'*Cousin Mary!*' I cried.

The child dropped the cat and ran forward to bring her tiny mouth to mine. But even as she kissed footsteps came, and she

172

drew back alarmed. I took the honeysuckle and flung it all into her apron, and she, as if fearing to be seen, made for another door and disappeared.

Then Lady Barbara entered. There was nothing of the patrician in her appearance. Clad in a plain brown dress with a narrow collar of lace, she might well have passed for a housekeeper who had no liking for bright colour. Her face was round and russet, with a broad low forehead that was covered with an intricate network of wrinkles. Her eyes were small and sherry-coloured, and her teeth, which (as I heard afterwards) were natural, glistened like regular pieces of ivory. Altogether she struck me as a sharp bargain-driving countrywoman, with a good deal of craft, and an underlying vein of sarcastic humour. As she saw me she courtesied very low.

'So you are Ralph, or Rafe, as I love best to say it,' she said. 'Well, you are very welcome here, though your father and I got across at our last meeting. But I suppose he has thought better of my proposal, and sent you now.' Here she looked at her watch, a massive gold and crystal globe that swung from her girdle. 'The girl is a long time!' she exclaimed.

Before I could open my mouth to declare the truth about my father, a rustling of silks came, and a girl swept through the doorway. She was about fifteen years old, but might well have passed for twenty. Tall and slender in figure, and with a face so perfectly, so strangely lovely, it compelled me to make a simile of a flame resolving at the lambent crest into a star. She moved towards me, and with no assumption of modesty, threw her arms around my neck and kissed me. I have no idea how she was dressed, but as I write comes a recollection of the flower called 'crown imperial,' lying on a web of red golden hair.

Lady Barbara shrieked in affected dismay. 'My dear Rachel!' she cried, 'you are forgetting yourself; Rafe is not a little boy—he's seventeen—he's a *man!*'

Rachel Verelst turned to her, uplifting luminous eyes: 'O aunt,' she said, with a sigh of relief, 'it is most delicious to see a *man*. I am Miranda—he Ferdinand. Cousin (mincingly), you're the first man I've seen for two years, except of course the servants, and they don't count with such people as your lowly handmaid.'

Something about her—perhaps the fact that her manner was so opposed to that with which I had endowed my ideal woman—fascinated me at once. Never before had I seen such radiant beauty: never before had I known a woman lay herself out so coquettishly to attract attention. She was unlike anything I had ever dreamed of, and even as I stood I felt myself become enthralled. There was such admiration, too, in her glance—admiration of the most flattering kind. All suddenly I sprang high in self-esteem.

'A handsome couple,' the old woman said pointedly. 'One fair as day: the other, as Shakespeare says somewhere, black as night. Yes, day and night! Now pray let me see you walk together to the breakfast-room. I will waive etiquette for once, and you shall take precedence. Ah, yes, sir, your arm was given gracefully; I am quite satisfied with your manner. You are a Verelst, though your name is Eyre.'

With many comments upon the picture we made, she followed us to a small parlour hung with red velvet, embossed with earl's coronets in gilt. A light meal was spread. The aroma of coffee filled the air, and after the footman had brought in the hot dishes, a gust of fresher sweetness came as Mary, shyly bedecked with honeysuckle, entered and sat at my side. Lady Barbara took no heed of her appearance, so bent was she on her own plans.

'So your father has really conquered his prejudices,' she remarked. 'I knew all the time that they meant nothing (poor Alston, he was always feather-brained!), and I did not believe that he would have held out so long. Well, forgive and forget. It does my heart good to see you and Rachel at table together; I am almost inclined to sing *Nunc Dimittis* at once!'

Something in the exultancy of her voice suppressed my avowal that, overpowered by curiosity and attraction, I had come clandestinely. It was not from kindness that my tongue refused its office, but rather of a dread of how she might act.

'Did he send any message, any writings?' she inquired sharply. I shook my head.

'Ah, the rogue!' she said. 'He's proud of you; he knows that your presence is enough to explain all. Ay, and a very good recommendation to my favour! Alston had ever a little of the diplomatist. Again let me assure you that nobody could be more welcome.'

So the meal passed. Often Rachel turned to me with proudly sweeping eyes, and brought her face so near mine that I could see my reflection in each apple. For one so young her wit was brilliant and sharp-edged, but the vivid outlines of her colouring prevented me from seeing anything unmaidenly in her demeanour. There was depth mingled with unstableness in her character; and although against my will I was allured, I could not help feeling a sort of oppression, as if the air were becoming too heavily perfumed. Two centuries ago she might have shone as a king's mistress. When I looked at her sister, timid, frail, and shrinking, it was as if a draught of cool air rippled across my temples.

Once the child essayed to speak. 'Cousin Rafe,' she said softly, 'will you tell me after breakfast what the world is like. I don't mean the country or the little market towns, but those places that one reads about. Is Venice like Mrs Radcliffe paints it in the *Mysteries of Udolpho*?'

Lady Barbara began to laugh rather coarsely. 'What is the girl raving about?' she said, turning contemptuously to Rachel. 'Does she think that at my age I've nothing better to do than to listen to puerile descriptions. My dear Rafe, do not trouble with her. Rachel, I wonder you permit his attention to be distracted.'

Great tears rolled down Mary's cheeks. I was angered. 'I like to hear her talk,' I said chivalrously.

At this my great-aunt laughed again, but Rachel, with wonderful tact rose and embraced her sister. If she had not done so I believe that I should have hated her. Even Lady Barbara was pleased.

'You are a good girl, Rachel,' she said, patting her shoulder. 'Now, Mary, you must forgive my querulousness.'

She took Rachel's hand and drew her from the table. As she reached the door she paused.

'Rafe,' she said, 'can you amuse yourself till noon? Rachel writes my letters and manages everything for me, so I must take her away. Mary, make your cousin's stay here as pleasant as you can: show him all over the house and gardens—or anywhere so long as he's entertained. If you care to ride order the ponies.'

But Mary, as soon as we were alone, led me to the open window. A flight of stairs descended from here to an old garden where busts and urns surmounted columns of fluted marble. A spring, prattling over many-hued stones, crossed the middle of this and deepened into shallow pools that were edged with irises and flowering rushes.

'Let us sit beside the dragon at the wellhead,' she said; 'it is my favourite dreaming-place, and I will ask you all I want to know. I am not tiresome to you, Cousin Rafe?' she added, with downcast eyes.

Our spirits rose. Ere long I was chasing her up and down the maze, quite forgetful of the gravity of seventeen, and attempting at each corner to grasp her flying skirts, but ever failing intentionally, out of compliment to her lightness of foot. Her paleness had quite disappeared, and as she laughed at me through the legs of the yew peacocks, she looked like a young nymph. She began to sing hurriedly, in a silvery voice, in imitation of some gaffer:—

'When first I went a-waggonin', a-waggonin' did go,
I filled my pairients' hearts full of sorra', grief, an' woe;
And many are the hardships that I ha' since gone thro'.
   So sing wo, my lads, sing wo. Drive on, my lads, Yo-ho!
   For ye canna drive a waggon when the horses wunna go.'

Every word came clear and distinct. Scarcely, however, had she begun the second verse than the sound of an approaching vehicle silenced her. We looked down the avenue, and beheld a trap drawn by a bony white horse.

It drew up near us. A familiar voice accosted me: 'Master Ralph.'

To my surprise it was old Jeffreys, very haggard, and with eyes more sad than reproachful.

'O Master Ralph,' he said, 'come back at once, for God's sake! There's just time enough to catch the boat, if you don't linger a moment. Word came this morning that my poor master was dying.'

His voice broke into sobs. Turning hastily to the child who stood aghast at my side, I gave her one quick kiss, and then sprang up to the seat, forgetful of all save the great catastrophe.

II

When I reached home it was to find my father dead. Had I arrived an hour sooner I should have had the gratification of holding his hand in mine during the parting moments, and have heard his last words. But my act of disobedience had prevented this, and by my secret visit to Furnivaux I had lost what would have been one of the dearest recollections of my life. He had died thinking of me, and as the last struggle began had stammered out that I was to yield myself entirely to the written instructions contained in the secret drawer of his writing-desk, and intended for my eyes alone.

Therein I found myself directed to spend the years intervening before my coming of age at a tiny estate in northern Italy. He had purchased it several months before his death, and having such use for it in view, had furnished the house comfortably and revived the faded glories of the library. Bound by a solemn command I was to live retired from the world, and not to present myself at Furnivaux whilst Lady Barbara Verelst lived.

The manuscript concluded mystically: 'I have known that in your youth she will cross your path; an unscrupulous woman who cares for nought so long as her heart's desire is fulfilled. The stars declare it. Perhaps, even as I write, she may be weaving the fatal web that is to destroy life and happiness. But the line of Fate runs on straightway. I cannot tell (for the evil destiny may overpower you) what to advise, but let justice and love ever sway you, and remember that earth's joy is nought in comparison with that which follows. Beware, Ralph, of her I write of, wherever she be.'

Overpowered with grief, my first impulse was a petulant and unreasonable fury against those with whom I had passed that delicious summer morning. So angry was I with the cause of my disobedience that I did not even write to Lady Barbara, and after my father's funeral I started at once for the home he had chosen.

Here I passed seven years of irresolute work. The management of the estate was entirely in my own hands, and I worked in a desultory fashion amongst my people, earning their affection, and being as happy as any man who has no aim in life. I had always my ideals and my recollections to think of, and I never felt a desire for stronger interests.

At last came a time when all this ceased, and I became terribly depressed. Who can trust presentiments? I have had so many—so many true and so many false, that I have alternately believed and disbelieved in the supernatural powers in which foolish people place such absolute trust. We spend many hours in mourning over catastrophes that never occur, whilst at the time that the greatest possible disasters are affecting our fortunes, we are plunged into the lightest ecstasy.

Yet I must confess that, when I received word from the Verelst's lawyer that on the opening of my great-aunt's will he had discovered a new codicil by which I was compelled to marry either Rachel or Mary, or to suffer the estates to pass entirely from our branch of the family, a long vista of ills opened before me, and I complained bitterly, because of the craftiness and self-will of the old woman, who would not believe that ought but worldly interest was necessary for marriage.

At first I determined not to go, but as the knowledge came that, unless I did so my cousins would be plunged into poverty, I gave instructions for my trunk to be packed, and left everything; in the hands of a steward. It was with considerable trepidation that I pondered over our meeting; and as I looked farewell on the gardens of my house, on the vineyards and the river, I execrated the memory of the old make-plot.

In four days I was on the platform at Carlrhys station, watching with a sort of amazement the train that had brought me disappearing at the curve, and wondering whether the letter I had written from Dover had forewarned the ladies, when a withered groom advanced and touched his hat in antiquated style.

'Be ye Mr Rafe?' he said. 'Why, God bless me, what am I sayin''—as if I couldn't tell him from his likeness to Mr Alston!'

'Yes,' I responded laughingly. 'I am Rafe Eyre. You are from Furnivaux Castle?' He wore the old fawn livery with pelicans wrought on the buttons, and a high white crape stock was tied around his neck. 'You are surely not Stephen, whom my father spoke of so often?'

'That I be!' he cried.

I remembered him perfectly now, from my father's description. In my boyhood, I had been told that he was at least ninety; yet he was still straight as a staff.

'Miss Rachel's waiting outside in the carriage, sir,' he said. 'Train's nigh upon an hour late!'

With this gentle hint that his mistress might be growing impatient, he seized my luggage and led me to the gate, where stood a large green chariot.

A woman's voice accosted me. 'I bid you welcome, cousin.' And before I could speak I felt my hand taken and held. The sunlight was gleaming so fiercely, that I could scarcely distinguish the features that smiled beneath the crown of red-golden hair; but when I did so it was with a start of astonishment, for Rachel Verelst's beauty had become transcendent.

She leaned back against the soft olive velvet cushions, and after insisting on my sitting at her side, she gave the order, and we were driven through the stretches of woodland and moor, and over the miles of park road that lead to Furnivaux. Half bewildered I continually turned to look at my companion. Strange to say she did not wear mourning, but a gown of yellow tulle, worked in high relief with golden flowers, and the outline of her splendidly proportioned figure was visible through the gauzy folds.

Whether it was that my arrival had excited her, or that it was her ordinary motion, I could not tell, but her heart was beating wildly beneath its coverings, and floods of a rich colour sped to and from her cheeks.

Her bizarre conversation related much to the object of my visit. The peculiarity of the circumstances she took little heed of, and having at the first moment leaped into the familiarity of an old friend, she tacitly refused to vacate the position.

'How delightful it is,' she remarked as we passed through the Headless Cross wood, 'to meet a man who knows something of the outer world! O the stupidity of our country gentlemen, whose noblest aspiration is to dine well; whose noblest possibility is to hide the mark of the ploughman and the lout! How definitely you refresh me, Rafe! Your presence here has already done me a world of good. If you only knew how stagnant—how wearisome life is! Bah! but you don't sympathise!'

This last observation was made because I had not replied, but to tell the truth I did not wish my voice to break the musical echo hers had left in my ears. I expressed a hope that she would not regard me as laconic, but rather as overwhelmed by the gladness of reunion.

Whilst I spoke the turrets of Furnivaux, just touched by the purple rays of the setting sun, gleamed above a cluster of gnarled elms. The mists from the sloping woods had ascended to the parapet of the roof and given it the aspect of a terrace in the clouds. A gaily-coloured flag fluttered in the Giant's Tower, and I could distinctly see the crest wrought in flagrant contradiction to the laws of blazonry.

''Twas I who did it,' Rachel said, 'in your honour. Mary wanted to embroider the pelican, but it was all my own idea, and I would not let her. However, she prevailed on me concerning the motto—see—you can just catch a glimpse of her *Nourrit par son sang*, in azure letters.'

The carriage stopped in front of the portico, and Stephen opened the door. My cousin laid her hand on my arm, and we entered the great hall together. As I paused to look up at the domed roof, with its pargeting of wyverns and cockleshells, a feeling of chilliness made me shiver.

'My dear Rafe,' Rachel said, 'the change of climate tries you. Had I imagined that the place would be so cold I would have ordered a fire to be lighted. This is the way to the dining-room. I wonder where my sister is;—ah, you are there, Mary.'

One dressed in the plainest of white muslins stood in an open doorway. She shrank visibly at the sight of my outstretched hand, and it was only by an effort that she placed her own in it; to lie there for too brief a space. Her figure was slight and insignificant, and she had not a feature worthy of comparison with her brilliant sister's. Rachel had taken away all the awkwardness of my involuntary visit; Mary had forced it back again, and I mentally accused her of inhospitality.

Rachel, seeing that I was hurt, turned with the intention of diverting my thoughts.

'Pray do not change your clothes this evening,' she said. 'We are very unconventional here, and it is nearly dinner-time. I will show you the state bedroom—it is at your disposal.'

So saying she led me to an immense upper chamber, with a gilt bedstead hung with watchet blue. Grotesque lacquered cabinets lined the walls, and in each corner stood a dark-green monster from Nankin. Here I made a few hasty alterations in my toilet, and after slipping a spray of honeysuckle from a bowl on the dressing-table into my button-hole I hurried down to the drawing-room. Mary sat within; her knees covered by a long piece of lawn which she was embroidering. It fell to the floor and she turned very pale as I entered.

'Cousin Mary,' I said reproachfully, 'why do you treat me so coldly? Have I offended you?'

Her eyes were slowly lifted to mine, and I beheld in them, despite her timidity, a look of the keenest pleasure. She held out her hand tentatively, and seemed relieved when I grasped it.

'I am sorry that you should have misunderstood me,' she murmured. 'The anticipation of this meeting has been so painful. I am not as strong as Rachel, and anything disconcerts me.'

Rachel's entrance prevented any further remarks. She had taken advantage of the short time to doff her yellow gown for one of pale green gauze, of the same hue as the sea where the sunlight falls over shallows. A pair of fancifully worked gloves were fastened to her girdle: they were made of a claret-coloured, semi-transparent skin. With a laughing reminder of the ceremony we had used as boy and girl at our first meeting, she accompanied me to the table, where the meal passed in delicious interchange of thought, during which, although Mary neither spoke nor seemed to listen I could well understand that she was appreciative.

When I returned to the drawing-room Rachel's look was mischievous: Mary had evidently been reproving her.

'You shall judge me, Rafe,' she cried, holding up her hands so that I might see what she had done. The gloves she had worn at her belt covered them now. They were awkwardly made, and on the back of each was worked a silk picture of a dagger and a vial.

'They are tragic accompaniments,' she said. 'Mary has been scolding me for wearing them—she declares that they will bring me ill luck. Do you believe in such nonsense?'

She did not wait for my reply, but continued: 'They were made of the skin of a murderess gibbeted in these parts a hundred and twenty years ago. Old Barnard Verelst insisted on having a piece: he wanted to cover a book with it, but his wife, whom tradition reports as a real she-devil, insisted on having these gloves instead. Between ourselves, the result was that she poisoned her lord, but as he was very old, nobody was much the worse.'

And mirthfully arching her mouth, she passed the gloves into my hand. A strong repugnance to touch them made me immediately drop them on a side table. Rachel's originality carried her into strange humours. I was not sorry when the lamps were brought. They were of curious Venetian make, with round shades of silver lattice work filled in with cubes of gold-coloured glass. Their soft and pleasant light enhanced Rachel's personal charm.

She went to the piano soon, and calling me to her side, began to play. Never had I heard such wild and fantastical music as the first three melodies. They were Russian; savage, rough airs, which fretted me to unhealthy excess of inquietude. After the third, by which the soul is wrought to such a pitch that it is hard to refrain from shrieking, she began a plaintive air with a grotesque rhythm.

'This is the tune the gnomes dance to on the hillside,' she said. 'Here they emphasise the step; now they float round and round in rings; now the king is performing alone and they are all watching. My favourite is that one with the white slashed doublet and crooked face, with a moustache so long that it pricks the others. Ah, well! (with hands brought down clashingly) they must all creep through the bronze door. *So!*' Then, playing another unfamiliar melody, she began to sing Shelley's 'Love's Philosophy.' I scarcely dare attempt to describe her voice. Poets have dreamed of its likes (heard them I may swear never); it was almost unearthly in its pathos, and tears were streaming from my eyes ere the first verse was ended. How she could sing so purely I cannot tell, but it seemed as if to the accompaniment of music all the dross were purged from her spiritual nature, and an innocence left, unsullied as that of our first mother ere she sinned.

As the song went on a fuller harmony sustained her, and looking around, I saw that Mary's hands swept delicately over the strings of a harp that stood in shadow. I leaned back, delivered to perfect delight, but just as my head pressed the cushion a sob came from Rachel's lips, and rising hastily, she pressed her hands over her face and hurried from the room.

Mary followed her, but returned almost immediately. 'Cousin Rafe,' she said nervously, 'forget that Rachel has broken down—her singing often overpowers her—she feels everything too acutely. She begs you to pardon her absence for the rest of the evening. Recent events—my aunt's illness and sudden death amongst them—have unnerved her; you must remember what great store they set on each other.'

The revulsion was very distressing. I had begun to regard Rachel as a woman of iron will, endowed with an intellect nothing could quail. This sign of weakness, coming so unexpectedly, surprised and pained me. Had I been more closely connected with her, I would have sought her chamber and drawn her head to my breast.

As I sat, the moon began to rise over the further hills. The rays slanted into the Italian garden, where, seven years before, Mary and I had played like young children. She had returned to her harp and was drawing forth soft chords. The night, however, became so beautiful that I felt I must breathe the outer air.

'Let us walk together,' I said. 'Show me the dragon and the maze where we ran, and the lilies and flowing rushes. The heat of the room oppresses me.'

She led me silently down the broad stone stairs. The dragon was unchanged.

'We will sit here,' she said; 'and you can tell me everything that has happened in the last few years. I have nothing to give in return, for my life has been placid from the very beginning, and the only great excitement I ever had was when you visited Furnivaux before. Rachel says that I have a small soul; it must be so, for the quiet content of this place suits me well. I suppose that I am one of those weeds that root themselves firmly anywhere. Each thing about here I love as if it were a part of me. Now, forgive me for my tediousness, and tell me everything!'

Thus bidden, I began the story of how I had spent the intervening time. There was little worth telling. It was a brief and simple record of dormant faculties and aspirations, when my highest desire had been for undisturbed sleep. Mary listened in silence, and when I had finished, looked up.

'But the awakening has come now,' she said very gently. 'A new future is thrust upon you:—your life will no longer be as it was.'

Somehow as she spoke my head moved nearer hers, and before she could draw back my lips had pressed her cheek. She rose, gasping, then turning on me a look of surprise and wonder, she hurried away. Perhaps some reminiscence of our former racing came to her, for I heard her laugh, light and long and silvery, as her gown glimmered through the yews.

When I retired to my room, it was not to sleep. A conflict was raging in heart and brain. Rachel was undeniably the more beautiful: indeed she was by far the most beautiful woman I had ever seen, and her wit and power of fascination were incomparably superior to Mary's. She evidently believed that I *must* choose her, and so I had fully intended to do until a tone in Mary's voice and a quick responsive beating of my own heart told me that it could not be. Mary had never imagined that I should take her in preference, but I knew now that whatever love lay in my nature must be placed in her keeping. I had discovered that I wanted no mental stronghold to surround me, but a wife, tender, loving, and dependent.

Uncertain whether a declaration would or not be premature, I decided to leave the castle early next morning, and to reflect for at least a month on my decision. Rachel had acquired a strong influence over me, and I dared not venture to free myself from her bonds without tightening my armour. So, rising almost before daybreak, I set out in secret, from the village inn despatching a short note:—

'My dear Rachel,—Do not attempt to fathom the motive which compels me to leave Furnivaux. Impute it, if you will, to flightiness. I was always fond of doing strange things. I shall return in a month—a month today.   —RALPH EYRE.'

My meditating place was Northen Hall, a small manor-house situated about two hundred miles away. I had inherited it from my mother. It stands in a little park, outside an antiquated market town. I had installed Jeffreys, my father's old friend, and he was living out the remainder of his years in ease and solitude.

He was standing in the walled rose-garden when I reached the place. Half his time since my father's death had been spent with me in Italy; but the climate had proved unsuited to him, and he had been compelled to return to England. The affection he greeted me with was very touching. Although I had always been very tiresome, I have no doubt that he loved me deeply.

A suite of rooms had been kept in readiness for me, and I was soon made comfortable therein. I had much writing to do, and for some days worked hard, so that I might drive away the thought of my dilemma. But after awhile, when I was idle again, the remembrance of Mary's timid loveliness haunted me from morning to night, and I began to long for the time of my return.

The momentous day came at last. Rachel Verelst, like another Fiammetta, clad in a gown of dull dark green, with scarlet lilies at the neck, met me on the terrace. There was a slightly puzzled look in her eyes, when I did not give her the warm greeting she evidently expected; but she slipped her arm into mine with as much graceful ease as if she were already my wife.

There was no sign of Mary, and when I inquired for her Rachel replied evasively. Not until I went to the drawing-room after dinner did I see her. She was alone, sitting near a window, with a book in her hands.

She gave a sudden start when she saw me. 'O Rafe,' she cried, 'when did you come? I did not know you were here: Rachel would not tell me anything about you, either where you were or why you went, and I have only just come in from riding to watch the sunset.'

Before she had done speaking I had clasped her in my arms and was showering kisses on her lips.

'Mary,' I whispered, 'I have come back for you!'

She began to extricate herself, but before I had released her the door opened, and Rachel herself entered.

III

She gave but little sign that she had seen the embrace. The bunch of white roses she held in her right hand were raised slowly, as if she wished to inhale their perfume, and beneath their shade her lips were convulsed for just one moment. Then with even more than the old grace she came near. Her skirt caught the gilded legs of a chair and drew it for a short distance, but she took no heed. She began to smile winningly.

'Has Mary told you of the naughty trick I played?' she said. 'I wanted to keep all the gratification to myself: it was so great a pleasure to know something of you that nobody else knew. Of course I was selfish! Now, my cousin, as you gave her a guerdon for waiting so patiently, do not forget that I also waited. Not with patience, for I have chafed terribly—but still, every awakening has been fraught with the knowledge that a day nearer our meeting had come.'

And she held up her mouth, sweet and ruddy as the lilies on her breast. I kissed her. Seeing that I made no motion to encircle her with my arms as I had done to Mary, she clasped her hands at the back of my neck, and again brought her lips to mine.

'There is nothing wrong in my kissing you?' she murmured inquiringly. 'When women kiss it is mere passionless duty and affection; but when I kiss you... O Rafe, Rafe, Rafe! I cannot say it!'

I saw Mary's reflection in a mirror. She was standing wan and wretched-looking by the window. When she knew that I was watching her she moved quietly from the room. Rachel laughed nervously as the door closed.

'It is well to be alone, Rafe! I never thought that I should feel the presence of a third person such a restraint, but so it is! I cannot breathe freely with you unless I have you entirely to myself. Now, I wish to know what you have been doing away from me, or rather (for, of course, I *do* know all about it), I am dying to hear the words you have to say to me.'

Not divining her meaning, I hesitated. 'I do not understand you,' I said.

She laughed again, this time very sadly. Somehow I felt that she was murdering her scruples. She raised her fan and struck me lightly on the shoulder.

'Dear Rafe,' she said, 'I know well that you are overcome with a kind of reluctance to declare yourself. Why then should we temporise? You have not known me for so short a time as not to see that—that—*I love you with my whole heart and soul.*'

The last words came in a hoarse undertone. Then with her flushed face downcast she left me, turning once at the door, to see if I followed. But, being almost petrified with amazement, I did not move. I had never thought sufficiently highly of myself as to believe that Rachel would really love me. I knew that she might marry me to retain the estates, but not for one instant had I imagined that I could stir her passion.

The knowledge filled me with dread. Although she charmed, nay, almost magnetised me, my pulse beat none the quicker because of her presence, and I felt blinded with excess of light. A desire came for the soothing Mary's voice alone could give, and I too left the room.

Old Stephen, stiff as the mailed figures in the hall, was pacing outside the door. His eighty years of service had given him the freedom of the house. He divined my intention. 'Miss Mary is in the garden,' he said.

I went to the Stone Dragon, convinced that I should find her there. I was not deceived: she was sitting on the sward beside the monster; her head resting on his scaly back. At my approach her face lighted up, and she rose to meet me.

'Forgive me for being so weak,' she murmured coyly. 'I could not bear to see you kissing Rachel. I am foolishly jealous and—it followed so quickly after—'

'Dear Mary,' I said, 'let us forget it all. Tonight I would leave the precincts of the house. Let us walk together to the moor. There is a British camp somewhere near: it will be just the place for a solemn vowing. Show me the way!'

She led me through the intricate maze to a door in a moss-covered wall, which opened on a barren path. This crossed a mile of park, and then reached a broad and hilly stretch of moorland. Here the track was sunken between gravelly banks. At some distance rose a mound, on whose top stood three cromlechs.

When we stood against the largest, I took her right hand.

'I, Ralph Eyre, swear solemnly that all my life shall be devoted to your happiness.'

Mary's voice, soft and trembling, followed. 'I, Mary Verelst, swear solemnly that all my life shall be devoted—'

A harsh cry interrupted her. Turning sharply we saw Rachel herself, covered with a long grey cloak, whose hood had fallen back. How she had followed so silently I never knew: it may have been that she had unwittingly chosen this as a night walk, but whether or no, her presence here was the work of some evil genius. She was haggard, and as the moonlight fell on her distorted face I saw that her eyes had contracted so much as to be almost invisible. One hand was tearing the flowers from her throat, the other moved automatically in front.

'Rafe!' she muttered, 'Rafe!'

Mary came closer, and passed her arm around my waist. She was nearly fainting, and required all my strength to support her, but I was impotent as a new-born child, and could only grasp her elbow with nerveless fingers.

'Is this the end?' Rachel asked. Her voice was dull and monotonous. 'Answer me quickly—don't you know what a woman's heart is? Is this the end of all I have prayed for—this refusal of my passion?'

I strove to speak: my teeth chattered.

'I am not an heroic woman, noble enough to wear the willow in peace, and to pass my prime in the doing of good deeds. God forgive me; my nature is small—so small that you have consumed its virtue! If only my love would change to hatred I could endure it better.'

With this she moved rapidly away. Some minutes passed in silence.

'Let us go in at once,' Mary said. 'I am afraid.'

We returned to the castle. As we reached the postern door Rachel's grey figure rose before us again. Her attitude was threatening now, and her voice clear and loud. She thrust out both hands to show that she had donned the skin gloves.

'Am I attired for tragedy?' she cried, 'or is it because of the devilry in my soul that I desire evil things about me? See, they fit better now—my fingers are swollen—with bitterness if you like!'

Nearer she came. Mary flung her arms around me, and despite my endeavours and entreaties that she should move, leaned closely on my breast.

'She shall kill me first,' she said quietly. 'My body is yours.'

Rachel's eyes were flaming sullenly. 'I am denied,' she said. 'Had you died before this moment I should have been a maid all my life; had you vowed celibacy, I would have loved you still, though the world lay between us. As it is—'

With one powerful effort I forced Mary aside and stood facing Rachel. 'How can I control my affection?' I cried. 'I had not the creating of it.'

She shook her head ominously. 'Since you are lost to me as the completion of myself,' she murmured, 'let us remain unwed, and choose poverty for the future. Who knows but we may rise to greater riches and state? I will be content with little—a pressure of the hand, nay to breathe the same air will be enough for me. Only give me your constancy! It is the thought that you will belong to another that hurts so cruelly now!'

Strung to the highest tension, I replied, '*It cannot be.*'

Rachel's hand toyed at her breast for an instant, then making a sudden upward movement, curved in the air and came glittering towards my heart.

A moan of horror was the only sound. Afterwards something bore down at my feet, and a fountain of hot blood gushed over the grass. Mary had sprung before me and saved my life. Forgetful of all else, I knelt, and lifting her in my arms, carried her to the house. Rachel was no longer in sight. As soon as the blow had fallen she fled.

*

The bells rang from daybreak. It was a hot autumn morning, and the after-math of honeysuckle was very rich. I had gathered great clusters for my bride, and was in my lightest humour. That morning I was to wed her whom I had watched so long winning her way back to health.

Together we walked to the damp old church: she in her simplest gown, I in my ordinary clothes. Mary had ever a fond belief that her sister would return to forgive her for her guiltless sin; and she would not agree to our leaving Furnivaux for even one day.

So we were married. No wedding party accompanied us: the clerk gave Mary away, and although money had been dispensed amongst the villagers, there was no merry-making. A few girls cast roses on the path,—that was all.

Home we went. Old Stephen was standing at the door. A senile resentment was on his face: he looked as if he hated us.

'She's come back,' he said in a broken voice. 'Poor lass! poor lass!'

Mary ran forward, her face glowing with joy. She had never harboured an ill-feeling against her sister.

'Where is she?' she asked. 'Did you tell her, Stephen?'

'No, Miss Mary, I didn't. She knew about it, though, I'll be bound! Perhaps Mr Eyre had best go alone to find her!'

But my true love clasped my arm. 'Let me come too,' she said. 'Stephen, tell us where she is.'

'She's sought you at th' old stone dragon, where ye were always a-sitting in th' old time. Ye'll find her there right enow.'

The man burst out sobbing as we hurried down the staircase. To me there came a terrible fear, but Mary had a bride's blitheness.

We reached the Italian garden. A travel-stained form lay beside the dragon. The face was buried in the thick wild thyme, but a bright web of red-golden hair was spread over the lichened stone.

Mary knelt and strove to turn her. 'My darling,' she said. 'How much I have missed you. It was tender of you to come today. Though I love Rafe so, you were always most dear and wonderful to me!'

After much effort she raised Rachel's head to her lap. The beautiful features had sharpened strangely and the skin was ashen grey.

'O my God! O Rafe!' my wife shrieked. 'She is cold; *she is dead!*'

PART III
Of Passion and of Death

This selection of stories deals with Gilchrist's overarching concern with doomed romance and passion in its most unrefined form; the physical and spiritual suffering caused by love. 'The Lost Mistress' and 'The Writings of Althea Swarthmoor' both tell similar stories—the former through traditional narrative while the latter uses a one-sided series of letters—where love is spurned and eventually spoils into something unbearably bitter. The corrupted desire of 'The Noble Courtesan' inverts this bitterness by raising the spirit of Auguste Villiers de l'Isle-Adam's *conte cruel* romances, with the very human monster of a serial killer replacing Gilchrist's previous vampires and ghosts. At first reading 'The Holocaust' is a confusingly circular narrative with a needlessly verbose narrator but it is, at its core, a touching meditation on the self-sacrificing lengths to which anguish will push someone who feels lost and abandoned. 'Roxana Runs Lunatick' and 'The Madness of Betty Hooton' are even more bleak as the eponymous subjects of the two stories are not even allowed the release of death but rather, due to the machinations of a jealous husband and conniving brother, linger in their torments. This blend of passion and death culminates in the melancholy 'My Friend', where two male companions walk 'hand in hand like small children' along a path that is both literal and philosophical. Indeed, the tale itself can be read both literally and more subtly. It is not far-fetched to see the narrator and his friend Gabriel as partners who are unable to fully express their love for one another—at some small slight the pair stop talking and 'there came a sequence of those drossy moments when silence is loathsome'—but 'My Friend' can equally be read as Gilchrist himself struggling with his own sexuality. The narrator repeatedly mentions the concept of metempsychosis—the belief that human souls leave the body at the moment of death to take residence elsewhere—and the narrative exudes a kind of bittersweet, cautiously hopeful belief that the pair, and by extension Gilchrist, might be reborn in a time when they can be themselves more fully, more joyfully. This section ends with 'Sir Toby's Wife' and its achingly Gothic tale of doubles and murderous obsession.

THE LOST MISTRESS

The Author's Study

half-dead *Spiræa Japonica* stood on the writing-table; reared against the pot was a miniature, which, as the only beautiful thing in the room, and, moreover, as the work of John Ravil himself, merits a full description. Not even the most ardent flatterer of the sex would have sworn that the woman was less than eight-and-twenty. She was reclining on a luxurious, shawl-covered chair, with a background of pale roses and quaintly shapen mirrors. One hand held a frontal of pearls just taken from the light-brown hair; the other a letter which she was reading with some tenderness. Her face was fair, her eyes of a rich blue. Firm and lustrous shoulders peeped through the smooth white muslin of her gown. Mother Eve could not have peered her physical charm.

John Ravil himself was grotesque even to ugliness. Of scarcely the middle height, ill-shapen in body, and husky voiced, his peculiarities were so marked that it was impossible for him to walk in the streets without exciting unfavourable comment. His complexion was neither light nor dark; and an odd look was given by a bushy copper-coloured moustache, whose ends had never known training. An overhanging forehead, with knitted brows and stiff white hair that stood on end, completed the list of his most noticeable faults. Despite the marks of age, however, he was as yet only in his twenty-third year, and evidences of his youth were visible in his large brown eyes that seemed at times to belong to a young child.

Today those eyes were full of terrified perplexity. A change had come into his life; the love that had sapped his fountain of inspiration, and hindered him in his struggle for bread, had grown more and more absorbing of late, and in proportion, the passion of the beloved one had dwindled. Life had nothing for him save this woman: fame could never come now, and in his unhappiness he felt himself degraded to the verge of the commonplace.

After awhile he rose, with a heavy indraught of breath, and opening the secret drawer of an old mahogany bureau took thence a small bundle of letters, each enclosed in its gilt-edged enve-lope. A band of white paper, whereon was inscribed 'Flavia's Correspondence,' was tied round all. This he loosened, and taking the topmost letter, reverentially unfolded the sheet. It had been written soon after their first meeting. Flavia's hand was eccentrically masculine. 'Forgive me,' it ran, 'for being so obtuse last night in not divining the meaning of your words. You stung me somehow when you laughed at my singing: it was not till afterwards that I understood your laughter—strange and harsh as it sounded—as a far greater compliment than any other man could bestow. Truth to tell, I half resented the little speech that followed. *Why should I sing only alone or only for one?* Heaven knows that I have not a beautiful voice, but still I believe (and I am not an egotist) that I have the power of expressing the predominant sentiment of the song. *Addio*, stay, I often visit that alley of firs you admire so—in the afternoon of most fine days—and a voice sounds infinitely more *spacious* there. Shall I sing there alone?'

Here John Ravil bit his white lower lip until the blood oozed in scarlet drops. O the midsummer noontide; the trembling air;

the golden dusk that clung around the fir trunks! Flavia had wafted towards him from the eastern glade, clad in azure and seeming like a cloud-borne cherub. Cherubs sing too, and she sang; but no cherub ever sang as she. Only one song—

> 'Oh turn, love, oh turn I pray
> I prithee, love, turn to me.'

But such memories add to one's agony.

The second letter, dated two months later, told of capitulation.

'You did not come,—some scruple withheld you? If you had known how utterly sick I grew as the hours passed you would have pitied me. At every sound I gazed from my window, craving to see you on the terrace, your head downcast as ever; your eyes waiting for the brightness that my presence alone can bring. You are very cruel; I could not bear you to suffer as I do. Even when absent you magnetise me. Nothing appeals to me now—the gorgeous sunsets of late; the autumn foliage; the knee-deep drifts of already fallen leaves. Come tonight, my lover, my—I had almost blasphemed! Just to let my heart spring to yours, my blood leap through my body, my beauty grow paramount.'

Ravil sat for a while with his hands covering his face. The blood trickled down his chin and fell on the white sheet; he wiped it away, replaced the letter in its envelope and took the next. The tide of love was flowing yet.

'Genius,' it began, 'poet-painter, genius of mine, I thank you for your idealising of me. But I was never as lovely as the picture. I am almost glad that you insisted on retaining it, for I should have become jealous of its excellence, and perhaps destroyed it in some frenzy. How lively must my image be to you in absence!

'To other people you are grotesque (what you said was true): to me you are the handsomest in the world. I and none other have seen that wondrous lighting of countenance, have heard that quickening of the voice. At this moment I could tear myself without a murmur from the vain world, to dwell in some remote garden where conventionalism triumphs not; where we should exist for each other, and let our lives form one perfection. Come tonight: I will sit with your head cushioned on my breast. Bring your story and let us cry together.'

Soon after this the woman's passion had begun to fade. Ravil knew what was in the other letters. She had wearied slowly of the genius. Her feeling had been too fervent to endure. She was healthy and full-blooded. Another, 'a swart-haired Hercules,' had taken her fancy; and with the admission of this second love all the old worship had grown lukewarm. In proportion, however, as she had become less infatuated, he had descended almost to madness: had craved over humbly that she would consider the wrong she was doing him; had sworn that if she were false to him, life would hold naught of goodness more.

Men as highly strung and as unfortunate have little sustaining strength. Fate, the evil godmother, bestows an excess of imaginative power, and Nature, angry in the unwelcome gift, takes her spite out of the unsinning god-child, and makes him timorous and unmanly.

Flavia's last letter must have cost her an effort. Each word was as a dart through his vitals.

'My love, there is a certain proverb which I am not powerful enough to disprove, that the constancy of women exists more in fiction than in reality. You accuse me of no longer loving you? In a measure you are wrong: your friendship will be more to me than anything in life. One way I have failed. Forgive me if I tell you that you will ever appeal to my spiritual part. We never could have married; in my cooler moments I have often acknowledged myself too cowardly to cross the bridge between our ranks. The homage of my kind is necessary after all. Let us regard the past as a pleasant episode.

'Apparently you have heard the rumour of my approaching marriage. Let me beg of you one thing: in honour you are bound to return my letters; yours are ready in exchange. I shall be much pained to part with what has given me almost preternatural pleasure. Why should we not meet and bid each other good-bye?'

II

The Lady's Boudoir

The chamber was softly radiant with mother-o'-pearl colours, all so blended that by contrast a woman's face might wear a heightened charm. Plants with pale leaves and white flowers filled the oriel; dusky mandarins leered in corners; chastened pictures hung on the silk-covered walls. Before each window was drawn a gleaming tissue.

Flavia rose from the piano with a great sigh: tears were rolling down her cheeks (evidently the song had suggested woe), and some fell on the brown cover of a volume that lay on the table. It was John Ravil's *Venus's Apple*, a romance which, he had once dreamed, was like to bring him fame. Flavia took it up and held it over her breast until it was warm. It should ever be the dearest book in the world! Although love was dead, gratitude remained. For his short hour her lover had been all-in-all; through him she had tasted of intellectual pleasures unknown before their meeting.

'He will bear it well enough in time,' she sighed; 'it will give him strength for his work; he will use his Oriental richness no longer,—will curb his luxuriance, and develop an epigrammatic style, which, being coupled with that fine imaginativeness of his, must needs fillip him into popularity.'

The thought gave consolation, and she became herself again in mentally comparing the two lovers: the one saturnine, ugly, oppressive; the other bright, laughing, and handsome—her ideal of manhood. Sure 'twas only in an unwholesome dream that Ravil had been victor?

She raised the lid of her cedar desk and took his letters from their nest amidst dried rose-leaves. Then she sank back to her favourite chair, leaning almost in the same posture as in the miniature. The collection was unfastened and placed in her lap, and soon, with a few more sighs, she raised the sheets for a last reading.

Even for letters of passion they were extravagant: the weakness of his nature, his need of a restraining power, was manifest in each. They were almost hysterical: no man healthy in body and mind could have written them. Yet Flavia's face grew troubled, and her lips moved pitifully.

'Why did you look at me so,' the first began, 'look at our first greeting as if I had been by your side all my life? You brought a strange fluttering to my heart; you stopped my breath; the room whirled round and round. You must have thought me a very fool in the incoherent words I spoke. You may guess the cause; my oppressed brain had never permitted me even to imagine such beauty as yours.

'Only once before in my life have I known such a feeling: I had read a story told of love and death under a southern sky. The hot malaria, the aroma of lilies, the thick water, seemed to envelop me, and I swooned. It was like rain on parched ground to find myself still in my own room, nodding my head to the bunch of yellow-flags I had bought of a child at the door.

'But now I swoon again, and the awakening can only come at the transition into the next world's darkness.

'I am in love's wine-press, shrieking at the weight that must descend and crush out new-born joy. Give me, in the name of God, one word of tenderness, and forget that I ever dared to lift my eyes.'

As Flavia read she smiled, as women smile upon a baby thrusting out a tiny fist with broken flowers. As free and natural a gift was Ravil's love. Her eyes grew tender: she looked at her shoulder just as if his head were resting there.

'Poor head, poor coarse hair!' she said.

The next letter treated of some dereliction.

'You have tortured me cruelly. When you rode past on the road, I stamped in the dust till my folly was manifest, even to myself. *Who is he? I insist on knowing.* When I saw him loose-mouthed and peering right into your pupils all the tigerish part of me sprang up, and I could have destroyed him for his temporary usurpation of my rights. How dared he look at you so? All night I lay awake, calling upon your name, praying for some miracle to bring you to my chamber.'

Flavia remembered her exultation when her fingers tore this sheet open: how she had been so merry as to sing and run and play like a young girl. She passed hastily over more, and came to that he had written after she had yielded him her honour. Her own letters had feebly echoed his at the time.

'Sweetest and noblest,' it ran, 'life has changed. The dense veil that shrouded my future has been withdrawn. Today I feel infinitely more inspired than ever I felt in my youth. A myriad rich ideas float from my brain, and were it not for very impatience of the hour of our meeting I would sit at my table and write some grand epic, or some romance that would shake the centre of every heart. Love! love!'

Flavia's eyes glittered now; but grew languid quickly as she fell to picturing old scenes. The minutes passed and passed, ere she returned to her task. The letter she took had signs of a lover's doubts.

'I awaken in madness; for the dread that grows in my companionless nights deepens towards morning. Suppose that Flavia had never really loved me;—suppose that I had been only her last dearly-paid-for whim;—suppose,—nay, now I have written it my fears go in laughter. Flavia is the paragon: I alone understand her mystery. Any man less initiated in the secrets of her character might declare that to me her outward demeanour was cold. But I glory in her apparent lack of feeling, conscious that my position is impregnable, and that her passion, though chastened, is still powerful.'

The white shoulders were shrugged. 'How lacking in discrimination!' Before he had written thus she had been absolutely discourteous, whilst he had ever refused to understand. It was her remark, that change is necessary to existence, which had evoked this strange protest. Besides, she knew herself to be inconstant in thought. The hours spent in his company, which at first were almost unearthly in their speed of flight, were dull and wearisome now, and she had grown to hail the time of his departure with something akin to pleasure.

Six more letters were passed unopened—much less unread. Then she unfolded the last—his reply to her renunciation.

'Flavia, it is hard to think that you of all the world should care to jest with me. That your letter is anything more than a jest I am struggling not to believe. After all your vows, breathed as you lay in my arms, whispered in a tone that made me vibrate like a harp-string, you should not play with my feelings. You know me, darling: it was unkind.

'O God in heaven, I dare not believe it! I will not! I cannot! My mind is not large enough to take in so monstrous a truth!

'We will meet tomorrow in the wood, and laugh together at the frightened fool you have made of me! and in revenge I will be sardonic and cruel.'

III

Love Lies Bleeding

Sloping fir alleys; bounded at one end by a darkly mantled fish-pond, at the other by an open park, with grazing deer and cattle. Birds avoid these fir-woods: this one was silent, save for a low boom of insects and the dwarfish whistling of shrew-mice.

Ravil was first at the meeting-place. He rested in a cathedral-like vista overarched with olive—the glade where Flavia had sung. The wiry grass was hot with the sun, the air thick with fragrance.

He waited in gladness. As the time had drawn near much of his dread had vanished, and although he still felt like a man who stands with his back to a pit, on whose verge his heels are pressing, the light beating on his brain so dazzled him that little save the maddest joy was left.

In the interval he conjured up visions of her beauty: his lips moved as if to kiss. He reviewed for the thousandth time the history of their passion. No false humility had ever troubled him; and despite the worldly distinction between noble and plebeian, he saw himself her equal at all points. In his egotistical belief, the highest patent of nobility should be bestowed on those with unplumbed depths of feeling, with superior capacities for suffering.

At last she came, not in azure this time, but in a gown of plain russet, such as any of the cottagers' wives on her land might have worn. But something exquisite in her manner of wearing it showed the gentle rounding of her breasts, the rise and fall of her breathing. A flush spread over her face as he rose to greet her; at the sight the old hunger came, and he bent his head to hers.

'Once,' she said very faintly.

There was a note of sublime renunciation in her voice. If she had loved him with all her heart, and had discovered that his future required the breaking of the unlawful bond, she could not have shown a nobler pathos. He flung his arm about her neck, and half-savagely kissed her ripe lips.

Soon she drew apart. 'You hurt me,' she said. 'There is not much time... I must return soon... there are people... He...'

He fell back with contorted mouth, for the lash had agonised him with its subtle poison. Pity filled her, and she soothed him with velvet caresses, tried to flatter him with hopes of fame. 'Twould be best for him; in after years they would meet, he jubilant with men's praise, she saddened and broken in by the legal bond. For his sake, all for his sake.

When he had recovered somewhat he strove to discover the truth in her eyes. It was a profitless task.

His chin began to tremble. 'Here are the letters,' he whispered huskily. 'Keep mine... Leave me here... Good-bye.'

Flavia went weeping away. Ere she had walked a mile a sudden thrill shook her from head to foot, and she sank down to the grass.

A wonderful light shone from her face. Life's greatness was upon her: her lover's child had stirred within her body.

Born of womanly ecstasy, born of the pain of parting, love that before had been a sickly dwarf, sprang up a ruddy giant. O the bliss, the tenfold bliss of passion revived!

She hurried to the place where she had left him, wild to pant out her secret on his breast. He was there still, but white and rigid, and with a purple wound in his temple.

THE WRITINGS OF
ALTHEA SWARTHMOOR

portrait of Althea Swarthmoor hangs in the library of the House with Eleven Staircases. She is depicted (by Kneller's brush) as a tall, thin woman of about thirty, somewhat sallow in the matter of complexion, and with deerhound eyes. Her crisp black hair is drawn plainly from an admirably arched brow, and there is a perplexed look about her lips.

Doctor Marston's miniature hangs beside—the presentment of a corpulent, thick-necked divine with a fair skin, pallid eyes, and a sensuous mouth. Herrickian curls lie flat on the temples. A suave grace is manifest in the dimpled chin and complacent cheeks.

The literary remains of Althea are coffined in sheepskin on the topmost shelf of the bookcase. The Swarthmoors have a strenuous objection to the opening of this volume, for the episode of their seven times great-aunt is supposed to reflect no honour on the family. However, a few specimens of her fantastic letters, culled at random, can harm neither them nor the reader.

*

ALTHEA SWARTHMOOR TO DR MARSTON

THE HOUSE WITH ELEVEN STAIRCASES,
19th May 1709.

Do not fear, good Doctor, that I shall ever lose the remembrance of those tender words you spoke in the maze t'other evening. It is not necessary to copy them down for me; for they seem part of some rich painting, whereof the hanging moon and the stars form the background—such a picture as shall ever remain before my view. Yet I thank you for your kind proffer, and, whilst I forbid you, entreat you to know that I am depriving myself of what would be a most valued souvenir. Commend me to madam your wife; and understand that I am most cordially your ever faithful friend to serve you.

DR MARSTON TO ALTHEA SWARTHMOOR[*]

BALTCOMB IN LANCASHIRE,
20th May 1709.

Honoured Madam,—I was writing my discourse for the Sunday when the messenger brought your most gracious epistle. Truly a great happiness hath fallen to me! When I declared myself as one whom the power of your presence and the fascination of your glances conquered, I felt the same spirit as is described by the lover in the Canticles—*Turn away thine eyes, for they have overcome me.* In the pulpit I shall next hold forth on the Shulamite and her would-be

---

[*]   This letter is the only one preserved.

spouse. A fig for those who fondly believe the Church is meant! 'Tis an idyllic cry of passion betwixt real man and real woman; the preparative for as rich a marriage song as the world ever imagined. Yet, madam, to you alone dare I acknowledge this idea. We are both freed (in mind) from the conventional; but the world is apt to be censorious with those who have strength to think apart from the multitude. Therefore my treatment of the old love-song must be in the usual veil of supposed prophecy. How rarely does it befall a man to have such a friend (if I dare think you my friend) as you! Let me see you soon: I have a thousand thoughts to elaborate—a thousand religious fears to overcome. My poor wife is at present sunning herself among the herbs; she is again threatened with a plethora.—I am, with the truest sense of gratitude and respect possible, your most humble, most obedient and most obliged servant.

ALTHEA SWARTHMOOR TO DR MARSTON

THE HOUSE WITH ELEVEN STAIRCASES,
30th July 1709.

Were it not that I had promised to write whene'er I had leisure, I might, perchance, choose rather to loiter about the pleasaunce with my brother's children, and to sit by the water basins, watching the goldfish, and paddling my fingers. But the strange impatience that has held me of late forces me to take pen in hand, and to write the wild thoughts that flee through my brain. If only the sound of thy voice came, the midday heat would disappear and I should be refreshed as by fountains.

Tell me of Love, not in the few words that almost make me swoon with their power, but in one long, uninterrupted recital. Fear not the censure of other folk (for the speech shall sink secret into my bosom) but drag it out of thy very heart—one drop of blood for each word. Thy miniature lies on my table; alas! my Bible hath grown dusty with neglect. May we not meet to talk of Passion and of Death, and how they oft walk hand in hand together?—Your most loyal and ever devoted ALTHEA.

THE SAME TO THE SAME

5th August 1709.

A trifle I have written I enclose. One at dinner chid me for never having loved. The verses were born of fevered heat during a restless night. I have named them 'The Secret Priestess of the Amorous Deities'

> Nymphs and Shepherds forthwith sing
> To Dan Cupid, Friend and King,
> Gamester with our wavering hearts,
> Giver both of joys and smarts:
>   Hail to Cupid! Hail!

> Hail to Venus! Mother Queen,
> Who, with eyes of glist'ning sheen,
> Sports him on, our souls to cheat,
> Laughs and sings at every feat:
>   Hail to Venus! Hail!

> But the Love, which dwelt inside
> My heart's core, had leifer died,

213

Than be praised and sung aloud,
For 'twas secret, wild, and proud.

THE SAME TO THE SAME

September 20th, 1709.

That we should truly admire what you were good enough to praise gives me pure joy. In my girlhood I had dreams of helping another by throwing my whole life into his. Am I really of service to you? Assure me that you did not flatter. Doubting is delicious only when one is certain that the doubts must be resolved. Another walk in the coppice, now that the nights are so sweet and so misty. Another of those fatal, delicious hours, wherein Love comes at the flood. Dear Marston, best and noblest of friends, believe me ever to be your devoted and very attached servant.

A MANUSCRIPT OF ALTHEA SWARTHMOOR, SUGGESTED BY SOME DREAD.

(Written about January 1710)

There is nothing in the world more sad than a Love that's dying. Profoundest melancholy comes when the gaudily-hued leaves drop from the parent boughs in Autumn, and leave the trunk gaunt, bare, and unlovely. Those trees are beautifullest whose fruit hangs bright and cheering through the Winter, but alack! they are rare indeed.

How the groaning branches weep when they see their offspring, yellow, crimson, and death-colour, lying beneath them, or carried off, dancing blithely, by every little breeze, to shrivel and decay as Nature demands, on some alien soil! The fairest lineaments of Devotion depart thus from us, and though we grasp a withered tenderness with such a palsied hold as an age-worn oak clutches its leaves, the unwilling thing passes away, floats through the thin air, and leaves us tearful.

We force ourselves to exact those little attentions given by the beloved one, and take an unhealthy gratification in such, believing, or striving to believe, that there is no gold and nought but baser metal in the world. But this cannot last. The Passions of some are destined to die quickly. To warm a corse on the hearth brings back no life. Bury the dead deeply, water its grave with streaming eyes, and in springtide pluck a withered violet or some other sweet-scented blossom from the green sod. Whilst cherishing the token in thy bosom, laugh and be merry in the knowledge that there is no attendant Spirit from the pined creature hovering near.

First desire is ever immature, and worthless in comparison with that which comes in after-life. It is not true that the nature understood to be the largest is capable of the grandest thoughts, for often the most selfish soul is lifted to the highest ecstasy. The strength given by powerful Love is Divine;—the sun warms and ripens Life; Earth is no longer Earth. Existence is a glorious gift.

Love that's true lasts for ever. Death *cannot* end it. My certain hope, nay belief, is that, whether the Afterwards be cast in a wondrous, lovely country or an arid desert, an arm will clasp my waist and feet pace beside mine, whose owner will share all my joy and all my pain.

ALTHEA SWARTHMOOR TO DR MARSTON

1st February 1710.

Day after day of wearisome snow! Interminable workings with my needle and discoursings on my sister's spinet! No interview in private to make me forget the staleness of life. When you come here I must needs sit with hands folded, to listen to the mouldy apophthegms my brother repeats, and admire the quiet courtesy wherewith you reply. A woman must think of nought but her still-room, her table, and the fashions. Even as it is they look upon me as a hawk amongst sparrows.

Ah me, to live with a squire who knows nought but Bacon, and knows him, alas! insufficiently; and a lady whose highest inspiration is to work tent-stitch better than her neighbours at Thundercliffe! Lord, how the children are bred! Barbary, who is twenty, sits demure, and fancies she was brought out of a parsley-plot!

Send me those writings of yours, that speak so curiously of happiness. Also those volumes of Suckling and Rochester you mentioned. 'Pigmalion's Image' I read with delight: it is a picture of such vivid, fruit-like loveliness as no modern poet could invent. Almost the reader believes in its truth—for me, my breath came quick and my cheeks grew hot as the Sculptor's desire was granted. Is there no other poem told in so sweet fashion? Have you not quoted one 'Hero and Leander' by Kit Marlowe; the story of a lover who swam the sea? Pray, if thou canst procure it, do so, for I am enamoured of verse.

Tomorrow night we go to the Assembly Ball. I have prepared a surprise for you. Such a gown as you swore would become me most has been devised, and you will see me in light green, with laces of dead-leaf colour. Let not scruples hinder your coming.

Lastly, for I was fain to finish with the taste of this, I am sending you a cravat, wrought by my own hands, of admirable point, of the kind Antonio Moro loved to paint. It has all been done in my chamber, and none knows of it save myself. Honour me by wearing it tomorrow, and understand me, as ever, your loving friend.

THE SAME TO THE SAME

24th June 1710.

Since your removal to Bath, life here has been trebly stagnant I trust the waters are improving the health of madam your wife, to whom pray commend me.

My godmother, Lady Comber, is staying near you. She wrote the other day to bid me come over, but—I cannot. You would be less *for* me, I less *to* you in the midst of a crowd of intellectual and fashionable folk. So I must endure the sweltering summer at home, but truly beg for all possible alleviation of the dulness by what letters your kindness may prompt you to send. As you ask, I have writ no more poetry. In a sardonic mood, such as I suffer at present, I am inclined to think all my past work neither rhyme nor reason.

This day I have been over all the walks we affected plucking flowers for our favourite seat, and kissing the lavender tree that grows at the lake-vista. It was a solemn pleasure to revisit these places; a pleasure illumined with the glad certainty that ere long you will be my companion again. Write to me soon, and tell me a thousand things of yourself.

Have you met the great wits? Have you played and won, or— God forbid—lost? What said you in your sermon before the Prince? BUT ABOVE ALL, HAVE YOU MISSED ME?

Last night I could not sleep. The heat was great, my imagination tortured. Ever and anon I fancied you were near, so rising from my bed at last I sat looking down the terrace, each moment anticipating your approach. By some miracle you were to arrive and to tell me that the strength of my affection had drawn you.

Dawn tore the East to tatters, Phoebus shook himself and leaped out golden. One by one the birds awoke. Yet my dream did not die until Hieronimo (for so I have named the young peacock) shrieked harshly beneath my window. Only then did I understand that you were still at Bath; and with the knowledge of the eightscore miles of separating hill and plain came the bitterest of tears—those from a lonely woman's eyes.

So, genius and divine, wipe out their remembrance with the tenderest, lovingest letter you ever wrote, and earn the everlasting gratitude of thy Bedeswoman   ALTHEA.

THE SAME TO THE SAME

Sept. 1st, 1710.

Since you chide me for my melancholy, dear, good Marston, tell me how I may avoid it. Stay, do not write. Your protracted absence will soon be over—'tis but a week to your return; a week of leaden hours whose passing I shall count one by one, and enjoy them in the same way that we enjoy crab-apples before a feast. The rapture of seeing you again, of hearing your voice, ay, of breathing the same air, must come in one overpowering excess. Because you love me I am crowned amongst women! What glorious, mad words were those ending your last letter: 'There may be no real happiness for us in this sphere, but in the next, whate'er betide, all my joy shall be with you.'

O fools that we be, not to dare to pluck the good which lies in our power!

Forgive me now, for I am a coward and need assuring. Art thou sure that after death thou wilt be mine? Nay, I could not live here under suspicion of having yielded to the sweetest temptation. Rest content then, dear heart. There is a particular Paradise for those denied joy on earth. *Addio*, I have kissed the spot of my signature.

FRAGMENT OF A DIDACTIC SERMON
BY THE ESTIMABLE DR MARSTON

Conquer then, I say, conquer the lusts of the flesh; trample them beneath the feet; crush them as men crush venomous reptiles. Live loftily and purely, admit no evil thought; do what good thou canst, and thou shalt inherit God's Kingdom. To the righteous evil desires never come, and the most lovely career is that which like the sun swerves not in its path and sinks to rest amidst the peaks of the country of Beulah. The only perfect man is he whose life is calm and passionless, etc. etc.

ALTHEA SWARTHMOOR TO DR MARSTON
15th November 1710.

It is harder than I dreamed to live without you, in the now uncertain hope of a meeting after this world. Yet when you ask me to meet you again in the fir-wood for a long and sweet discourse such as we were wont to have, I cannot but say nay; for my brother's eyes have oft been set upon me lately, and he has questioned me in strange fashion concerning my abstraction and frequent absences. Dearest, I lied to him, and said, with all the blood of my body rushing to my heart, that I was much engaged in meditation and writing. I dare not meet you tonight, but if you rise betimes in the morning I will be in the Long Spinney. Till sunbreak then, yours,

ALTHEA.

FROM THE SAME TO THE SAME

16th November 1710.

Let it be now, my lover, let us not wait until age or disease brings us together. To die in the full expectation of joy, without one thought of the gloomy past, with its lurid clouds and too-scorching light—to die in the strongest appreciation, uncaring for men's calumny—is my hope and heart's desire. And even if there be no future but eternal sleep, 'tis eternal sleep at thy side. What more can a tired, loving woman wish for than rest by the man she adores? But there is another country, of that I am assured. So we will brave it together, seize Death at the height of Life, and enter, with unwarped souls, a new existence.

I have been to gaze upon our old trysting places for the last time. Shall we be permitted to visit them when, existing for each other, we pass hand in hand through the air?

At midnight Althea Swarthmoor will be counted amongst the Dead. She calls thee—she bids thee welcome.

*

Tradition is silent as to the precise manner of the lady's end. Suffice it to say that she died violently at the appointed time. Dr Marston survived her by forty years; becoming in turn Dean of Barnchester and Bishop of Norbarry. Besides twelve volumes of sermons, he wrote a 'Dissertation on the Human Feelings,' which is still notorious for its triteness.

THE NOBLE COURTESAN

he *Apology of the Noble Courtesan* was fresh from the printers; the smell of ink filled the antechamber. The volume was bound in white parchment, richly gilt; on the front board was a scarlet shield graven with a familiar coat-of-arms. Frambant turned the leaves hastily, and found on the dedication page the following address:—

> '*To the Right Honourable Michael,*
> *Lord Frambant, Baron of Britton*

'MY LORD,—It is not from desire of pandering to your position as one who has served his country wisely and well that I presume to dedicate to you the following Apology. A name so honoured, a character so perfect, need no illuming. 'Tis as a Woman whose heart you have stirred, into whose life you are bound to enter. For know, my Lord, that women are paramount in this world. In the after-sphere we may be Apes, but here we are the Controllers of Men's fates, and so, in the character of one whom you have stricken with love, I profess myself, my Lord, your Lordship's Most Obliged and Most Obedient Humble Servant,

THE NOBLE COURTESAN.'

Frambant flung the book angrily across the room. What trull was this who dared approach him so familiarly? His brows contracted;

his grey eyes shot fire; a warm dash of blood drove the wanness from his cheeks. The very thought of strange women was hateful: it was scarce a year since the wife he had won after so much striving had yielded up life in childbed, and he had sworn to remain alone for the rest of his days. Catching sight of his reflection in a mirror, he saw resentment and disgust there.

But when he looked again at the book he found that a note had been forced from its cover. Curiosity overcame, and he stooped and took it in his hand. Like the dedication it was addressed to himself: he unfolded it with some degree of fear.

'You will infinitely oblige a distressed Lover,' he read, 'if you meet her at Madam Horneck's bagnio. Midnight's the time. She will wear a domino of green gauze, a white satin robe braided with golden serpents.—CONSTANTIA.'

This communication fascinated him, and sitting down by the window he began to read the wildest book that ever was written. It was a fantastic history of the four intrigues of a fantastic woman. Her first lover had been a foreign churchman (an avowed ascetic) who had withstood her sieging for nearly a twelvemonth; her second, a poet who had addressed a sequence of amorous sonnets to her under the name of Amaryllis; her third a prince, or rather a king's bastard; and her fourth a simple country squire. Some years had elapsed between each infatuation, and madam had utilised them in the study of the politer arts. The volume teemed with quotations from the more elegant classic writers, and the literature of the period was not ignored. The ending ran thus:—

'It has ever been my belief that love, nay, life itself, should terminate at the moment of excess of bliss. I hold Secrets, use of which teaches me that after a certain time passion may be tasted with the same keen joy as when maidenhood is resigned. But, as the lively L'Estrange declares, "the itch of knowing Secrets is naturally accompanied with another itch of telling them," I fling aside my pen in fear.'

As he finished reading his brother Villiers entered the room. He was ten years Frambant's junior, and resembled him only in stature and profile. His skin was olive, his eyes nut-brown, his forehead still free from lines. He leaned over the chair and put a strong arm round his brother's neck.

'What is this wondrous book, so quaintly bound?' he said. 'By Venus, queen of love, a wagtail's song!'

Frambant flushed again, and raising the *Apology* flung it on the fire, where it screamed aloud.

'It is the work of an impudent woman,' he replied. 'Tomorrow all town will ring with it. She has dedicated it to me.'

'Surely a sin to burn such a treasure! Let me recover it.'

Villiers took the tongs and strove to draw the swollen thing from the flame, but it collapsed into a heap of blackness. The note, however, which Frambant had replaced, lay uncurled in the hearth, and the lad read its message.

At that moment one came with word that Sir Benjamin Mast, an old country baronet whom Frambant held in high esteem, lay at the point of death. 'The water crept higher and higher, and my lady thought you might choose to be with him at the last. The coach waited.' Frambant hurried downstairs, and was soon with the dying man. Sir Benjamin's hydropsy had swollen him to an immense size, but his uncowed soul permitted him to laugh and jest with heart till the end. His wife, a pious resigned woman of sixty, shared the vigil.

Darkness fell, and the chamber was lighted. Forgetful of all save his friend's departure he never remarked the passage of time, and not until after midnight when Mast's eyes were closed in death did his thoughts recur to the *Apology*. He took his seat in the coach with a grim feeling of satisfaction at the imaginary picture of the wanton waiting, and waiting in vain.

After a time, being wearied with excitement and lulled by the motion of the vehicle as it passed slowly along the narrow streets, he let his head sink back on the cushion, and fell asleep almost instantly. Five minutes could not have passed before he woke; but in the interval a curious idea had entered his brain. He remembered Constantia's account of her lovers, and her belief that life should wither at the moment of love's height, and simultaneously there came upon him the recollection of four tragedies which had stricken the land with horror. So overwhelming was the connection that he could no longer endure the tediousness of the journey, but dismissed his coach and walked down the Strand.

The first case was that of the Cardinal of Castellamare, who had been exiled from Italy, and who, after attending a court ball and mixing freely with the dancers, had been found dead on his couch; his fingers clutching the pearl handle of a stiletto, whose point was in his heart. Then, in the same conditions, Meadowes the laureate, the Count de Dijon, and Brooke Gurdom the Derbyshire landowner, had all been found dead. No trace of the culprit had been found, but in every case was the rumour of a woman's visit.

He reached the old road where stood his house, and stumbled against a weird sedan that waited in a recess by his gateway. An arching hornbeam hid it from the moonlight. Two men stood beside it attired in outlandish clothes. Frambant stopped to examine the equipage, and at the same moment a link-boy approached. He called for the light, and to his wonderment found that the bearers were blackamoors with smooth-shaven heads and staring eyes.

The sedan was of green cypress embellished with silver; a perfume of oriental herbs spread from its open windows. Frambant asked the owner's name, but the men with one accord began to jangle in so harsh a tongue that he was fain to leave them and go indoors.

In the antechamber a great reluctance to pass further came upon him, and he halloed for a serving-man. Frambant was merciful to his underlings, keeping little show of state. Rowley, the butler, came soon, half-dressed and sleepy. On his master's inquiry if any visitor had entered the house, he protested that he knew of none, though he had waited in the hall till past midnight. So, at the word of dismissal, he retired, leaving Frambant to enter his chamber alone.

He took a candle and went to the place where hung the portrait of his wife. There he paused to gaze on the unearthly loveliness of face and figure. His eyes dimmed, and he turned away and began to undress; but he was wearied and troubled because of his friend's death, and when his vest was doffed he threw himself upon a settle.

Presently the ripple of a long sigh ran through the sleeping house. Frambant sprang to his feet and went to the antechamber. There he heard the sound again: it came from the west wing, which for the last year had been reserved for Villiers's use. He caught up the candle and hurried along the cold passages. At his brother's door he paused, for through the chinks and keyhole came soft broken lights.

A woman was speaking in a voice full of agony:—

'Infamous, cruel deceiver! I have loved another, and given myself to thee!'

Again came that long sigh. Well-nigh petrified with fear, he fumbled at the latch until the door swung open. A terrible sight met his eyes.

Villiers lay stark on the bed, a red stain spreading over his linen. On the pillow was a mask that had been rent in twain. Beside him stood a tall, shapely woman, covered from shoulder to foot with a loose web of diaphanous silk. Her long hair (of a withered-bracken colour) hung far below her knees; a veil of green gauze covered the upper part of her face. She was swaying to and fro, as if in pain.

'Dastard,' she wailed. 'Thou hast attained the promised bliss unjustly. In my arms all innocently I slew thee, praying for thy soul to pass to my own heaven.'

Frambant's lips moved. 'My brother! my brother!'

The woman turned, glided towards him, and sank to her knees. She laughed, with the silver laughter of a child who after much lamentation has found the lost toy.

'It is thou,' she murmured. 'Let us forget the evil he hath wrought against us—let us forget and—love.'

She put out her hand to grasp his, he lifted his arm and thrust her away.

'Touch me not!' he cried.

She rose and faced him, supporting herself by grasping the bedpost.

'He has wronged us foully,' she said. 'The last love—the flower of my life—he would have cheated me of it!'

'Murderess! murderess!'

Her breath came very quickly; its sweetness pierced her veil and touched his cheek.

'What evil thing have I done?' she asked. ''Tis my creed to love and to destroy.'

Frambant went to the further side of the bed, and felt at his brother's heart. It was still, the flesh was growing cold. He flung his arm over the dead breast and wept, and Constantia stole nearer and knelt at his side.

'God,' she prayed, holding her hands above her head, 'pervert all my former entreaties, let all the punishments of hell fall upon the dead man! Sustain the strength that has never failed, that I may conquer him who lives.'

Frambant staggered away; she locked her arms about his knees.

'Listen,' she said. 'I loved thee from the first moment... When we met at the bagnio, he was disguised—not until I had killed him and looked on his brow did I know the truth.'

He made no reply, but considered the corpse in stony horror. So she released her hold and stood before him again.

'O cold and sluggish man! Why should I faint now? Cleopatra bought as hard a lover's passion.'

With a sudden movement she undid her robe at the neck, so that it whispered and slipped down, showing a form so beautiful that a mist rose and cloaked it from his eyes,—such perfection being beyond nature.

He moved towards the door, but she interrupted him. 'Is not this enough?' she cried. And she tore away the green veil and showed him a face fit to match the rest. Only once before had he seen its wondrous loveliness.

Again his eyes were drawn to Villiers. How he had loved the lad! Very strange it was: but at the instant his mind went back to boyhood, when he had made him hobby-horses.

'You have killed my brother! you have killed my brother!'

Constantia laughed wearily. 'Enough of that mixture of iron and clay. What is the penalty?'

'The law shall decide.'

She sprang forward and drew the knife from Villiers's breast. Frambant, however, forced it from her hand.

'For love of the wife who died, who even now is pleading at God's throne for me?'

Frambant's fingers relaxed. 'Hush!' he said.

'If I must die let it be at thy hands.'

'As you will: here… write.' He took a quill from the table and dipped it in the pool of stiffening blood.

Then he dictated, whilst she wrote in a firm hand.

'*I, Constantia, the Noble Courtesan, after slaying five men, meet with a just punishment. Seek not to know further.*'

She pressed close to him, smiling very tenderly. Her eyes were full of passionate adoration. As he raised the knife to her breast she caught his disengaged hand between her own…

Frambant wrapped her in the gauze. Then after pinning the paper at the head, and covering all with the gown of white satin that was braided with golden serpents, he carried her through the house and garden. Dayspring was near, the light appalling.

He reached the cypress sedan and laid his burden inside. The two blackamoors, who had gibbered sleepily the while, caught up the poles and bore the Noble Courtesan away.

THE HOLOCAUST

y husband and master the Bishop being called to Court, I journeyed yesterday to Broadlow. This morning my cousin's second lady vehemently desired me to tell all I know of her who once held the place she adorns so brightly. We were in the still-room, and the bantlings played on the floor, pulling the buckles of their mother's shoes and croodling like culvers. The request was over-sudden; to gain time, I opened the green lattice, and looking out to the herb-garden, said that little Bab herself had mounted by Neptune in the empty tank, and that in the sun-haze her countenance bore a plain likeness to one dead. And the row of clarifying waters in the window span round and round, and I swooned in madam's arms. But she consoled me, and now to her will, I write the following history, in trust that my lord may never be permitted to read. The fustian preface I will omit: 'tis but a record, unprofitable to the would-be adventurer, of life among the Barbary Rovers, of voyages to Feginny, of the saving of a ship's crew. Its six volumes are in the library, bound in pigskin, and revered by all. Of my cousin's three years in Bologna—years devoted to the joys of Italian gallantry—little is known, for on that score he hath ever been silent.

Thirteen years ago he returned for good—even then scarce more than a youth—with the Princess Bice. As you know report tells that ere he travelled to Italy he and I had had love passages. The grandams teased me, and (for I am assured, madam, that you have heard) once I stole away from Broadlow for a month, and came back lightened. We were close akin, and Bible patriarchs enjoyed their handmaids... When news came of his marriage I prayed for a renewal of his ardour; but at the first sight of the Princess Bice, as she sat at his side in the big chariot, I knew that all hope was unavailing. Yet she was not more beautiful than you, dear lady; indeed her face lacked the mysterious and tender charm that shines from a woman whom nature has intended for motherhood. Where you are snowy, she was olive, her black hair was dull and lifeless, not all quick with gold. If at any time Bab be taken into a darkened room, and the curtain lifted aback of her head some faint resemblance may be seen. Once, peeping unawares to the Princess Bice's dressing-closet, I saw her naked afront of the mirror—her wondrous hair unbound and tumbling to the floor. At my appearance her body flushed, and methought I watched a rushlight burning in a grove of firs.

Her manner was haughty: at first it seemed as she mistrusted me, looking from her spouse to me and back again with some suspicion. He leaned on her shoulder, and it was as though I heard, 'This is she—was not I foolish? nay, sweetheart, trust me!' The roses I had greeted her with were put carelessly aside.

My lord took my band with ancient friendliness. 'Diana is your gentlewoman,' he said. 'She will conduct you to the chamber.'

She smiled wryly, and laid her fingers on my palm, with a look bidding me kiss, so I raised their daintiness lothfully to my lips.

Then I led her through the lines of servants, past stately old Mother Humble—God rest her—and along the upper gallery to the bedchamber; and there, when the door was shut, she put her hands on my shoulders and drew me to the hearth.

'You were...' she said. 'He hath told me all, and I forewarn you—that if—again—I can be an enemy worse than Satan himself.

Yet, since you are his kinswoman, I had liefer you were my friend.'

At her girdle was a pouch made of silk, inwrought with a curious device of seed pearls; this she untied, and emptying to her table the comfits held therein, begged me to accept it as a token of her desire to act in all things well. From that even I became attached after a fashion: she held me as the flame holds the jenny-spinner. I strove to abhor her, yet was never happy save in her presence. 'Tis to her I owe the accomplishments that commended me to the fancy of my husband the Bishop. True, in my girlhood I could strum on the harpsichord, but my music was never more than picking the tune with ray forefinger and making base haphazard; and the Princess Bice taught me the rich *fugues* and solemn *adagios* of the Italian masters. The golden tissues that hang in the with-drawing-room we worked together on her toy-loom of ivory; and amongst my cousin's books are many vellum scrips of our illumination.

Months passed, and the gossips began to grow impatient, for the couple had already spent nigh upon a year in Paris, and yet there was no sign of my lord's happiness being consummated by the birth of one to inherit. The land, as you know, madam, goes with the title, and Sir Cadwallader, our Welsh kinsman, vowed, if 'twere ever his, to divide the park into farms and to chop down every tree. My lord did not hate him (Sir Cadwallader being a fool), but it tore his heart to think of such beauty being destroyed. Day by day—hour by hour—the desire for a lawful child grew upon him, and she herself became impatient beyond measure, questioning minutely all the matrons and perusing all that has been writ. Several false alarms were given, and these of themselves depressed the husband, for the continual deferring of hope fretted his soul. The chaplain spent long afternoons in prayer; and she harped on the idol-creed in which she had been bred, and sent to foreign shrines offerings of jewels and gold.

My lord's demeanour changed, and, although he was never harsh, her caresses grew distasteful to him, and I have often seen him take away her hands from his brow, and crave leave to meditate. Then she would sigh like one demented, and for awhile in her voice as she sang I could find notes of anger and of bruised tenderness, that wetted my eyes with tears, and made the fascination wherewith she held me deepen into love.

Three years after the return, my cousin was despatched to the Hague with secret messages for the Princess Mary of Orange, now—Heaven be praised—our queen, and in his absence, I saw her linger fondly over all that brought him to mind. She would sit in his chair, study his favourite books, and even kiss the breast of his coats, as if, perchance, she might detect some lingering aroma.

Once she strove with the women in the harvest-field, hoping thus to cast away the curse of barrenness. At sunset—she had gleaned from noon—a wench passed by with her by-blow, and she turned pale and sick, and came back to the house.

'Diana,' quoth she. 'God's mercy it unduly dispensed. Yon beggar with her babe is starving. Go privately and bring the woman here, and feed her in my room!'

So I went and filled the strumpet with good things. Whilst she ate, the Princess Bice stole the babe away, and when the half bemused mother noted its disappearance and cried out, I ran to the cabinet, and found madam, with the child patting her naked breasts and chuckling most jocundly.

Sometimes days passed without her making comment on her grief, but anon she would lament. ''Tis not that I love children, Diana, but that I love my spouse. Love him—said I—marry, I adore him! Such is my devotion that were I to die in travail I should be tenfold more happy than to live unchilded.'

Each morning she writ an account of how the preceding day had been spent; once by chance I tumbled on the unlocked book and read: 'I am indeed weary, for what I know of his past assures me that I alone am to blame. Nay, I would yield up everything—cast away my riches—turn to the humblest wife in the land could I but once again wear him in the flower of our passion. Yesterday I pondered, 'twas as if between heaven and me hung a curtain of rusty steel God might not hear through. I have prayed and prayed and naught answers! I am tempted to turn to the Powers of Darkness. Are there no necromancers—no half-devils in human form who may help me? For now I am desperate and would travel over red-hot plough-shares to compass my desire.'

A thousand preparations were made for my cousin's home-coming. Every friend and kinsman of note was ordered, for the earldom had been given to reward his successful embassy. The Princess Bice grew paler and paler as the day approached, and mention of him brought the poppies to her cheeks. She had devised quaint entertainments, and the thought of his return made her heart beat so loudly that I might hear.

On an October evening she and I, hearing the beacon fired on Comber Knab, where had been stationed a watcher, set out to drive across the park, where in the abysses writhed white vapours, like the steam from ever-shifting pots. She leaned from one window of the chariot; I from the other. The air was soft, but permeated with some subtle dulness; in the far landskip the basin-shaped depression of the Black Rake, surrounded by its tree-fringed cliffs, resembled an immense, solitary mere, with blackly glazed surface. The oaks of Hollym Chase wagged their heads above the underwood: the drowsy rooks wheeled to and fro. Twice the scritch-owl cried, and hills and valleys caught the horrid sound and echoed it with many reverberations: once a pike in the sullen stream sprang up and fell with heavy splashings. This was the good-night of all wild things; for after it the gloom deepened into inkiness, and across the sky was drawn a web denser than that of all former nights.

At the Cammer-Gate, where the wooden bridge crosses the gulf, the chariot drew up sharply, for an old man barred the way. He spake no word to the drivers, but moved slowly to the door from which my mistress leaned, and in the glimmering light of the lamp I marked his strangeness. His countenance was that of a physician, his attire of velvet edged with sable. He spoke in a foreign tongue, and she answered, her voice full of sharp gladness. 'Twas not Italian—that I knew full well—but rather a barbarous lingo. Soon he threw into her lap a small packet, and pointing with a yellow hand to a copse of beeches, allowed the vehicle to pass. In a few minutes my lord had met us, and taken his seat by his wife's side.

That night he was mightily loving. After supper, when the dance was opened, he was even handsomer than in the days when he had been lord of my own heart; and the Princess Bice seemed transfigured with delight. All the folk noted it; and many lamented that so fit a couple should be so unprofitable. Then, the morrow being Sunday, Dean Bastler, my mother's uncle, who was deaf and decrepit, read his sermon on the relationship of Elkanah and his wife, taking for his text '*Penninah had children, but Hannah had no children.*' He had never been a respecter of persons, and the discourse was little qualified to please, though, forsooth, the gaffer was eloquent enough. He told naught of Hannah's joy, but recounted from history many instances of unprofitable wedlock, and declared that SIN alone was the cause. At the end he offered a lengthy prayer that the Almighty would see fit to bestow children on his host and hostess; and my lord, covering his face with his hands, which thing he was not wont to do, cried out *Amen!* As we left the chapel his lady fell on his bosom and whispered, 'Am I not better to thee than ten sons?' But he put her from him in silence.

An hour later I was sent for to her chamber, where I found her worn out with the frenzy of weeping. 'All is over,' she said. 'For love's sake be it done.'

My lord had cause to set out for London soon afterwards, and she bade him farewell with much tenderness. That night she drew me to a private place and undid before me the packet the old man had flung into her lap. 'All it holds I know,' she said, 'but 'twill be strange to you.' And she showed me a handful of pastilicos. 'Light one,' she said.

I did as she bade me, and instantly a silence fell upon the place, so that even the crackling of the sea-coal was no longer heard. The air became redolent with marvellous perfumes, and I heard one tap-tapping at a door I wot not of, and felt unseen hands touching mine. She laughed. 'Tonight I will lie in the state-bed,' she said. 'A whimzie has taken me: see that the purest linen is laid, and every window tightly fastened.'

Midnight was near when she withdrew from the company that was still in the house. At the foot of the staircase she trembled violently, and would have me clasp her waist; and when I had helped her undress she delayed me with a thousand pretexts, sitting uneasily in her chair by the fire and talking feverishly. On a table I saw in a copper chafing-dish a charm of pastilicos; I made as though I would disturb its symmetry, but she called me to her side. 'Nay, Diana, do not destroy my plan!' she gasped. 'Give me the taper.'

I placed it in her hands; she lighted it, and moved to the chafing-dish and touched the pastilicos one by one. Then I flew to the door, but she followed me open-mouthed and caught me in her arms. Her lips said, though no sound came, 'Stay with me! stay with me!'

My limbs lost all power and I fell to the floor. The Princess Bice crawled into the bed. From the pastilicos arose an angry melody; then all was silent. Soon the air of the chamber trembled and gathered together over the smoulderings; and hovering there I beheld the figure of a man so fearfully and so miraculously beautiful that my eyes were dazzled. The curtains parted and fell to, and I saw no more.

At daybreak I felt her breath on my cheek, and heard her command of silence. Some time before noon all the servants were called together in the Council Room, where my mistress, very haggard but full of triumph, sat in the great seat from which Mall of Broadlow had dispensed judgment. 'Friends,' she said softly, 'for I may call you friends, I have news of import. Your master's trouble will soon be removed, for I have cause—and 'tis not hope now—but truth certainly—to believe that in due time I shall bring him a child.' So unexpected was her announcement that even those who had regarded her with disfavour, fell to their knees, and, as she passed through their midst, caught the edges of her skirt to kiss. Dean Bastler had stood at the door and one had repeated her words loudly, and he raised his hands in benediction; but she passed without any sign, and, although she spoke not of it to her guests, all matrons divined the cause of her vapourish spirits. And when my lord returned 'twas to find the house mad with delight. The months passed quickly; all preparations were made for the lying-in; but the Princess Bice herself took interest in naught save her husband's devotion.

The night of her lightening came at last, and by her request I sat with her before her labour. She had instructed me to light at a certain time the pastilico that still remained. As the clock struck I obeyed, and saw her rise from her bed and leave the chamber, ever increasing the space between us: I followed—sank upon the stairs—strove vainly to cry for succour.

Afterwards I crawled on hands and knees through many long-deserted passages, and into the open park. Her bare feet passed hurriedly over the grass in the distance, then turned across to the road, and to the wooden bridge where we had met the old man. She reached the beech copse, and ere she entered a flame leaped forward to embrace her; I heard a long and terrible sigh. From the house came a crowd of searchers, headed by my lord: amidst the heart-burnt wood they found Bab lying on a bed of charred leaves.

ROXANA RUNS LUNATICK

mongst the May poetry in the ninety-first volume of the British *Review* is the following composition by Lady Penwhile, whose Roxana had shaken the town for a whole season.

'Placed in the hand of the Satyr who guards the Puzzle-Pegs at N——, with a tress of hair for Hyperion.'

> *If so be that Hyperion visit thy stately lawn on the anniversary of our parting, O Satyr, wilt thou tell him that R—— hath often sigh'd for him there, and that, tho' she has worn green Hellebore, such as he gave her a year agone—when he vow'd an early return—her hopes grow ever fainter and fainter. Say to him that she is bound in golden chains, but that her heart sings when she thinks of him—(ay, her heart is ever singing)—whisper that she loves him more as every moment passes. And when thou hast done all this, bid Pan trill from his pipes, whilst thou chantest this ditty.*

Five halting verses follow, wherein 'tis told that the lovers had parted, that Roxana had wedded an old man, that she felt incapable of expressing in words the vehemency of her passion. But dear, pleasing ghosts haunted her chambers day and night.

My lord's cast-off doxy sent the journal, with a venomous letter bidding him rub his forehead, for fear of the cuckoo. So he pondered in his book-room, his half-blinded eyes fixed upon the logs; and, after many struggles with his better nature, he devised a plot worthy of Satan himself.

For Roxana was a prize worth keeping. She was pale, exquisitely pale. One forgot her eyes, but remembered that somewhere in her face was seen the sudden starting of a timid woman's soul... Hast ever watched the heart of a palm-catkin when a wanton hand has fired it? Lurking under the outer blackness are red and yellow intermixed. Such was the colour of her hair that fell from nape to heel. Hands that alone might have quenched lawless desires: of a subtle pink, like the ivory that comes from Africk.

Few women could have given such devotion as she gave my lord. By some stratagem, some wild persuasion in her moment of wavering, he had gained possession. Compassion weakens distaste, and he had posed long as one broken-hearted. How daintily did she acknowledge his requirements, how sweet her service had become! When he had decided concerning Hyperion, his punctilio was greater than ever: the house rang with shrill commands for madam's comfort, and he sat hour after hour listening to her tenderest songs. She was a lutanist too, and great in the Italian masters.

On Oak Day, when men and maids bore the garland through the park, a country fellow came to mistress and delivered her a note. My lord was not present, but she grew faint and chill, and had much ado to applaud the pageant. With unseemly haste she withdrew to her chamber and read there—

'Many days have passed ere I could summon courage. At twilight tomorrow we will meet; I have discovered the place. What manner of love was mine erstwhile that thou wert false?'

In her cabinet were many choice silks. She made a bag of the richest, and put the folded sheet inside, and spread ambergris upon it, then hung it between her breasts. That night as she slept her fingers relaxed, and my lord took thence the token, and read it, gnashing his teeth. He put it back: so that in the morning flush, when her hand sought the thing, it seemed untouched.

That day passed so wearily! In her spouse's company she was gay and brilliant; all her paleness had disappeared, and a feverish red pulsed in her cheeks. And he was brimful of paradox and of jesting, but sometimes she trembled because of the fearsome coldness of his looks. Once, when she fawned upon him he put her away, not untenderly.

'Sweetheart,' he said towards sunset, 'an' if thou wert false!'

'Ay, me,' she faltered, for the repetition of Hyperion's words struck her with terror. 'False! false!'

It was growing dusk; he peered close to the clock-face. 'More than two months have passed since we came here,' he noted, breaking the ominous silence. 'And yet this place is strange to you. Let us visit the old house—see, here are the keys! Dearest, lean on my arm.'

They passed through the garden to the porch and so to the mildewed avenues of the pre-Elizabethan part where all the lumber was stored. My lord saw Roxana's bodice swell as if the threads would burst. Soon they reached a great hall lighted with green windows, whose dimness scarce revealed the many sacks of too long-garnered grain, where the mice ran in and out. There, near the foot of a staircase that led to the gallery, he left her, and she heard the clicking of a lock.

My lord went to an upper chamber whence he could see the outlet of the maze. The belling of his red-eyed dogs as they strutted in their leash tickled his ears: he laughed and rubbed his forehead. The moon rose, and he could hear Roxana clamouring in the hall. After a while he descended by another way, and took out his death-hounds, and went towards the trysting-place.

Roxana could not know what happened in the darkness. The agony of the man whose every vestige of clothes was torn away, and whose white flesh gaped bloodily, was hidden from her by the seven feet of masonry that parted them as he leaped madly into the courtyard. Nor could she hear his worn, querulous cry—such a cry as the peewit makes before dawn. Yet, withal, her hands began to drum in her lap.

When the darkness was intense my lord came back. He felt for Roxana in the place where he had left her. She was not there: an hour before she had climbed to the gallery. He groped painfully round the walls.

In one corner soft delicious things like nets of gossamer fell on his fingers. He stooped to the floor, and touched more of them. Above was a sound of tearing, but no panting nor indrawing of breath. Another web fluttered past his face; his lips began to quiver. It was Roxana's hair.

THE MADNESS OF
BETTY HOOTON

hen the postchaise had borne old Basil Constable to the gate of the park that surrounded his ancient home, he alighted, choosing to revive the bittersweet of memories in solitude before passing to the house. The post-boy he bade drive on and instruct the housekeeper (of whose name he was as yet ignorant) to feed him, by the new master's orders, on the best of her larder. As soon as the horses, which had galloped all the last stage of fifteen miles, had passed out of sight in the hollow of the avenue he turned abruptly into a narrow alley of drenched lilacs, all white and heavy with bloom. An hour ago the heavens had closed their gates, and after a week of continuous rain, the sun, with a mighty effort, had thrust aside the heavy clouds and made the air hot as that of a glass-house.

The lilac walk led to a mausoleum with a green copper cupola. Basil found the door ajar, and entered the chapel. There was a deep marble well in the centre, and on the eastern side a brass and ivory crucifix, before which stood a *prie-dieu* chair, covered with moth-eaten tapestry.

He knelt on the cushion and buried his face for a few moments; then rose and descended by a spiral staircase to the vault where his dead kinsfolk lay, with their feet against the circular outward wall of the well. Alabaster slabs elaborately gilt concealed the head-piece of each coffin save that of his brother, which looked oddly out of place in the gloomy light that came through the rusty gratings; for the crimson velvet was as yet unsullied, and the ornaments glistened as brightly as when they had left the silversmith's hand. A wreath of withered flowers, placed there for decency's sake by some hireling, lay softening upon the floor in front. The air was tainted with a charnel smell; flies with blue-shotten wings boomed to and fro.

As Basil stood glancing half-wistfully at the two empty receptacles that still remained, his hand moved involuntarily to his breast, and brought forth the miniature of Betty Hooton, the girl whom he had loved forty years ago, and whose rejection of his suit had driven him to the East, there to enter commerce as a Smyrna merchant, and increase by a hundredfold a cadet's patrimony.

A black beauty, with thick ringlets, one shading either temple, the others falling to flushed plump cheeks and elegantly-curved neck. Eyes deep blue and languishing, a straight thin nose, upper lip bow-shaped—lower lip pouting like a ripe fruit, a chin made surely for no other aim than to nestle in a lover's palm.

She wore a bodice of oyster-coloured silk, cut so low that the dint of her back was visible; a crimson scarf drooped from her left shoulder. The right arm fell gracefully from a butterfly sleeve, caught in the middle with a garnet lozenge from which hung one great pearl and two sapphires. This trinket her mother, Anastasia Dornton, had worn in her stage triumphs, ere she had won, modestly and with good repute, the favour of, and soon enough the honourable conjugal estate with, Charles Hooton, seventh Earl of Longstone.

Basil had kept this, Betty's only gift to him, always hanging from a thin gold chain over his heart. She was the only woman he had ever loved, and her dismissal of him in his youth had killed all desire for womankind. Yet he had borne no malice, being a gallant gentleman, true as steel, and endowed with a good man's best gift—the power of bearing grief and physical pain without outward lament. Of the finest blood in England; but, as he was wont to declare, 'an ugly devil—ugly as Punchinello!' But such as study physiognomy would have been vastly delighted with his countenance, for all its hooked nose and wry mouth, because of the truth and tenderness of the sunken grey eyes.

After a while he replaced the miniature and moved again to the staircase. ''Tis a vastly unwholesome place for the recalling of a woman's beauty,' said he—'a beauty that, if she herself be not food for worms, must have long since faded in bleached hair and deep wrinkles!'

A profound depression overcame him as he thought of the past. He had felt but little affection for his dead brother, who had ever wilfully wronged him, and the vicinity of his corse was not accountable for this melancholy humour. Perchance it was the sudden cessation of his journey, taken hurriedly, after four decades of work so strenuous that he had scarce allowed himself breathing space; perchance a stagnancy created by the utter barrenness of his present life. He had dwelt so entirely apart from his own country that, save for his colleagues in London town, he knew none with whom he could claim even the title of acquaintance. A wall of ice had risen between him and his youth; even the old pleasaunce in which he had spent his earliest years seemed almost as unfamiliar as though he had never beheld its vistas before.

The lean old man hurriedly retraced his steps along the alley and entered the avenue. Between each lichened elm stood the leaden statue of a pagan deity, brought from France more than a century ago. He remembered them as brightly gilded and stately in their erectness; but now all were covered with a purple bloom. Olympus was no longer Olympus—the gods and goddesses had lost all dignity and grown pitifully ludicrous with age. Here and there a jagged gap showed on breast and shoulder; hanging from the thunderbolt of Jove and the quiver of Diana the paper-making wasp had fashioned her nest.

His melancholy increased to such a degree that he reached the great red-brick house and passed through the open doorway of the hall without casting his eyes over the frontispiece to discover what rack time had made. An elderly woman, whose head was covered with a crimped linen cap, stood curtseying beside the open gallery that led to the servants' quarters. She wore a mourning gown, and mittens of fine thread. A kindly, puckered-faced creature.

'I bid you welcome, Sir Basil,' she said, 'sure there's no liberty in taking so much upon myself, since I have served here from the time I were a wench grown.'

The new master nodded courteously. 'But that was long after I went away,' he responded. 'I have not seen Dalton Constable for forty long years.'

'Dear heart!' cried the woman, 'when you were a lad, I were still-room maid—young to the work, but apt to improve. Please you to come this way, master—there's a meal ready served in the dining-parlour.'

She conducted him to a vast saloon hung with Lely's portraits. A table at the further end, covered with damask and embellished with gilt glass and silver, was laid for his use. When he had taken his place, she removed the covers.

'We be under-served here, Sir Basil,' she said. 'For years and years, there's been none save myself and three wenches; and an old groom and keeper who sleep, gun by side, in the plate-room at night. I be Mrs Humble, the housekeeper. I wedded Nathan—him that held the butler's post when you were young. God rest him—but he's in Abraham's bosom, where a man should rest! The last butler Dalton Constable ever saw; and he, poor soul, cooled in his linens two-and-twenty years ago.'

Her garrulous officiousness warmed his heart; when she prepared to retire, he bade her stay longer and tell him of all the changes in the country—of who had died and who had been born. The question concerning the woman he had loved he dared not ask.

Mrs Humble was a devout woman, and her rigmarole was besprinkled with many pious ejaculations. Her master found it of pathetic interest. All the lads with whom he had hunted in his boyhood were dead and gone; some families were extinct, others had sunk into utter oblivion.

'There be none left,' she said at last—'none but the ladies Anastasy and Betty Hooton, who still live in Camsdale, and ne'er quit the bounds of their own valley.'

Basil looked up suddenly. 'Unwed!' he said, half to himself. 'How came it that two such girls should live unmated—two of the fairest creatures ever made?'

'Alack, master,' replied the housekeeper. 'Have you ne'er heard that Lady Betty lost her senses soon after your going, and that her sister e'er refused to budge from her side? A harmless, gentle madness, to be sure. Sir Digby, my late master (Heaven be his bed!), ne'er missed an evening without driving over in the chariot. 'Tis said as the playing blood in her veins (madam, the countess, being a stage-actress), warms up at such times. Lord! the serving folk tell the tale that she hath a little theatre for puppets true as life, to do the same thing over and over again.'

The old man filled his glass to the brim with generous wine. He held the reddened crystal above his head.

'Here's to her health!' he cried hoarsely. 'Here's to the health of Betty Hooton!'

Then he drank thirstily to the dregs, and, the tears gushing from his eyes, flung the glass against the mantel, covering the hearth with fragments.

'The chariot—the chariot,' he said, 'and at once, for I cannot rest until I have seen her!'

An hour later, in the blue parlour at Camsdale, after Basil had sat for some minutes in the midst of lac cabinets and tall Nankin vases and sandalwood screens, he saw Lady Anastasia, an ashen white ghost, attired in black paduasoy. She had entered so quietly that he was unaware of her coming until she laid her hand upon his shoulder.

'Ah, Basil,' she said mournfully, 'you have come at last! Come to two unfortunate women whose sole virtue is their remembrance of you.'

He had not forgotten the courtly fashion of his young manhood; he raised her smooth be-ringed fingers to his lips.

'I did not know,' he said. 'Had I known, my coming had been a lifetime ago.'

'But even then,' she said, ''twould have been too late. When you went away, you bore with you all my sister's happiness.'

The old man found the perfumed atmosphere intolerably oppressive; he moved to the oriel (where the moonlight and the dull flickering of haloed candles fought for supremacy), and threw open the lattice. Then he caught Anastasia's sleeve.

'I cannot understand,' he said. 'What does it mean? Betty drove me from her with harsh words—drove me—who have loved her all the days of my life!'

She covered her thin face. 'Do not ask for the whole truth,' she said. 'One came to her with lies of you—brought forged proofs of your inconstancy—so cleverly wrought that she might not doubt therein you had spoken of her as a wanton. And he, afterwards, feigning compassion, piqued her into a promise to wed.'

'God!' groaned Basil. 'My brother!'

'One summer eve, as they sat together in this very place, the demon of confidence came to him, and in the belief that her love was too great to be shaken, he told her of his baseness. And that night, as she lay stunned—silent as death—within my arms, her wits left her... Ah, do not cry out, Basil, we are all old—and she has never known unhappiness since that hour. Her eyes became for him the eyes of a basilisk—from then, until the time of his death, he came here night after night—not missing once in all those years—to gaze upon her and listen to her fond talk.'

'Let me see her!' he cried. 'My Betty!'

'First must I forewarn you,' she replied, 'that she has not changed as you and I have changed. Time has used her with miraculous kindness—you will find her to outward view as beautiful as when you went away. And she hath a strange recreation—even since his death she hath not ceased to delight in it. The puppet-stage, with which my mother solaced herself after her marriage, stands in the midst of the withdrawing-room; and thereon she plays with mannikins of wood her own piteous tragedy.'

She took him by the hand and led him up the oaken staircase to a state saloon, at whose further end, beneath a canopy of purple velvet, stood the chair of the first Earl of Longstone, who had risen to greatness and riches as the lover of an unmarried Queen. The walls were adorned with tapestry of Flemish weaving; along the frieze vividly coloured beasts and birds and trees and hills capered to the music of Orpheus.

''Tis nigh upon her time of entering,' said Anastasia. 'I pray you sit beside me afront her theatre, and together we will watch the play.'

As she spoke, the hangings of a side-door were thrust aside, and Betty entered, light-footed and merry, and ran towards her toy. The old man's breath came in gasps; all the muscles of his heart were knotted together. For Anastasia had spoken sober truth, and her sister had lost no jot of her loveliness. Oh, it was strange—strange to see her thus—it was unnatural and beautiful and hurtful. Still with her jetty ringlets, still in lustrous silk and crimson scarf.

She drew a taper from its sconce, and held it to the wicks of the footlights. This done, she confronted her audience, and began to speak in a whimsically tender voice.

'Good people,' she said; 'if you but have patience, you shall see here the story of *Love Betrayed, or the Virgin Deceived*, writ by—I know not whom, and played by little creatures with human souls.'

She hastened to the back of the theatre, and began to jerk two little dolls—dressed as a swain and his sweetheart. The water burst from Basil's eyes, for the words each spoke were the words he and she had used in the days of their courtship. His affection was so wrought upon that he saw nought foolish in the stilted movements of the puppets as they strutted to and fro, with a background of gaily painted trees, and a foreground of terraced walk and mere.

The same soft, cooing voice for each—not a sentence, not a word but he already knew by heart...

Down tumbled the drop-scene, and the worker of the puppets came again to the front.

'The first act's ended,' she said, 'and now I will sing.'

She took up an ancient lute that lay near by, and lifted the green riband over her ringlets. Then she sang, very fantastically, with sudden hushings and swellings, the second verse of a lyric of Aphra Behn's:—

> 'Because Edymion once did move
>   Night's goddess to come down,
> And listen to his tale of love,
>   Aim not thou idly at the moon.
> Be it thy pleasure and thy pride
>   That, wrecked on stretched desire,
> Thou canst thy fiercest torments hide,
>   And silently expire.'

'Friends all,' she continued, gently laying aside the instrument, 'the love of our two folk turns to tragedy. We shall see how a false villain—ay, a false, false villain—bred ill-feeling in the maid, and how she, finding that all his tales were but slanderous lies, took her heart between her hands thus, and broke it clean asunder!'

Basil could bear the strain no longer; in spite of Anastasia's hindering grasp, he rose from the settee and went to the back of the theatre, whither she had again retired.

'Betty!' he faltered. ''Tis I, Betty—I, your Basil—Basil who hath always loved you!'

The beauty arched her white neck haughtily. 'Sir,' she said, 'the Lady Elizabeth Hooton, at your command.'

'Nay, Betty, my life, my love! See, here rests the miniature you gave to me' (he tore open his vest) 'here against my heart! Each breath of mine hath stirred it, Betty, for more than forty years. No hour hath gone by without a dear thought being yours, my

Betty—no dream came but with you in't. 'Tis I, Betty, your poor, lonely Basil.'

For one brief moment her eyes were resplendent with the fire of wondering joy, then the veil fell once more.

'There is no Betty,' she whispered, 'no Betty and no Basil. The wretched Betty lies buried under the deep grass in the greenwood—at the very spot where she sent away the lad she loved… Good friends—the second act.'

MY FRIEND

hey have just told me that I cannot live beyond midnight. But this is no confession of guilt. Knowing that I was soon to see an unknown land, and that the friend I had won (the first and the last) loved me so dearly that he would be unhappy unless his hand were clasping mine—did I sin in my desire that he should go forth, and be waiting for me?

A fortnight ago I met him in the street. His head was hanging, his gait dejected, he was talking to himself. I stood watching him. As he approached, long before he really saw me, a change came over him: his figure grew erect, his face sharpened, his lips closed. He smiled strangely as our eyes met, and I felt exultant in the knowledge that such spontaneous gladness should never degenerate. I took his hand, and held it so long that the townsfolk looked and laughed.

'Gabriel,' I said, 'I have been dreaming of you again. I thought we had gone together to spend Sunday on the Naze of Blakelow.' A warm flush of pleasure spread over his face. 'Yes,' I went on, 'and you said in my dream that it was the last of the vignettes' (he had a way of calling our short holidays 'vignettes'), 'and I replied that this was on a grander scale.' He laughed, though I am sure he did not understand. 'If only you *would* go,' he made answer, 'I feel that I should be so much better for the mountain air. I am out of tune with all the world but you. I can start soon—in two hours, if you will.' So we met later. I looked on his dark face, and my heart leaped out to him. I forgot the acrimony of living with those whose only feeling for me was one of relationship; forgot the Dead Sea apples of my past, and felt joyful beyond expression: often pressing my hand to my heart, where the toy I carried nestled in its scarlet sheath.

Something in his face told me that he was sad. 'You are not happy now?' I said. 'I am not,' he replied. 'I am envious of you. Your life is so free: you have no business affairs to drag you to earth. But I shall be happy soon; it is good to be with you.' As for myself, I never was happier. My spirits rose quickly; from the far recesses of my brain I brought the wildest thoughts to lay before him. Flashes of inspiration that only showed in his presence (sparks of divine fire, perhaps) spun themselves into one glittering string for his sake.

We were to sleep at the Eagle, a hostelry whose prosperity began dwindling with the decline of coaching. It lies eighteen miles from our town, midway between the hamlets Ashstraw and Glosboro. Neither of us had been there before; but the guide-book was explicit. The weather was dull; but it took no hold on me. We left the precincts of the town and reached the great moorland with its bridle-path. When the dense smoke of the furnaces had given place to fresh, heather-scented air, I essayed a question.

'Are you still depressed?'

'No,' he cried, with his brown eyes full of mirth.

'Then you are perfectly happy?' said I. (It was always gratifying to be assured of this.)

'I cannot be otherwise when I have left the town with you,' he said.

And at this I took his arm, for it was always less painful to myself when I walked close to him. We began to talk of our dreams. Circumstances had bound him to a profession that chafed his very core; but Nature had given him aspirations, and miraged him a future as great (if as worthless) as my own.

How daring I grew! Farther and farther I had ventured down the heretical abyss. Gabriel's face gleamed with amazement: he drank it all in greedily. Was it not curious that I, who knew how fast the end was nearing, should have dared to relax my hold upon those snatches of hope which are as straws to the drowning man? After a time I turned the discussion—if you may call a monologue discussion—to my favourite theme, which is death. I had grown so morbid that I could pile horror upon horror. I gloated on the orthodox eternity: I drew brave pictures of my childhood's Satan in his environment of fire and gloom. But after the sunset rain came down in torrents. In five minutes we were wet to the skin. My clothes were old, my shoes let water; I had no umbrella, but walked under Gabriel's. Just before twilight the path left the heath, and descended abruptly to the grass-grown coach-road that runs along the side of the hill they call the Silver Patines. Evening fell. The rain hissed on the heather, and the wind, catching the few gnarled thorns, drew from them a dull, sonorous cry. The river, somewhat in flood, rushed over jagged stones; a few moorland sheep were sheltering under the rocks that lined his banks. Owls, so unfamiliar with man that they rattled their wings well-nigh in our faces, went whirring through the air. They started a train of abstract reasoning in me as to the doctrine of transmigration.

'Ah, Pythagoras's metempsychosis!' I said to myself. I am certain that my tongue was silent; yet Gabriel smiled. I was slightly hurt, and, drawing my arm away, walked to the other side of the road, refusing to shelter beneath the umbrella. Soon came the knowledge that his smile contained no touch of contempt, but was only a glad movement for that he knew himself in such sympathy with me as to apprehend my unvoiced fancy. I hastened to his side, and begged him to forgive. But the charm was broken for a time. My thoughts had withered, my words were grown unpregnant. So his happiness fled, there came a sequence of those drossy moments when silence is loathsome, yet must be. We felt them keenly. My head grew hot with grief: I it was who had snapped the golden cord. We had not walked much further before Gabriel stopped and leaned his cheek on the wet stones of the wall.

'I wish that I were dead,' he murmured. 'I am tired.'

'Then shall we go back?' I said. 'Perhaps it would be best. We are both wet through: the inn may be uncomfortable—the rooms damp.'

He turned and gave me his hand. 'Go back?' he gasped: 'go back? Why—I wish—that I might pass—all my life thus!'

'With the shadows and the rain and the wind's howling,' I added laughingly, 'and no home, but inn after inn, strange bed after strange bed?'

'No home, and you with me!' he cried. 'Ah! I could forget everything if you were with me.'

By now we could see nothing afar from us. At intervals a sound as of heavy hoofs a-splash on the road warned us to go warily. Ever and anon we waded tiny gullies. Thrice blasts of warm air, from the airt in which we were going, fluttered about my cheek and my hands. I fancied, and said, that these were disembodied souls hustled by the storm. Gabriel could not feel them; and when I said that another and yet another had touched me, held out his hands without avail. The wind piped with a shriller sound, changing its tone to one that mystified me, for we had passed the region of trees. Long-drawn sighs came first, then chords of broken melody, then whisperings as it were in a foreign tongue. Why, we were nearing some Druid stones! Ten yards to the right they stood, in a perfect circle, stately and tall, their bases hid in ling.

Again a change in the wind's song: a thousand shrieks as though men were being tortured with sharp knives. I turned to Gabriel, and spoke; it seemed as if my voice leaped with the storm. 'Gabriel,' I cried. 'What is it?' His wan face came near to mine. 'I hear nothing,' he said. 'Come, let us hurry; it is getting late—they may not let us in.' And a change had come into his voice too; a troubled note, as if a dread had swept over him. 'You are not afraid?' I said lightly. He made no reply.

Suddenly, as I listened, the heavens were rent from end to end, and a flash of lightning leaped out: to laugh and dance and gambol on the hilltops, and then skip hissing across the river.

A sacrificial hymn was beginning at the Circle—a naked and bleeding victim was bound to the altar—fire and water were there—the long-bearded priests shook their white robes—the sharp knife glittered—and my own stiletto waxed heavy, as it strove to draw me downwards. I lifted my hand: just to touch the smooth pearl handle! Again the skies opened, but with only a momentary gleam; one glance of the Almighty Eye. But it was not so swift as to prevent me from seeing the face of the Sacrifice. 'They have taken him away,' I faltered. 'He was at my side an instant ago.' Gabriel drew me away.

He was shivering. For the first time that night I thought of his health. 'Let us run,' I said. 'Give me your hand.' He lowered his umbrella (it was of small use now, for the wind had risen—risen!) and then, hand in hand like young children, we ran together. It was delightful; but we were tired. So our feet were soon stayed, and, standing at an abrupt turn of the valley, we were aware of a lonely light agleam in the darkness—the light of the first house we had remarked since our nightmare town. It disappeared ere we reached the threshold. A sign-board flapped uneasily, and we found that our journey was done. It was a vision of gables, with dormers and oriels; immense beams here and there upheld a sodden thatch; the chimney stacks, huddled and incongruously set, gave forth no friendly smoke. With a mad desire to harangue, I ascended the perron-staircase, and grasping its scrolled balustrade, began:—'Friend Gabriel, who listenest with the night bats and the darkness—what is the soul?' (Heedless of the pelting rain and Gabriel's tender lungs: brute that I was!) 'Nay,' I continued, 'rather what is the body? That I can define: husks—husks—a frippery of flesh!' The light came again, this time at an upper window. I struck the door with my fist; but nobody heeded.

A few nights before Gabriel and I had seen a strolling company play *Cymbeline*: so I began to mimic the stentorian voice of the Imogen. The keyhole, which was hard to find, was covered with a stiff and rusty scutcheon, which I had some difficulty in moving. At last, though, I could press my lips to the void, and 'What, ho, Pisanio!' I cried. Gabriel was too tired to smile; but footsteps came along the passage, and after a wearisome time the bolts were all undrawn, and the door opened as wide as the chain would run. A harsh and feeble voice came forth upon the night: 'What do you want?' 'Supper and a room,' I said. Another minute, and we stood in a yellow-washed hall, hung at even distances with dusty stags'-heads. A few paintings of scriptural scenes, done in Guercino's style and framed in black, were fixed between queer oak carvings, the subjects taken from the superstitions of Holy Church, for in the first I saw Christ, crowned with a great golden aureole, descending a ladder into flames that coiled snake-like about the bottom rungs.

I showed it to Gabriel; but he scarce seemed to heed. His eyes and mind were fixed on the woman who stood looking at us, the candle held above her head. To tell the truth, I never saw a stranger creature. She wore a long gown of amber cloth, padded voluminously, but unbuttoned at the bosom and showing her brown, wrinkled throat. Her feet were shoeless, and were covered with grey stockings. Her face was profoundly unhallowed. There were remains of marvellous beauty; unparalleled eyes, pure and light blue and unfathomably deep, under white, knotted, bushy brows. No other feature did I note, save loose, prehensile lips and rippling flaxen hair that fell, like a young girl's, in great locks over her shoulders. In truth, she had sinned monstrously; and in punishment thereof Nature had gifted the most alluring of her sweetnesses with a perenneity of youth: so making her a frightful anomaly—a terrifying Death-and-Life. She stood bowed; her mouth twisting, her eyes falling with inquiry on me. Gabriel she scarce observed; and I know not what in myself attracted her. I was excited, and could scarce repress my mirth. Yet, when I think of it, how oddly laughter would have rung along that mildewed passage! How Sara in the painting of the Angel's Visit would have smiled a grimmer smile!

After a while, sighing heavily, she turned and led the way to a great room. Here she lighted two candles on the central table and, bidding us wait for a little, disappeared. We could hear her movements grow more and more distant. I sat on a tiny settee—(bah, how cold it was!)—whilst Gabriel wandered about, lifting the candle at times to the Italian landscapes painted on the panelling. 'The Colosseum!' he cried suddenly—'and not ruined, but in its full pride. See, I can't understand this!' He drew me towards the picture (poor Gabriel was always a lover of art),—I looked, and was amazed to see the building I had so often dreamed of glistening in the moonlight. But my gaze was not so deeply interested as his, and, leaving the picture, it fell upon the miniature of a young girl above the mantelpiece. A host of memories came, my eyes grew dim, my chin trembled. Surely—surely—the likeness was familiar? Yet it could not be. The woman with the web of flaxen hair, Lenore whom I had lost, but never loved, Lenore whom I had forgotten years ago. Lenore with a rose—a lust-flower—a flower of volupty—warming the iciness of the breasts it glowed between! *Lenore! Lenore! Lenore!*

I could not show it to Gabriel. It was not Lenore. How should the portrait of the holy witch, who slept so peacefully, encounter me here of all places? Fie! An instant, and I had fallen to speculating as the jack-o'-lanthorn of my folly bade, when the hostess came back. She bore a pan of live coals and a bundle of fagots; these she threw on the hearth, so that a bright flame was soon leaping giddily up the chimney. 'Gentlemen,' she said, 'your chamber is making ready. Supper shall be laid anon.'

Gabriel and I went to the fireside now, and stood in the heat. He was silent but not unhappy: indeed the gleaming of his sunken eyes went far towards dispelling the passion awakened by the miniature. Again the woman entered, this time with a laden tray. She drew the table nearer the fire, and, having spread the cloth and arranged the quaint china, produced from a large press dishes of old-fashioned confections—rose-petals, clusterberries, and almond comfits. Also, there were birds dressed in a way that I had never seen before. We grew very hungry at the sight. A sense of possession came over me: I was the host, Gabriel the guest. I assumed the honours. 'Pray, make yourself comfortable!' I said, and we both laughed until the lamplight fluttered. He could laugh best—with the most singleheartedness. Outside the wind cried like a beaten child, and the gusts in the corridors were as mournful as the last breaths of a dying man. As no rain beat upon the windows, I surmised that the weather was fair, and I drew one of the sombre curtains. But I could see nothing but blackness: so with a shudder and a joyful thanksgiving that we were indoors, I went back to the table.

The collation done, I rang for the dishes to be removed. When, after a long time, the woman came, her suspicious curiosity was gone, and she moved in apathy. As she left us for the last time, after placing two logs across the andirons, she courtesied foolishly. 'Gentlemen,' she said, 'the door of your chamber opens on the first landing. A fire is burning there: you will see the reflection when you wish to retire.'

Beside the hearth were two great leathern armchairs, shaped like sedans. Gabriel took one, I the other. They were padded deep, and exquisitely comfortable. I leaned back, gazing dreamily on my friend's face; for I wanted his features burned into my brain. He enjoyed the examination, but soon distracted me by speech.

'It seems a hundred years since we left the town,' he said; 'we are in quite another world—in a realm full of romance—'

'Gabriel,' I interrupted, as if I had not heard his remark, 'will you tell me the perfect truth if I ask you something?'

'Yes,' he replied. 'I promise seriously.' I covered my forehead with my handkerchief. I was fain to hide my look. 'Then,' I said, 'it is this: *Do you really care for my friendship?*'

'My dear fellow,' he cried impetuously, 'why do you ask? I thought you knew before now. There is nobody else on earth for whom I care a thousandth part as much.'

'Have I been of any use to you?' I asked: unnecessarily, for I knew what his reply would be. He reiterated my words.

'Any use to me—any use to me? Why I had sunk into a dreadful slough before I knew you. It had been a sleep of years and years, and you helped me out of it all, and made me human again. You have brought me ideal happiness in our friendship.'

I was silent a moment, then I said tentatively: 'Suppose that I had to take a long journey—one with no chance of returning? What of your friendship then?'

His face grew very white. 'If you take such a journey,' he said, 'I go with you.'

A stillness followed, so profound that I was afraid lest the beating of my heart should attain to him and stir his sympathy. The gleaming logs on the hearth were as quiet as if the lapping flames were magical; and a dull, subtle perfume spread from the wisps of azure smoke that came winnowing down the chimney. The mantel was wonderfully wrought—a masterpiece in carven oak. Lilith, the wife of Adam, stood to the left; the Queen of Sheba, her feet on Solomon's Mirror, to the right; on the transome, clustering and grotesque, were angels and fiends. It was in accordance with my imagination—wild and fantastic, and with no unity. I bent towards Gabriel to point it out, but seeing that, drowsy with the heat, he had let his head fall back to the cushion, and was already well-nigh asleep, I strangled my remark, and began conning his face once more. What a curious forehead! It was high: not narrow, but oddly misshapen, particularly above the eyes, where the great black brows, bristling on penthouses, gave a fiercely kind look. His nose was good, his moustache coarse and with bitten ends; his lips were full and unequal; his chin was square. Here was nothing fascinating, save the fact that it was the face of my only friend.

Soon, impatient that he should sleep when I was wide awake, I rose from my chair and began walking about the room. Not daring to look at the miniature again, I turned to the opposite wall. A cry of delight burst from me, for standing there was a satin-wood spinet with open lid. I read the label of Johannes Pohlman, and the date, 1781. I had cherished from my earliest childhood the desire of playing on such an instrument, and I drew out the needleworked stool, and ran my fingers lightly over the keys in an attempt to harmonise my thoughts. To my surprise the tone was neither discordant nor decayed, but echoed with a charming tinkling. In a minor, on a numbed undercurrent of bass, a melody like a thin gold wire began its incantation. I lost myself: I was the Spirit of the Music—not the fragile fool whose life should be required of him so soon! But the vein was soon exhausted, and I turned to Gabriel to find him awake and looking at me. 'What are you playing?' he said eagerly. 'I was dreaming unpleasantly, and the sound brought me to myself. I never heard anything like it' (he passed his hand over his forehead as if perplexed): 'it reminds me of twilight vapours in June, wind-borne across a marshy pool to die among foxgloves and wild aniseed on the farther shore.'

'You are right,' I replied. 'It is a requiem.'

Looking at my watch, I saw that it was now midnight, so I took up a candle and, lighting it at the fire, suggested sleepily that we should go to bed. Gabriel rose, and ascended the staircase at my side. The fagots in the bedroom had burnt low: only a dim red gleam was mirrored on the panelling of the landing and on the glossy door of a clock, above whose dial a curious arrangement showed the waxing and waning of the moon. Our chamber was large, and apparently was over the supper-room. No carpet covered the worm-eaten floor; but a few discoloured skin rugs, irregularly shapen, lay about, chiefly round the cedar bedstead in the middle, where on a volant angel, blowing a gilt bugle, leaned from the top of every post. I threw logs on the hearth, and while Gabriel undressed I lay on a couch from one of the recesses in the wall. As I rested, hot tears ran down my cheeks.

Gabriel drew aside the bed-curtains. I sprang to his side and took his hands. 'Stay,' I said gravely; 'you have not said your prayers.'

He laughed blithely. 'I never say them,' he replied. I did not relax my hold.

'For God's sake,' I muttered, 'say them tonight of all nights.'

His mirth died quickly: 'If you will sleep better with the knowledge, I will say them;' and he began to pray with a surprising beauty. I said *Amen* when all was done. In less than ten minutes he was fast asleep.

For me, I sat listening to the deathwatch sound in the region of my heart; the nearly silent drip-dropping of blood from the vessel, now well-nigh exhausted, whose emptiness means freedom. Its ticking alternated with the clock's, and each one brought a separate vision to my fancy—visions that I had thought ripped from my heart years ago. Visions of Lenore! O damned miniature! But Gabriel's breathing soothed me. Once he murmured: 'Friend!'

The gleaming of the hangings startled me. Some dull metal was interwoven with the wool, so that, as the light rose and fell, figures sprang from the folds and leaped down chasms, eyes gleamed and dimmed, arms were uplifted and struck. Soon, in my curiosity, I began to consider the chief subject, and was amazed to find it that scene in *Tamburlane*, where Bajazeth and Zabina lie with their brains dashed out. It was wrought on the side nearest the fire, and on the other (which I saw by candlelight) was an uncouth picture of the tent of Heber the Kenite, with Jael in act to use the lethal hammer. Suicide and murder, each grimly figured—suicide and murder: here were strange subjects for a temple of rest! Yet Gabriel's dreams were happy. Often during my vigil I drew the curtain, and laid my hand tenderly on his forehead, and watched the lines of care fade out and away. As the night passed, he seemed to realise my presence: so, not wishing to break his rest, I was content to listen to the rise and fall of his breath.

The wind lulled before dawn. I looked from the window, and high above (for the opposite hill walled out all but a narrow slit) was the sky, dark blue and nebulous. On the sill a thin-voiced bird chirped a few odd notes. Another light began contending with the gleam from the fire. A solemn grey took the place of the gloom outside—a grey that brightened and brightened.

… 'Gabriel,' I said aloud. 'Let us see the sunrise together. Come, dress yourself! We will go to the crest of the Naze.'

He sat up in bed yawning.

'Nay,' he answered. 'I am too lazy to walk far before breakfast. It is not time to get up yet. I am sleepy.'

But, seeing me fully dressed, he sprang to the floor with a bound that made things shake, and, clamouring that he was no sluggard, began to put on his clothes.

The sun rose; a long ruddy haze trembled above the hill. All the stars faded, and the glitter began to creep down the side of the valley. Streamlets were leaping in the tiny cloughs, and spreading before they reached the melancholy river into brown and white mare's tails. Only that one bird, with the same acid piping! When we descended, breakfast had just been laid. There was nobody to wait at table; but everything you needed was there. 'Twas a still stranger meal than that of the night before. The food was impregnated with a strong flavouring, as of cinnamon; the coffee smelled deliciously; but a dish of scarlet poppies, with hearts like fingers, effused a close and sleepy perfume. We ate in silence; and, having sat a while, I rang for the reckoning.

The woman came, as evil-looking as ever; still wearing the amber gown. Moreover, the interest she had in me was greatly heightened, for she stood a minute gazing open-mouthed at my face, and her words were mystical. 'I trust that you have slept well here,' she said dreamily, 'for he who sleeps here needs no more sleep on earth. But this is not your last visit!' Had she seen anything in my eyes? Was she a witch? I turned to Gabriel, my heart panting. Thank God, he had not heard! But when I had paid her she plucked my sleeve, and led me to a great mirror between the windows. There she pointed to the reflection of my face, which I had never seen so impassive before. I turned half-angrily away, aghast but not surprised at her familiarity (for I knew her now), and she cackled drily, with a sound that better suggested wickedness than the most insidious speech. Even Gabriel was startled, and walked quickly to the door. As we stood on the threshold, to which she followed to speed us with courtesyings, I asked the nearest way to the village of Esperance, whose church, with its priest's chamber and its bells, I wished to see.

''Tis fourteen miles from here, gentlemen,' she said. 'Pass for a good step along the river; cross at the leppings, where the water lies broadest; and when you reach the hilltop eight miles of barren moorland lie before you. The path is a Roman road, swarded and wide. Turn at the pillar with the snake-rings. Go straight through the clough to the right, and there is Esperance, with the Featherbed Moss betwixt.'

She closed the door with a loud bang, and left us standing in amaze. The guide-book showed me that the village was at most some seven miles off, and that by a straight road. But the sound of drawing bolts prevented us from asking any more: so we started for the river-side. Suddenly Gabriel turned to look at the quaint cluster of buildings. A cry burst from his lips: 'By Jove, we've come to the wrong place! This is not the Eagle—just look at the sign!' We returned. It was a long swinging hatchment, a lozenge with proper supporters, whereon was painted an ungainly mythical creature, half dog and half bird. An inscription—*Ye Gabbleratch Inne*—in faded gilt letters gleamed below. But that was not all; for through a small mullioned window to the left the old woman was peering at us, and looking over her shoulder was the face of the handsomest man I have ever seen: youthful, white, and with auburn hair: but so sinister withal that his gaze seemed as petrifying as a cockatrice's.

We turned and fled, breathless almost, but with a fleetness I should not have believed attainable to one in my condition. Ere long we turned the foot of a crag, and to our common relief passed out of sight of the inn.

'The Devil and his Dam!' quoth Gabriel, half in earnest.

The river broadened until it filled the bottom of the valley, whose walls grew more and more precipitous. Moss-covered stones, that bore the marks of ancient carving, met the path soon; and, though in places they were somewhat under water, they were distinct enough to make crossing safe. They ended at the entrance to a gorge, along whose side a path, built of clamped flags, rose sharply to a level platform. When we reached the top there lay a prospect of utter barrenness: an immense plain with an horizon of jagged peaks; a few scant patches of heather relieving the sameness of the red earth; the Roman road, with its green, velvety turf, stretching, like a stagnant canal, from where we stood to the furthest crevice in the sky-line.

A queer memory awoke in me. 'Gabriel,' I said, 'do you know the secret of this earth?' He did not: so I told him of a place, something akin to this, where, in my own childhood, the body of a girl, murdered in the first year of Queen Anne, was discovered perfectly intact and supple. The tale pleased him. 'This is just the place I should like to be buried in,' he remarked. His words excited me. At that instant I could have done it—painfully. But I wished above all things to spare him pain.

Once I paused; between myself and the sun a hawk was grappling with a smaller bird, whose feathers floated down like snowflakes. My tongue formed the word 'metempsychosis' again, and Gabriel understood once more. A taint of sorrow came at the thought of our brief parting. And then I was possessed of an unutterable joy.

At midday he lay sleeping beside me on the moor. With my own hands I made his bed: with my own hands smoothed the sheet. Evening had fallen, when, alone and pensive, I heard the sweet bells of Saint Anne of Esperance, and saw the dim valleys of Braithwage and Camsdell with their serpentine streams.

SIR TOBY'S WIFE

he road sloped abruptly to a river green as emerald. Near the bridge was a ford, where the waters pulsed amongst the pebbles as though it were affected by the distant sea. On the left bank were two empty cottages with rounded gables. One had a strip of neglected garden, riotous with almost sapless, etiolated roses; the other a balustraded court, where valerian red as blood rose from the chinks of the broken pavement. The right bank, whence the road climbed to the strangest of sleepy villages, was embellished with a vast church and an imposing archway with a turret at either end. The grille was absent, its place filled with lichened masonry; beyond, one caught sight of the fantastic dormers of a Jacobean house.

Mary Winterbourne bade the chauffeur stop, and, turning to her companion, a vivacious elderly spinster, expressed her intention of spending a short time in the weird grey town that rose from the bridge to the summit of the hill.

'Never have I seen such a forgotten place,' she said. 'Nothing can have changed for hundreds of years. I'm not sure that it's real. I believe that, if I closed my eyes for a moment, it would all disappear.'

'There's a very real child teasing a cat over yonder,' said the chaperon, who boasted a strong American accent. 'See, the young wretch is coming along!'

The fat little girl with the pallid face released the struggling kitten and came hobbling along towards the car. Beside a worn mounting-block she stopped and gazed stupidly. The companion held a penny between thumb and forefinger, and asked the name of the place.

'Melton Barnabas,' said the child, in the dreariest of voices— 'Melton Barnabas.'

Once possessed of the coin, she retired without a word of thanks, disappearing in the narrow opening of a winding jennel. The only living thing left in that mediæval street was a great white rooster with a comb bright as fresh blood. Mary Winterbourne left the car and opened the worm-eaten gate of the churchyard.

'Don't follow me, Miss Andrews,' she said. 'I know you're tired of these old churches.'

'I'll be glad to rest, my dear,' said the elder lady. 'You needn't hurry. I shall probably take a nap. I'm surfeited with these ancient places of worship; there's too strong a scent for my taste.'

Mary Winterbourne did not seem to heed her words. She went along the narrow path to the porch, where she heard a faint sound of music, wheezy and wiry as of any hurdy-gurdy. On the opposite side of the aisle a dwarfish old man with a white, fan-shaped beard was slowly turning the handle of a quaintly decorated barrel-organ, the tune being 'Sun of my Soul.' At the sound of the girl's footsteps he ceased and came to meet her, his feet clicking dully against each other. The nearer he came, the more gnome-like grew his appearance. He effused a strong odour of snuff, and the hair of his upper lip was stained to a bright golden. His black eyes were small and protuberant, the whites crossed with a choleric network.

'Miss, would like to see the tombs?' he said, simpering. ''Tisn't often anyone comes, Melton Barnabas being off the main road. But our tombs—they're grand, and no mistake.'

Mary Winterbourne took out her purse, found a coin, and dropped it into his palm, careful that her finger-tips should not come into contact with his yellow, hardened skin. He mumbled copious thanks, then drew her attention to a font all carved with centaurs and wreathed snakes—a font that might once have been the fountain of some patrician Roman's courtyard.

'Ever since I was a little lad I've wondered about it,' said the custodian. 'You'd be fair mazed if you knew how many hours I've spent watching the things. There's been times when I could swear I'd seen 'em move!'

The oddness of his speech interested Mary Winterbourne, who, in spite of a fine share of common-sense, was not without love of the fantastic. She eyed him more closely, and her repulsion increased. At moments he suggested the freakish carving of a hidden miserere. She asked him to show her the other objects of interest, since her car was waiting, and she must continue her journey.

'Hurry no man's cattle,' said the fellow. 'There's enough in Melton Barnabas Church to keep you for days and days. I've been sexton for forty good years now, and I've been learning all the while. If I'd had education with my knowledge, I could write such a book about dead-and-gone folk as has never been writ before. Come this way, miss, and you shall see the Warnard tombs.'

He led the way into a dusty side-chapel, whose walls were hidden with altar-tombs of the seventeenth century, the carving as fresh as though of yesterday. Each of these—from beginning to end they covered a period of eighty-five years—was inscribed with 'I know that my Redeemer liveth,' and with the names of prolific sires and dames.

'A grand family, for sure,' said the sexton. 'Maybe you noticed their hall, or what's left of it, beside the river? Oliver Cromwell destroyed it—all but one end, where Sir Toby lives now. Eh, dear, I'm blest if here isn't Sir Toby himself!'

A tall and handsome young man came from the porch. He was dressed somewhat shabbily in Norfolk jacket and knickerbockers, but he wore his clothes with excellent grace. Mary Winterbourne marvelled at the pleasant freshness of his face. He bowed slightly as he passed, and the sexton raised a hand obsequiously to his curiously protuberant forehead.

'You're after your keys, Sir Toby,' said the latter. 'They'd dropped to the floor o' the pew. You'll find 'em on the seat... If you'll follow me, miss, I'll show you the old glass where St Anthony's training his pig to climb the staff.'

The young woman only gave a vague interest to this singular relic, being for the nonce singularly impressed by the personality of the upstanding Sir Toby. A minute later, however, he had left the church, and she was able to give all her attention to the sexton's talk.

'As honest and upright a gentleman as anyone might seek and not find in a twenty miles' march,' he said. 'That's what I always say, and always shall say, about Sir Toby. Poor as a church mouse, but none the worse for that. And proud as he's poor. Well, he may be proud, seeing as his fore-elders have lived at Melton Barnabas for a good six hundred years. Grand doings, too, there were at the Hall, from all accounts, before Oliver Cromwell's day. The first Sir Toby was a great man at Court. Look ye through this screen and you'll see his tomb.'

They had reached a massive screen of worm-eaten oak, whose bosses still bore faint traces of colouring. In the midst of the chapel beyond rose a magnificent altar-tomb of alabaster and Purbeck marble. Beneath the great canopy, charged with warm-hued heraldic bearings, lay the figures of the great Sir Toby and his wife. The sexton, after watching the girl's face in silence, chuckled hoarsely, then drew from his breeches pocket a brightly polished key.

''Tisn't usual to let strangers in,' he said, 'particularly since these Suffragetters are ramping about. But for sure you're not one of 'em, and there'll be no harm.'

He turned the key in a lock, and part of the screen swung aside, admitting Mary Winterbourne into the dusty chapel. There he pointed with a stubby thumb to the ornate canopy.

'One, two, three, four,' he said half to himself. 'There's some folks as 'd kill 'em, but, as for me, I love 'em better nor any birds!'

Observing that his companion was somewhat perplexed, he explained that the chapel was frequented by a colony of bats. 'Flitter mice we call 'em in these parts,' he added. 'Innocent things as do no harm.'

He climbed beside the figures and unhooked one of the little animals, holding it in his palm quite near Mary's face. 'Witty things they are—you'd be surprised to know what tales they do but tell!'

The bat piped shrilly, and Mary drew back in repugnance. He smiled grotesquely and laid it on Dame Warnard's left breast. Then he fumbled in his pocket for another key, and moved towards the wall, where a huge square of black slate was framed between twisted columns of Siena marble.

'The second Sir Toby's tomb speaks for itself,' he said. 'If ever there was a story, 'tis written there.' He looked anxiously towards the outer door, then hastened to the porch and closed it gently.

''Twouldn't do for Melton Barnabas folk to know I'd shown it to a stranger,' he observed, as he returned. 'For the matter of that, nobody's seen it but myself for a good twenty years. You'd like to see it, I reckon?'

'To see what?' said Mary in perplexity.

'You ought for to see it,' said the sexton, without paying heed, 'since for certain you're vastly like the portrait of the second Sir Toby's lady. It hangs in the picture gallery. You'd be surprised if you looked at it. Why, I declare, if you was dressed in old-fashioned outlandish garments, and your hair was all in ringlets, you'd say as you was her reflection!'

Thereupon he inserted the key in the middle of the black panel, which proved fashioned of two leaves like a stately door. The ancient hinges groaned and shrieked, then each side moved slowly forward, and Mary Winterbourne found herself gazing on the second Sir Toby's fantastical tomb.

The young man, carved life-size in marble of startling white-ness, was attired in a loose and flowing shroud. He stood beside a bronze chair, the seat of which was covered with crimson velvet; his right hand was outstretched, as though he were in the act of assisting some invisible person to rise. The Italian sculptor must have been a genius—the whole figure suggested vigorous life rather than death. The head was passably handsome, the features bearing curious resemblance to those of the Sir Toby of today.

'See the velvet!' said the old man excitedly. 'Who'd believe as 'twas the very same as was put there when yonder gentleman was laid to rest? There's 'broidered on the under-part the date. You'll scarce believe me, miss, but these doors they fit so tight that the leastest moth couldn't enter. When he's closed up, he might as well be in a corked bottle!'

'Why is Sir Toby alone? What is he waiting for?' inquired the girl curiously. 'I've never seen anything so strange in my life.'

'You may well say that, miss. Why, he's waiting for his wife, and for none other—the madam who's your own picture. Eh, but 'tis a queer story, and no mistake. A rare good-looking, upstanding chap he was—'tis plain to the eye.' He turned suddenly and stared into Mary's face. 'If you'd been wedded to such a lad, you'd have done what he'd wished. Heavens, but how your cheeks do flame!'

If Mary had been less ardently interested in the whimsical and odd, perhaps the weird gaffer's familiarity might have excited her disgust. As it was, she felt conscious of nought but a powerful desire to know the history of the empty chair.

'I cannot stay here long,' she said. 'Please tell me all you have to tell.'

'If I were to do that, 'twould take me a year and a day,' replied the sexton. 'It all comes down by hearsay. I had it from my father; he had it from his fore-elders. Sir Toby's waiting for his wife!'

'Was he married?' said Mary, in a voice that sounded in her ears as a stranger's.

'Married? Why, haven't I told you as you might be the woman he chose? Married! Ay, of course he was married, and as happy as a bird on a bough for twelve months only; then he was shot by Cromwell's men when they pillaged the house. He didn't die straight off. I did hear as he lay three days and three nights in his bed.'

'His wife was with him?' said Mary.

'Ay, and nearly all the while she sat aside of him, holding his hand. 'Twas then as he planned the tomb—him to wait there till she came. She was to be carved in stone and sit in the chair, and there their images were to bide till the Day o' Judgment.'

'And, since he's alone, she never came?' said the girl.

'That's plain enough to see. She mourned him for another twelvemonth, and then, belike thinking the times unsafe for a widow, she fixed her choice on another—a great lord, too, who

275

carried her away from Melton Barnabas. Lies buried in Salton-by-the-Water church, t'other side o' the county. I did hear as she survived Sir Toby by fifty odd years. When Sir Toby died, she'd a bairn a few weeks old. 'Twas by him the line was kept up.'

'What does the tomb mean?' said Mary.

'I'd have thought you'd known. After her ladyship 'd been put aside of him, her marble hand in his, him standing just as if he'd heard the last trump, the doors were to be riveted together and never opened again. Poor Sir Toby, I always say, waiting there with his look so expectant!'

Mary Winterbourne was no sentimentalist, yet this bizarre story moved her to a strange compassion; her eyes became dim with a veil of tears. She turned aside as though about to leave the chapel; the sexton abruptly placed himself between her and the opened screen.

'Nay, miss,' he said, in a hoarse voice. 'Nay, you'll not leave Sir Toby yet awhile. Poor lonely lad, left by himself all these years! And he looks different, somehow. I could swear he's smiling. Do but look at him!'

'I must go,' said the girl. 'Please stand aside.'

'And you're the living picture of his dame. See, he's well aware as you've come at last. 'Twould be cruel hard to leave him so soon!'

He caught her roughly by the arm and turned her again towards the open tomb.

'I saw his hand move as plain as plain can be; it pointed to the chair where you're to sit.'

'How dare you touch me?' cried Mary in alarm.

'Bless my soul, 'tis a pity if I can't please myself,' he chuckled—'at my time of life, when I'm getting on for eighty years! Eh, but 'tis a grand thing, knowing as Sir Toby's wife's come at last!'

For the first time came the conviction that the old man was mad. She was alone with him in the church; in all probability, if she cried out for help, her voice would not be heard. A struggle was out of the question—in spite of his age, his arms were as strong as a chimpanzee's. She had read somewhere that mad folk must be humoured; if she meant to escape uninjured, she must fall in with his whims.

'I'll stay a few minutes longer,' she stammered.

'Ay, and that you will,' he said. 'What do you say to me lifting you to his side, so as you can sit on the chair and hold his hand? My word, but 'twill please Sir Toby to know as you're got back!'

'I'll sit beside him for a moment,' said Mary, only half conscious of her words. 'I'll climb up; it's easy enough.'

Without any further delay, she rose to Sir Toby's side and sat down and took his hand. And the sexton, after a leer of pleasure, forced together the two leaves of slate and turned the key in the lock.

The sexton retired to the west end of the church and began to turn again the handle of the barrel-organ. This time the tune was 'Vital Spark of Heavenly Flame.' A faint crying might have been distinguished occasionally—a sound such as a lost child might make in the midst of a dense forest. After the tune had been wheezed thrice, he sauntered nonchalantly into the churchyard, where he was met by Miss Andrews, the chaperon, who, having enjoyed her nap, was now somewhat uneasy concerning her employer's protracted absence. She addressed a question to the old fellow; he giggled foolishly and jerked his thumb towards the porch. She entered the church and sought everywhere, but found no trace of Mary; then, filled with uneasiness, she prepared to examine the churchyard. As she was passing through the doorway, she heard the vague sound of one in mortal fright, and, rushing towards the gate, stumbled into the arms of Sir Toby himself. After a few hurried and almost inarticulate words, he seemed to understand, and, moving abruptly to the sexton's side, asked him what devilry he had been engaged upon. For reply, the man, choking with hoarse mirth, gave him the key to the Warnard tomb. ''Tis the second Sir Toby's wife as has come to him at last,' he said. 'Last I saw of her, she was sitting aside o' him, and he'd hold o' her hand!'

'The poor fellow's been strange for years,' said the baronet, turning to Miss Andrews. 'Please come with me. Heaven forbid that any harm has befallen your friend!'

Although by this time Mary Winterbourne was filled with greater terrors than ever assailed her in any nightmare, she did not cease calling for help. It is true, however, that the air of the closed tomb was oppressive in the extreme, and that the chill of the marble had already begun to impede the movement of her blood. She heard not a sound save that of her voice, and, when she paused for breath, the beating of her heart. The minutes seemed hours; breathing became almost impossible; unconsciously she clung closer to the marble hand. And at the moment when the door was opened, she fainted, and her face was as white as the second Sir Toby's own. His descendant took her gently in his arms, and, followed by the companion, carried her across the churchyard and through a postern that opened to the most wonderful of old-world gardens. There she recovered consciousness and spoke feebly of departing; but the young man insisted on both going indoors to rest. It was as she sat beside a lacquered tea-table, her beautiful colour returned, that he first became aware of a marvellous resemblance. Later he showed the portrait of his Cavalier ancestress, and Mary realised the old lunatic was justified in imagining that she might have been the lady for whom the second Sir Toby had waited so long.

So romantic a meeting might without question end in no commonplace way. Before another six months had gone by, the young folk were married, and although they move little in fashionable society, notwithstanding that Mary's fortune restored the Warnard name to its old lustre, they are as happy a couple as anyone might wish to know.

PART IV
Peak Weird

As a kind of appendix to the preceding sections I've included these three examples to showcase the 'tales of the Peak' that Gilchrist was more well known for in his time. Although many of his Peak Tales are simple reflections on the lives that Gilchrist would have encountered in the Derbyshire countryside—an article in *The Derbyshire Countryside* of 1951 calls them 'as real as Derbyshire oat-cake and sage-cheese'—some maintain a weird glimmer. The story-within-a-story of 'The Panicle' and the rogue's come-uppance in 'A Witch in the Peak' give a tongue-in-cheek glimpse of both Derbyshire folklore and also the disapproval the county's inhabitants have for fools and misers. Finally we have 'A Strolling Player', whose genial title belies the tale of a forlorn, funeral vigil. Perceptive readers may remember the deceased, Michal, from 'Witch In-Grain' and wonder what specific shame it was that she brought home with her. Yet there is an irony that it is this tale, one where Gilchrist talks most clearly not just of death but of the grief of those who remain alive, which closes the collection with a rare happy ending.

THE PANICLE

he farmhouse parlour faced the north, and the cold light, made dimmer by the bubbles of green glass in the heavy lattice, gave the place a grotto-like aspect. The floor, raddled round the sides, and covered in the middle with a knitted carpet of yellow and black cloth, was made of uneven flags; as much of the walls as was visible between the rows of memorial cards and samplers, and the engraved portraits of eminent divines, from John Wesley to James Caughey, nauseated the unaccustomed beholder with a monstrous design of livid roses, festooned with ribands of pea-green.

At the door Mrs Ollerenshaw paused and gazed inward with the devotion of one who prepares to enter a temple. She stooped and held her head sideways to discover if any dust had settled on the highly-polished, gate-legged table. Its cleanliness proving satisfactory, she folded her checked duster into the smallest compass and replaced it in the beaded bag that hung at her side, and went to the harmonium that stood between the two windows.

She was a fine, middle-aged woman, with prominent teeth, a hooked nose, and a pallid complexion. This evening she wore her most imposing gown of steel-grey poplin. As she sat on the high music stool, her back view was like that of a well-developed girl, and her dull, crimped hair seemed as luxurious as in the days when, as the Methodist local preacher's young daughter, she had caught the fancy of the wealthiest farmer of the countryside.

She played the tune of *Miles Lane*, and began to sing in a voice which, despite its Peakland accent and great unpliability, was sweet and clear and strong, a doggerel hymn written by her father in denunciation of all creeds save his own.

A maid clattered along the passage and stood waiting until Mrs Ollerenshaw had finished the second verse, which condemned superstitious fools and Unitarian and Roman Catholic fiends with equal bitterness.

'Theer's Mester Bateman Middleton coom, mam.'

Her mistress rose and closed the lid of the harmonium.

'Yo' can bring him here, Libby,' she said. 'Be sure an' see as he wipes his feet well.'

Then she sat composedly in the leather-covered armchair with the big legs, in which her husband had slept away his last days. She had just straightened her skirt when Bateman appeared. He was a tall, well-proportioned lad, with a broad, tanned face. He had donned for the occasion his fawn-coloured holiday suit and his brightest necktie. Mrs Ollerenshaw shook his hand and made him take the chair at the other end of the hearthrug. After they had discussed the weather and the seed-crops, she came suddenly to the point.

'Emma towd me as yo' were coomin' up to ask leave to coort,' she said, 'an' so I thowt et 'ld be best for her to be aat o' the road. Hoo's ridden ower to her uncle Pursglove's, and hoo's none comin' beck till morn.'

The young man's face saddened; he had hoped for a pleasant family scene, of the kind he had read about in the novels of Mrs Sherwood's day, which are still in vogue in the Peak country. He was not uncertain of the mother's favour. There was no complaint to be urged against his position; the farm of The Hallowes was his own property, and his brood mares had won three consecutive year's prizes at the Noe Valley Show. Emma was his first love, and he foresaw no disappointment.

'Et's a faith-trial as I'm goin' to test yo' by,' Mrs Ollerenshaw explained. 'My feyther tried et on my husband, an' his answer were satisfyin', an' ef yor's es—then yo've my consent off-hand.'

'I'm willin',' the lover replied, feebly. 'Em said et 'ld be no use aar walkin' together onless yo' gev leave.' His tone became more conciliatory. 'Hoo's a good dowter, an' hoo'll be guided by yo'r will.'

'Well, then, et's this,' said the widow. 'Theer were a farmer as used to coom to aar haase when I were a wench, an' he said as it happed to his wife ere they wedded. I wunna gie my opinion o' et: soom b'lieves et an' soom doesna…

'Et fell abaat this way. Th' young woman were goin' to Tidsa Market wi' butter, an' her röad lay 'cross Middleton Moor. Et were a hot forenoon i' hay-time, an' hoo were dry as a cricket, an' theer werena ony quick wayter to slake wi'. Well, hoo went on an' on, till at last hoo couldna beer et ony longer, an' hoo set daan her basket an' looked abaat. Th' Deep Rake's up theer, wheer fowk used to dig for lead i' ancient times, an' all th' pit-whöals are full o' green wayter covered wi' scum. Et were filthy, but hoo couldna forebeer, an' hoo just stooped her daan an' supped an' supped like a cawf till hoo were full. Then hoo got up, tuk her basket an' started on again, but afore hoo'd walked ten steps summat stirred abaat i' her stomach… Th' owd man said as et twisted inside like a live horsehair! Th' long an' th' short o' et were as hoo didna go to Tidsa Market that day, nay, nor for long enaa afterwards. Hoo grew white an' flabby, an' i' less nor a month were that bad as hoo couldna leave whöam!'

Bateman's mouth opened. 'Eh dear!' he exclaimed. Mrs Ollerenshaw sighed when she saw his consternation.

'Doctors could do nowt for her,' she continued; 'an' her fowk 'gan to think hoo were deein'. At last someone suggested as th' wise man as lived Whetstoneway might be o' soom service. So they sent for him, an' he cem, an' said et were a panicle hoo'd swallowed. A *panicle*, but yo'll find et i' no book! An' next day at th' edge o' dark he med 'em build up th' brew-haase fire wi' fir baughs, an' then he tuk th' lass an' fas'ned her i' a chair wi' ropes, an' tied her hair to th' back-bars an' turned all aat, an' locked th' door. He kep' her afront th' fire till hoo were well-nigh roasted. Th' owd man reckoned he were lis'ning aatside an' her mooans were summat fearful!

'All o' a sudden th' panicle popped ets yead aat o' her maath an' looked raand. Then et drew back 'gain, but th' wise man hed sin et, an' he picked up th' potter as lay gain, an' shoved et into th' heart o' th' fire. But th' brute wouldna coom aat again, so he moved th' young woman till her knees welly touched th' grate… Hoo were all covered wi' blisters afterwards, th' owd chap said, an' hoo hed a bad baat o' 'rysiplus. At last th' wise man saw th' panicle's yead coom aat again, so he popped behind th' chair an' hid. An' et crawled aat, bit by bit—a beast th' picture o' a fat effet, wi' six claws like honds, an' a swelled body abaat an arm's-length long, an' een blood-red. Et let etsel' daan to her bresses, an' afore ets tail were aat o' her maath, ets fow yead were lyin' i' her lap. After a while et drew ets tail daan an' coiled up i' a knot. An' then, wi' one hond, th' wise man nipped up th' potter an' clapped t' other hond to th' wench's lips, an' 'gan to bren th' panicle to dëath!'

The lover's legs were trembling; his arms slipped from the sides of the chair and hung nerveless.

'O Lord! O Lord!' he ejaculated.

Mrs Ollerenshaw shook her head resignedly. She had heartily wished him to pass unscathed through the faith-trial; but she was not a woman to be soured by disappointment.

'When he touched it wi' th' potter, et writhed abaat like a bit o' crozzlin' worsted, then et stood up on ets hindmost claws an' tried to get beck, but his hond—which it bit, cowsin' him to use costick—were i' th' way, so et tumbled daan an' lay on th' harstone... He set th' potter 'cross et length-wise... Et 'gan screetin' like a child... But et soon were a lump o' cinder.'

A long silence followed. Bateman broke it with a tremulous inquiry.

'Did th' young woman get better, mam?'

'Th' man as towd us married her, onyhaa, Bateman.'

'I never heerd o' such a awesoom thing! I'd liefer hev died!'

Mrs Ollerenshaw rose. 'So yo' b'lieve et, Bateman?'

'That I do, mam! Et's as ef I could see et naa.'

'Well, I'll say good-neet to yo'. Onyone as b'lieves such a thing esna fit to wed wi' Emma.'

He crept, dumbfounded, from the room. She watched him pass through the garden, then, moved by some careful impulse, she followed to the door.

'Bateman,' she called, 'coom beck a moment!'

He returned hastily, with a glad flush driving away his wanness. 'Ay, mam?'

'On'y this, Bateman; yo' munna coom coortin' Emma ony moor.'

A WITCH IN THE PEAK

t was the evening after old Johnny White's funeral, and Elizabeth sat by the low fire in the house-place, wondering how she could manage to exist for the remainder of her days without him who had never spent a whole day apart from her since their wedding, fifty years ago. The bitterness of her spirit was increased by the knowledge that at the end of the week the little farm must be sold to pay the money which the dead man had owed for standing surety for a dishonest cousin. The original sum had been thirty-five pounds; but the lender, Luke Flint, a shoemaker, who was known as 'the Milton Spider,' from his knack of wrapping a web about such unwary folk as craved aid from him, had stipulated on an interest of fifty per cent until all was repaid. This interest had eaten up all the profits of the stony acres, and Johnny had died heart-broken because one year's payment was in arrears.

Elizabeth had dismissed all her neighbours. She desired to be left in solitude for such short time as she remained in the house, so that she might recall scenes of bygone happiness. She was quite alone in the world, so that there was none save herself to suffer; but still the outlook was so depressing that the source of her tears was dried.

'I can see yo' again, Johnny lad,' she murmured, 'walkin' wi' me fro' church on aar weddin' morn, as coomly a man as were i' th' whöal Peak... But yo' looked just as coomly i' yo'r shroud, wi' all ets pratty gimpings, tho' yo'r cheeks hed lost theer red, and yo'r gowd hair were gone as white as snow. Ay lad, ay lad, I do wish I might hev gone wi' yo'! When I think o' all our good life together; how yo' thowt nowt were too han'some for me, an' as whate'er I did were th' reet thing, I'm like to go mad. An' now I'm to be turned aat o' th' place wheer aar wedlock's bin spent! Et's hard, et's very hard!'

As she lamented, the latch of the door was lifted and the creditor entered. He was a dark, squat man of middle-age, with a bullet-shaped head and blue, close-shaven jowls. His arms and legs were unnaturally long, and his broad shoulders were so much bent as to suggest deformity. He strode forward to the hearth, and without invitation plumped down in the armchair which Johnny had always used.

Elizabeth rose in excessive anger. Her thin face flushed crimson, her toothless lower jaw moved oddly from side to side.

'I'll thank yo' to get aat o' that!' she cried. 'Et's always bin set in by a honest fellow, an' I canna see ony other sort use et! Ef yo' mun sit, sit on th' sattle.' He assumed an air of bravado; but her aspect was so threatening that he rose sullenly and took the corner to which she pointed.

'Yo' needna be so haughty, 'Lizbeth White,' he said, with an unpleasant sneer. 'This spot'll be mine soon, for I'm agoin' to buy et, an' happen yo'll coom a-beggin' to th' door.'

'I'ld liefer starve nor beg o' yo'. What d' yo' want, a-coomin' rattin'?'

'I on'y want to mind yo' as yo' mun tek none o' th' things aat o' th' place. My papers 'low me to sell all, an' if yo' touch owt—off yo' go to Derby.'

She cracked her fingers in his face. 'I'll be more nor thankful to get aat o' yo'r debt,' she said. 'Et's yo'r cheatin' simple lads like my John as keeps yo' alive. Yo're none fit to be 'mongst decent livers. I do be'lieve as th' law wouldna favour yo'.'

His sallow skin grew white and then purple.

'Yo' try th' law, 'Lizbeth White, an' yo'll find as et canna touch me. Yo'r man signed th' agreement to pay me my money, an' ef he couldna pay et, I were to be at lib'ty to sell th' lond. Th' lond, say I?—et esna lond—nowt but three akkers o' stone an' moss, wi'aat a real blade o' grass! Et wunna fetch thretty pun', an' I'm certain sure as th' furniture esna worth ten. Yo'll still be soom pun's i' my debt. I reckon yo'll hev to go to th' Bastille, an' I may mek' up my mind to losin' some o' th' good money!'

'I'd go to th' Bastille forty times ower, sooner nor be behowden to yo' for owt. But as long as I'm stoppin' i' th' haase, I wunna stond yo'r jaw! Aat yo' go, yo' brute yo'!'

She unfastened the door, and held it wide open. It was a dark night, and the air was heavy with the scent of withered leaves. The prattle of the spring as it leaped from the moor-edge to the trough in the paddock was distinctly audible.

'Yo' owd wretch!' he muttered. 'I'll see as yo' suffer for yo'r brazzenness. Yo' beggar! When yo'r a-hoein' taturs i' th' Bastille garden, I'll set th' others laughin' at yo'.'

He moved leisurely across the floor; she sharpened his gait by picking up a besom-stale.

'Whiles I'm mistress here, I'll hev none o' yo'. John's paid yo' time an' time again. Be off, yo' skin-a-louse! I beg an' pray God to punish yo' this very neet. Ef et hedna bin for yo' theer'ld hev been no buryin' here for mony a year. I'm none one as es gi'en to cursin', but yo' deserve whatten yo'll get.'

He slunk out into the darkness. She closed the door and bolted it carefully, and when the clatter of his footsteps had died away, she returned to the chair by the hearth, where a choir of crickets was now singing cheerfully, and delivered herself to the melancholy satisfaction of meditating on past joy and present sorrow.

Meanwhile the Spider walked down the lane in some trepidation, for her violence had unnerved him strangely.

'I do b'lieve hoo's really a witch,' he said. 'Her eyes brenned that red! Ef hoo'd lived i' my greet gran'feyther's days hoo'ld hev bin faggotted, sure enow!'

His mumbling was suddenly cut short by some terrible thing catching the hinder-part of his waistband and plucking him up from the ground. When he recovered his senses in some measure he was on a level with the tree-tops. His voice rose in a harsh shriek.

'Help! All o' yo' help! Jack-wi'-th'Iron-Teeth's gotten howd o' me an's draggin' me to Hell!'

But as it was late, and the Milton folk were abed, none heard. He flew swiftly through the air, his long arms and legs sprawling frog-like. Once he caught hold of the thatch of a barn and clung for a moment, but the rotten wisps came away in his hands. He gave himself up for lost. The demon was dragging him over the moor in the direction of the river.

'O Lord, forgi'e me, forgi'e me, an' I'll tek' advantage o' innocent fowk no more. I'll do my best to set things reet as I've set wrong, ef only Thou'lt let me off this time!'

He fell with a heavy splash into the marsh of the Wet Withins. For a long time he lay, half-swooning, on a tussock of bent-grass. Then, when his strength returned, he crawled blindly over the heath to the road.

Instead of making for home, he went straight to Crosslow Farm and knocked feebly at the door. Elizabeth was sleeping in her chair. She had been dreaming blithely of years of good crops. She rose, drowsily, and drew back the bolts. In the dim firelight she looked more like a witch than ever.

'Yo've coom back again!' she said, sharply. 'Be off! I wunna hev et said as I let yo' in at this time o' neet!'

He was trembling like a paralytic.

'Gie me a bit o' paper, 'Lizbeth White,' he stammered, 'an' I'll write a quittance. Yo're a wicked woman, an' I'll hev nowt more to do wi' yo'. Yo're on'y fit to bren!'

'I reckon et's conscience,' she said, as she took paper and pen and ink from the corner cupboard. 'Write whatever yo' like an' go to—'

'Dunna say thatten, for Lord's sake!' he yelled.

He took the paper and wrote: '*I, Luke Flint, do hereby forgive Elizabeth White her husband's debt as she owed me, and I trust as she will bear no further malice.*'

Then he hastened from the place, as though it held a creature accursed.

Two days afterwards he returned to Crosslow, in a cajoling, lachrymose humour.

'Gi'e me that quittance back again,' he said, with a painful giggle. 'Yo're an honest woman, I reckon. I thowt yo' were a witch, but et were a b'loon hook as picked me up an' carried me to th' wayter-holes. Soom chaps droppin' advertysements for gin an' whisky 'ld gone astray an' were tryin' to fix on a spot. Summat hed gone wrong wi' th' machine. Gi'e me et back, wench, yo're a reet-dealin' woman, an' I'm sure yo' wunna do but whatten's just.'

She laid hold of the besom-stale again.

'I'll breek yo'r back ef yo' dunna go,' she cried. 'Yo' thowt I were a witch, but yo' munna think I'm a fool!'

A STROLLING PLAYER

t the bend of the hill-road, where one loses sight of the distant village, a stream had overflowed before the last frost, and the limestone cartway, with its smoothly-worn cobbles and its lattice of red and yellow and black leaves, was covered for many yards with a transparent sheet of ice. In daylight it resembled a mosaic of arabesque device, but now, reflecting the last scarlet shred of the afterglow, it suggested a river of blood. All around grew dwarf sycamores and elms and silver birches; their bare timber streaked with ribbons of frozen sleet.

When the waggon reached this perilous place, Joe Ascham got down from the high shaft, and, with a few sad clucks of encouragement, strove to make the young white horse proceed. Its shoes had not been sharpened, however, and at the first attempt it slipped back with such violence that the thing inside the waggon was jolted roughly against the side. At the sound the old man winced and crept to the back and drew the burden again into the middle, covering it neatly with the strip of clean sacking.

'Theer munna be a scrat on et,' he muttered, 'else Johanna 'll breek her heart altogether. Ef et's all reet, hoo'll be pleased, poor soul, for et's th' best whöak I've ever seen! Dane said as et cem off one o' th' big trees i' Whitstone Dale.'

He caught the bridle again and pulled with all his might, and the horse felt its way very slowly, without lifting its hoofs from the ground. The road turned abruptly again, at a corner with a steep and barren acclivity on the right hand, and on the left a danger-ous ravine filled with ancient firs and rough stones. The wind was rising, and the place seemed full of whispers.

There the horse slipped for the second time, and the sacking fell in a heap at the back. In the waning light was visible a short and narrow coffin, with a bright metal name-plate. Joe covered it again, and jerked the bridle almost furiously, but the horse would not move.

'O Boxer, my lad, dunna fail me at such a time,' he cried, querulously. 'Johanna's waitin' theer all alone, an' we're late enaa already!'

Some one rose from the low wall and came towards him. His eyes were wet, and he could only distinguish the outline of a woman's figure.

'Can I help you at all?' she inquired, in a thin, eager voice.

'I'ld tek et very kindly, mam, ef yo'ld set inside an' howd et i' position. I dunna want et spoilin'. I could mek Boxer go, ef on'y I werena afeard o' shakin' et.'

'What is inside?' she said, lifting her bundle and preparing to climb.

'Et's a coffin, mam... my poor Michal's—my dowter's.'

The woman shivered, but got in without a word and knelt and clasped her arms about the thing. Joe dragged Boxer forward, and in a few minutes they had reached the level. There the woman rose to alight; but the old man put out his hand.

'I reckon yo're goin' my way over th' moor,' he said. 'Et's five mile to my house—midway across, an' yo're welcoom to ride ef yo' will.'

She thanked him. 'I want to reach Great Hucklow tonight, if I can,' she said. 'I'm a strolling player, and I'm trying to get an engagement with Bainbridge's company. I shall be very glad to ride with you, for I've walked ever since daybreak.'

Darkness fell and the air grew thick with the oncoming of snow. Ascham struck a match and lighted his lantern and walked on in front. The woman saw that they had reached the moorland: on either side was a low bank of heather-covered turf, broken here and there with frozen water holes. A few ragged sheep followed in the wake of the waggon. The road was no longer of limestone, but of brown sand and pebbles; the shadow of the wheels stretched behind and broke amidst the moving sheep.

A few snowflakes fluttered downwards. Ascham stopped the horse and came again to the side. The woman was still crouching with her arms about the coffin.

'I reckon et were a strange thing o' me to ask,' he said, 'but yo' see I were baffled. Et's getten' mortal cowd. I've got th' horse rug i' front—yo' may's well put it on an' sit on the shaft. Yo'll hev to step daan first.'

She obeyed. He put the lantern on the ground and found the rug. He saw that she was very wan and exhausted. Her face was a wasted oval; the skin about her eyes was blue with weeping and sleeplessness. She wore a shabby black silk cloak, trimmed with moth-eaten fur; the hat that shaded her forehead was of dingy yellow lace. She might have been any age between thirty-five and fifty.

When Joe had pinned the rug over her breast, he helped her to the shaft and she sat there with her feet dangling. The snow was falling heavily now; the sheep had retreated to the hollows, and even the sides of the road were invisible. Suddenly the old man lagged and fell behind to walk beside the stranger.

'I want to talk, mam,' he said. 'I want to forget things. Yo've seen misfortun', hevna yo'.'

'Yes, I've seen misfortune,' she replied. 'So much misfortune that I wish the coffin had been made for me. But all of us have our share. Do you go much farther?'

'Abaat a mile, but I'd liefer yo' cem' up to th' haase wi' me. I dessay et'ld do Johanna good. An' happen—ef I may tek' th' liberty o' askin' yo'—we could carry th' coffin in betwixt us.'

The woman nodded.

'Ay, et's Michal's coffin, an' Michal's aar on'y child. Such a rare wench too hoo were afore hoo went away. But such were her will, an' there were no howdin' her in a' whöam. Yo' should hev seen her! Hoo were just as pink an' white as th' inside o' a peony-pod. An' et were a bad year wi' th' crops, though things bettered afterwards... Hoo wouldna coom whöam till a month ago, an' then hoo were heavy wi' trouble.'

He was obliged to go forward again: a track, diverging to the right, crossed a frozen brook and climbed, between stunted hedges, to the farmstead. He turned the horse safely and came back.

'I want to ask you something,' the woman said, anxiously. 'When she came back to you—were you kind?'

'*Kind*, mam? Ay, that we were. Et were th' happiest an' yet th' saddest day o' aar lives. Prethee wheer else should hoo hev' gone, ef none to her own fowk? Hoo browt shame wi' her, but hoo were Johanna's dowter, an' my dowter, an' th' shame were all forgi'en.'

The woman's eyes swam in scalding tears: she pressed her hands over her heart; then she quaked, remembering a casting from a door and a shouting of curses.

A dog barked softly. The wind was whirling the snowflakes in wreathed columns that passed in front of the house like veils of smoke. From the window of an upper room a clear streak of light stretched over the croft. The dog came bounding from a shippon and jumped up to Ascham's waist.

'Hush, Gyp, we munna hev a noise,' he said, stooping to stroke its head.

He 'put up' the horse, leaving the stranger standing in the open air; then he unlatched a door in that side of the house that abutted on the stable-yard, and beckoning her to help, silently drew the coffin from the waggon. They carried it through the kitchen, not without difficulty, for the oak planks were thick, and into the house-place, where they laid it on the lang-settle.

Ascham went to the foot of the stairs. 'Johanna,' he called, gently. 'I've gotten back, an' theer's a lady coom wi' me—hoo's bin helpin' me wi' et.'

Mrs Ascham came down very slowly. She was a stout little woman, with clear blue eyes and brown wrinkled skin. The outline of a goitre showed through her black and white neckerchief. She held out a cold hand.

'Et were good o' yo', mam,' she said. 'I were afeared my lad couldna manage et by himsen.'

'Th' lady's an actress,' Joe explained, 'on th' way to Greet 'Ucklow. Hoo held th' coffin for me when Boxer slipped.'

Johanna tried to unbutton the ragged silk cloak, but the stranger held it more tightly together.

'Lend me a lantern,' she said, 'and let me go on. If I am not there early tomorrow, my chance will be lost.'

The old woman threw open the window. The snowfall had thickened; it came down so quickly that it seemed as if a white sheet hung outside.

'Yo' see et's impossible, mam,' she said. 'Yo' mun stay wi' us an' hev soom o' Joe's supper. Th' way's hard to find i' broad dayleet, an' to-neet, e'en my lad, who's lived here all his life, wouldna dare to venture. Yo' dunna wish to freeze to dëath?'

The player smiled painfully. 'It would not matter much,' she replied; 'but if you will have me stay I must do something. Is there any sewing—I am good with my needle.'

'No, mam, nothin'. I med shroud an' all mysen,—i' fact they were th' very things I'd put by for when my own time cooms. Thank yo' very kindly, but all's doon.'

Her husband drew her attention to the coffin. She examined it carefully, feeling the polish of the wood and the weight of the metal handles with divers murmurs of pleasure.

'Et's a beautiful thing,' she remarked, at last. 'Ah, ef on'y aar Michal could see et, hoo'd be more nor satisfied!'

She took from the oven a huge bowl of hot porridge. Joe drank buttermilk with his share, but Johanna poured over the stranger's a jugful of rich cream. After supper, man and wife began to wrangle soberly concerning which should sit up in the death chamber. Johanna had done so on the preceding night, but knowing that her husband was weary with the journey, she wished to take his turn.

The actress broke in, during a pause, with—'Let me watch with your dead. I will keep awake all night.'

It was only with considerable difficulty that she prevailed. Johanna told her that it had been the custom of the family for many generations.

'Michal's th' third I've watched,' she said, proudly. 'Theer were Joe's mother first, an' then my own lad as died thretty year ago. But Joe an' I'm growin' old an' worn aat, an' et'll be best for us to sleep, for tomorrow'll be a hard day... What may your name be, mam?'

'Call me Violetty; that is the name my parents gave me—a foolish name, like tinsel and sawdust.'

Johanna opened the staircase door. 'Coom, then, Violetty,' she said. 'This es th' way to Michal's chamber.'

She led her up the broad, worm-eaten stairs to a great room, where stood a large four-post bedstead, hung with blue and white gingham. She drew the curtains aside reverentially, and after removing a crocheted cloth, showed Violetty the face of a young girl, whose long glossy hair spread from the frilled nightcap in strands over the pillow. Johanna peered into Violetty's hollow eyes before drawing down the counterpane and showing her the baby lying in its embroidered gown, like a doll, with its head resting between the mother's left breast and arm.

Violetty's face worked; she turned aside.

'Esna hoo a pretty yen?' Johanna said. 'Twenty-one year, but et's just as ef hoo were ten or 'leven, an' hoo'd gone to sleep wi' her moppet.'

There was a low fire on the hearth. She put on a dried peat and turned up the lamp.

'Yo' wunna be scared, Violetty? Hoo never did ony harm to onyone. My owd man an' me'll sleep wi'aar door ajar—et's just across the landin'. Ef yo' want owt, yo' need but call, for I warrant yo' we shanna sleep heavy to-neet.'

Violetty sat quietly in the armchair, with her hands folded in her lap. The old people went to bed soon: she heard them undress, and for a while caught sounds of sobbing and whispering. When they were asleep the silence of the place became too oppressive, and she walked to and fro, looking at the pictures that covered the walls. Most of these were sombre-hued chap-paintings, done on thin glass: the scene of Nelson's death hung above the funeral of Pitt, and a ruined castle surrounded by a moat beside a basket of impossible flowers. Over the mantel was a sampler, embroidered in faded silks—a prim cottage with a formal garden, on whose lawn was wrought a verse from the dialogue of *Death and the Lady*.

Soon she drew her chair to the bedside and took away Michal's face-cloth.

'If only I were dead instead of you, poor child,' she said. 'I have nobody and you had those who needed you.'

She folded her hands again and sat gazing at the curves of the girl's body. A clock downstairs struck hour after hour; the muffled wind stroked the windows with snow. A feeling of content filled her now; it was like a dream—a dream of quietness and rest. Her life had been one long turmoil of excitement and of shame and of repentance. Michal had known only one short sorrow; hers had been many and protracted through years and years.

'There is no rest but death,' she murmured.

Yet, all the time, her heart was craving for warmth and peace. She wished no longer for love: all that desire was burned out long ago: all that she wanted was a perfect calm.

The wind fell and a grey dawn broke. She heard the old couple stir in their bed, then fall asleep again. The nights of watching before and after Michal's death had taken away all their strength. She did not waken them, although she knew that unless she reached Great Hucklow before noon, all her chance of an engagement would be lost. But she felt no pang for herself, for were they not oblivious of all their trouble?

At last Johanna came, half-dressed, into the chamber. She leaned over Michal's uncovered face and kissed it twice.

'My dear deary,' she whispered. 'Thy nose were always cowd; et doesna seem as thou wert dead. An' i' a little while thou'lt be put away fro' thy owd mother.'

She beckoned Violetty to follow her down to the house-place.

'I mun ask yo'r pardon,' she said; 'but we slept on an' on. Why didna yo' waken us? I'm afeared yo'll be too late. Yo'd best stay till noon an' go wi' us to Highlow for the buryin', et's on th' way to Greet 'Ucklow. Theer'll be none theer—we wanted to put her away by aarsens. Besides, we hevna ony frien's.'

Joe came downstairs soon and they breakfasted in silence, then Violetty, seeing that he wished to take the coffin upstairs, took hold of the end. Johanna followed, and between them they lifted Michal and the child by the towels that were spread underneath, and spread the gimped cotton-wool evenly from head to foot.

'We mun start at twelve,' Joe said. 'Parson'll be waitin' at two. Et'll be a white buryin'.'

He raised the lid. Violetty left them to say their last good-bye, and waited downstairs. At noon the waggon started, with the two women sitting on either side of the coffin, whilst Joe rode on the shaft. The father and mother had donned rusty black garments and big, half-mouldy gloves. Violetty still wore her silk cloak, but Johanna had lent her an uncouth scuttle bonnet that almost concealed her haggard face. The track was deep with snow, but at even distances the heads of roughly-chiselled boundary stones kept them from straying on the moor. Johanna, who held the actress's hand in hers, wept silently all the way.

When they reached the churchyard, which lies in a hollow at the end of a scattered hamlet, they found the clergyman waiting in the porch. Two gravediggers came forward to carry the coffin, but the Aschams and Violetty lifted it themselves and laid it on the trestles in front of the altar. None of the villagers were present: they knew but little of the moor-folk, and it was much too cold to venture out of doors for such a trivial sight. The clergyman's voice rang hollow amongst the stuccoed arches. Joe and Johanna trembled as if ague-struck.

The grave had been newly dug: Violetty saw on the mound, not yet covered by the falling snow, some little white bones and the shreds of a long-decayed coffin. It was all that remained of the boy that Johanna had lost thirty years before. The player buried her badly-shod feet in the snow and covered these relics hurriedly, so that they might not hurt the mother's eyes. In a few minutes the service was over, and ere the gravediggers began to throw back the soft clayey soil, Violetty drew the old people away.

When Johanna had got into the waggon, Violetty leaned over the side and kissed her.

'Good-bye,' she said. 'God bless you for your comfort of me.'

Johanna threw her arms around her neck.

'I wunna let yo' go, Violetty, wench,' she wailed.

'Coom whöam wi' Joe an' me—coom an' stop wi' us for good. Aar Michal 'ld hev wished et.'

Joe put his hand over his eyes. 'Ay, dunna leave us, Violetty. We'n got nob'dy left us.'

Violetty turned faint; everything reeled before her eyes. Then she flushed as if overcome by some great and unexpected happiness, and clambered into the waggon.

NOTES ON THE TEXT

DEAD YET LIVING

The Crimson Weaver (p. 19)

Beldam: An archaic and pejorative term for an old woman, equivalent to crone or hag.

Asphodels: A flower of the genus *asphodelus*. In Greek legend the asphodel is the flower of the dead; Homer, in *The Odyssey*, describes part of the Greek Underworld as meadows of asphodel, 'where the spirits dwell, phantoms of men who have done with toils'.

Actaeon's horns: Actaeon was a hero of Greek mythology who accidentally saw the goddess Artemis naked as she bathed in a woodland spring. As punishment he was turned into a deer and torn apart by his own hunting dogs, foreshadowing the events of *The Crimson Weaver*. Gilchrist uses Diana here, the Roman name for Artemis.

Culver: An archaic term for a pigeon or dove.

Pleasaunce: A secluded garden, designed and planted purely for sensory experience rather than crops.

Mannikin: This is sometimes believed to refer to a small African bird of the genus *spermestes* but based on Gilchrist's use of the word in other stories and the more uncanny image it creates I believe this to be an intentionally archaic rendition of mannequin.

Columbary: A dovecote or other housing for birds. The etymological link with columbarium, a structure used to store funerary urns, implies that the Weaver's doves are in fact the souls of her previous victims.

Marplot: Someone who spoils the plans of others.

Yew-mast: All parts of the yew tree, except for the red flesh of the berries, are toxic to humans and even small doses can cause hallucinations. Sleeping under one, in the 'mast' or scattered seeds of the tree, no doubt causes the narrator's dreams. The dreams themselves reference works of William Blake and Edgar Allan Poe.

Bartizan: The corner turret of a castle, which often overhangs the wall beneath it.

Feet shaped as those of a vulture: With this Gilchrist appears to relate the Weaver to the harpies of Greek myth. The harpies, their name meaning 'snatcher', would accost evil-doers who had gone unpunished and deliver them to the vengeance of the Furies.

Clew: A thread or cord that leads to a goal. Ariadne helped Theseus kill the Minotaur by giving him the clew that allows him to navigate the monster's Labyrinth. Gilchrist uses the term ironically here, as it leads to a grisly fate and not safety.

The Return (p. 28)

Yarrow: Known colloquially as nosebleed plant or soldier's woundwort, yarrow (*achillea millefolium*) contains blood-clotting compounds that can prevent bleeding. The way this makes the plant appear to suck up blood, combined with the blisters its sap can cause on human skin, give it an indisputably vampiric 'evil omen'.

Spinet: A small harpsichord.

I no longer live in this house: If read literally this seems obvious as Bretton Hall is derelict and uninhabitable but Rose's statement also foreshadows the revelation that she is now dead.

Golgotha: The 'Skull Hill' outside Jerusalem where Jesus was crucified.

At four cross-paths: According to folk belief the restless spirits of suicides would rise from their grave to torment their living relatives. Burial at a remote cross-roads was thought to confuse the spirit, making it harder for them to find their way home.

The Lover's Ordeal (p. 36)

Hoyden: A boisterous, spirited girl.

Endymion: This Greek figure is mentioned repeatedly by Gilchrist. Endymion was so beautiful that Selene, goddess of the moon, fell hopelessly in love with him. Tormented by the fear that her mortal love would die, Selene petitioned Zeus to grant him eternal life. Zeus did so, but only by making Endymion fall into an eternal sleep. The link between the moon, eternal slumber and vampires is clear. Gilchrist again prefers to refer to Diana rather than the more accurate Selene.

Abigail: A handmaid or other female servant, taken from the Biblical story of Abigail who describes herself as a servant of God in the book of Samuel.

A Night on the Moor (p. 46)

Ling and sphagnum: Types of heather and moss, respectively.

John Peel: Possibly a reference to the song *D'ye ken John Peel*, written by John Woodcock Graves around 1824. The song's chorus features the line 'Peel's "View, Halloo!" could awaken the dead', which acts as a piece of foreshadowing.

Faggot: A bundle of sticks bound together for firewood.

Joskins: A condescending term for country folk, similar to bumpkin.

Mr Wycherley: An English dramatist of the late sixteenth/early seventeenth century. Wycherley's plays, particularly his later works *The Country Wife* and *The Plain Dealer*, were considered risqué to the point of obscenity.

Midsummer Madness (p. 59)

Hebe's urn: Hebe, the Greek goddess of youth, is often depicted with a vessel with which she serves the other gods their drink of nectar.

Anne Killigrew's portraits: Anne Killigrew was a poet and painter of the seventeenth century. Many male critics of the time believed that a woman could not write poetry of her level and so she must be a fraud. In response, she composed the poem 'Upon the saying that my VERSES were made by another' where she complains about being derided and ignored but finishes by defiantly stating that 'I willingly accept Cassandra's Fate / To speak the Truth, although believ'd too late'. Killigrew died of smallpox at the age of 25.

Ruines of Time: A poem by Edmund Spenser, published in his 1591 collection *Complaints*. It ends with the line 'So unto Heaven let your high Mind aspire / And loath this Dross of sinful World's Desire', echoing Phyllida's final words.

The Pageant of Ghosts (p. 75)

He held the diamond which he had brought from the East: The figures in this procession appear to be entirely fictional but Nabob Darrington's story also echoes that of the narrator in 'The Return'.

Althea approached: Again, this is a possible allusion to 'The Writings of Althea Swarthmoor', which appears later in this collection.

The Priest's Pavan (p. 80)

Hippogriff: A creature with the front half of an eagle and the rear of a horse, invented by the sixteenth-century poet Ludovico Ariosto in his epic poem *Orlando Furioso*.

Galliards, lavoltas, pavans: Various forms of formal dance from the sixteenth century.

Virginals: A musical instrument, related to the harpsichord.

Cachinnations: Over-boisterous and inappropriate laughter.

Gobelins: A then-famous family of French dyers and tapestry makers.

Bedizened: Decorated, often gaudily.

Dame Inowslad (p. 88)

Sward: An area of grass.

Lady-smocks: A flowering plant (*cardamine pratensis*), also known as the cuckoo flower, which folklore deems sacred to fairies.

Religieuse: An eighteenth-century novel by Denis Diderot in which a young woman is forced into a convent against her will.

Lyke-wake: A vigil, or wake, held over the dead prior to their funeral. Lyke is a Northern English dialect term for corpse, derived from the German *Leiche*.

USELESS HEROES

The Manuscript of Francis Shackerley (p. 97)

Alembic: A piece of glassware used in the process of distillation, often associated with the work of alchemists.

I would leifer: An archaic form meaning 'I would willingly', implying a preference.

Simples: A herb used on its own, rather than those which are mixed together.

Cuckoo and a child mocking cuckoo: The cuckoo, a bird which lays its eggs in the nests of others, is symbolic of adultery. This section acts as foreshadowing of the tale's finale.

Jetto: A fountain, derived from the French *jet d'eau*.

Nappy-ale: Strong beer.

Quaestio Curiosa de Natura Solis et Lunae: A treatise by the twelfth-century alchemist Michael Scot. Tradition holds that it is Scot who petrified a coven of Cumbrian witches, turning them into the standing stones known as Long Meg and her Daughters. Scot also appears in Dante's *Inferno* where he is held in the section of Malebolge, the Eighth Circle of Hell, reserved for seers and sorcerers.

Cockatrice: A mythical creature depicted as a blend of a dragon and a rooster, with a deadly gaze similar to that of a basilisk.

Se'nnight: Seven nights, or a week.

The Basilisk (p. 115)

Basilisk: A mythical reptile, sometimes called the 'king of snakes' and depicted wearing a crown, which is so venomous it can kill simply by looking at its victim.

Sege of bitterns: Sege is an alternate spelling for the marshland plant sedge, which is often used as a nesting place for waterfowl like bitterns and so has also become the collective noun for such birds.

Cabalistic: Literally secretive or mysterious but possibly also an allusion to the Kabbalah of Jewish mysticism.

Ballad of the Witch Mother: This appears to be the traditional song known as *Willie's Lady*. Willie marries against the wishes of his mother, a witch, and the knots, trouble-combs and master-kid refer to curses used by the Witch Mother to punish her unwanted daughter-in-law with childlessness.

Oberon, Titania and Robin Goodfellow: Fairies and major characters from Shakespeare's *A Midsummer Night's Dream*.

Witch In-Grain (p. 123)

Quincunx: An orchard with the trees planted in groups of five, arranged as the five spots on a die.

I dreamed that I fed the Dragon of the Hesperidean Garden: Michal refers to the serpentine dragon Ladon who guarded the golden apples in the garden of the Hesperides, the Greek nymphs of evening and twilight. Some mythic traditions see him eventually slain by Hercules. Although not necessarily an evil creature in his mythical form, the image of a serpent coiled around an apple tree has satanic implications that befit a witch's dreams.

Mammet: A despicable thing.

Costard: A large, sour apple used for cooking.

Runnion: A pejorative term for a woman.

Beldering: Loud crying, weeping.

Prick her arm: Folk belief holds that all witches are marked on their body by the Devil and that this patch of skin is numb to pain.

The Grotto at Ravensdale (p. 127)

Chirurgeon: Archaic term for a doctor or surgeon.

Brown holland: Plain, unbleached linen used for dust covers.

Lusus naturae: Rare, albeit natural, forms.

Almost to an anatomy: A euphemistic term, implying someone to be as emaciated as a cadaver.

Excerpts from Witherton's Journal: Also a Letter of Crystalla's (p. 142)

Malkins: Rough or uncultured people.

Domino: A small mask which often covers little more than the eyes and nose.

A quoit's-cast: Quoits is a game where players throw rings of rope or iron a short distance onto a target.

Pictor: The Latin for 'painter', referring here to Witherton.

Bubble Magic (p. 151)

Massinger's Maid of Honour: A tragicomic play from the early seventeenth century, with a plot involving intertwined romances.

Turk's-caps: A flowering lily (*lilium martagon*).

Repeater: A timepiece that chimes the hours and minutes on demand at the press of a button, allowing it to be used in darkness.

Reremice: An archaic term for bats.

Dryas and Lady Greenleaf (p. 160)

Ceres: The Roman goddess of agriculture.

Hakluyt: Possibly the sixteenth-century English writer, and Secretary of State to Elizabeth I, Richard Hakluyt. His name lives on in the Hakluyt Society, which publishes primary accounts of important voyages.

Mompesson: Very probably an allusion to William Mompesson. Mompesson was the parish priest of Eyam when an outbreak of plague struck the Derbyshire village in 1665 and then again in 1666. After the second outbreak, Mompesson called for Eyam to be quarantined to prevent further spread of the disease to neighbouring villages. This was successful but not before over 200 villagers, including Mompesson's wife, succumbed to plague. Eyam is only a few miles distant from Gilchrist's home of Holmesfield.

Pantoufles: Slippers.

Jove and Semele: The god Zeus fell in love with his priestess Semele and visited her in disguise. Due to doubts sown by Hera, Semele started to think she had been tricked and eventually demanded that Zeus reveal his true form, which he did. No mortal can gaze fully upon the gods, however, and Semele was consumed by his lightning. Gilchrist uses the catch-all Jove, or 'Father-God', rather than Zeus.

The sculptor and the maid of stone: The story of Pygmalion, a Greek sculptor, who created a statue so beautiful he fell in love with it. The goddess Aphrodite, moved by the sculptor's emotion, brought the statue to life.

Verrio: Antonio Verrio, an Italian painter of the seventeenth century who is largely responsible for introducing Baroque art to England while under the patronage of Charles II.

The Stone Dragon (p. 169)

The misty outline of Man: The Isle of Man, which lies in the Irish Sea between England and Ireland.

Crown Imperial: *Fritillaria imperialis*, which grows as a thin stalk with an explosion of red-gold flowers at the top.

Miranda and Ferdinand: Main characters from Shakespeare's *The Tempest*.

Nunc Dimittis: A hymn which begins 'let your servant go in peace', implying that Lady Barbara believes her work is done.

The Mysteries of Udolpho: Ann Radcliffe's classic work of Gothic romance, first published in 1794.

When I first went a-waggonin': Taken from the traditional ballad *The Jolly Waggoner* which ends, in a piece of foreshadowing, with the line 'and every lad shall take his lass, so loving and so kind'.

The laws of blazonry: The laws which guide the creation of a blazon, or coat of arms.

Nourrit par son sang: 'Nourished by his blood'. Traditional belief held that, in times of famine, pelicans would cut their own breast and nourish their young with their blood. The pelican therefore became a symbol for self-sacrifice and, by association, for Jesus Christ.

Another Fiammetta: Lady Fiametta is the narrator of Giovanni Boccaccio's *Elegia di Madonna Fiametta*, written in the mid-fourteenth century. She recounts the despair of waiting for her lover to return, only to discover he now loves another.

Guerdon: A small reward.

Wear the willow: To grieve. The drooping form of the 'weeping' willow is often associated with sadness.

OF PASSION AND OF DEATH

The Lost Mistress (p. 199)

Spirëa japonica: A flowering shrub native to Japan, China and Korea.
Yellow-flags: The yellow iris (*iris pseudacorus*).
Love Lies Bleeding: A plant (*amaranthus caudatus*) whose long, tassel-like
flowers look like flowing blood. In the flower language of the Victorian
era they were an indicator of hopeless or unrequited love.

The Writings of Althea Swarthmoor (p. 210)

Kneller's brush: Potentially Sir Godfrey Kneller, a German-born portraitist
of the late seventeenth century. He found patronage in England and is
known for portraits of Isaac Newton, John Locke and King Charles II.
Herrickian: Relating to the seventeenth-century poet Robert Herrick. His
poem *To the Virgins, to Make Much of Time* is known for its cautionary
opening line 'gather ye rosebuds while ye may' which, ironically,
Althea does not heed.
Turn away thine eyes: A line from *The Song of Solomon*, a controversial and
sensuous section of the Hebrew *Tanakh*, which Dr Marston then discusses.
Threatened with a plethora: In this context, plethora is used to mean a now-
discredited illness once believed to be caused by an excess of blood.
How they oft walk hand in hand: Love and Death—Amor and Mors—are
sometimes poetically described as siblings or even lovers.
Mouldy apophthegms: Trite sayings or mottos.
Suckling and Rochester: The seventeenth-century poets Sir John Suckling
and John Wilmot, 2nd Earl of Rochester, both known for their
extravagant lifestyles.
Antonio Moro: A Dutch portraitist of the sixteenth century, known professionally as Anthonis Mor.

Phoebus: An alternative name for Apollo, Greek god of the sun.

Bedeswoman: Someone employed through donation to pray on behalf of others and by extension a loyal follower.

The Noble Courtesan (p. 222)

Bagnio: A bath-house, also a euphemism for brothel.

Villiers: A probable allusion to Auguste Villiers de l'Isle-Adam, the French writer whose 1883 collection of sinister short stories *Contes Cruels* appears to have been a major influence on Gilchrist and on 'The Noble Courtesan' especially.

A wagtail's song: Wagtail was a Victorian euphemism, albeit a derogatory one, for a prostitute.

The Holocaust (p. 230)

Holocaust: A deeply troubling word to see for modern readers, though one without its modern connotations at the time of the story's publication in 1894. Gilchrist is likely to be referring to the Greek *holokauston*, a ritual offering which is wholly (*holos*) burnt (*kaustos*), rather than symbolically consumed, as part of the sacrifice.

Bantling: A young child.

Fustian: Pompous or long-winded.

Rushlight: A kind of candle made from dried rushes dipped in fat.

Comfit: An early kind of sweet often consisting of a mix of nuts, fruits and spices encased in sugar.

Jenny-Spinner: A dialect term for various small, flying insects.

Princess Mary of Orange: Mary Henrietta Stewart, the daughter of Charles I. Mary, like Princess Bice, was sent to live in a foreign land where she was largely unpopular—her Dutch hosts being more sympathetic to Oliver Cromwell, who executed her father when she was eighteen years old—and who also had difficulty with childbirth.

By-blow: An illegitimate child.

Elkanah and his wife: Elkanah is a figure from the Book of Samuel. His first wife, Hannah, could not bear children so he took Penninah as a second wife. Dean Bastler appears to intend this as a slight on Princess Bice, despite Hannah being Elkanah's favourite wife and mother of the prophet Samuel.

Am I not better to thee than ten sons?: Elkanah's attempt to comfort the childless Hannah (1 Samuel 1:8) is here reversed as a plea from Princess Bice.

Pastilico: Something which has been pastilicated, or rolled into a ball. The implication here is that they are balls of resin or incense.

Roxana Runs Lunatick (p. 239)

Hyperion: The Titan of heavenly light in Greek mythology, father of both the sun and moon.

Peewit: A bird, also known as the northern lapwing.

The Madness of Betty Hooton (p. 243)

Postchaise: A small, fast carriage.

Prie-dieu chair: A low chair which can be rotated to kneel on when at prayer.

Smyrna: Modern-day Izmir, Turkey.

As ugly as Punchinello: A notoriously coarse character from Italian *commedia dell'arte*, perhaps now better known as the inspiration for Mr Punch, foreshadowing the story's latter puppet show.

Lely's portraits: Probably Sir Peter Lely, Dutch-born portraitist to both Charles I and Oliver Cromwell. After his death in 1680 he was replaced as court artist by Godfrey Kneller (see notes for 'The Writings of Althea Swarthmoor').

Aphra Behn: Poet and author of the seventeenth century. One of the first English women to write professionally, Behn was friends with John

Wilmot (see notes for 'The Writings of Althea Swarthmoor') and her support for sexual liberty for women was as contentious as his libertine lifestyle. Behn was an influence on later writers such as Montague Summers and Virginia Woolf. One of the most famous portraits of Behn was painted by Sir Peter Lely (see note above).

My Friend (p. 253)

Dead Sea apple: The fruit of *calotropis procera*, which appears green and succulent but contains a poisonous and viscous sap. The fruit is also known as the Apple of Sodom.

Metempsychosis: The belief that souls can move into a new body at the time of death. Pythagoras popularised the theory after learning of it from either Egyptian or Indian thinkers.

Cymbeline: An early seventeenth-century play by William Shakespeare in which Imogen is a visibly gender-fluid figure and, when disguised as the young boy Fidele, a source of homoerotic desire for other characters.

Angel's visit: Sara, the wife of Abraham, is described in the Book of Genesis as 'laughing within herself' when she is told by a group of angels that, despite the couple being 'well stricken in age', she will soon bear a son.

Tamburlane: A late sixteenth-century play by Christopher Marlowe. Bajazeth, Emperor of the Turks is defeated by Tamburlaine and kept in a cage. Humiliated, Bajazeth eventually kills himself by beating his head on the cage's bars. Zabina, Bajazeth's wife, does the same when she discovers her dead husband.

Jael: A figure from the Book of Judges who killed the oppressive Canaanite commander Sisera by hammering a tent peg through his skull, thus fulfilling the prophecy that a woman would defeat his army.

Ye Gabbleratch Inne: A gabbleratch is a dialect term for a group of noisy birds, often geese. Folk belief held that the sound was either made by the souls of the unbaptised dead or warned, in a manner similar to the banshee, of an approaching death. The sinister figure whose 'gaze seemed as petrifying as a cockatrice' is reminiscent of the being encountered at the end of 'The Basilisk'.

Sir Toby's Wife (p. 269)

Jennel: A narrow alleyway, often between two houses.

Sun of my Soul: A hymn, written in 1820 by John Keble. The third verse consists of the lines 'Abide with me from morn till eve / for without Thee I cannot live / abide with me when night is nigh / for without Thee I dare not die', which take on a sinister air in the context of this story.

Miserere: An alternate name for a misericord, a small ledge on the underside of a folding church seat intended as a support for long periods of prayer. They are often extravagantly carved with grotesque or outlandish figures.

Vital Spark of Heavenly Flame: A hymn with lyrics written by Alexander Pope in 1712 and which ends with lines from 1 Corinthians: 'O grave! Where is thy victory? O death! Where is thy sting?'.

PEAK WEIRD

The Derbyshire dialect used in these stories can seem impenetrable to readers not accustomed to it. Reading the dialogue out loud often makes it more comprehensible.

The Panicle (p. 283)

Mrs Sherwood: Very probably Mary Martha Sherwood, a nineteenth-century author of children's books.

Panicle: A confusing term, perhaps intentionally so, which properly means a cluster of flowers on a branch but here is apparently used as the name of a salamander-like creature.

A Witch in the Peak (p. 288)

Besom-stale: A long-handled broom, ironically the kind that witches are
alleged to fly upon.

Hoo'ld hev bin faggotted: 'She would've been burned at the stake'.

Jack-wi'-th'Iron Teeth: Either a local piece of folklore or a reference to the
poem *Jenny Wi'the Airn Teeth* by Scottish poet Alexander Anderson.

A Strolling Player (p. 293)

Shippon: A barn or shed.

Lang-settle: A long bench.

Death and the Lady: A late seventeenth-century ballad more formally titled
The Great Messenger of Mortality, or a Dialogue betwixt Death and a Lady.
The Lady suffers an early death—'I did not think you would have
come so soon / Why must my morning sun go down at noon?'—but
attempts to convince Death to give her a reprieve; 'Fain would I stay,
if thou my life wouldst spare / I have a daughter, beautiful and fair /
I wish to see her wed, whom I adore / Grant me but this, and I will
ask no more?'

STORY SOURCES

Unless otherwise noted below, all stories have been sourced from *The Stone Dragon and Other Tragic Romances* (London: Methuen & Co., 1894).

'A Night on the Moor', 'The Priest's Pavan', 'Bubble Magic', 'Dryas and Lady Greenleaf' and 'The Madness of Betty Hooton' are sourced from *Lords and Ladies* (London: Hurst and Blackett, 1903)

'The Panicle', 'A Witch in the Peak' and 'A Strolling Player' are sourced from *A Peakland Faggot* (London: Faber & Gwyer, 1926)

'The Crimson Weaver' is sourced from *The Yellow Book* Vol. VI

'The Lover's Ordeal' is sourced from *The London Magazine*, June 1905

'The Holocaust' is sourced from *The National Observer*, February 1894

'Sir Toby's Wife' is sourced from *The Windsor Magazine*, November 1914

British Library Tales of the Weird collects a thrilling array of uncanny storytelling, from the realms of gothic, supernatural and horror fiction. With stories ranging from the nineteenth century to the present day, this series revives long-lost material from the Library's vaults to thrill again alongside beloved classics of the weird fiction genre.

From the Depths: And Other Strange Tales of the Sea – ED. MIKE ASHLEY
Haunted Houses: Two Novels by Charlotte Riddell – ED. ANDREW SMITH
Glimpses of the Unknown: Lost Ghost Stories – ED. MIKE ASHLEY
Mortal Echoes: Encounters with the End – ED. GREG BUZWELL
Spirits of the Season: Christmas Hauntings – ED. TANYA KIRK
The Platform Edge: Uncanny Tales of the Railways – ED. MIKE ASHLEY
The Face in the Glass: The Gothic Tales of Mary Elizabeth Braddon – ED. GREG BUZWELL
The Weird Tales of William Hope Hodgson – ED. XAVIER ALDANA REYES
Doorway to Dilemma: Bewildering Tales of Dark Fantasy – ED. MIKE ASHLEY
Evil Roots: Killer Tales of the Botanical Gothic – ED. DAISY BUTCHER
Promethean Horrors: Classic Tales of Mad Science – ED. XAVIER ALDANA REYES
Roarings From Further Out: Four Weird Novellas by Algernon Blackwood – ED. XAVIER ALDANA REYES
Tales of the Tattooed: An Anthology of Ink – ED. JOHN MILLER
The Outcast: And Other Dark Tales by E. F. Benson – ED. MIKE ASHLEY
A Phantom Lover: And Other Dark Tales by Vernon Lee – ED. MIKE ASHLEY
Into the London Fog: Eerie Tales from the Weird City – ED. ELIZABETH DEARNLEY
Weird Woods: Tales from the Haunted Forests of Britain – ED. JOHN MILLER
Queens of the Abyss: Lost Stories from the Women of the Weird – ED. MIKE ASHLEY
Chill Tidings: Dark Tales of the Christmas Season – ED. TANYA KIRK
Dangerous Dimensions: Mind-bending Tales of the Mathematical Weird – ED. HENRY BARTHOLOMEW
Heavy Weather: Tempestuous Tales of Stranger Climes – ED. KEVAN MANWARING
Minor Hauntings: Chilling Tales of Spectral Youth – ED. JEN BAKER
Crawling Horror: Creeping Tales of the Insect Weird – EDS. DAISY BUTCHER AND JANETTE LEAF
Cornish Horrors: Tales from the Land's End – ED. JOAN PASSEY
I Am Stone: The Gothic Weird Tales of R. Murray Gilchrist – ED. DANIEL PIETERSEN

We welcome any suggestions, corrections or feedback you may have, and will aim to respond to all items addressed to the following:

The Editor (Tales of the Weird), British Library Publishing,
The British Library, 96 Euston Road, London NW1 2DB

We also welcome enquiries through our Twitter account, @BL_Publishing.